DATE DUE

10/18/21			
1/10/22			
2/9/22			
2/23/22			
8/26/22			
9/20/22			
EP 0 6 2023			
9/21/23			

Form 392— SUPREME SCHOOL SUPPLY CO., ARCADIA, WI

CHARACTERS

STAR WARS: LOST STARS

On the day the Galactic Empire assumes control over the remote, rocky planet of Jelucan, where two distinct social classes (first-wavers and second-wavers) wage a fierce rivalry, second-waver Thane and first-waver Ciena have a fateful encounter that changes their lives forever. They dream of joining the Imperial Academy.

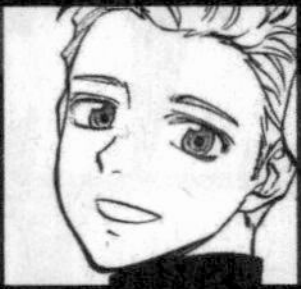

Thane Kyrell

Joins the Academy to be an Imperial pilot. After graduating, he is assigned to the defense fleet for a new space station.

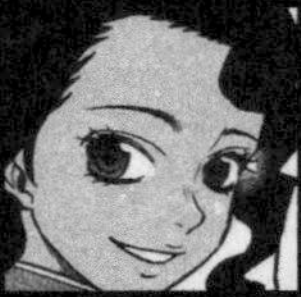

Ciena Ree

Joins the Academy to be an Imperial officer. After graduating, she is assigned to the Star Destroyer *Devastator*.

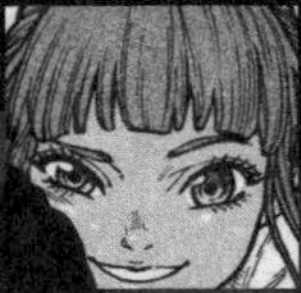

Kendy Idele

Ciena's bubbly former roommate.

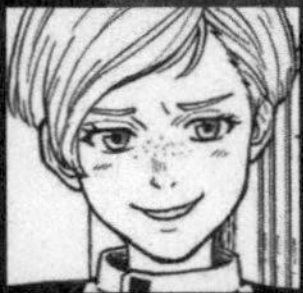

Jude Edivon

Ciena's former roommate, a whiz at data analysis.

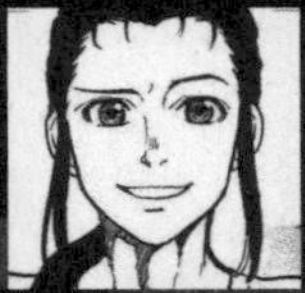

Nash Windrider

Thane's former roommate, a citizen of Alderaan.

STORY

STAR WARS: LOST STARS

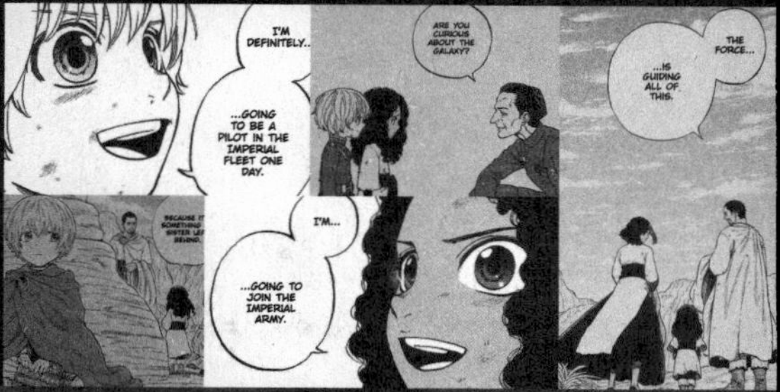
THE FORCE...
...IS GUIDING ALL OF THIS.
ARE YOU CURIOUS ABOUT THE GALAXY?
I'M DEFINITELY...
...GOING TO BE A PILOT IN THE IMPERIAL FLEET ONE DAY.
I'M...
...GOING TO JOIN THE IMPERIAL ARMY.

On the day of Jelucan's ceremonial annexation, Grand Moff Tarkin rescues young Thane and Ciena from a troop of local bullies and allows them aboard an Imperial spaceship.

Struck by the greatness of the Empire, Thane dreams of being a pilot one day, and Ciena hopes to be an officer. They make a promise to pursue their dreams and, years later, enter the Imperial Academy with excellent marks.

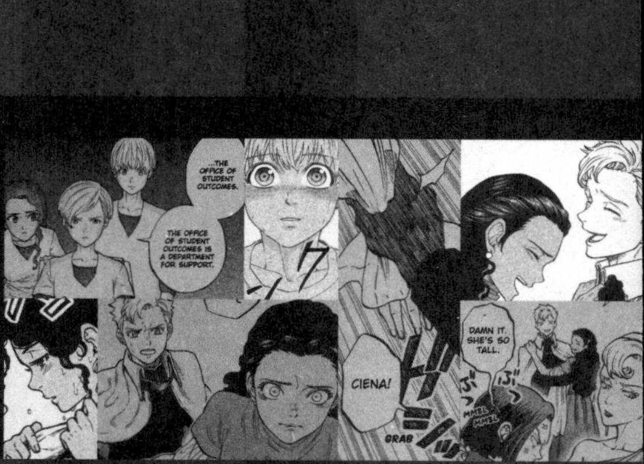
...THE OFFICE OF STUDENT OUTCOMES.
THE OFFICE OF STUDENT OUTCOMES IS A DEPARTMENT FOR SUPPORT.
DAMN IT. SHE'S SO TALL.
MMBL MMBL
CIENA!
GRAB

As students, they gradually find their friendship blossoming into love, but that emotion grows strained as Thane begins to doubt the Empire's ways, while Ciena steadfastly trusts in the righteousness of its cause.

The two graduate from the Academy and earn assignments in the Imperial Fleet. One day, the space station known as the Death Star tests its fully operational weapon systems by obliterating the planet Alderaan to send a message to the Rebel Alliance.

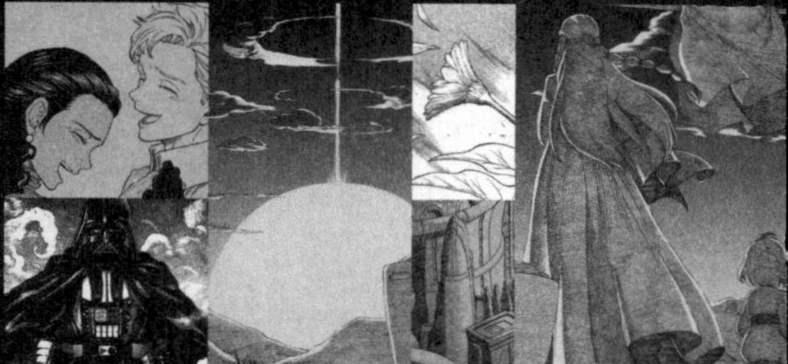

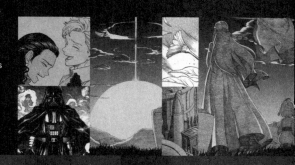

This shocking act transforms Thane's suspicion of the Empire's nature into outright despair...

STAR WARS  LOST STARS

VOLUME 2 CONTENTS

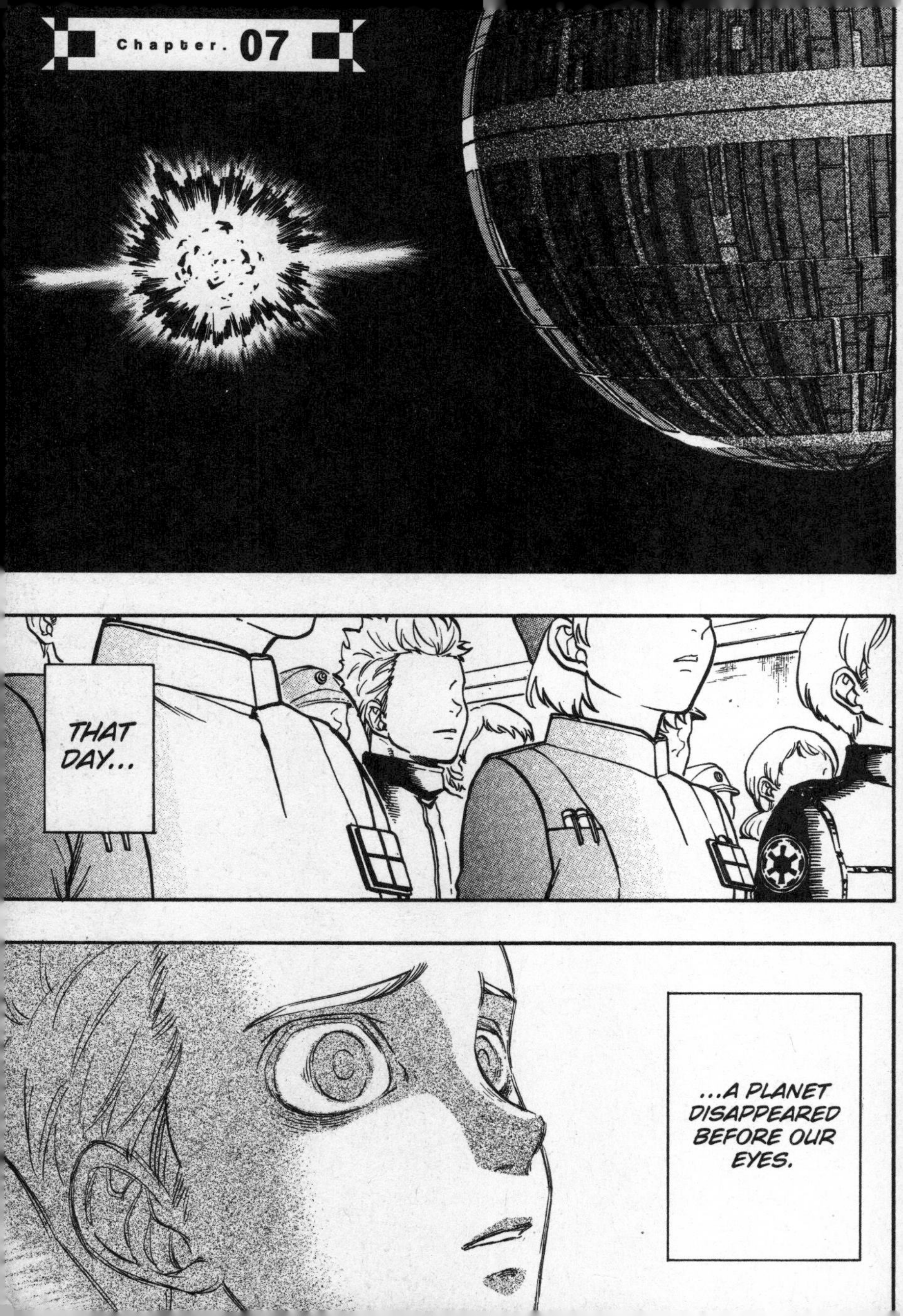
Chapter. 07
THAT DAY...
...A PLANET DISAPPEARED BEFORE OUR EYES.

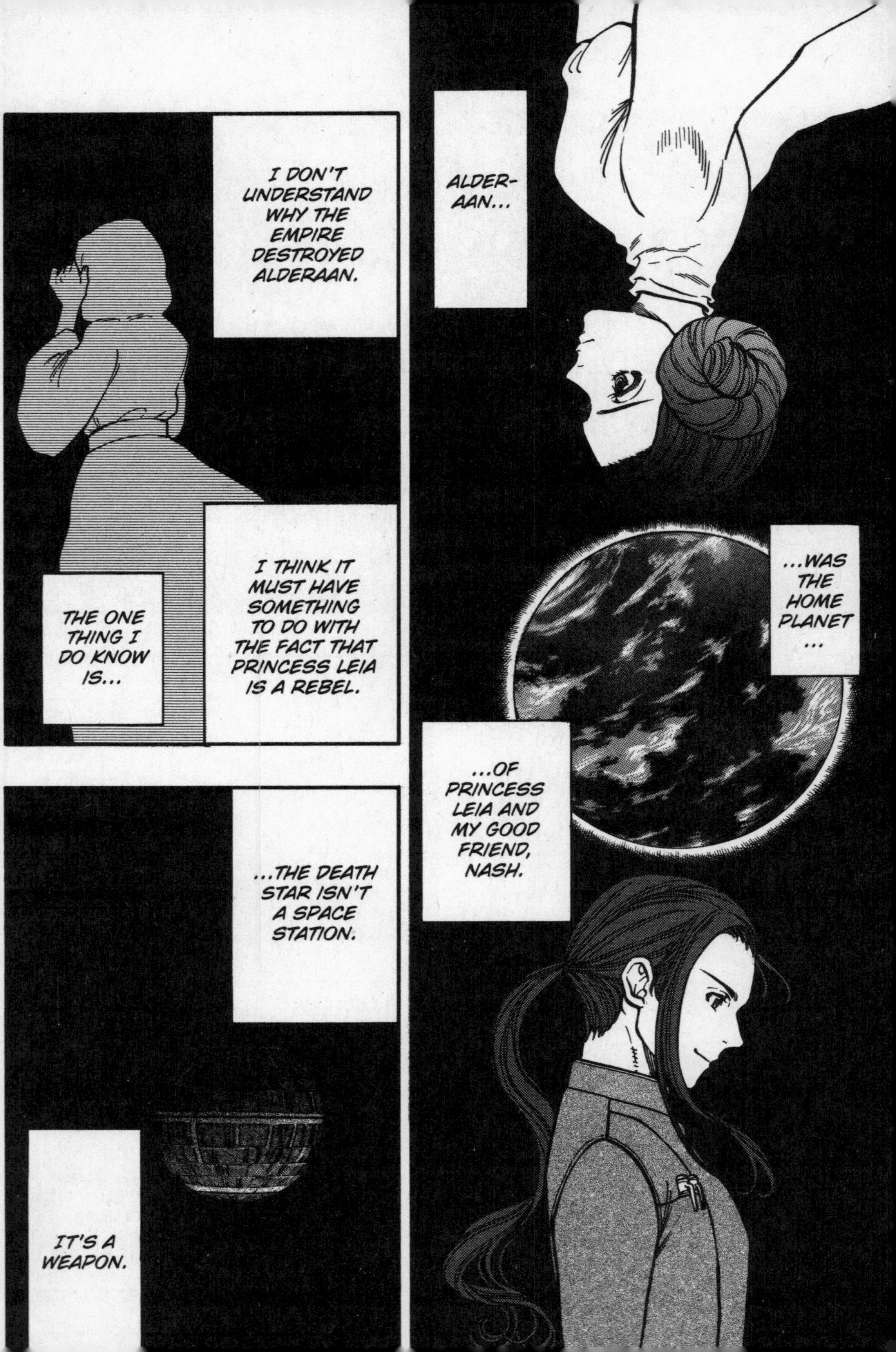
ALDER-AAN...
...WAS THE HOME PLANET...
...OF PRINCESS LEIA AND MY GOOD FRIEND, NASH.
I DON'T UNDERSTAND WHY THE EMPIRE DESTROYED ALDERAAN.
I THINK IT MUST HAVE SOMETHING TO DO WITH THE FACT THAT PRINCESS LEIA IS A REBEL.
THE ONE THING I DO KNOW IS...
...THE DEATH STAR ISN'T A SPACE STATION.
IT'S A WEAPON.

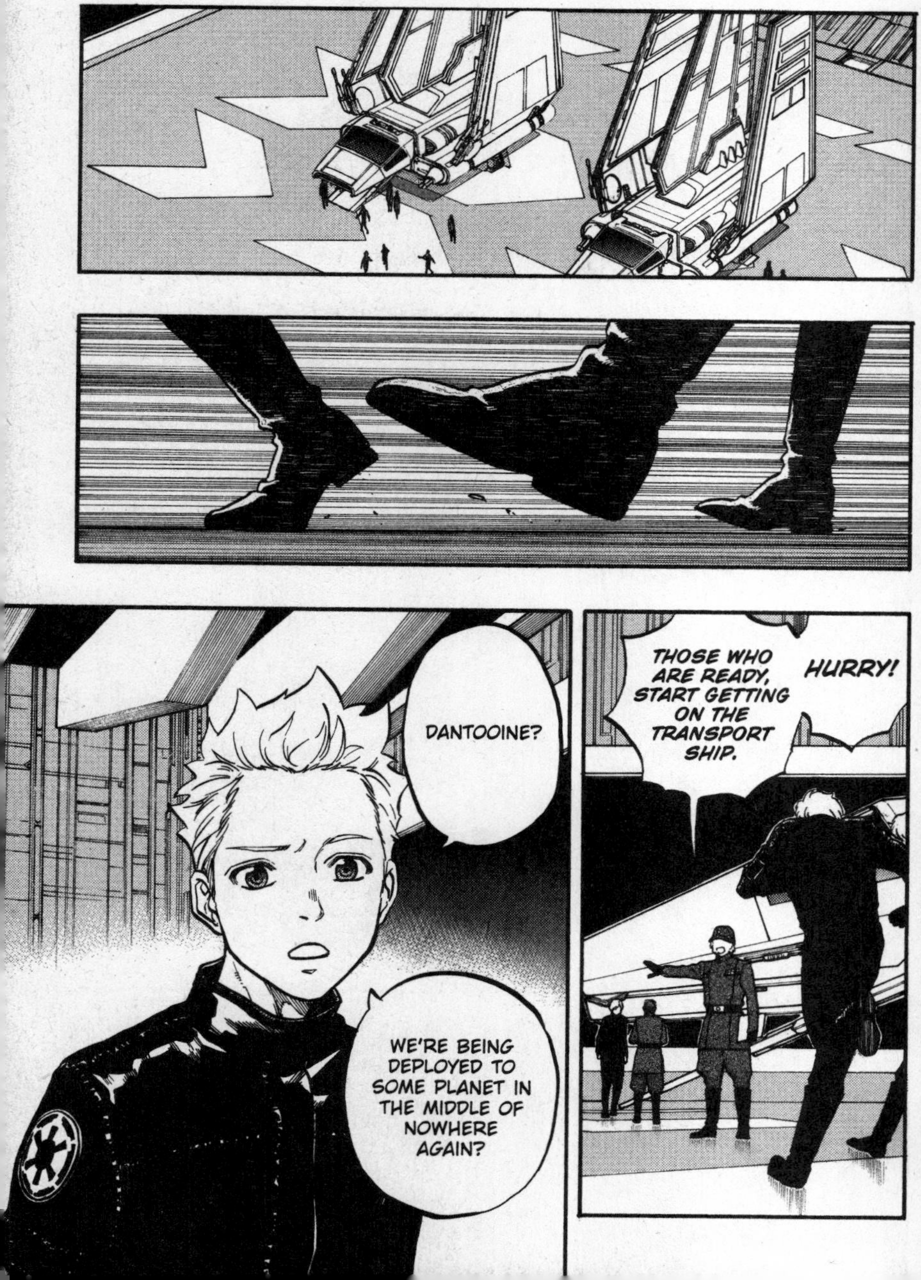
HURRY!
THOSE WHO ARE READY, START GETTING ON THE TRANSPORT SHIP.
DANTOOINE?
WE'RE BEING DEPLOYED TO SOME PLANET IN THE MIDDLE OF NOWHERE AGAIN?

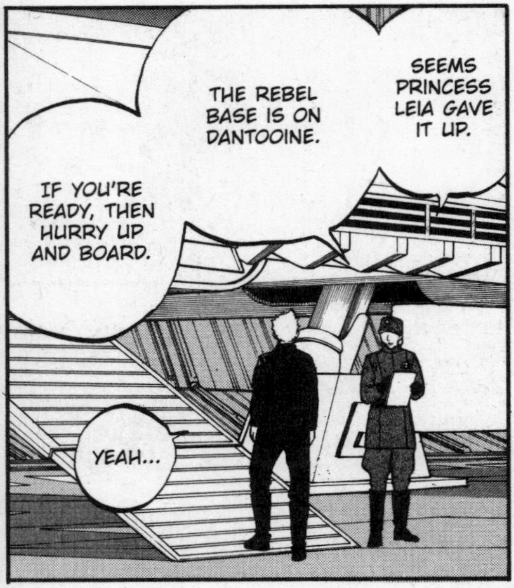
SEEMS PRINCESS LEIA GAVE IT UP.
THE REBEL BASE IS ON DANTOOINE.
IF YOU'RE READY, THEN HURRY UP AND BOARD.
YEAH...

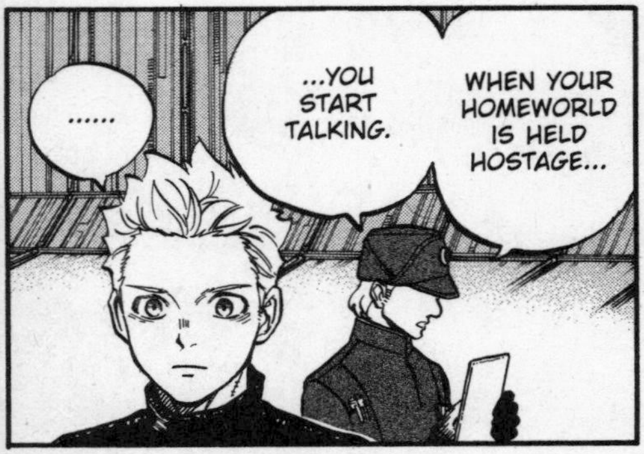
WHEN YOUR HOMEWORLD IS HELD HOSTAGE...
...YOU START TALKING.
......

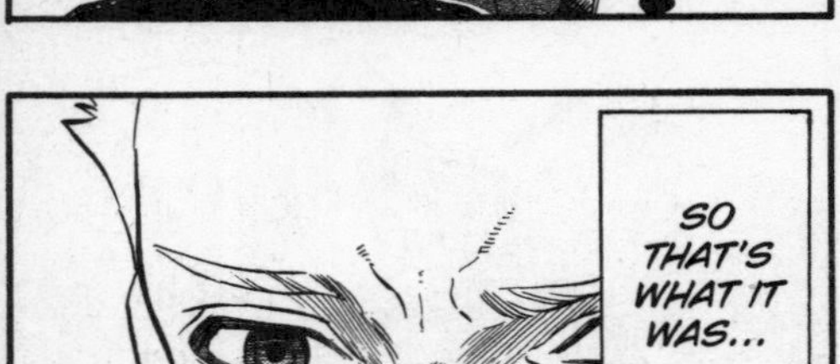
SO THAT'S WHAT IT WAS...

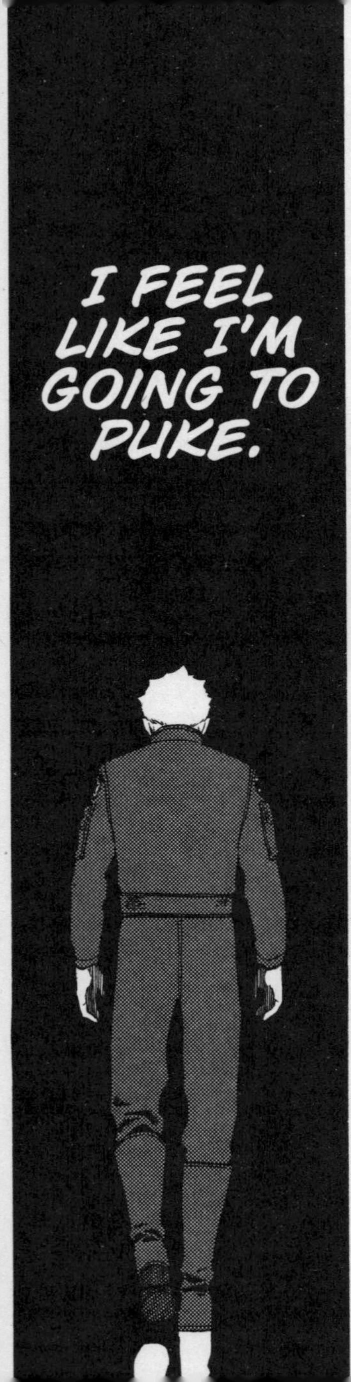
I FEEL LIKE I'M GOING TO PUKE.

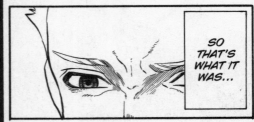

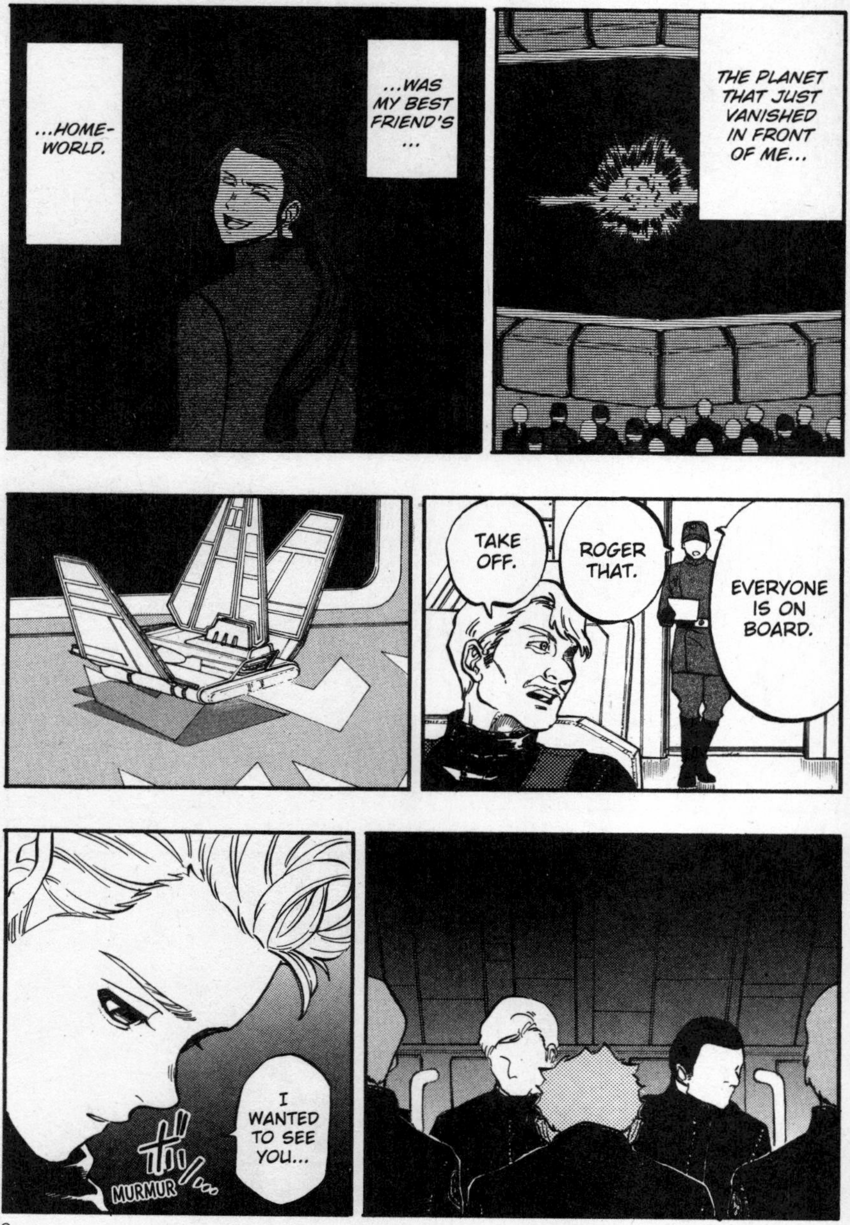
THE PLANET THAT JUST VANISHED IN FRONT OF ME...
...WAS MY BEST FRIEND'S ...
...HOME-WORLD.
EVERYONE IS ON BOARD.
ROGER THAT.
TAKE OFF.
I WANTED TO SEE YOU...
MURMUR

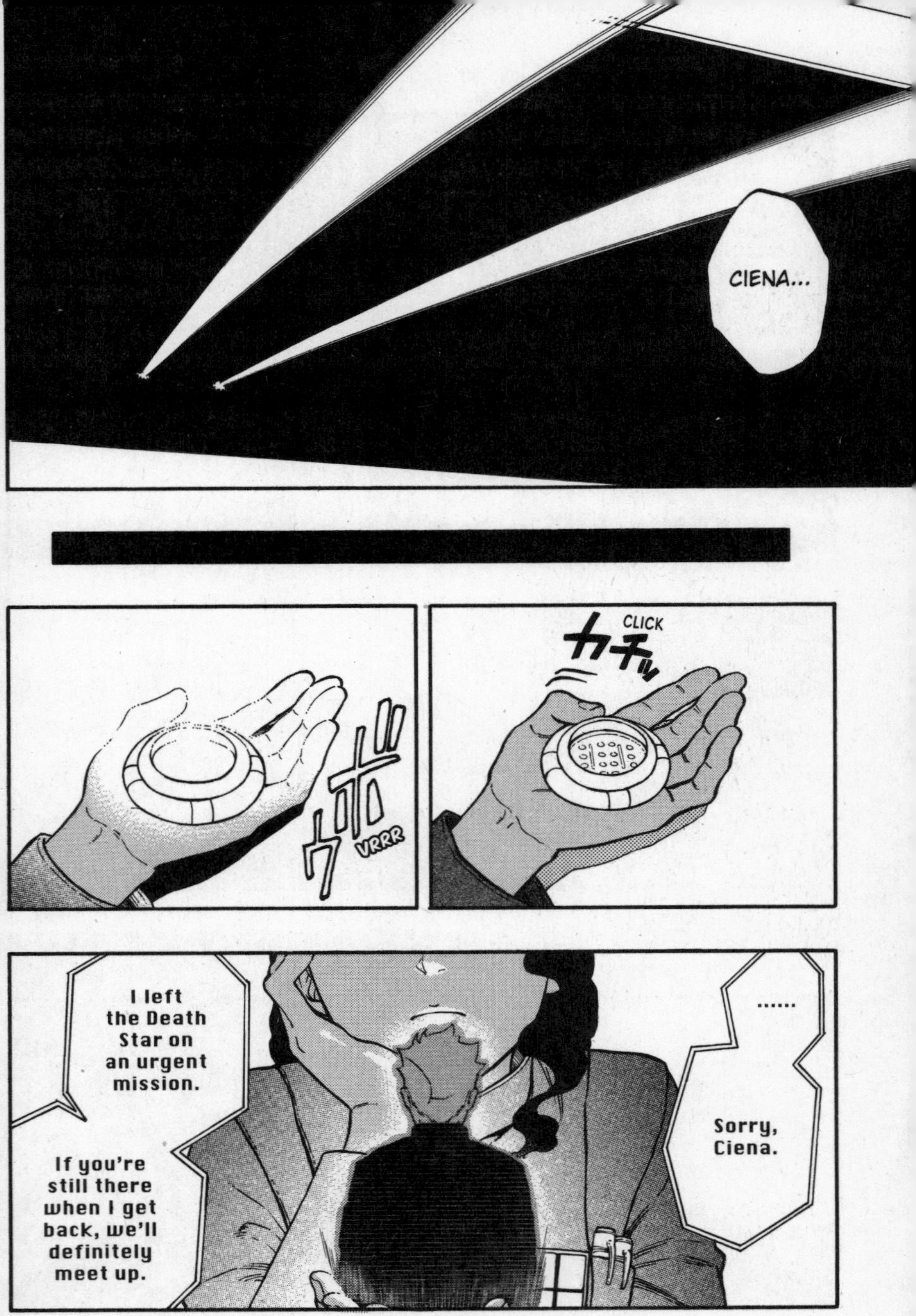

CIENA...
カチッ
CLICK
VRRR
......
Sorry, Ciena.
I left the Death Star on an urgent mission.
If you're still there when I get back, we'll definitely meet up.

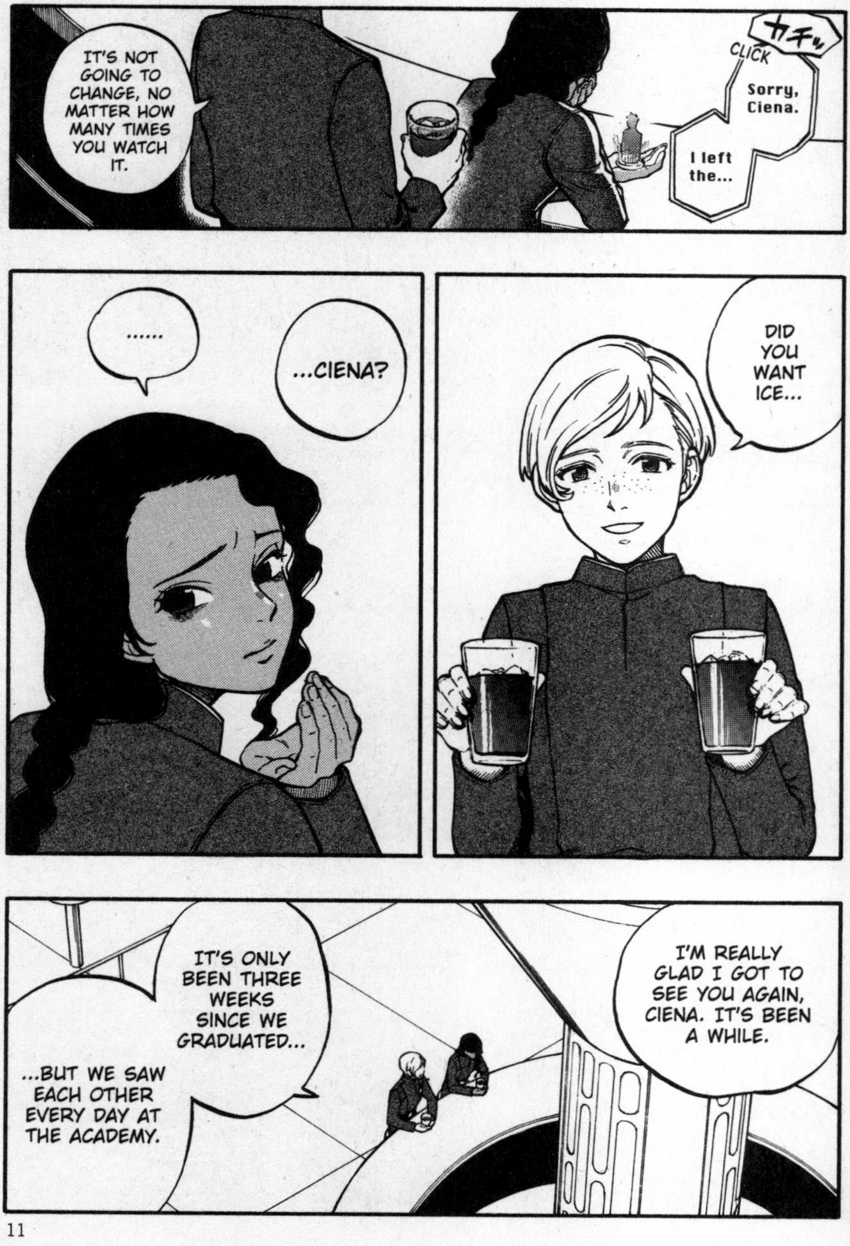

カチッ
CLICK
Sorry, Ciena. I left the...
IT'S NOT GOING TO CHANGE, NO MATTER HOW MANY TIMES YOU WATCH IT.
DID YOU WANT ICE...
...CIENA?
......
I'M REALLY GLAD I GOT TO SEE YOU AGAIN, CIENA. IT'S BEEN A WHILE.
IT'S ONLY BEEN THREE WEEKS SINCE WE GRADUATED...
...BUT WE SAW EACH OTHER EVERY DAY AT THE ACADEMY.

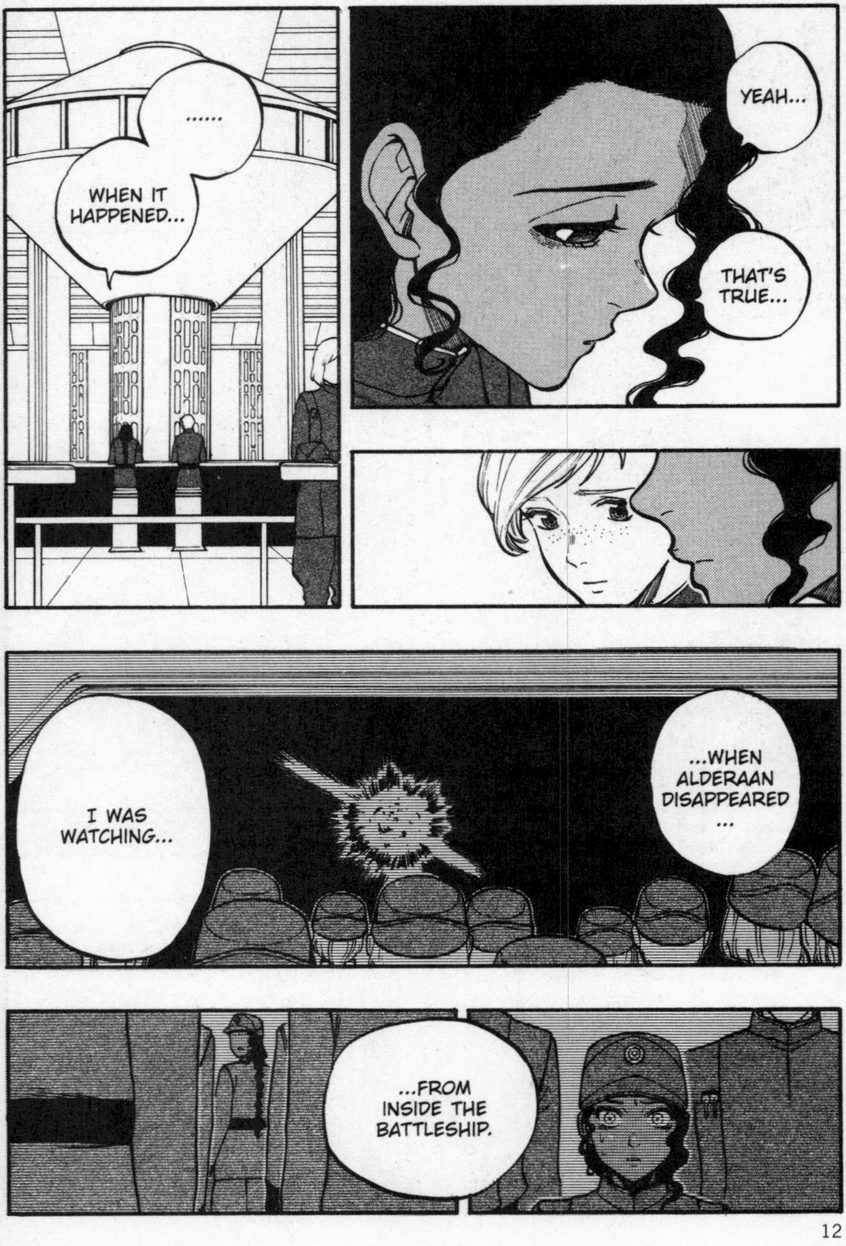
YEAH...
THAT'S TRUE...
......
WHEN IT HAPPENED...
...WHEN ALDERAAN DISAPPEARED ...
I WAS WATCHING...
...FROM INSIDE THE BATTLESHIP.

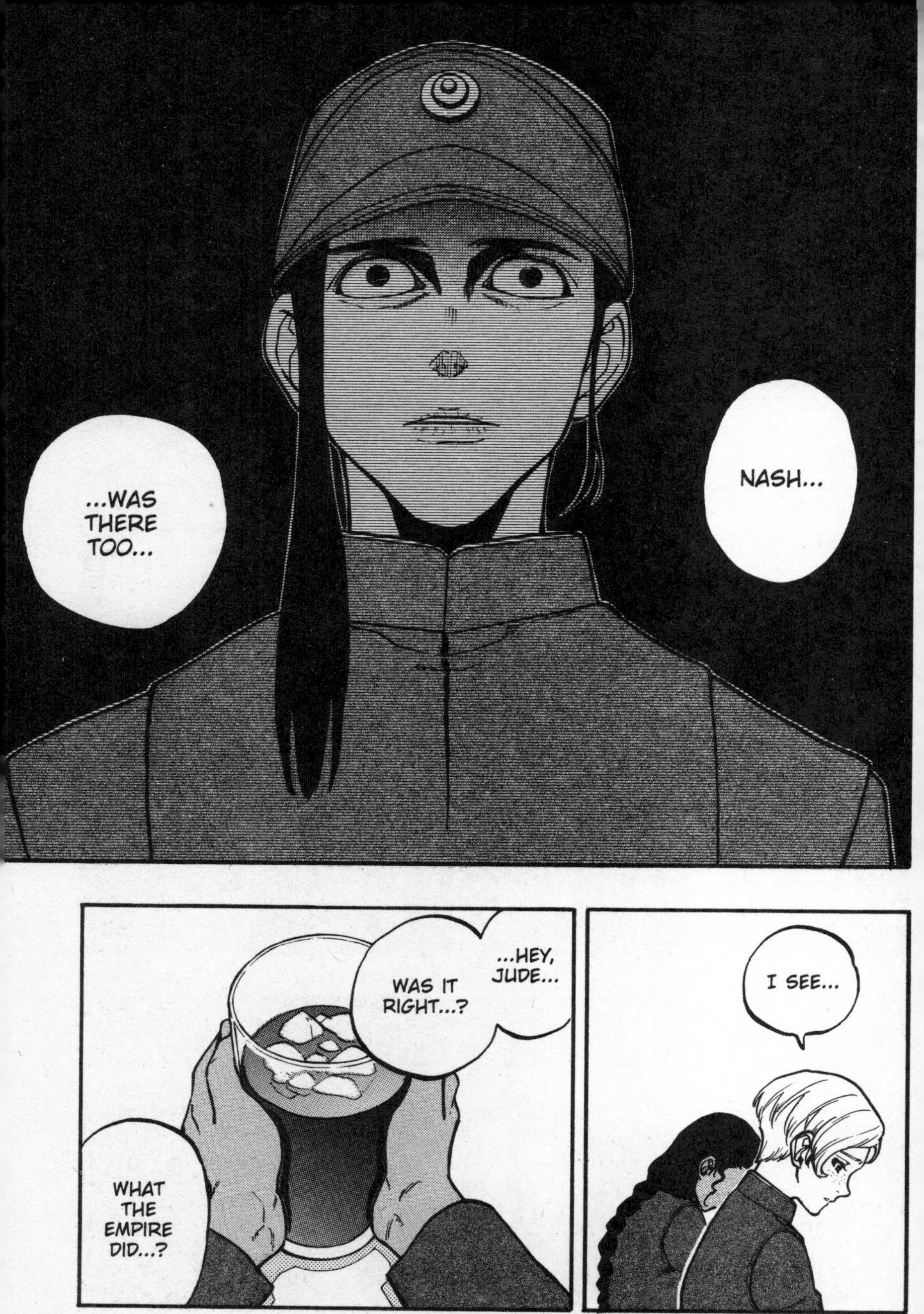
NASH...
...WAS THERE TOO...
I SEE...
...HEY, JUDE...
WAS IT RIGHT...?
WHAT THE EMPIRE DID...?

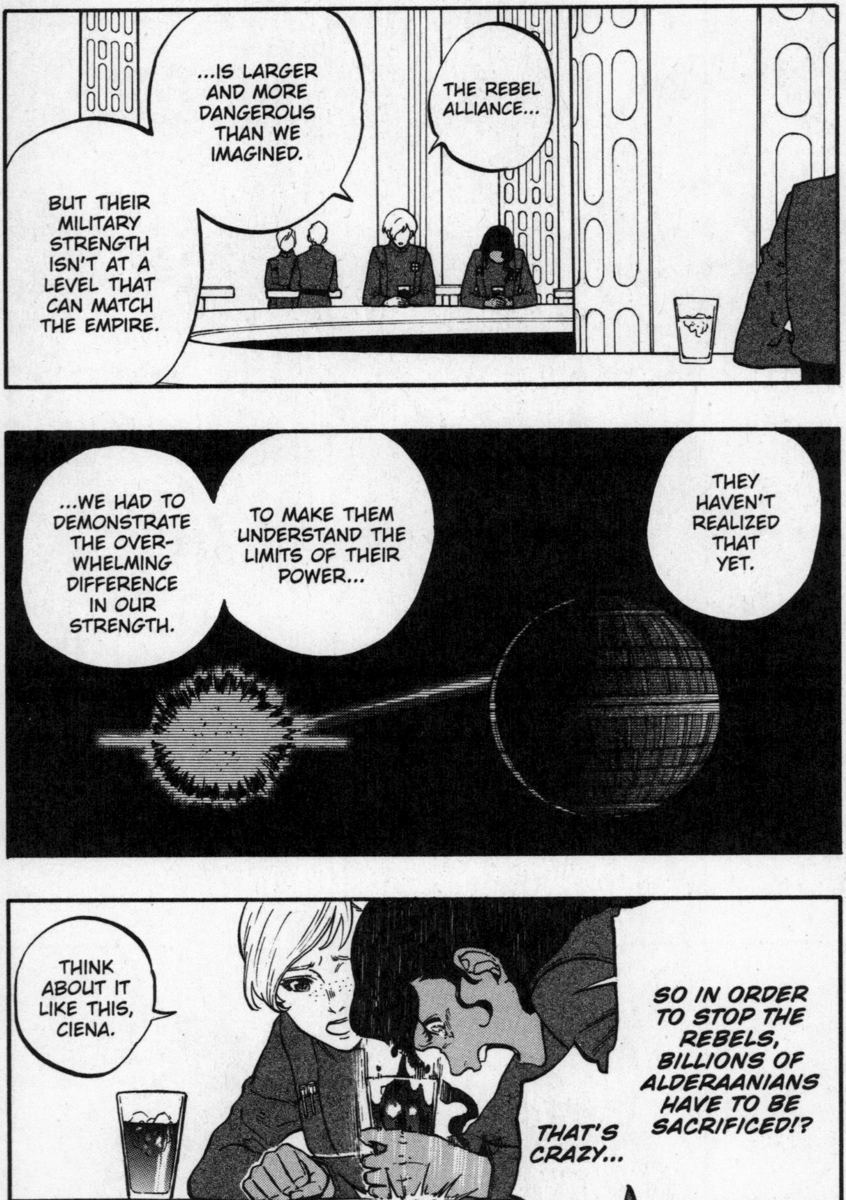
THE REBEL ALLIANCE...
...IS LARGER AND MORE DANGEROUS THAN WE IMAGINED.
BUT THEIR MILITARY STRENGTH ISN'T AT A LEVEL THAT CAN MATCH THE EMPIRE.
THEY HAVEN'T REALIZED THAT YET.
TO MAKE THEM UNDERSTAND THE LIMITS OF THEIR POWER...
...WE HAD TO DEMONSTRATE THE OVER-WHELMING DIFFERENCE IN OUR STRENGTH.
SO IN ORDER TO STOP THE REBELS, BILLIONS OF ALDERAANIANS HAVE TO BE SACRIFICED!?
THAT'S CRAZY...
THINK ABOUT IT LIKE THIS, CIENA.

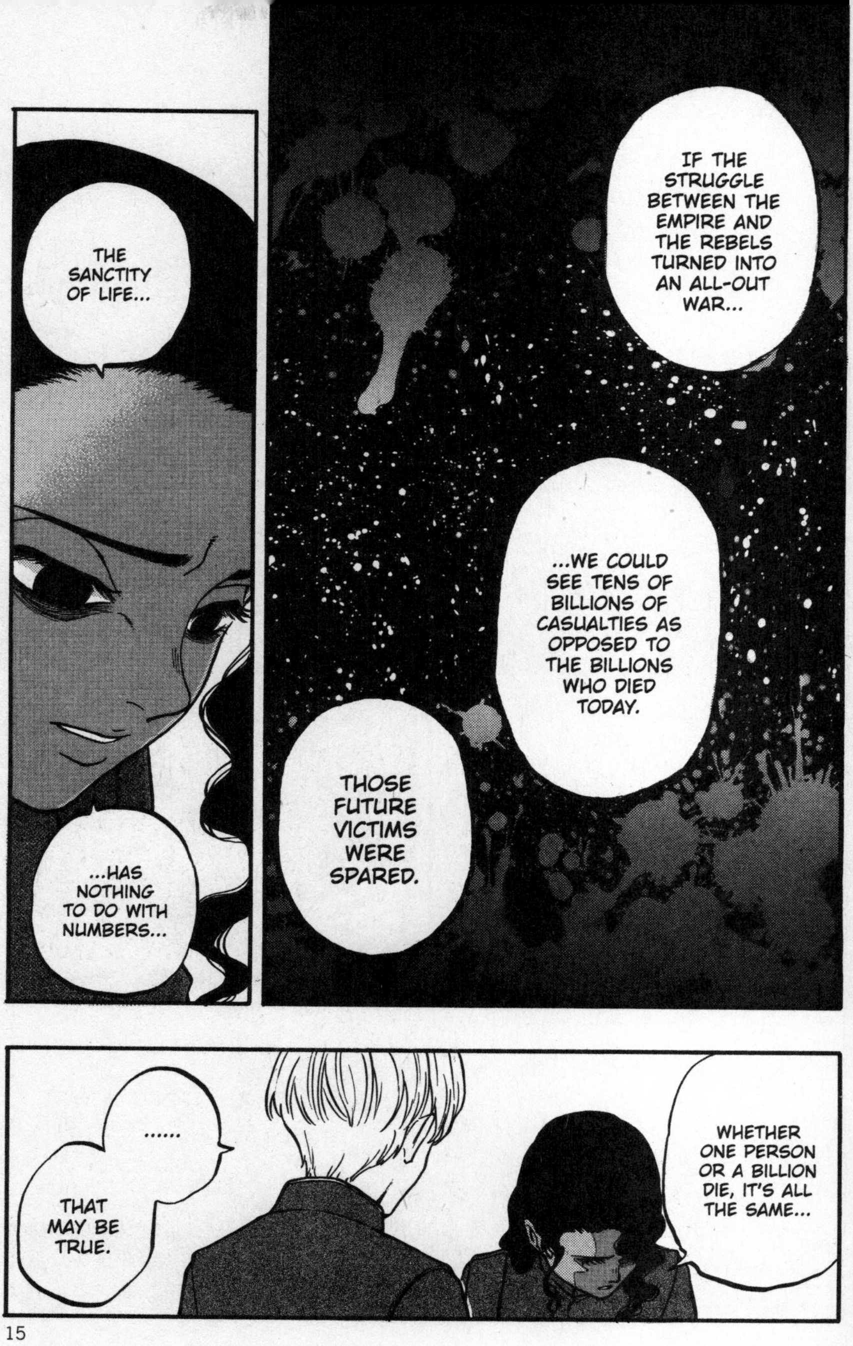
IF THE STRUGGLE BETWEEN THE EMPIRE AND THE REBELS TURNED INTO AN ALL-OUT WAR...
...WE COULD SEE TENS OF BILLIONS OF CASUALTIES AS OPPOSED TO THE BILLIONS WHO DIED TODAY.
THOSE FUTURE VICTIMS WERE SPARED.
THE SANCTITY OF LIFE...
...HAS NOTHING TO DO WITH NUMBERS...
WHETHER ONE PERSON OR A BILLION DIE, IT'S ALL THE SAME...
......
THAT MAY BE TRUE.

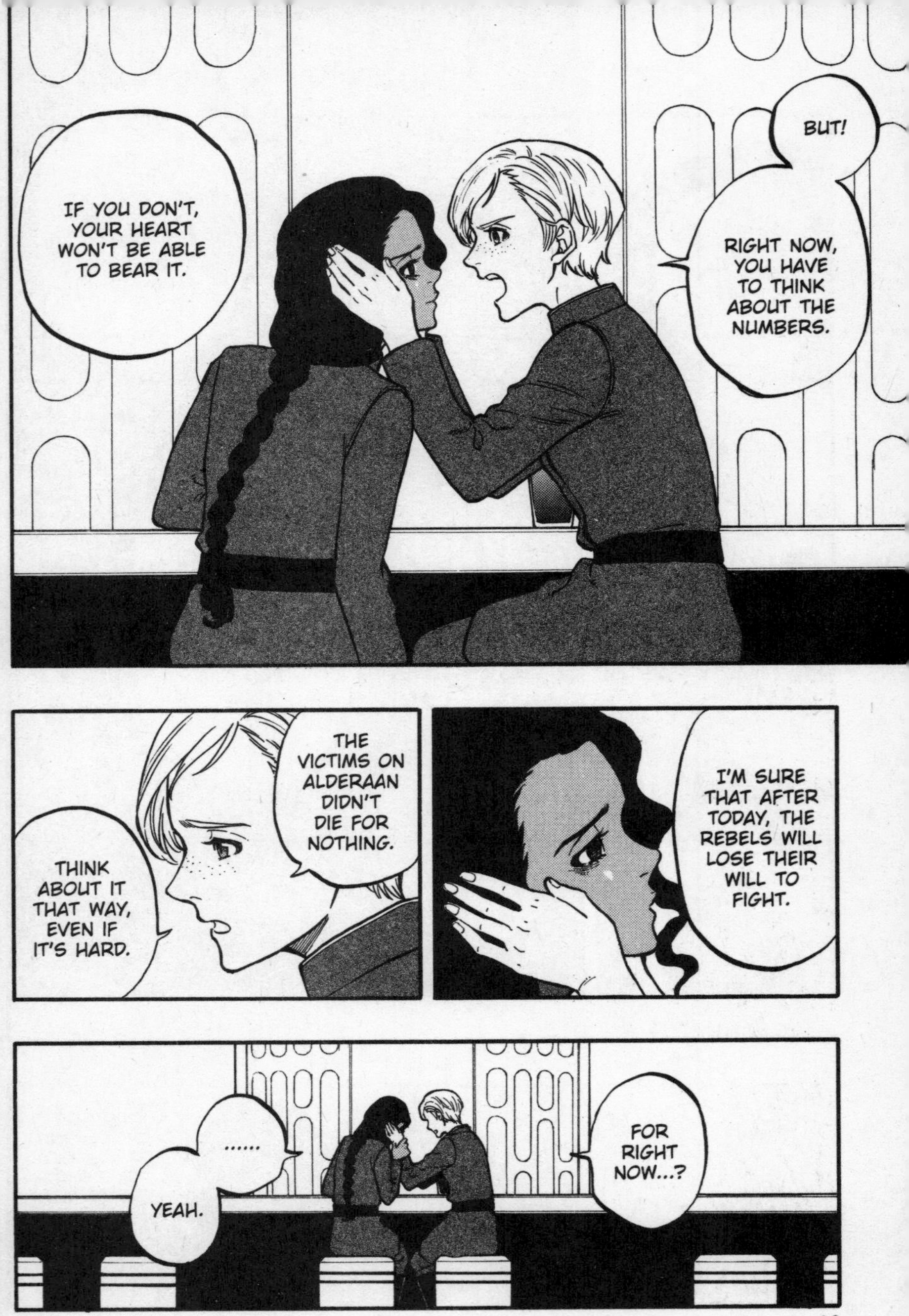
BUT!
RIGHT NOW, YOU HAVE TO THINK ABOUT THE NUMBERS.
IF YOU DON'T, YOUR HEART WON'T BE ABLE TO BEAR IT.
I'M SURE THAT AFTER TODAY, THE REBELS WILL LOSE THEIR WILL TO FIGHT.
THE VICTIMS ON ALDERAAN DIDN'T DIE FOR NOTHING.
THINK ABOUT IT THAT WAY, EVEN IF IT'S HARD.
FOR RIGHT NOW...?
......
YEAH.

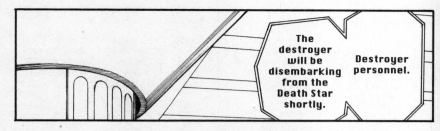

The destroyer will be disembarking from the Death Star shortly.

Destroyer personnel.

SQUEEZE

THE DESTROYER... THAT'S YOUR SHIP, RIGHT?

YOU HAVE TO GO.

All personnel should get themselves on board.

......

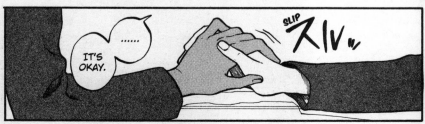

......

IT'S OKAY.

SLIP

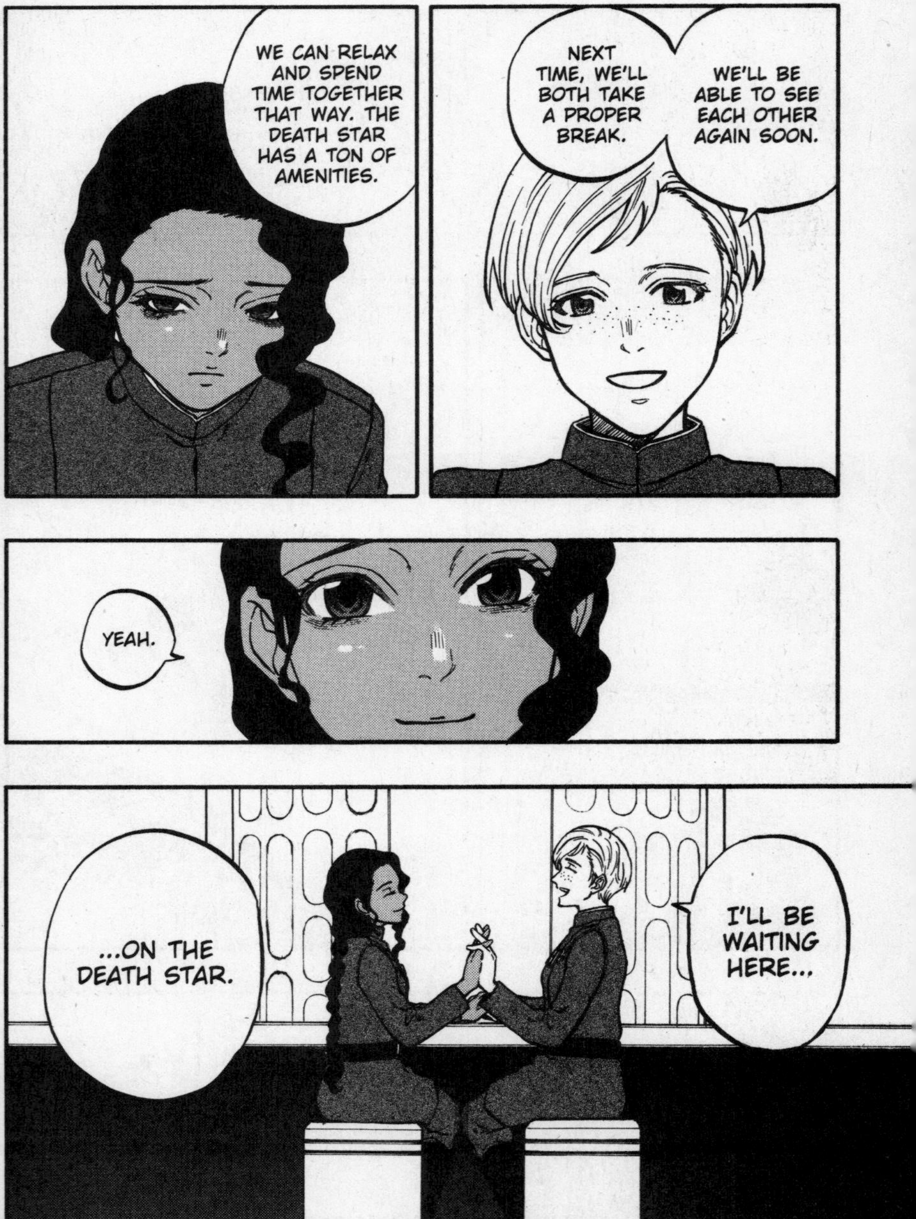
WE'LL BE ABLE TO SEE EACH OTHER AGAIN SOON.
NEXT TIME, WE'LL BOTH TAKE A PROPER BREAK.
WE CAN RELAX AND SPEND TIME TOGETHER THAT WAY. THE DEATH STAR HAS A TON OF AMENITIES.
YEAH.
I'LL BE WAITING HERE...
...ON THE DEATH STAR.

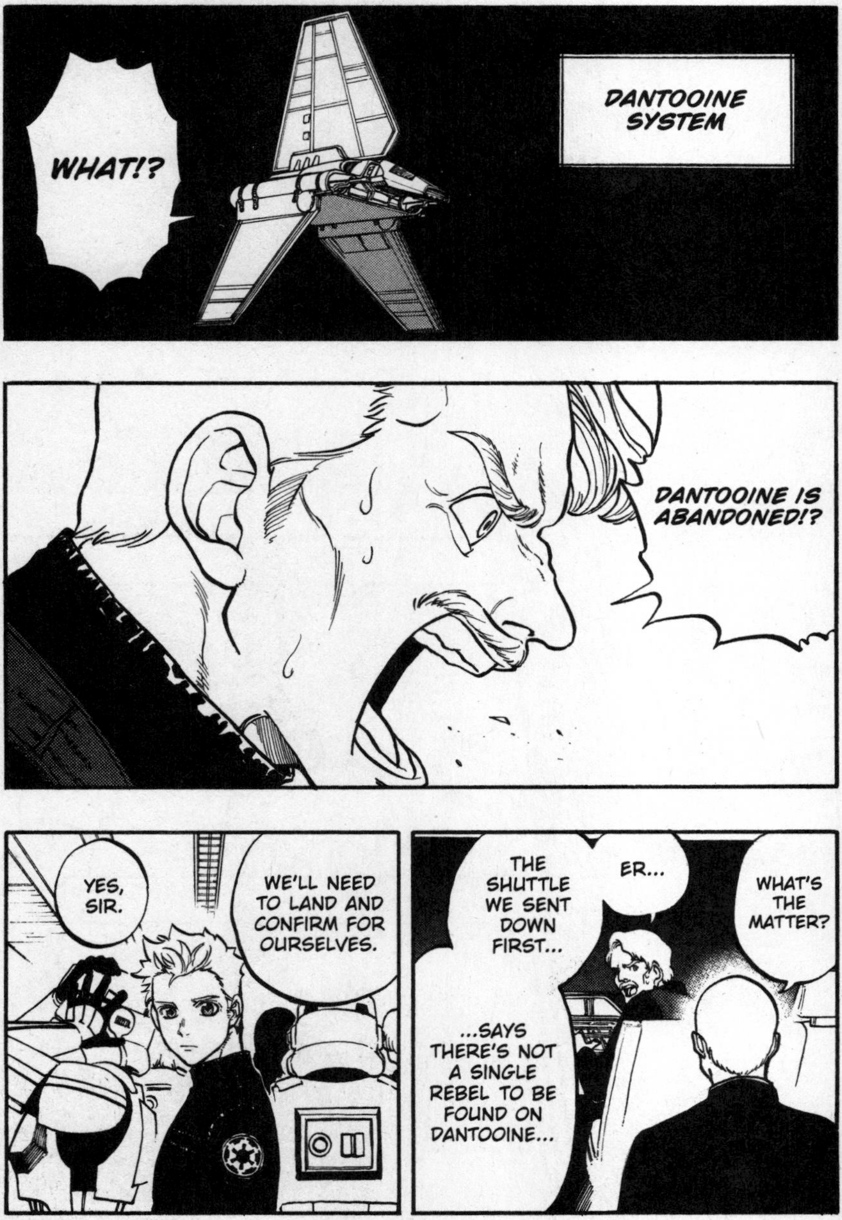
DANTOOINE SYSTEM
WHAT!?
DANTOOINE IS ABANDONED!?
WHAT'S THE MATTER?
ER...
THE SHUTTLE WE SENT DOWN FIRST...
...SAYS THERE'S NOT A SINGLE REBEL TO BE FOUND ON DANTOOINE...
WE'LL NEED TO LAND AND CONFIRM FOR OURSELVES.
YES, SIR.

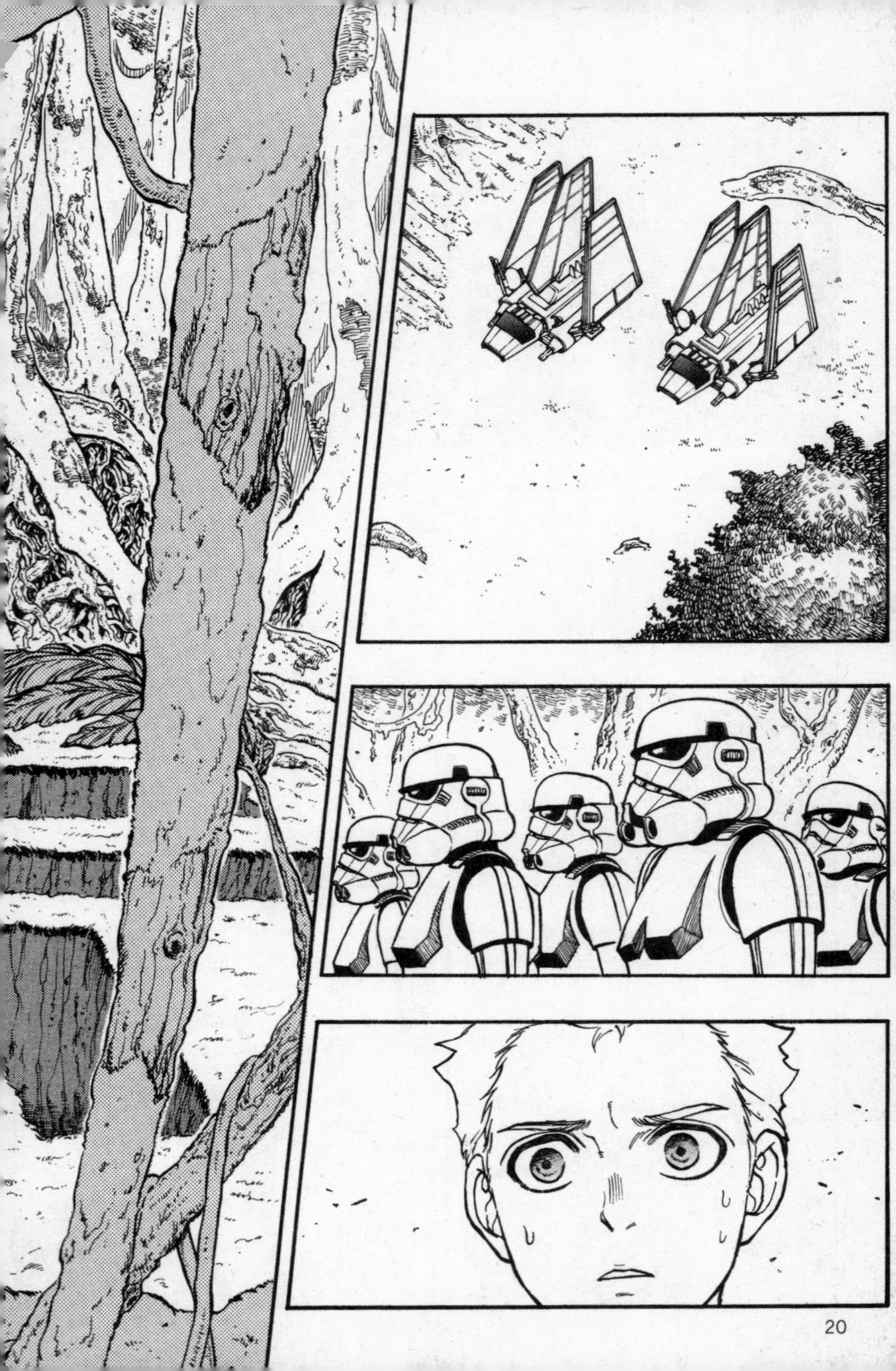

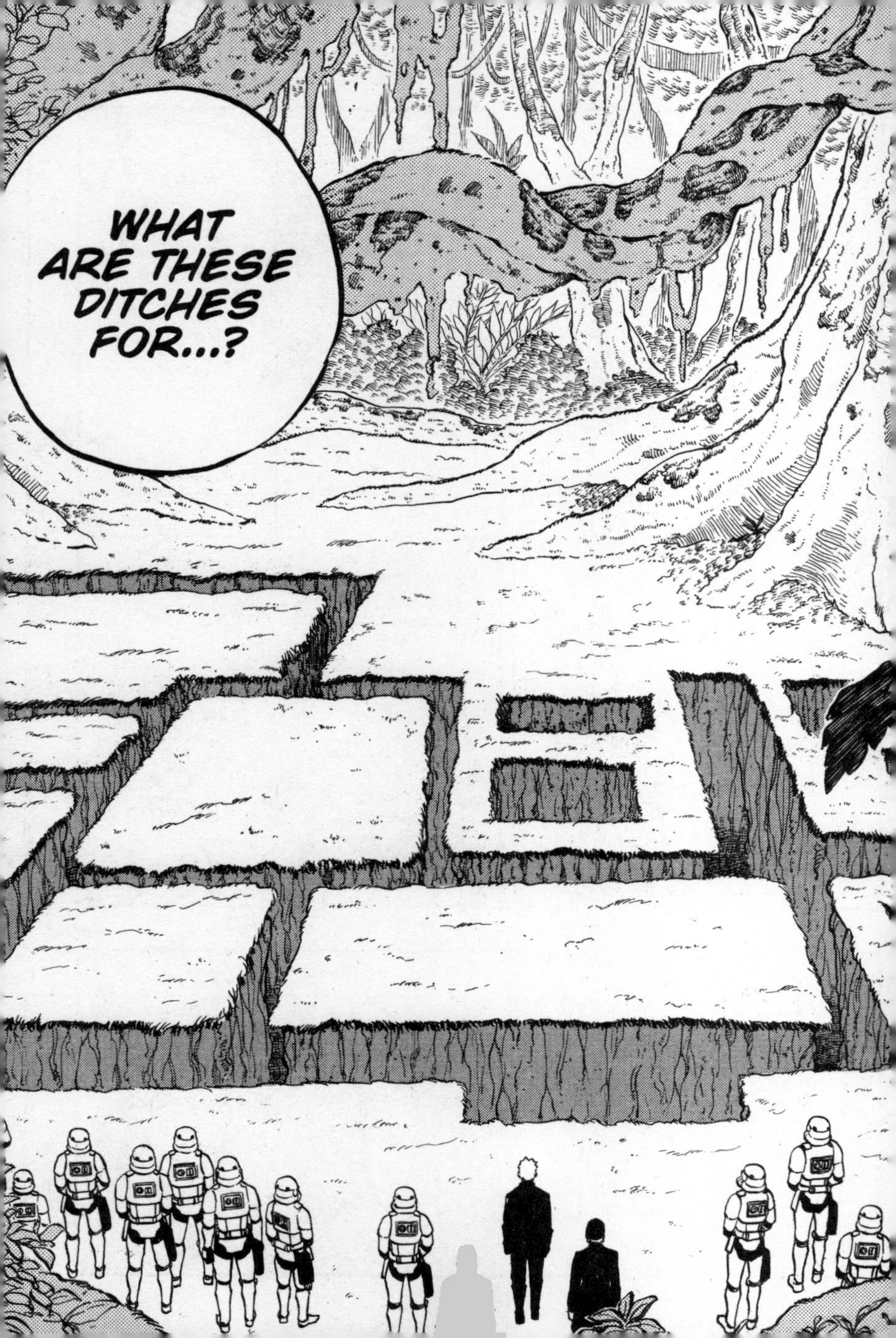
WHAT ARE THESE DITCHES FOR...?

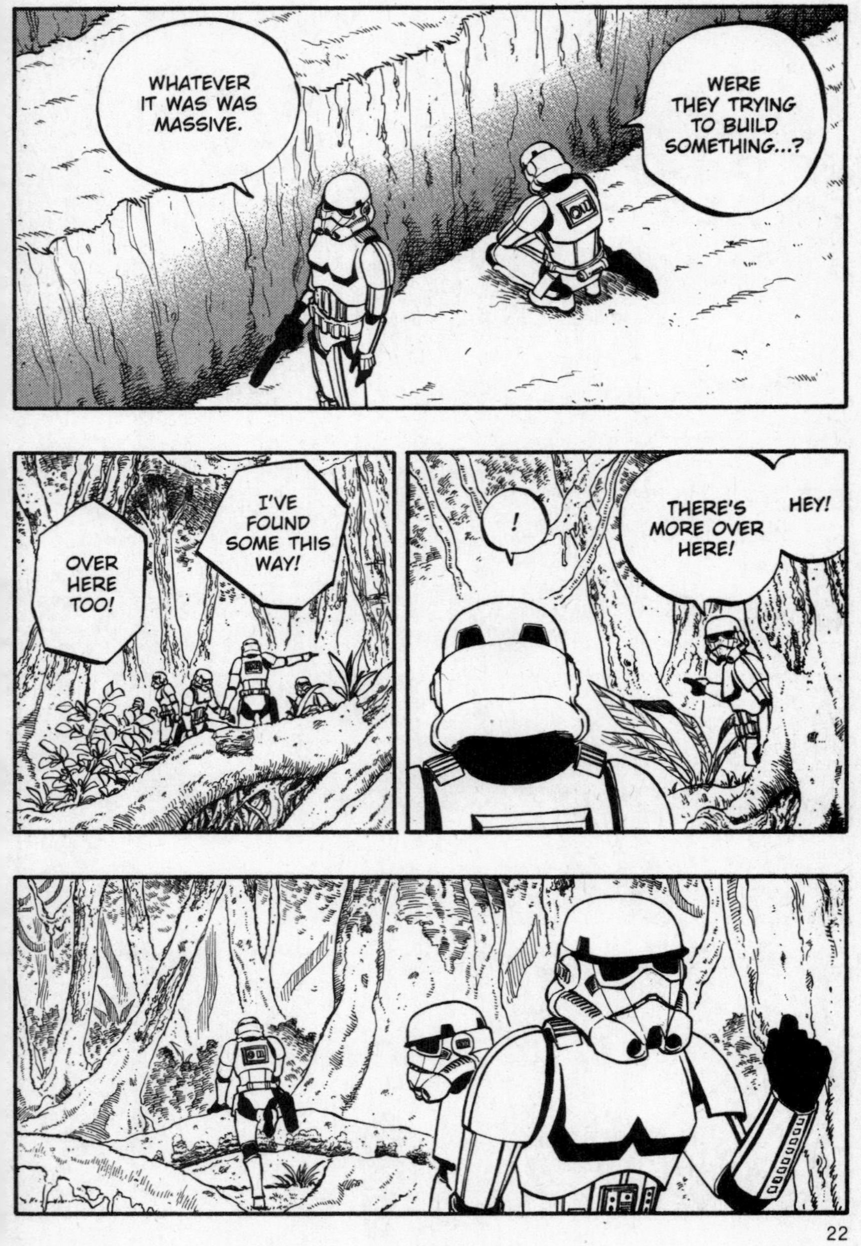
WERE THEY TRYING TO BUILD SOMETHING...?
WHATEVER IT WAS WAS MASSIVE.
HEY!
THERE'S MORE OVER HERE!
!
I'VE FOUND SOME THIS WAY!
OVER HERE TOO!

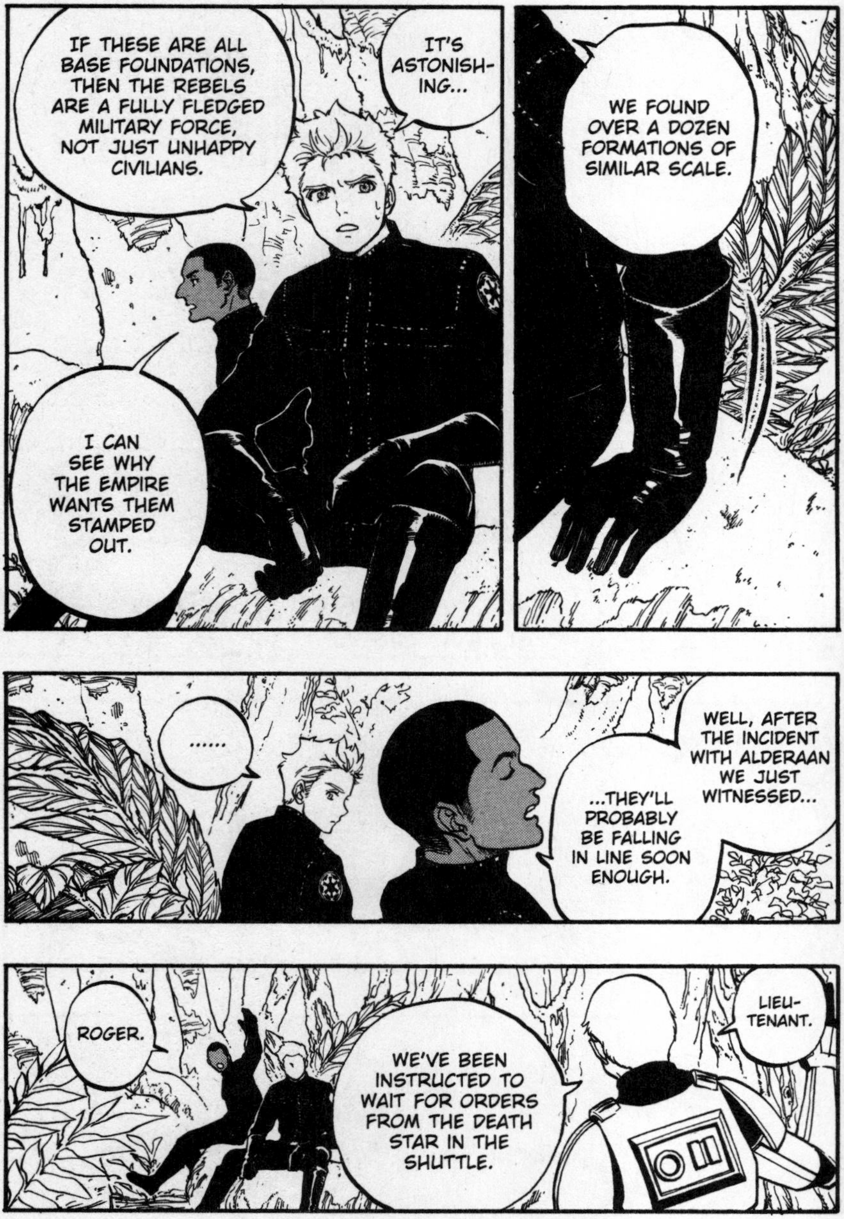
WE FOUND OVER A DOZEN FORMATIONS OF SIMILAR SCALE.
IT'S ASTONISH-ING...
IF THESE ARE ALL BASE FOUNDATIONS, THEN THE REBELS ARE A FULLY FLEDGED MILITARY FORCE, NOT JUST UNHAPPY CIVILIANS.
I CAN SEE WHY THE EMPIRE WANTS THEM STAMPED OUT.
WELL, AFTER THE INCIDENT WITH ALDERAAN WE JUST WITNESSED...
...THEY'LL PROBABLY BE FALLING IN LINE SOON ENOUGH.
......
LIEU-TENANT.
WE'VE BEEN INSTRUCTED TO WAIT FOR ORDERS FROM THE DEATH STAR IN THE SHUTTLE.
ROGER.

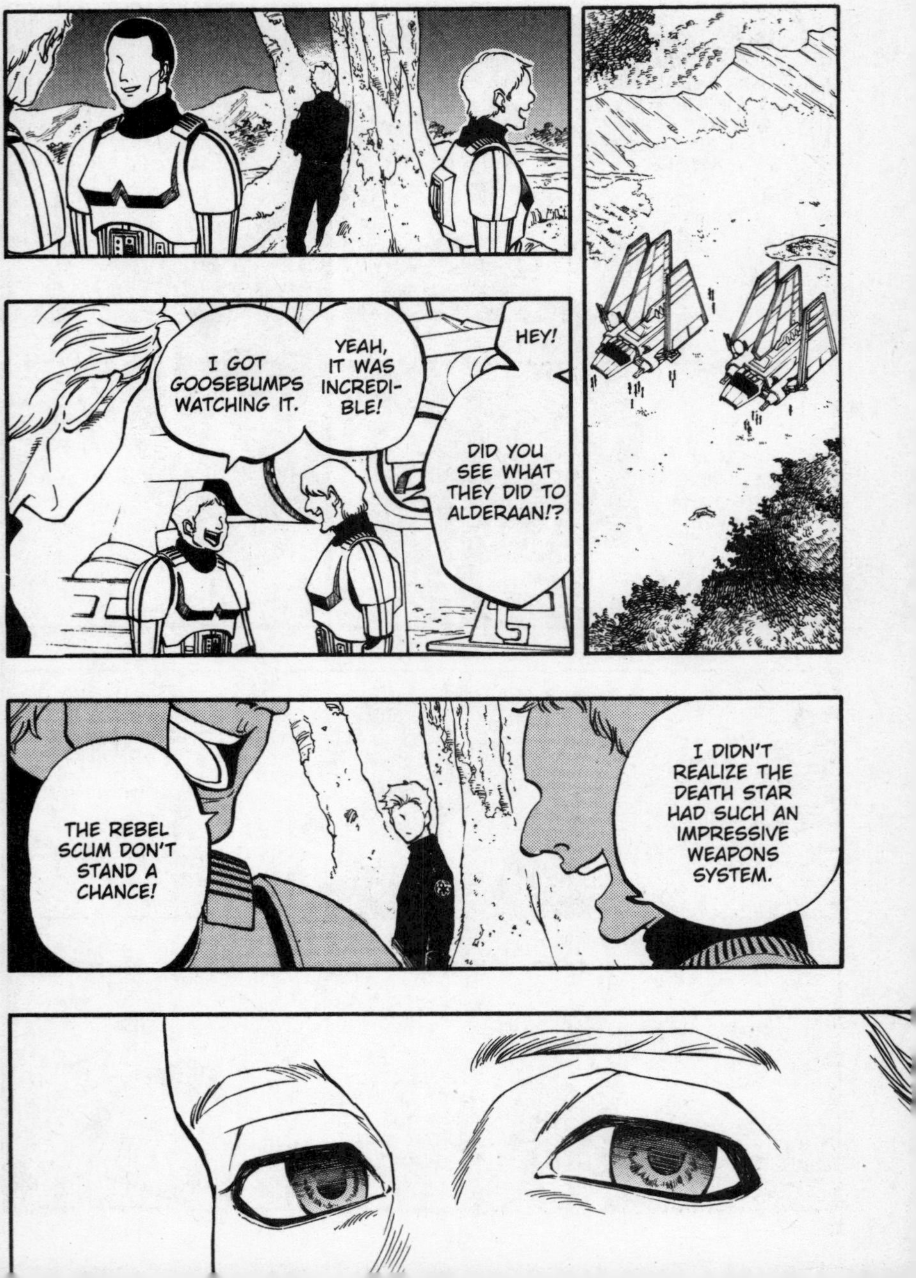
HEY!
DID YOU SEE WHAT THEY DID TO ALDERAAN!?
YEAH, IT WAS INCREDI-BLE!
I GOT GOOSEBUMPS WATCHING IT.
I DIDN'T REALIZE THE DEATH STAR HAD SUCH AN IMPRESSIVE WEAPONS SYSTEM.
THE REBEL SCUM DON'T STAND A CHANCE!

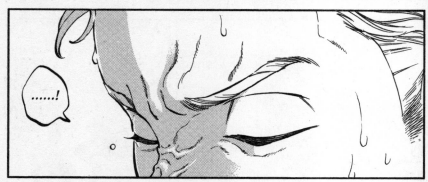

……!

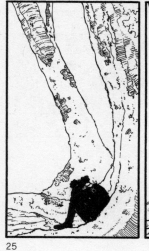

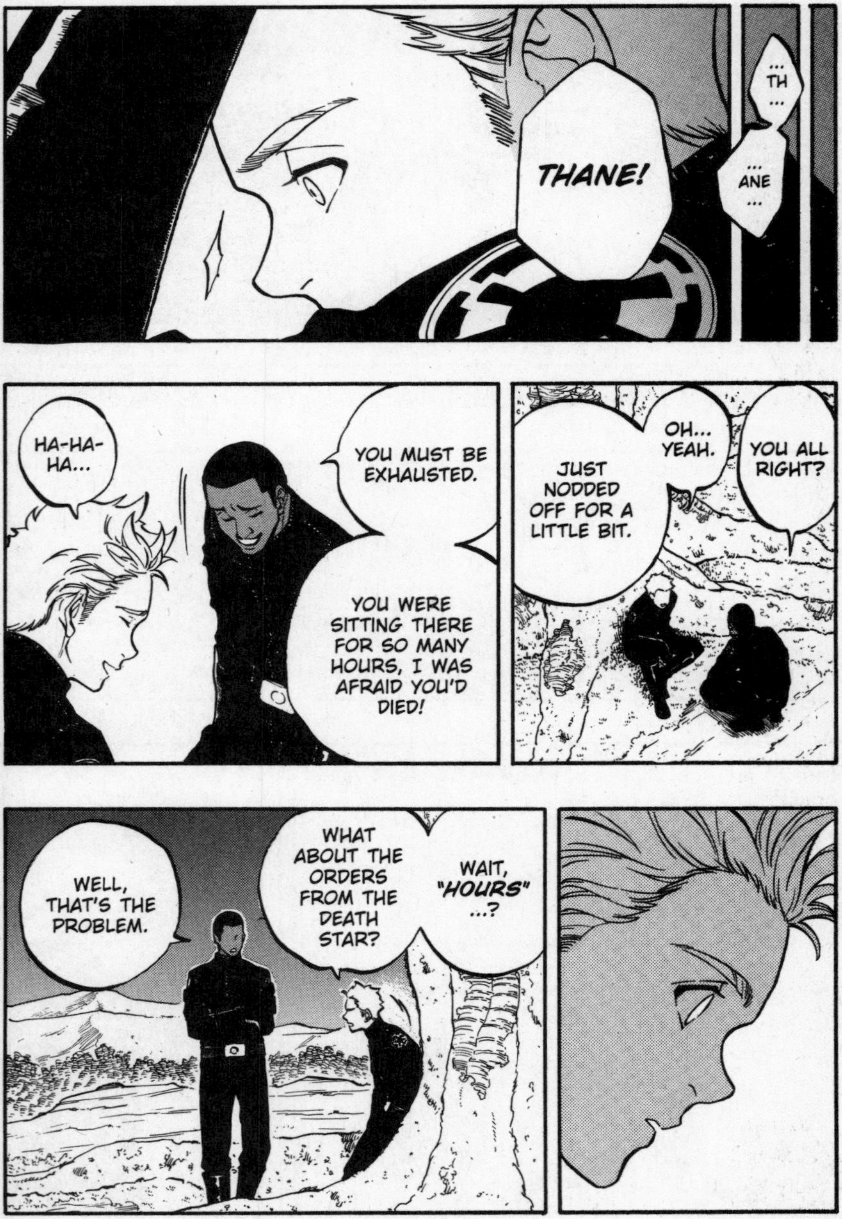
...TH... ...ANE...
THANE!
YOU ALL RIGHT?
OH... YEAH.
JUST NODDED OFF FOR A LITTLE BIT.
YOU MUST BE EXHAUSTED.
YOU WERE SITTING THERE FOR SO MANY HOURS, I WAS AFRAID YOU'D DIED!
HA-HA-HA...
WAIT, "*HOURS*" ...?
WHAT ABOUT THE ORDERS FROM THE DEATH STAR?
WELL, THAT'S THE PROBLEM.

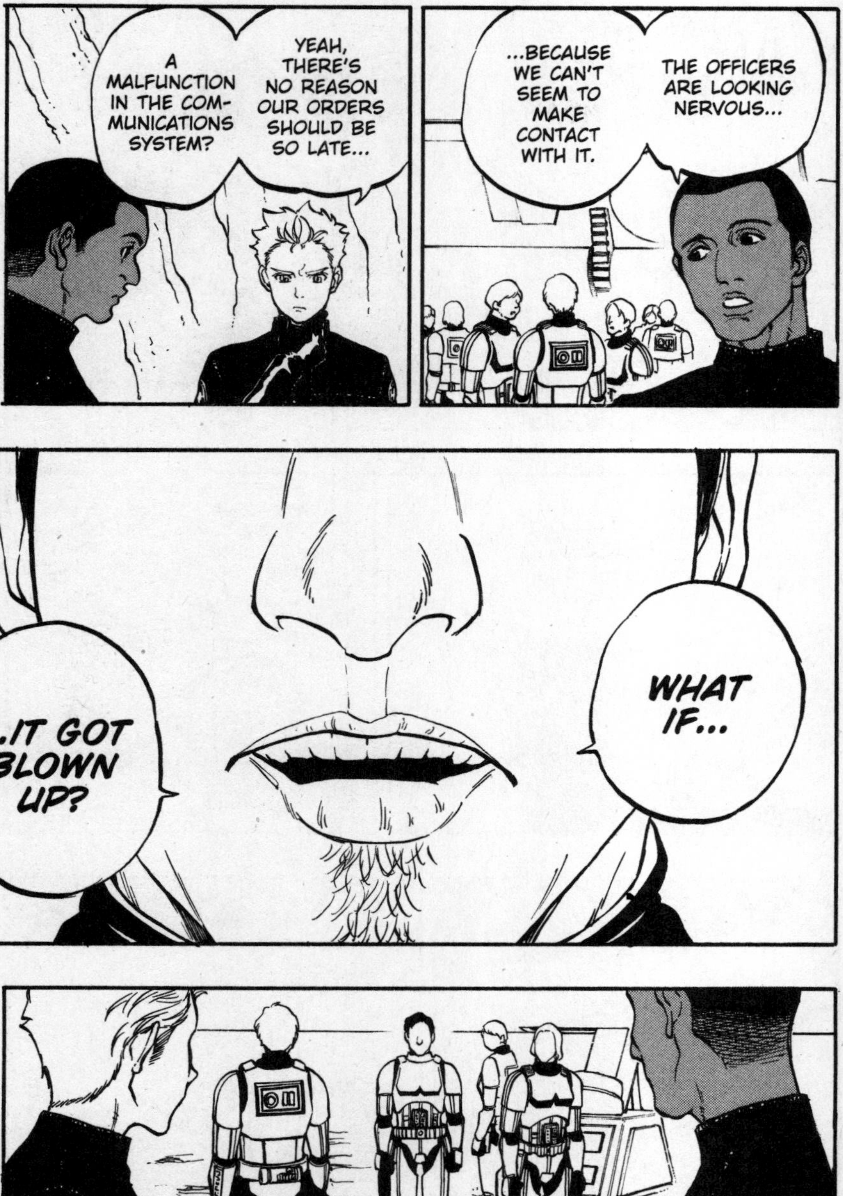
THE OFFICERS ARE LOOKING NERVOUS...
...BECAUSE WE CAN'T SEEM TO MAKE CONTACT WITH IT.
YEAH, THERE'S NO REASON OUR ORDERS SHOULD BE SO LATE...
A MALFUNCTION IN THE COM-MUNICATIONS SYSTEM?
WHAT IF...
...IT GOT BLOWN UP?

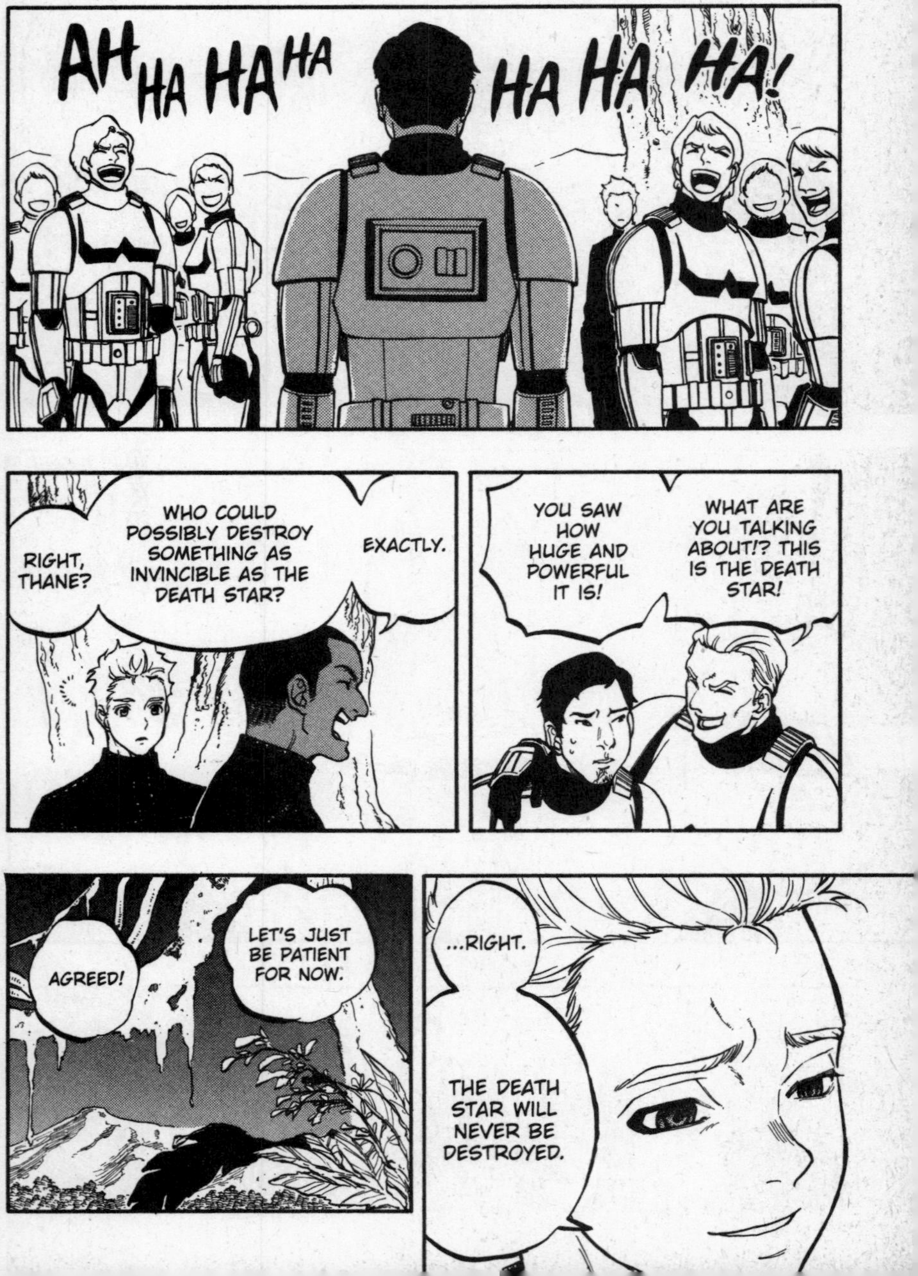
AH HA HA HA
HA HA HA!
WHAT ARE YOU TALKING ABOUT!? THIS IS THE DEATH STAR!
YOU SAW HOW HUGE AND POWERFUL IT IS!
EXACTLY.
WHO COULD POSSIBLY DESTROY SOMETHING AS INVINCIBLE AS THE DEATH STAR?
RIGHT, THANE?
...RIGHT.
THE DEATH STAR WILL NEVER BE DESTROYED.
LET'S JUST BE PATIENT FOR NOW.
AGREED!

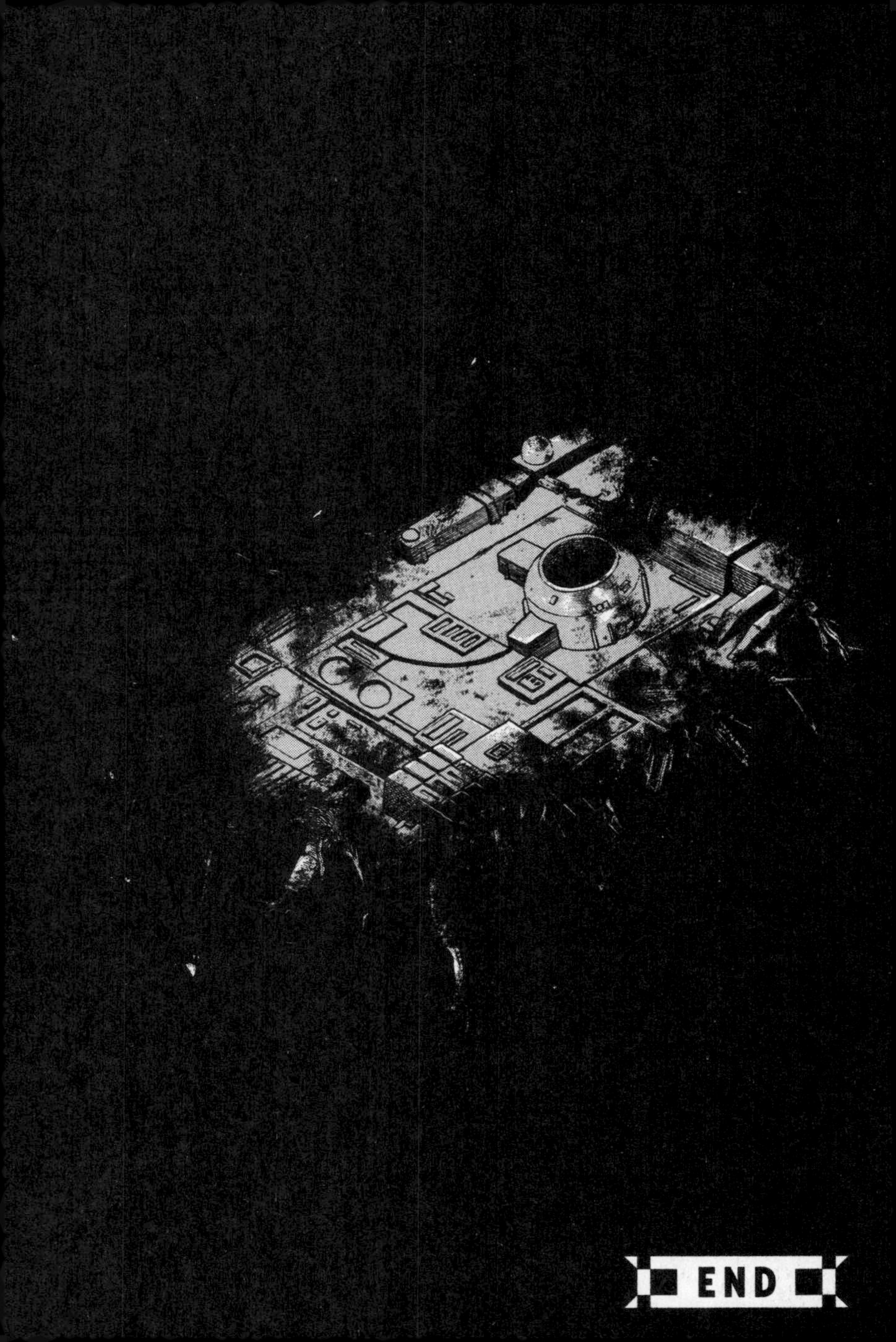
END

STAR WARS
LOST STARS
ロスト・スターズ

STAR WARS
LOST STARS
ロスト・スターズ

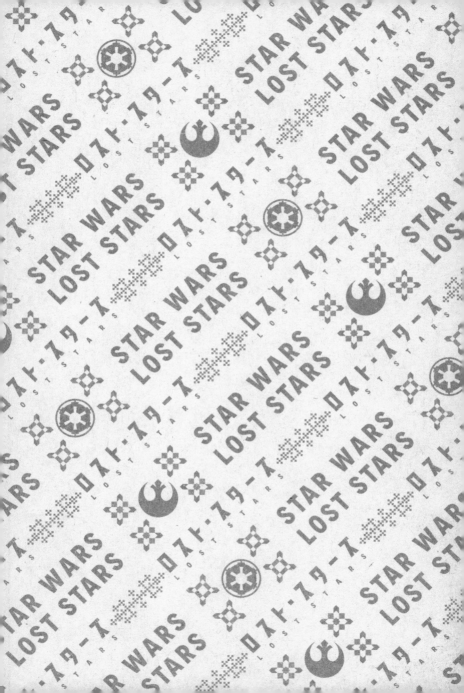

Chapter. 08

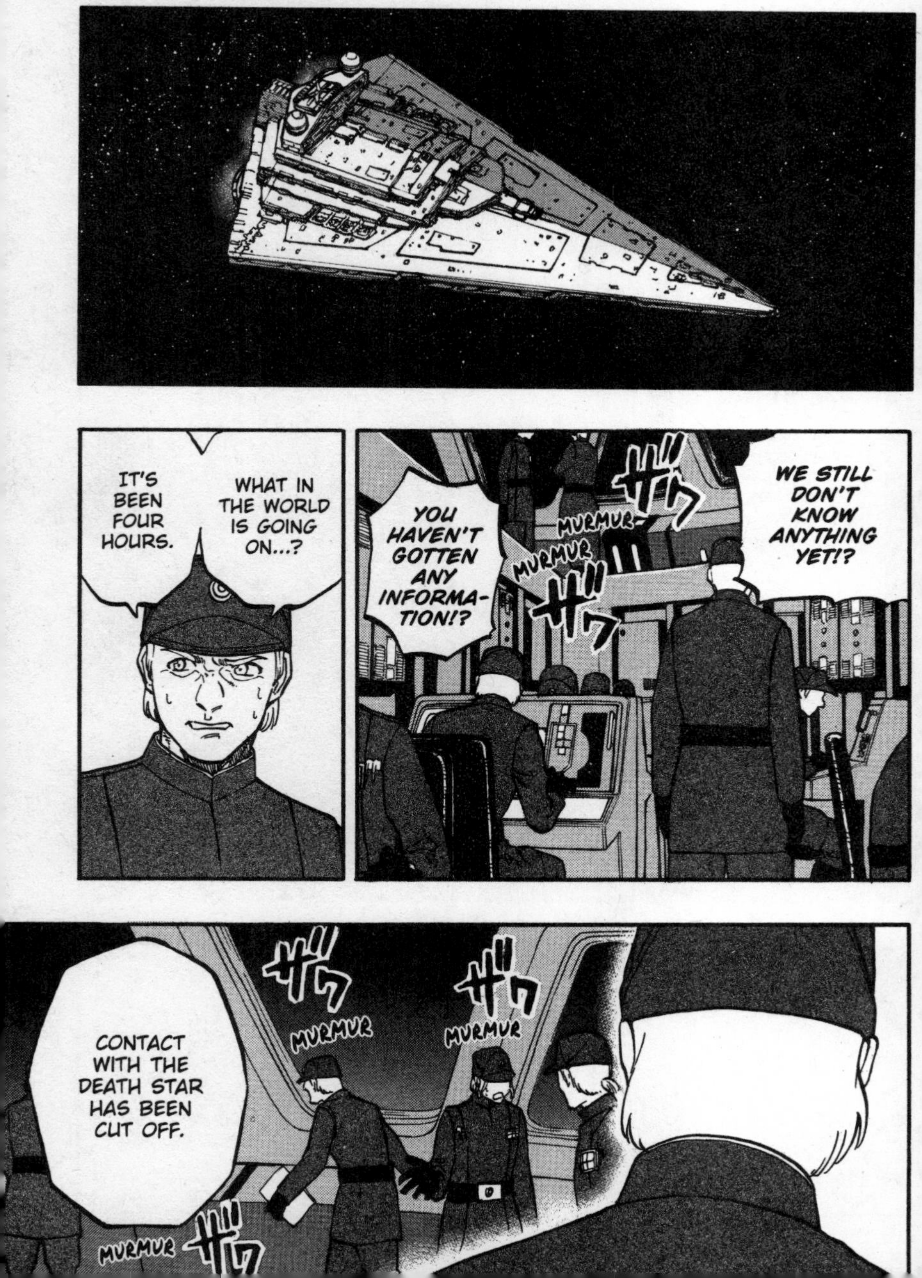
WE STILL DON'T KNOW ANYTHING YET!?
ザワ
MURMUR
YOU HAVEN'T GOTTEN ANY INFORMATION!?
MURMUR
ザワ
WHAT IN THE WORLD IS GOING ON...?
IT'S BEEN FOUR HOURS.
ザワ
MURMUR
ザワ
MURMUR
CONTACT WITH THE DEATH STAR HAS BEEN CUT OFF.
MURMUR
ザワ

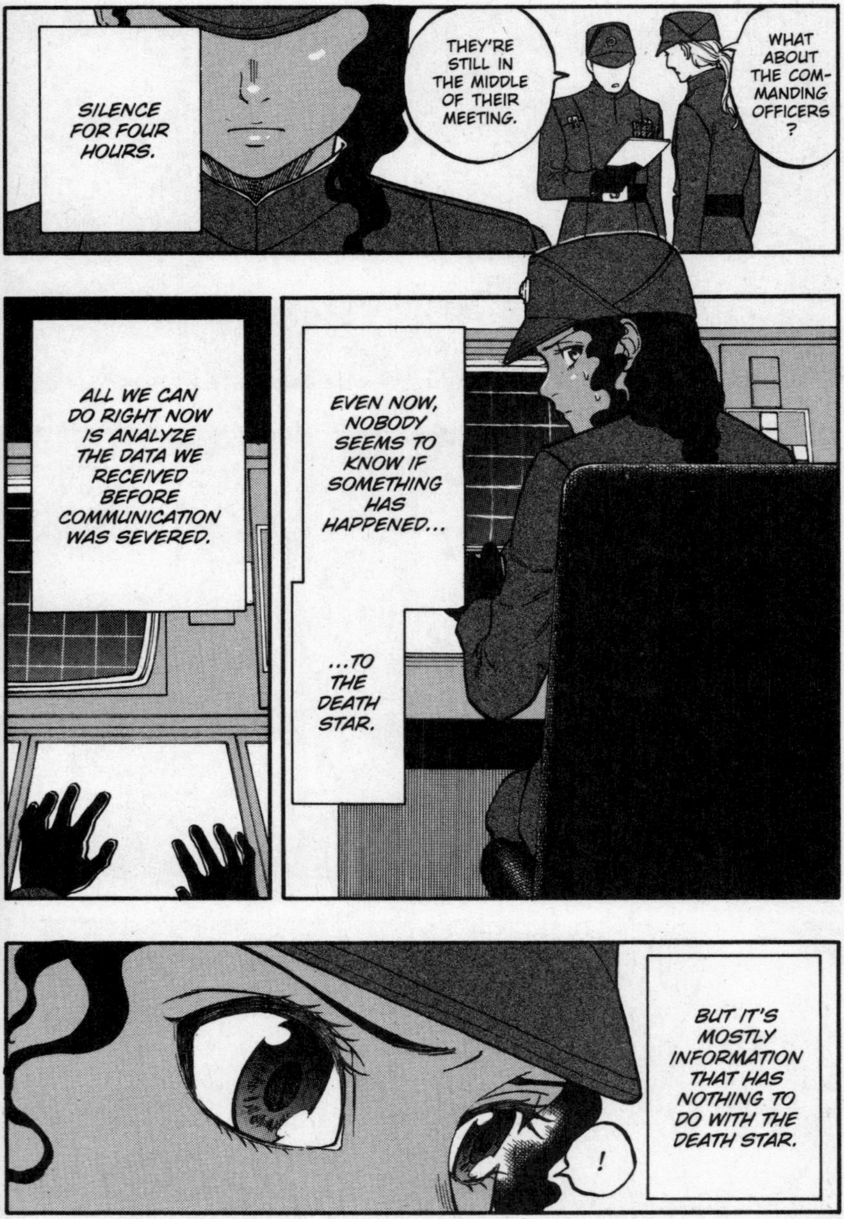
WHAT ABOUT THE COM-MANDING OFFICERS?
THEY'RE STILL IN THE MIDDLE OF THEIR MEETING.
SILENCE FOR FOUR HOURS.
EVEN NOW, NOBODY SEEMS TO KNOW IF SOMETHING HAS HAPPENED...
...TO THE DEATH STAR.
ALL WE CAN DO RIGHT NOW IS ANALYZE THE DATA WE RECEIVED BEFORE COMMUNICATION WAS SEVERED.
BUT IT'S MOSTLY INFORMATION THAT HAS NOTHING TO DO WITH THE DEATH STAR.
!

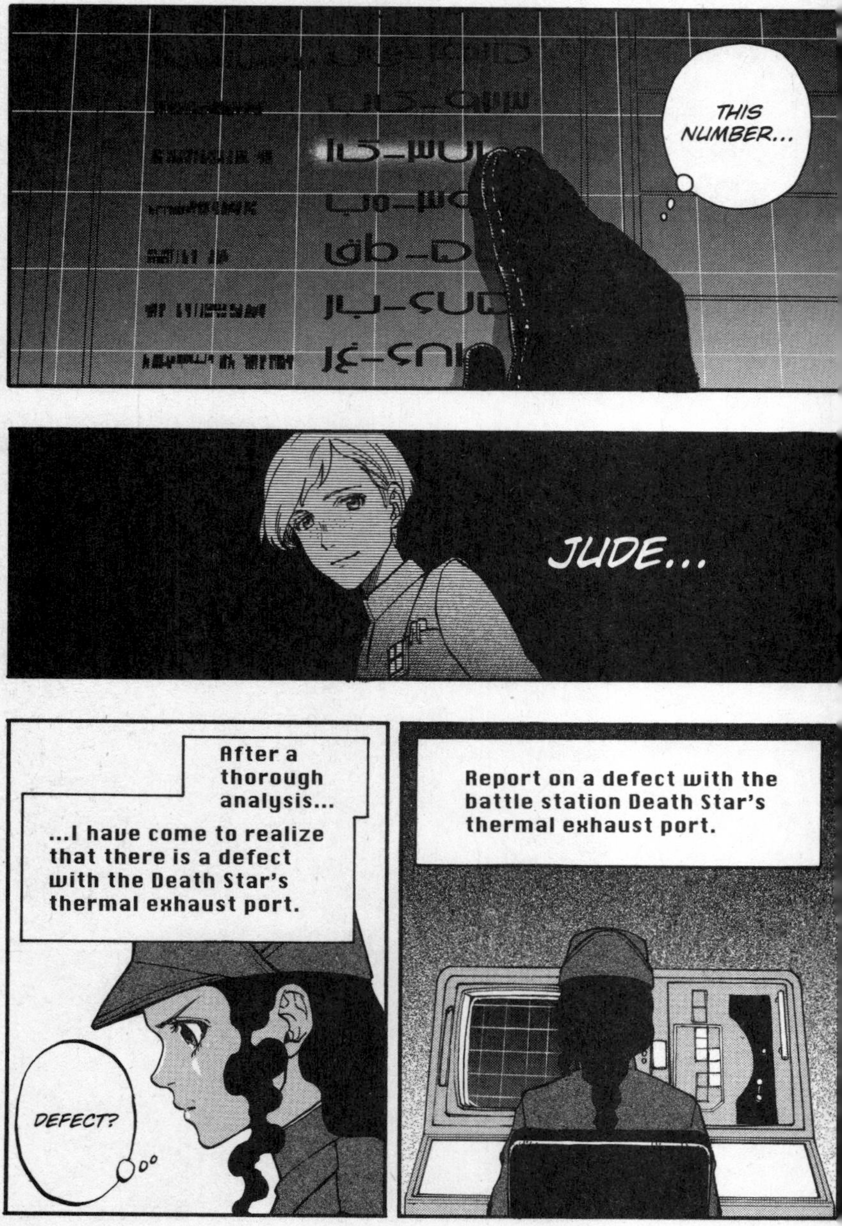

THIS NUMBER...
JUDE...
Report on a defect with the battle station Death Star's thermal exhaust port.
After a thorough analysis...
...I have come to realize that there is a defect with the Death Star's thermal exhaust port.
DEFECT?

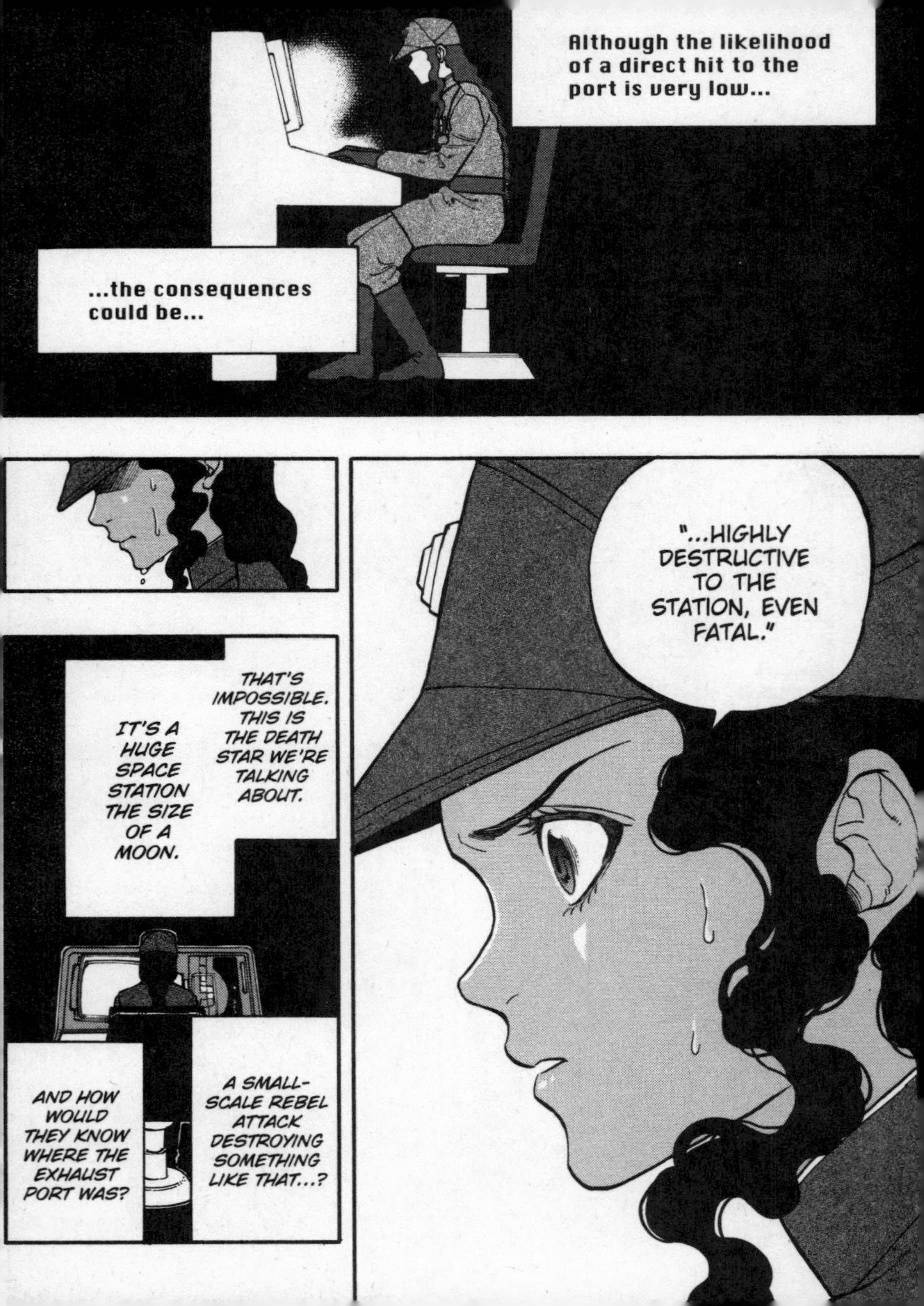
Although the likelihood of a direct hit to the port is very low...
...the consequences could be...
"...HIGHLY DESTRUCTIVE TO THE STATION, EVEN FATAL."
THAT'S IMPOSSIBLE. THIS IS THE DEATH STAR WE'RE TALKING ABOUT.
IT'S A HUGE SPACE STATION THE SIZE OF A MOON.
A SMALL-SCALE REBEL ATTACK DESTROYING SOMETHING LIKE THAT...?
AND HOW WOULD THEY KNOW WHERE THE EXHAUST PORT WAS?

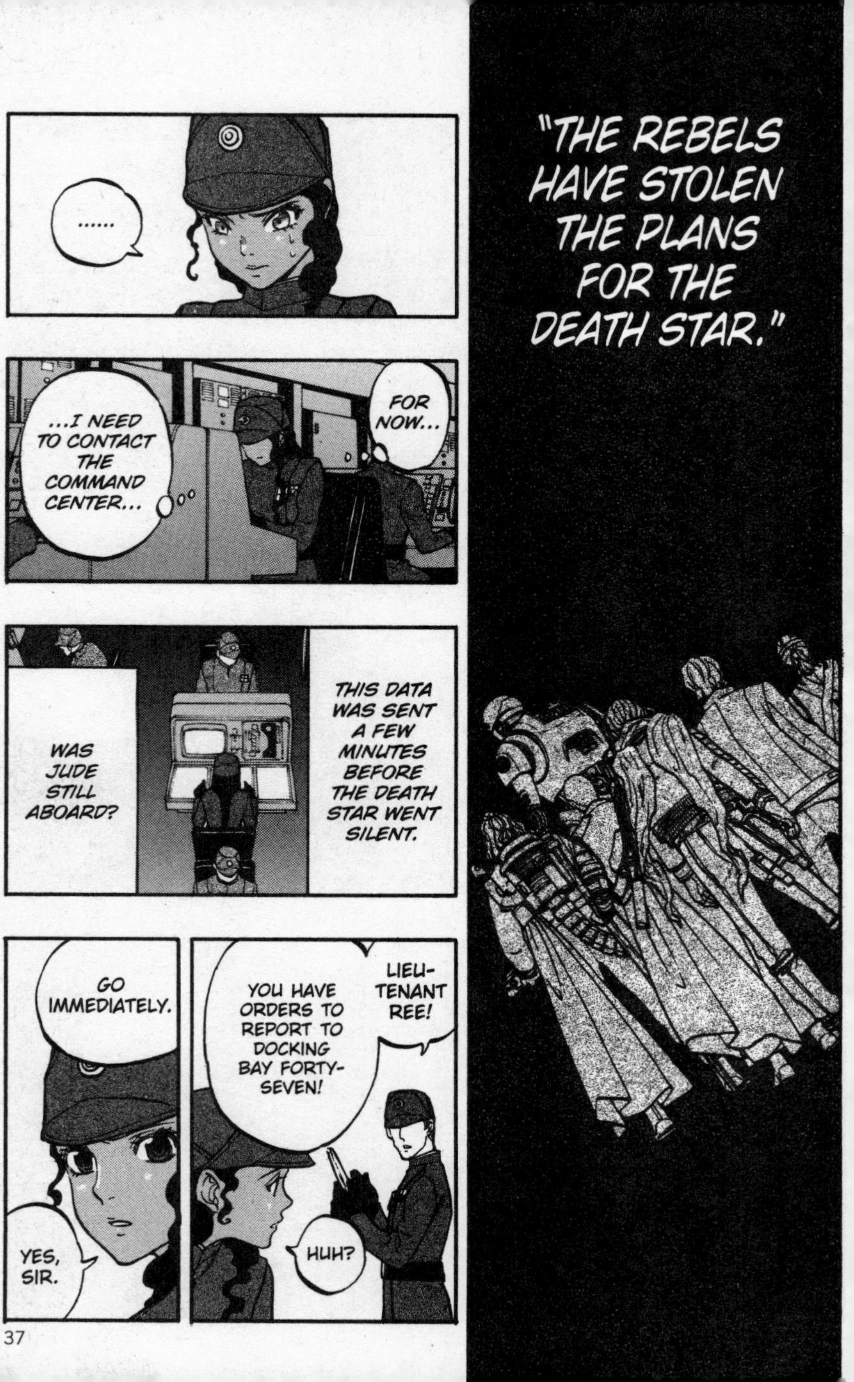
"THE REBELS HAVE STOLEN THE PLANS FOR THE DEATH STAR."
......
FOR NOW...
...I NEED TO CONTACT THE COMMAND CENTER...
THIS DATA WAS SENT A FEW MINUTES BEFORE THE DEATH STAR WENT SILENT.
WAS JUDE STILL ABOARD?
LIEU-TENANT REE!
YOU HAVE ORDERS TO REPORT TO DOCKING BAY FORTY-SEVEN!
HUH?
GO IMMEDIATELY.
YES, SIR.

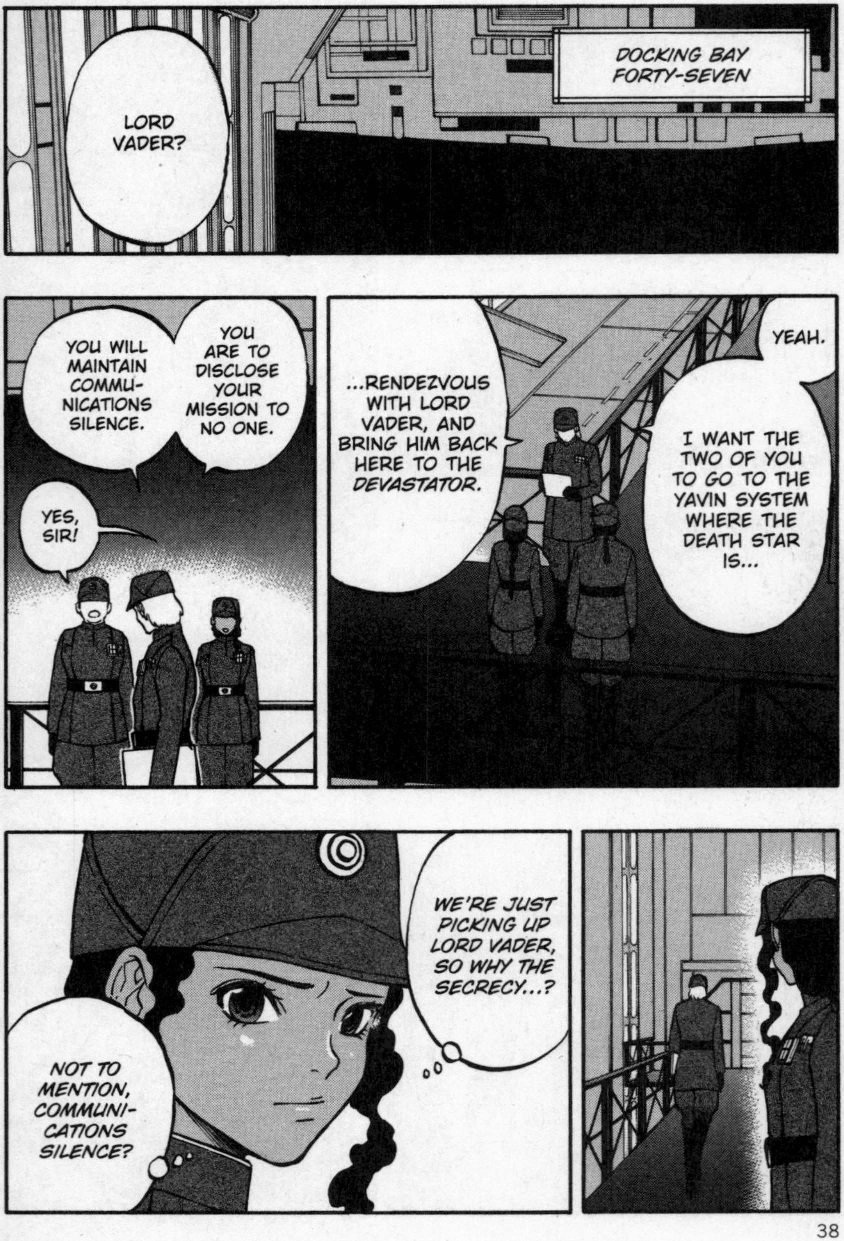
DOCKING BAY FORTY-SEVEN
LORD VADER?
YEAH.
I WANT THE TWO OF YOU TO GO TO THE YAVIN SYSTEM WHERE THE DEATH STAR IS...
...RENDEZVOUS WITH LORD VADER, AND BRING HIM BACK HERE TO THE *DEVASTATOR*.
YOU ARE TO DISCLOSE YOUR MISSION TO NO ONE.
YOU WILL MAINTAIN COMMUNICATIONS SILENCE.
YES, SIR!
WE'RE JUST PICKING UP LORD VADER, SO WHY THE SECRECY...?
NOT TO MENTION, COMMUNICATIONS SILENCE?

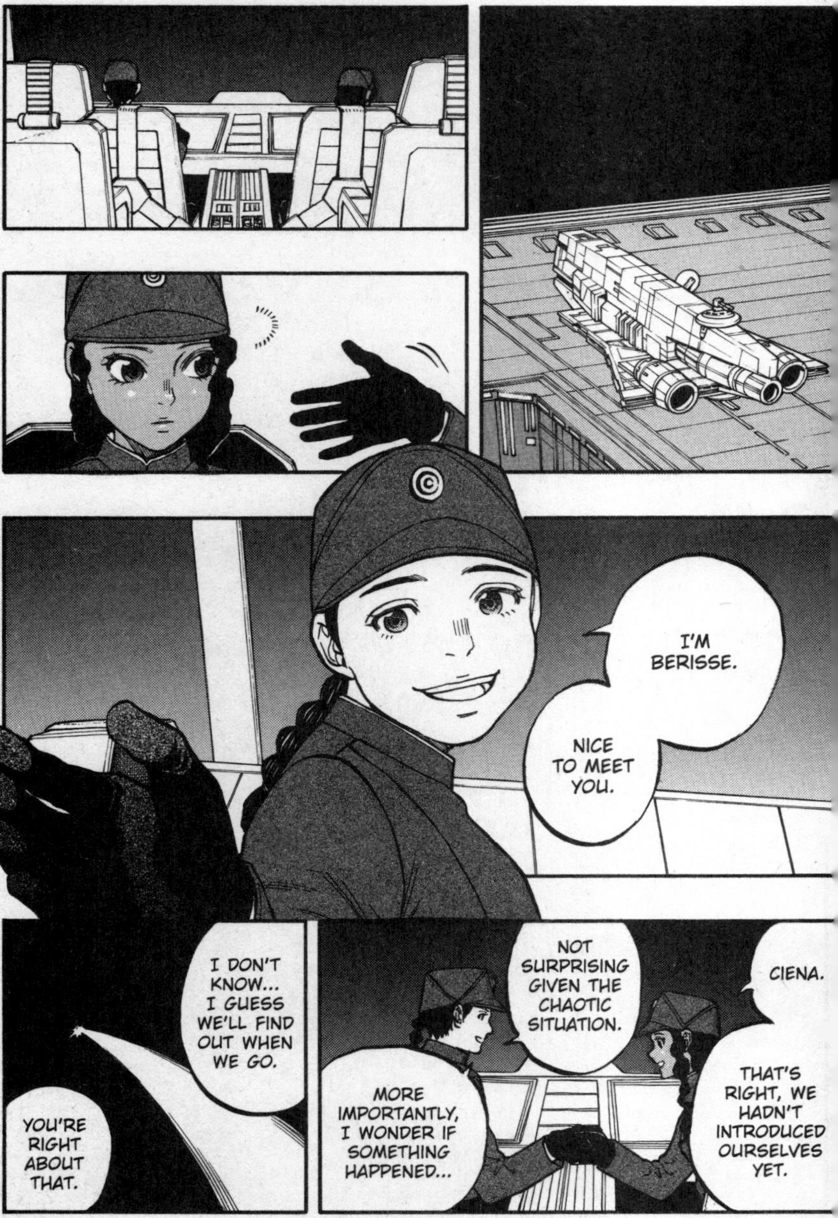
I'M BERISSE.
NICE TO MEET YOU.
CIENA.
THAT'S RIGHT, WE HADN'T INTRODUCED OURSELVES YET.
NOT SURPRISING GIVEN THE CHAOTIC SITUATION.
MORE IMPORTANTLY, I WONDER IF SOMETHING HAPPENED...
I DON'T KNOW... I GUESS WE'LL FIND OUT WHEN WE GO.
YOU'RE RIGHT ABOUT THAT.

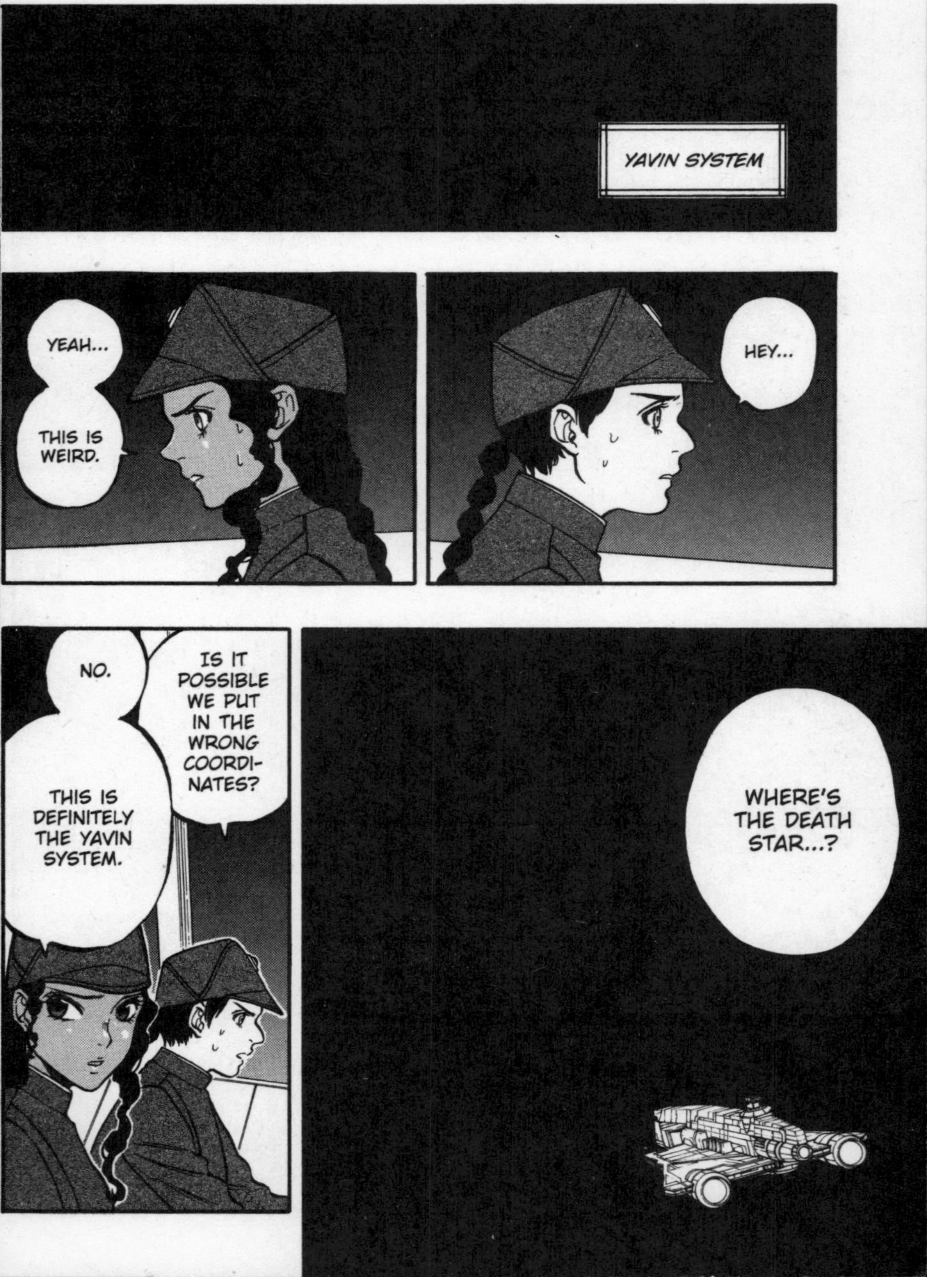
YAVIN SYSTEM
HEY...
YEAH...
THIS IS WEIRD.
WHERE'S THE DEATH STAR...?
IS IT POSSIBLE WE PUT IN THE WRONG COORDI-NATES?
NO.
THIS IS DEFINITELY THE YAVIN SYSTEM.

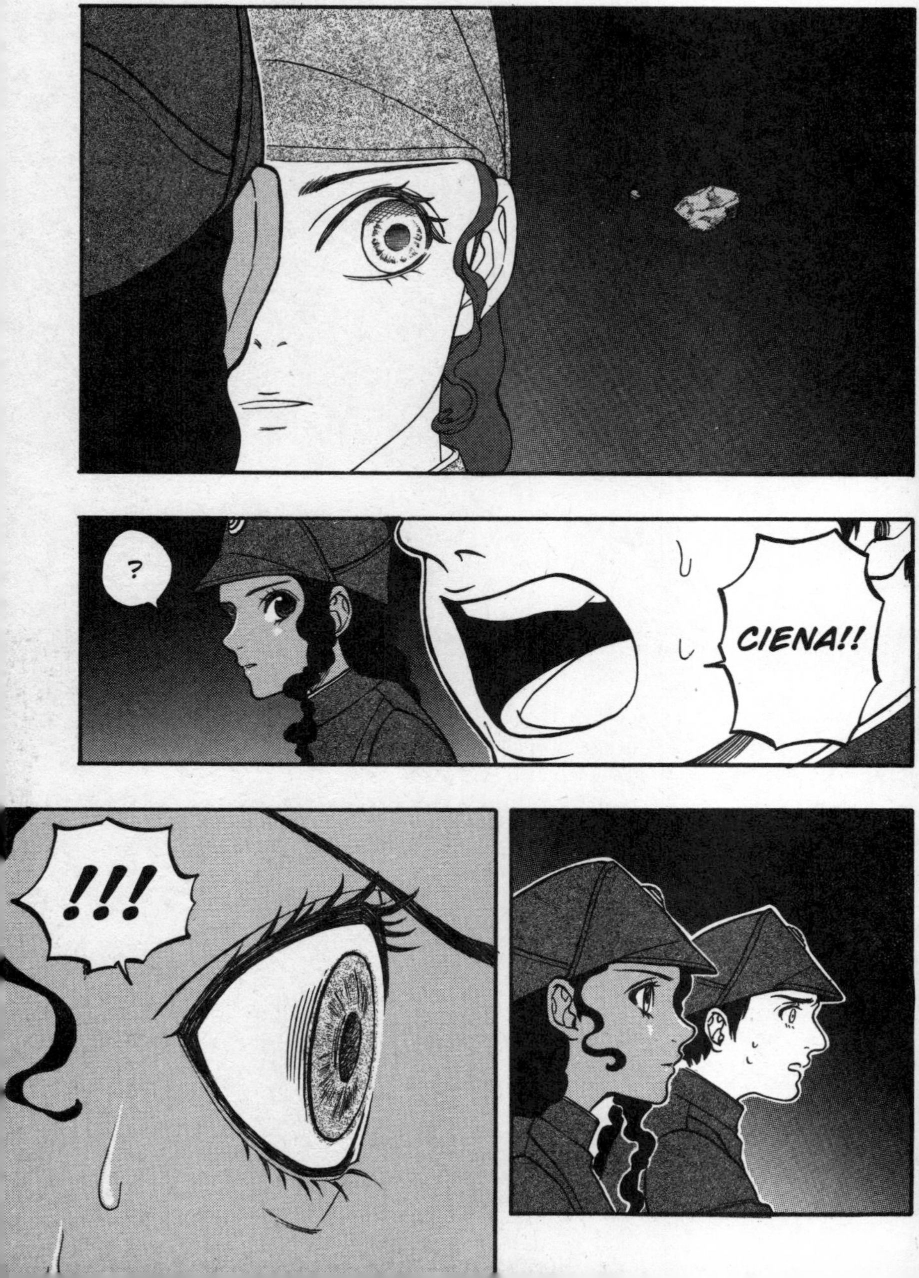
CIENA!!
?
!!!

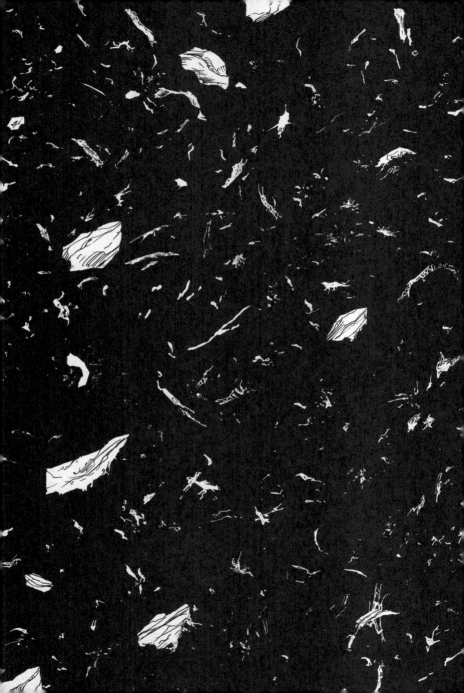

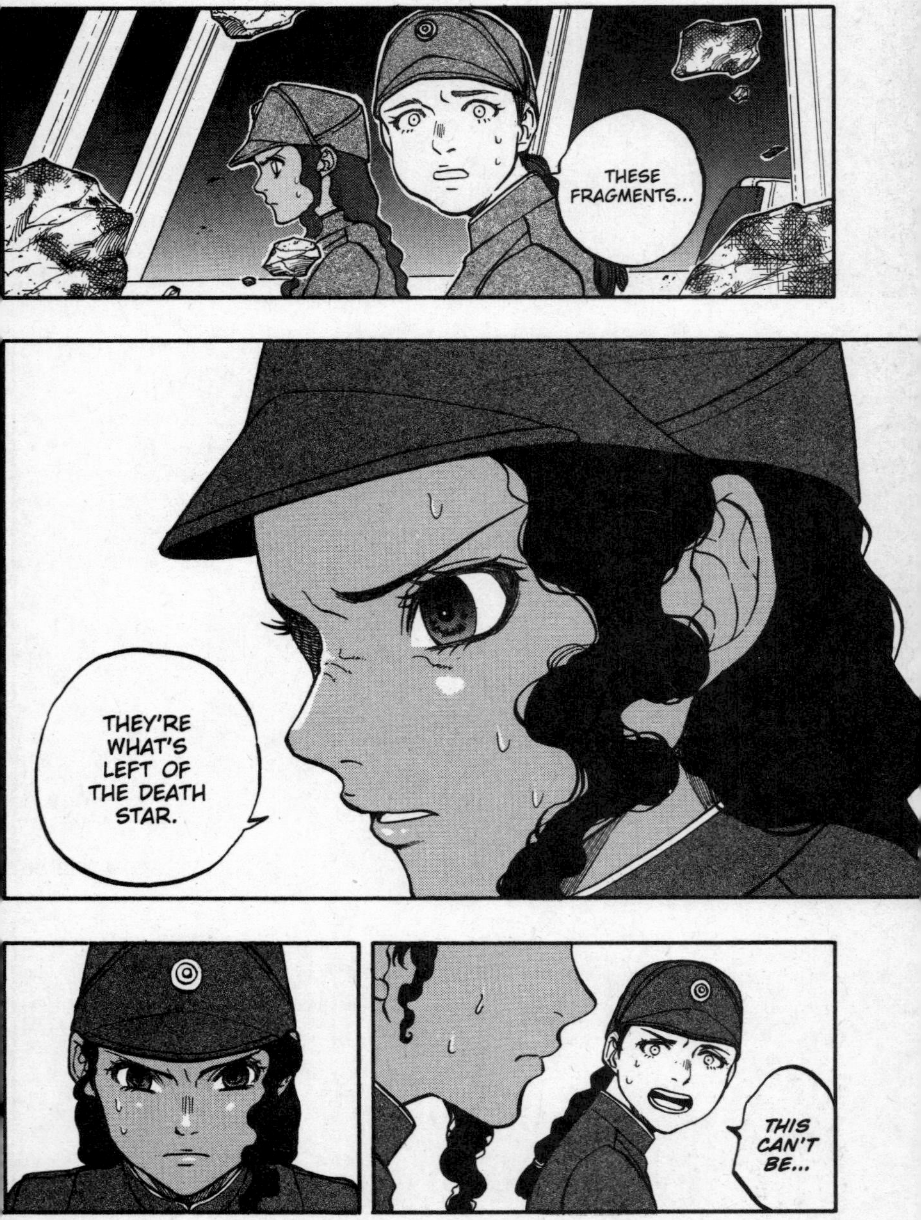
THESE FRAGMENTS...
THEY'RE WHAT'S LEFT OF THE DEATH STAR.
THIS CAN'T BE...

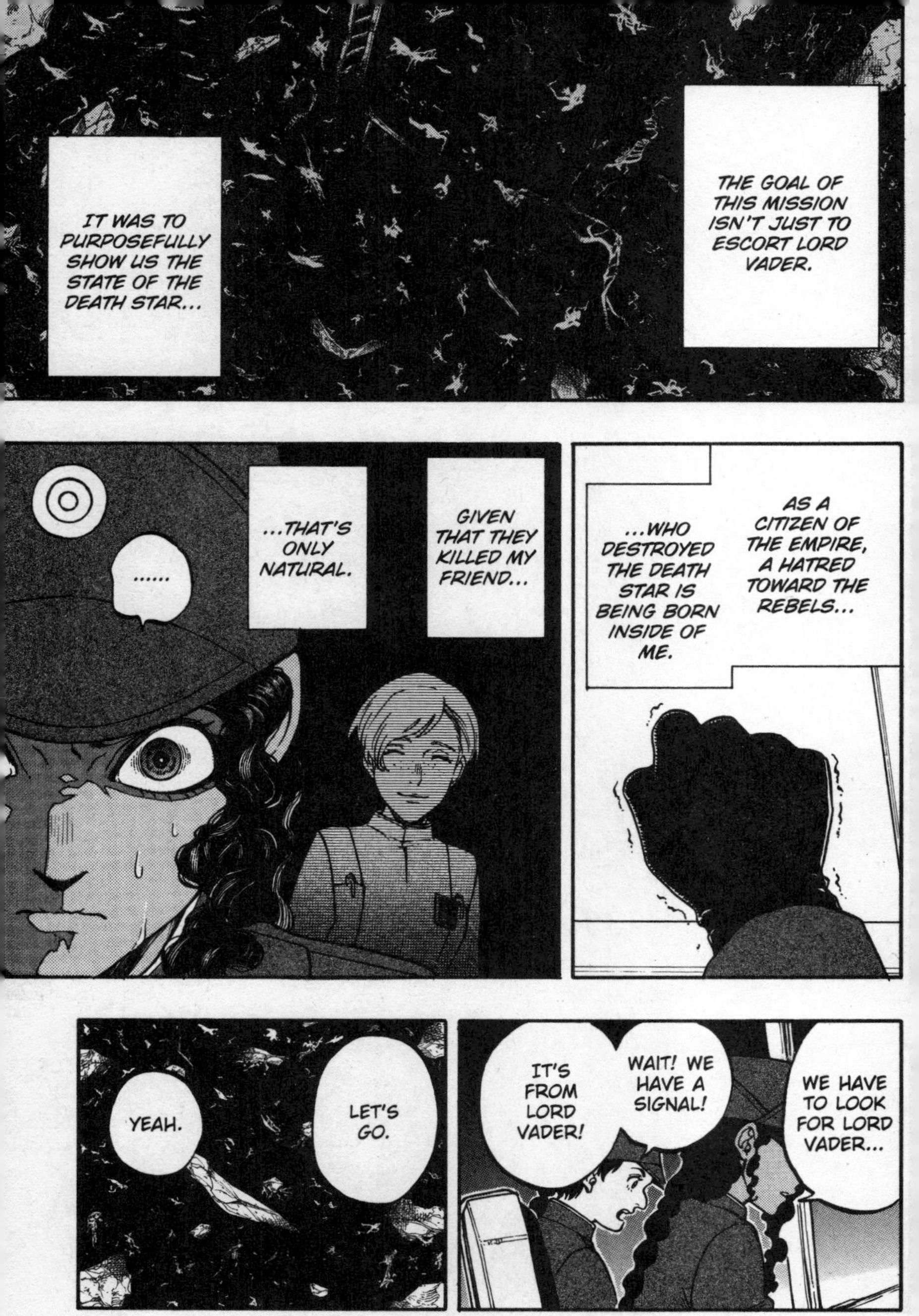
THE GOAL OF THIS MISSION ISN'T JUST TO ESCORT LORD VADER.
IT WAS TO PURPOSEFULLY SHOW US THE STATE OF THE DEATH STAR...
AS A CITIZEN OF THE EMPIRE, A HATRED TOWARD THE REBELS...
...WHO DESTROYED THE DEATH STAR IS BEING BORN INSIDE OF ME.
GIVEN THAT THEY KILLED MY FRIEND...
...THAT'S ONLY NATURAL.
......
WE HAVE TO LOOK FOR LORD VADER...
WAIT! WE HAVE A SIGNAL!
IT'S FROM LORD VADER!
LET'S GO.
YEAH.

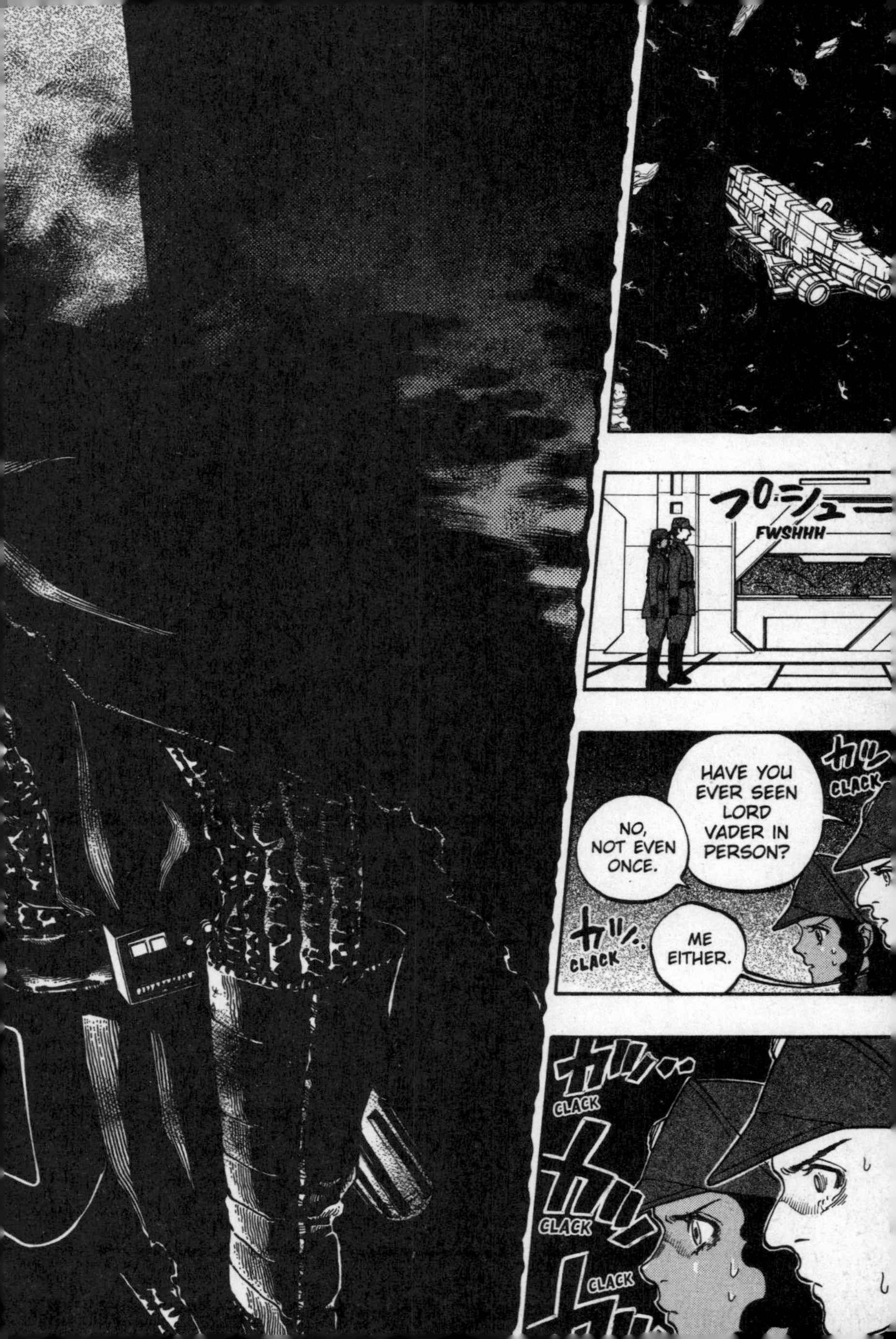
プシュー
FWSHHH
カッ
CLACK
HAVE YOU EVER SEEN LORD VADER IN PERSON?
NO, NOT EVEN ONCE.
カツ…
CLACK
ME EITHER.
CLACK
CLACK
CLACK

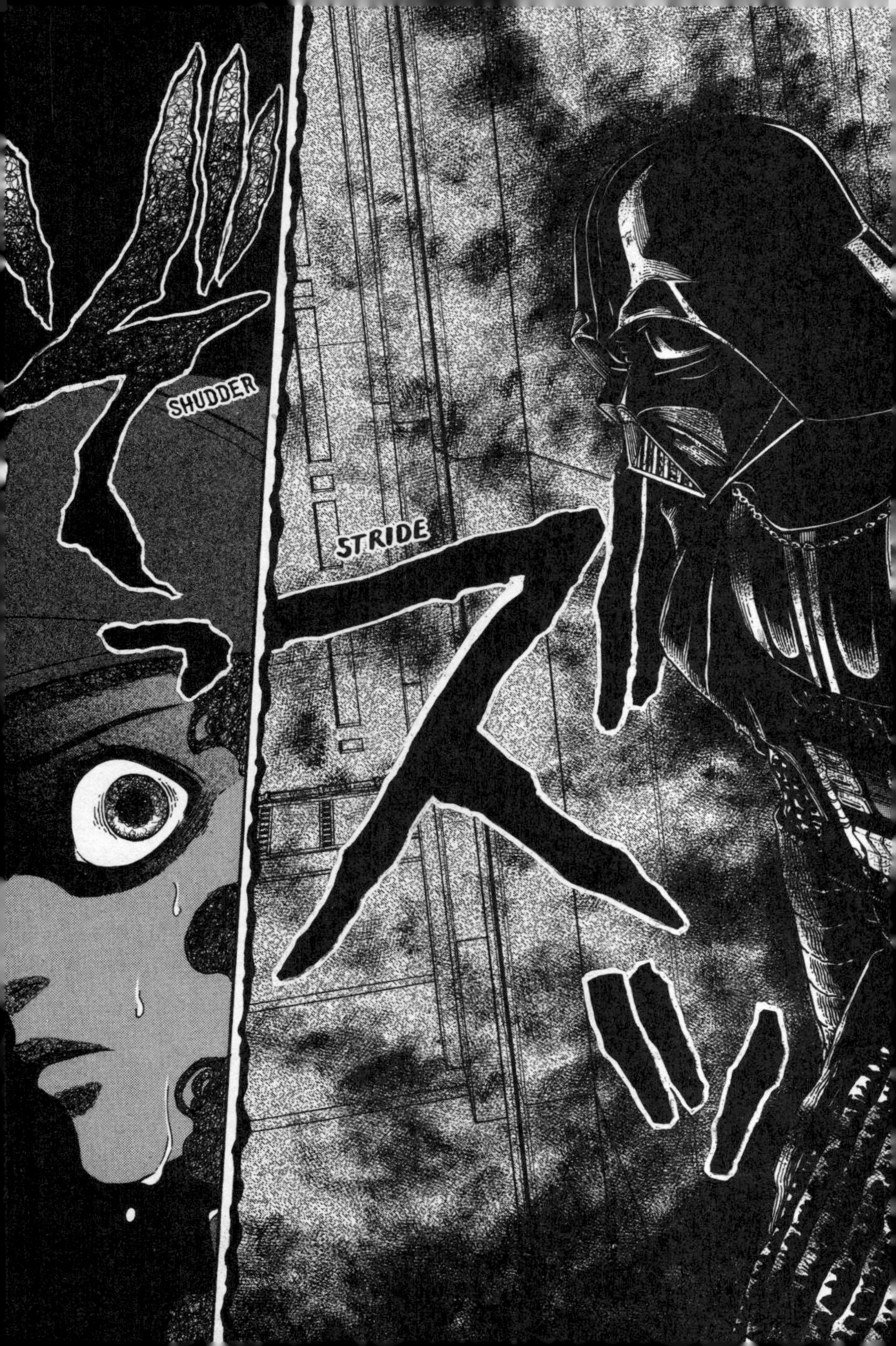
STRIDE
SHUDDER

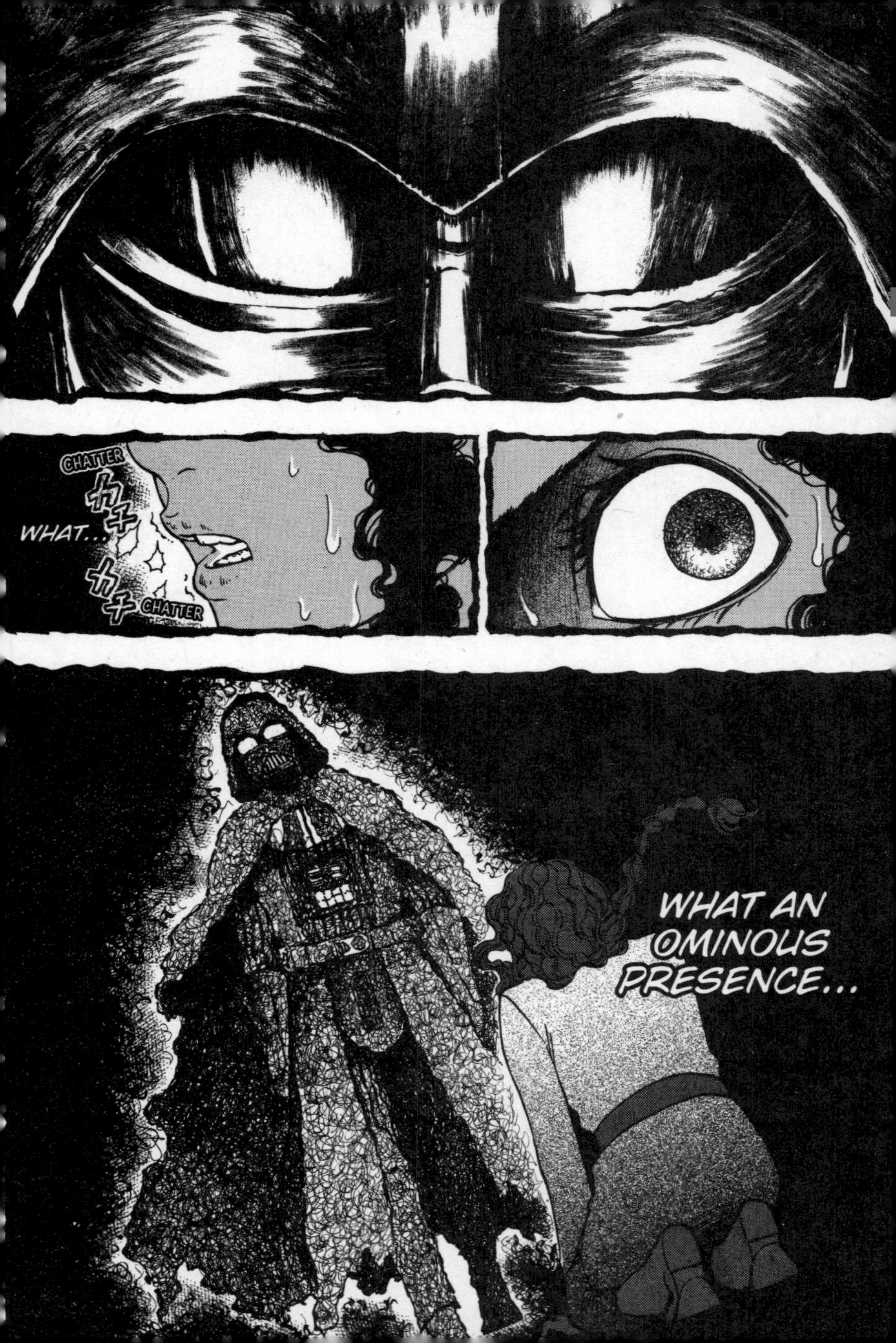
CHATTER
カチ
WHAT...
カチ
CHATTER
WHAT AN OMINOUS PRESENCE...

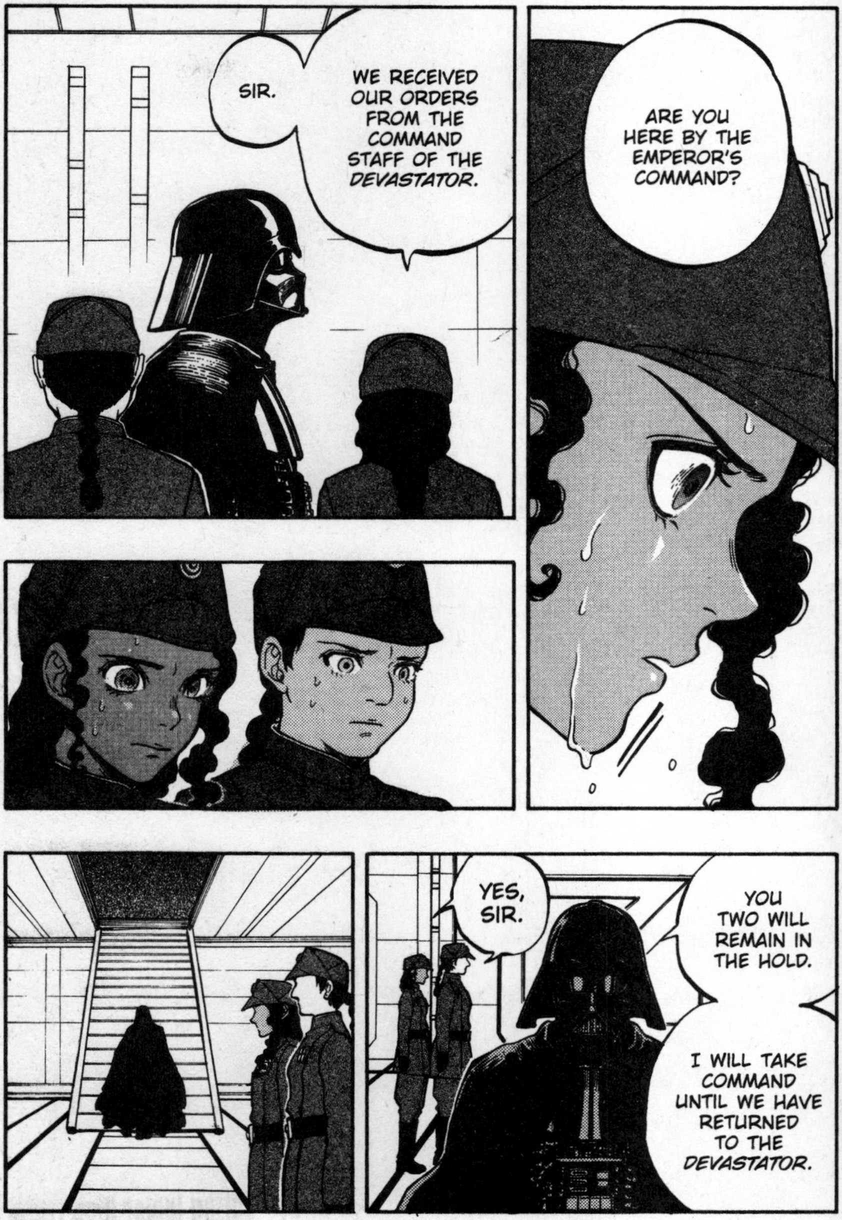
ARE YOU HERE BY THE EMPEROR'S COMMAND?
SIR.
WE RECEIVED OUR ORDERS FROM THE COMMAND STAFF OF THE *DEVASTATOR*.
YOU TWO WILL REMAIN IN THE HOLD.
I WILL TAKE COMMAND UNTIL WE HAVE RETURNED TO THE *DEVASTATOR*.
YES, SIR.

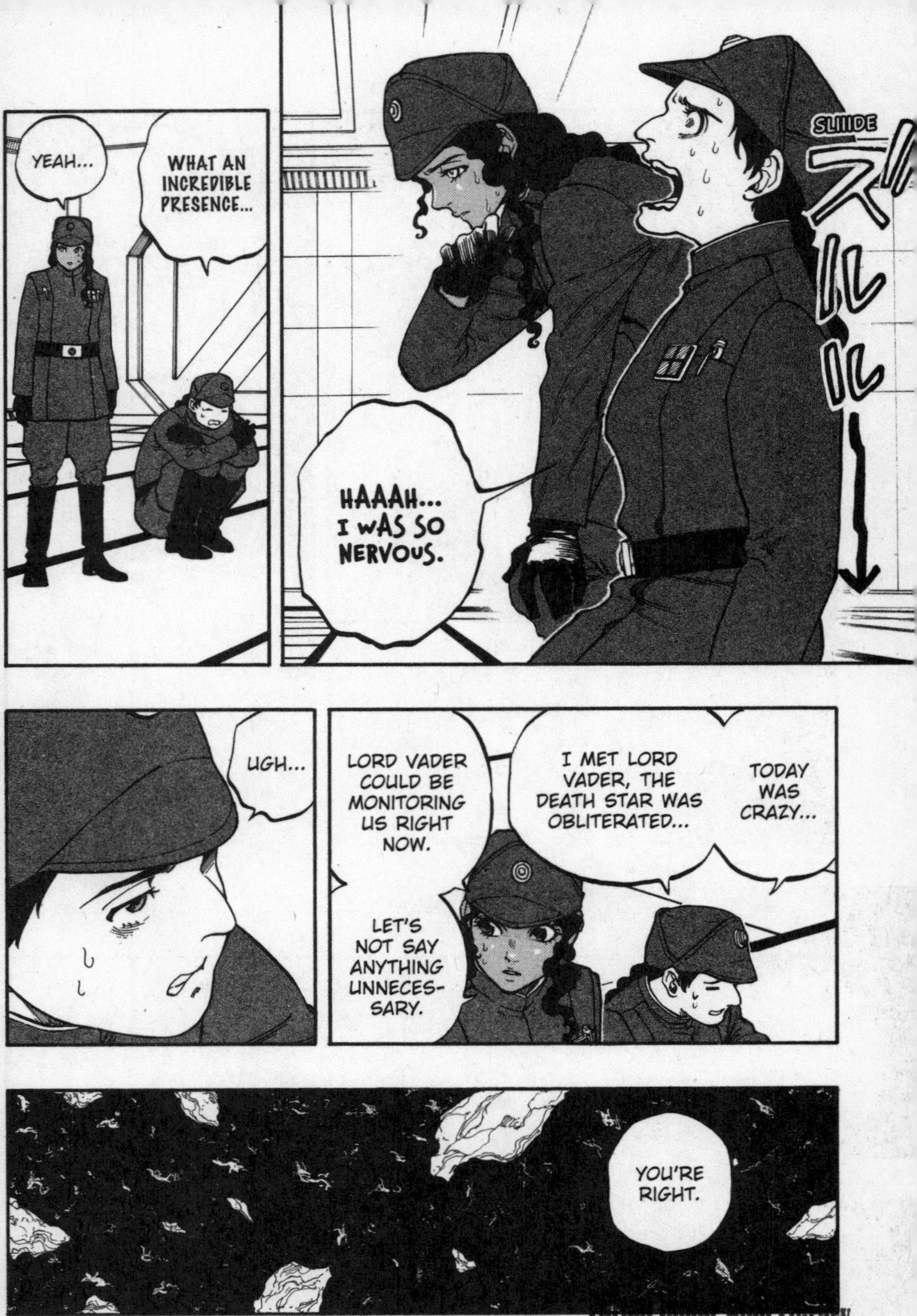
SLIIIDE
ズルル
HAAAH... I WAS SO NERVOUS.
WHAT AN INCREDIBLE PRESENCE...
YEAH...
TODAY WAS CRAZY...
I MET LORD VADER, THE DEATH STAR WAS OBLITERATED...
LORD VADER COULD BE MONITORING US RIGHT NOW.
LET'S NOT SAY ANYTHING UNNECES-SARY.
UGH...
YOU'RE RIGHT.

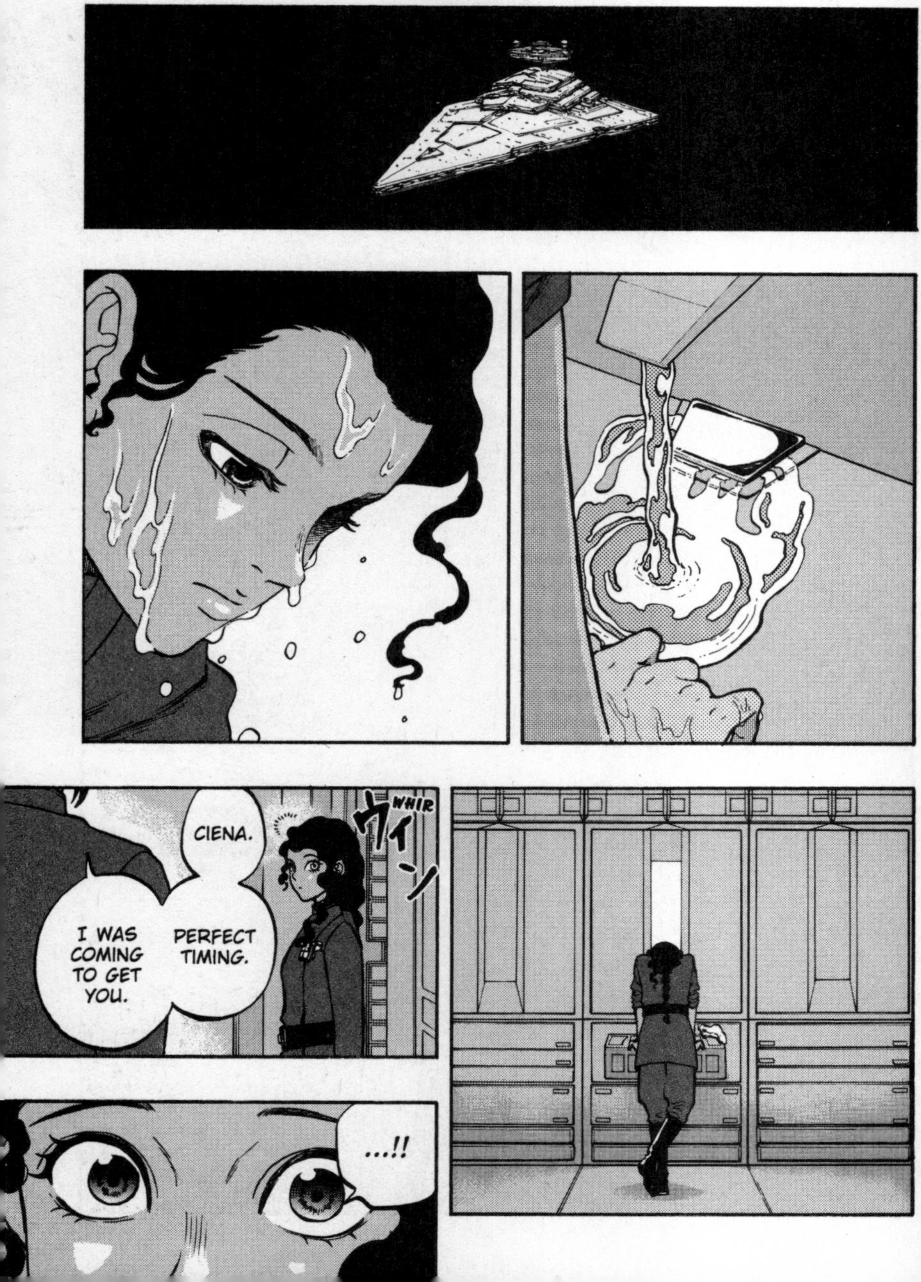
ヴィーン
WHIR
CIENA.
PERFECT TIMING.
I WAS COMING TO GET YOU.
...!!

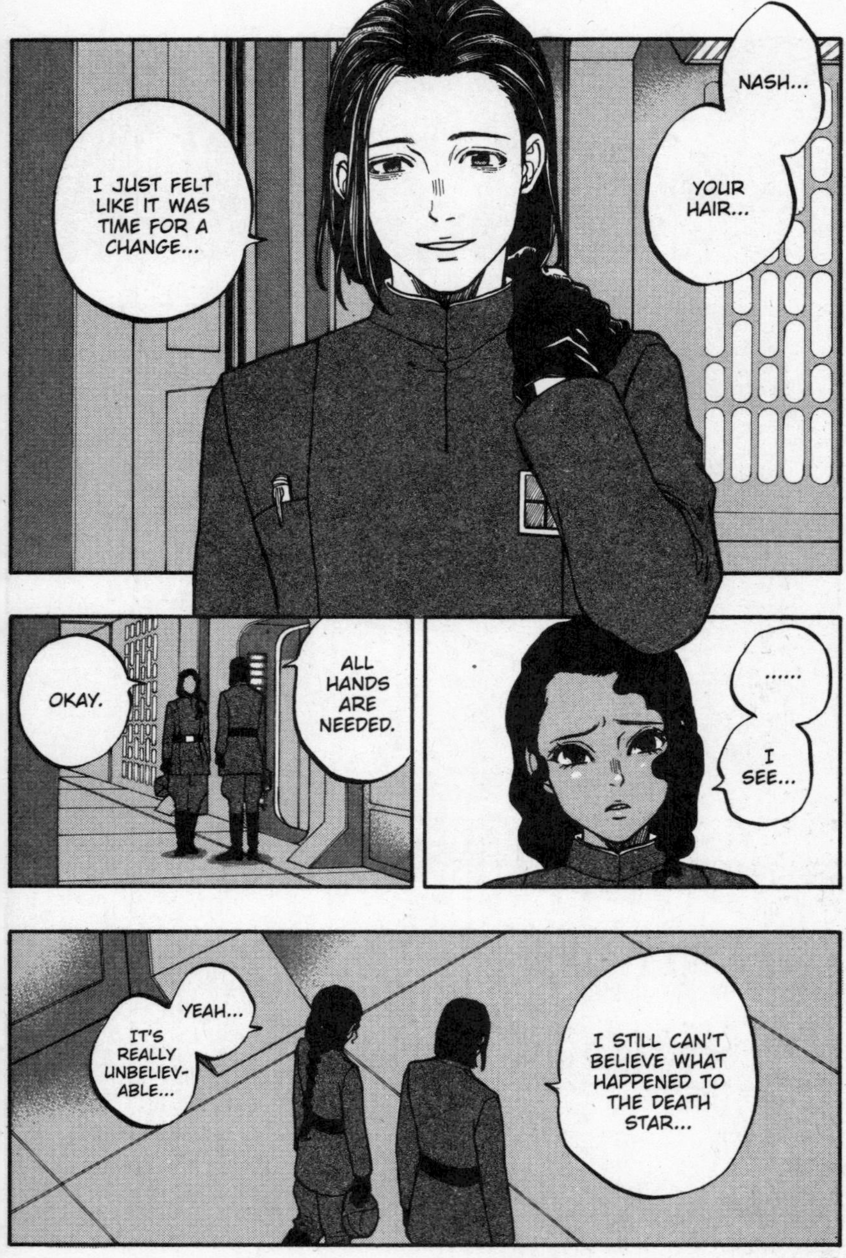
NASH... YOUR HAIR...
I JUST FELT LIKE IT WAS TIME FOR A CHANGE...
...... I SEE...
ALL HANDS ARE NEEDED.
OKAY.
I STILL CAN'T BELIEVE WHAT HAPPENED TO THE DEATH STAR...
YEAH... IT'S REALLY UNBELIEV-ABLE...

I'M OKAY...

I'M OKAY.

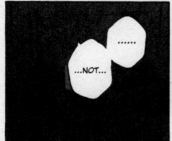

....

...NOT...

CIENA.

ARE YOU OKAY?

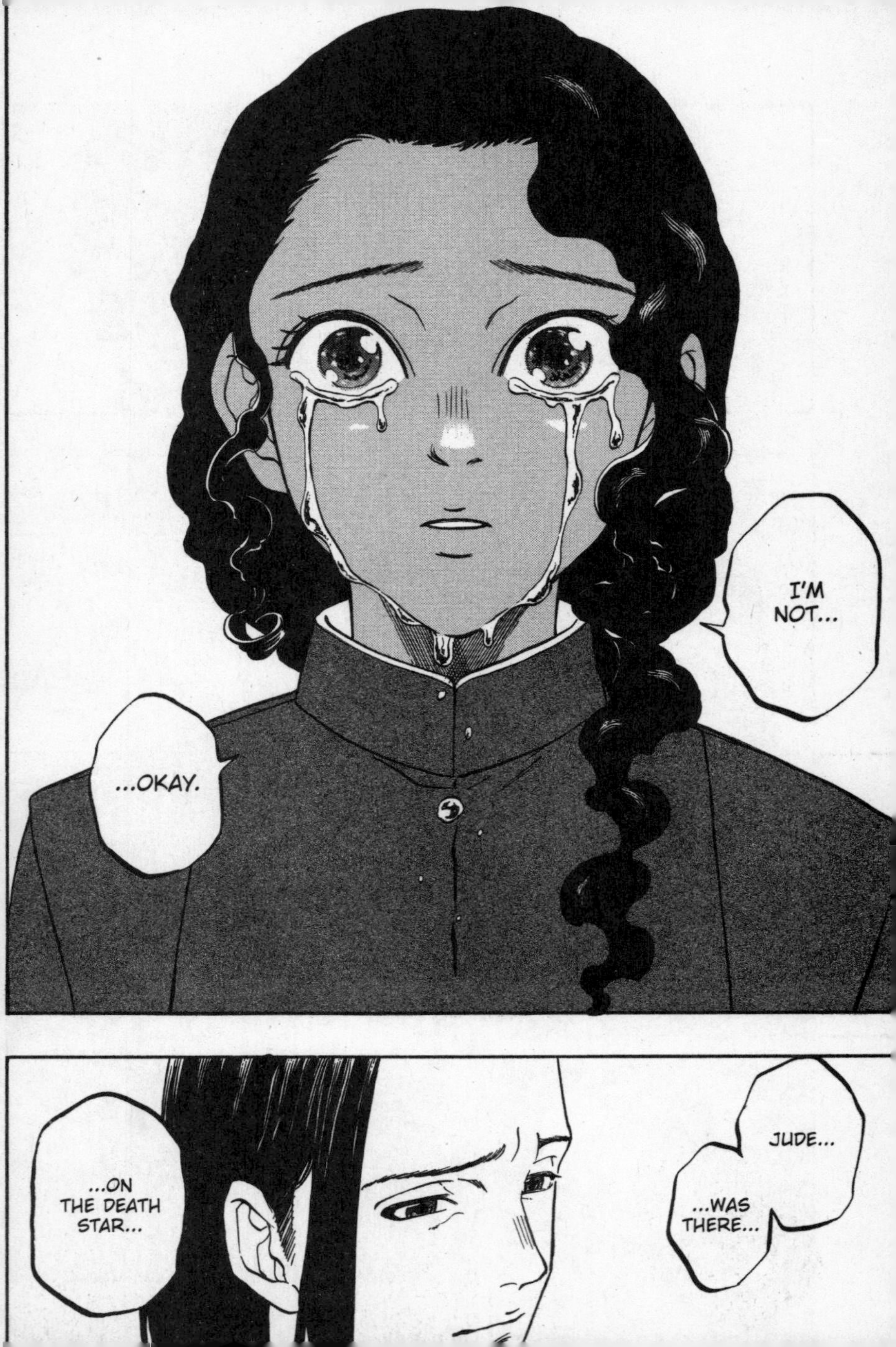
I'M NOT...
...OKAY.
JUDE...
...WAS THERE...
...ON THE DEATH STAR...

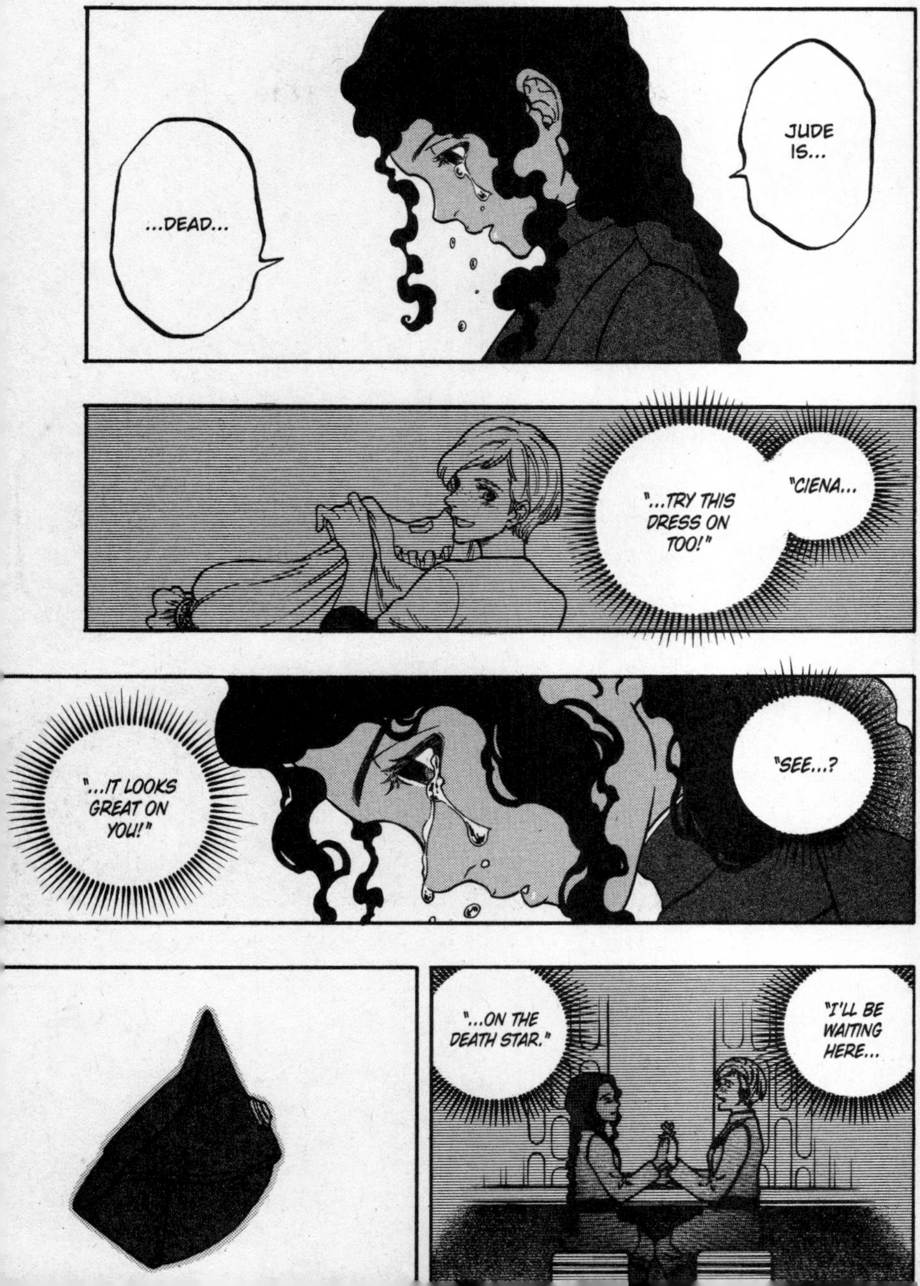
JUDE IS...
...DEAD...
"CIENA...
"...TRY THIS DRESS ON TOO!"
"SEE...?
"...IT LOOKS GREAT ON YOU!"
"I'LL BE WAITING HERE...
"...ON THE DEATH STAR."

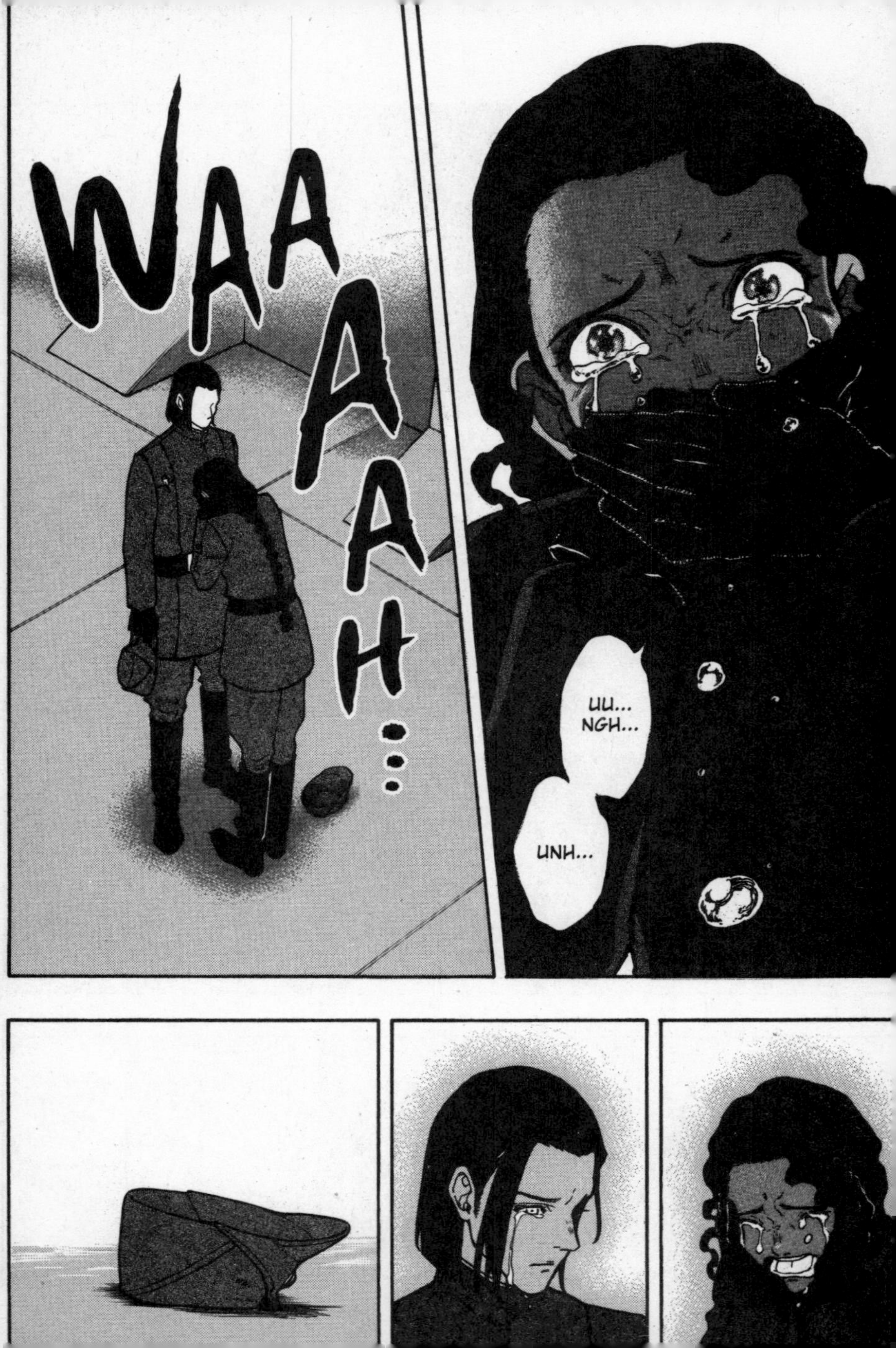
UU...
NGH...
UNH...
WAAAAAH...

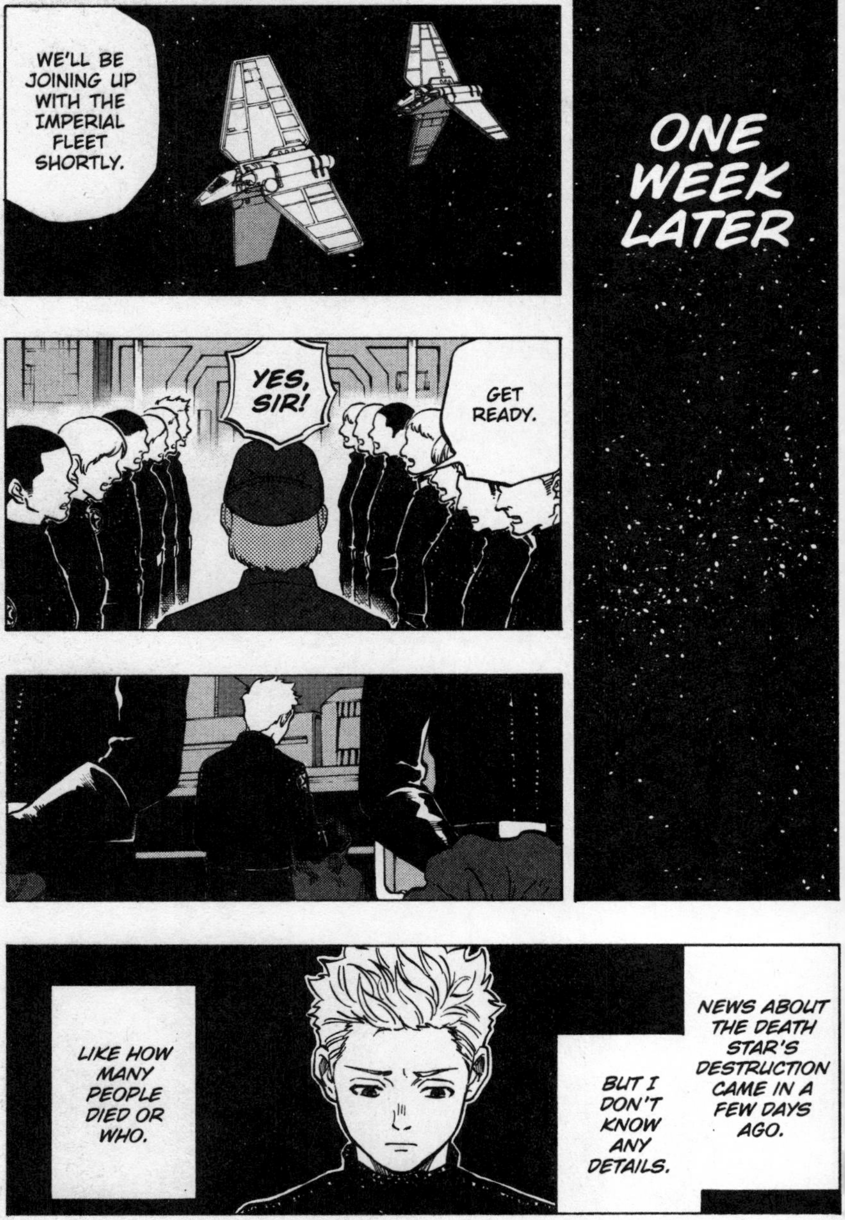
ONE WEEK LATER
WE'LL BE JOINING UP WITH THE IMPERIAL FLEET SHORTLY.
GET READY.
YES, SIR!
NEWS ABOUT THE DEATH STAR'S DESTRUCTION CAME IN A FEW DAYS AGO.
BUT I DON'T KNOW ANY DETAILS.
LIKE HOW MANY PEOPLE DIED OR WHO.

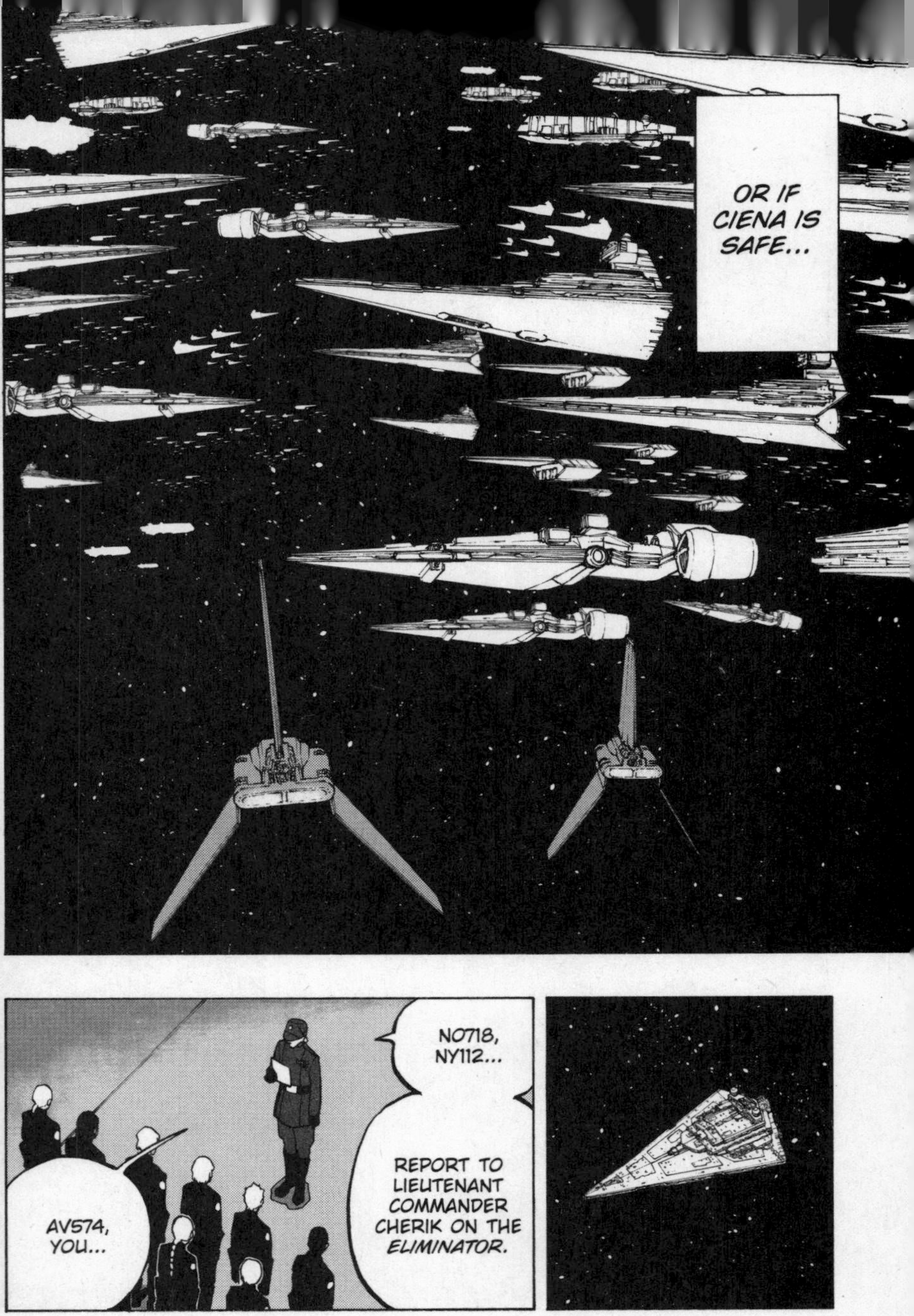
OR IF CIENA IS SAFE...
NO718, NY112...
REPORT TO LIEUTENANT COMMANDER CHERIK ON THE *ELIMINATOR*.
AV574, YOU...

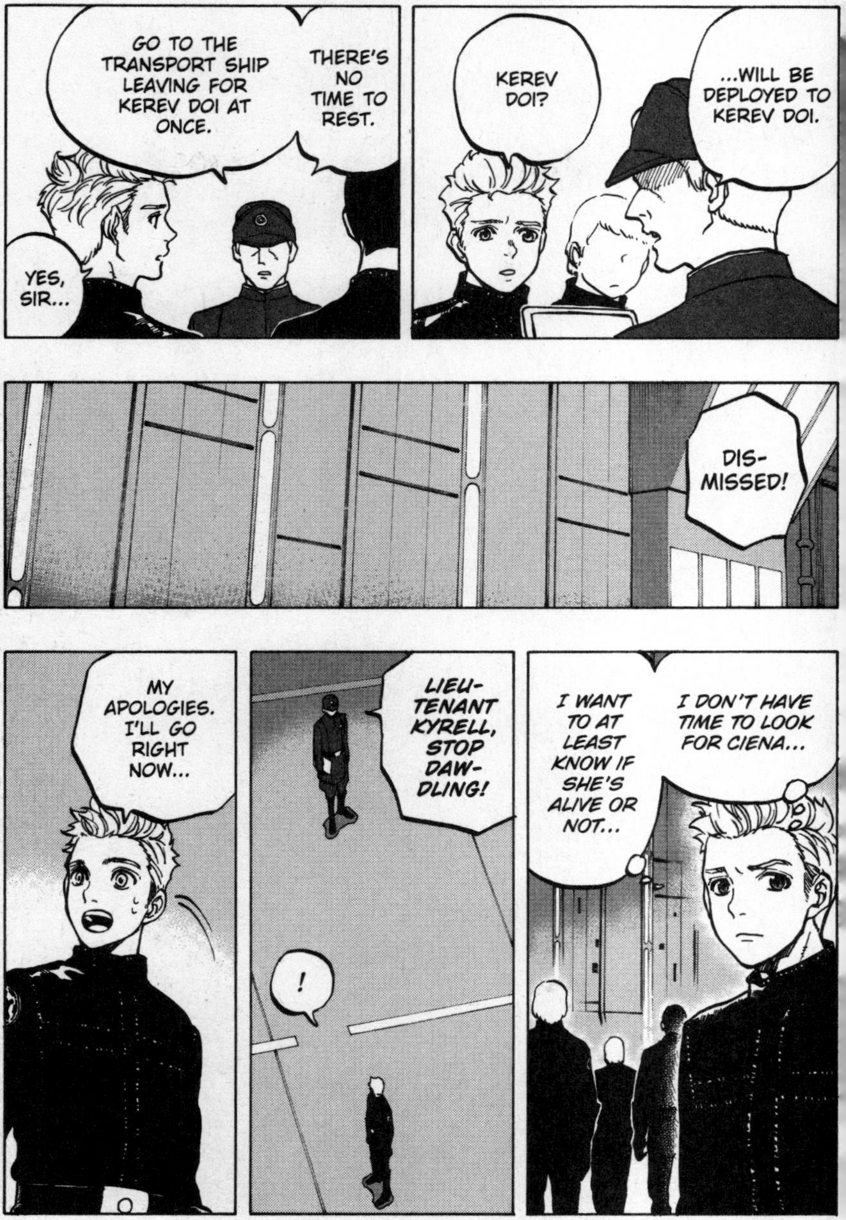
...WILL BE DEPLOYED TO KEREV DOI.
KEREV DOI?
GO TO THE TRANSPORT SHIP LEAVING FOR KEREV DOI AT ONCE.
THERE'S NO TIME TO REST.
YES, SIR...
DIS-MISSED!
I DON'T HAVE TIME TO LOOK FOR CIENA...
I WANT TO AT LEAST KNOW IF SHE'S ALIVE OR NOT...
LIEU-TENANT KYRELL, STOP DAW-DLING!
!
MY APOLOGIES. I'LL GO RIGHT NOW...

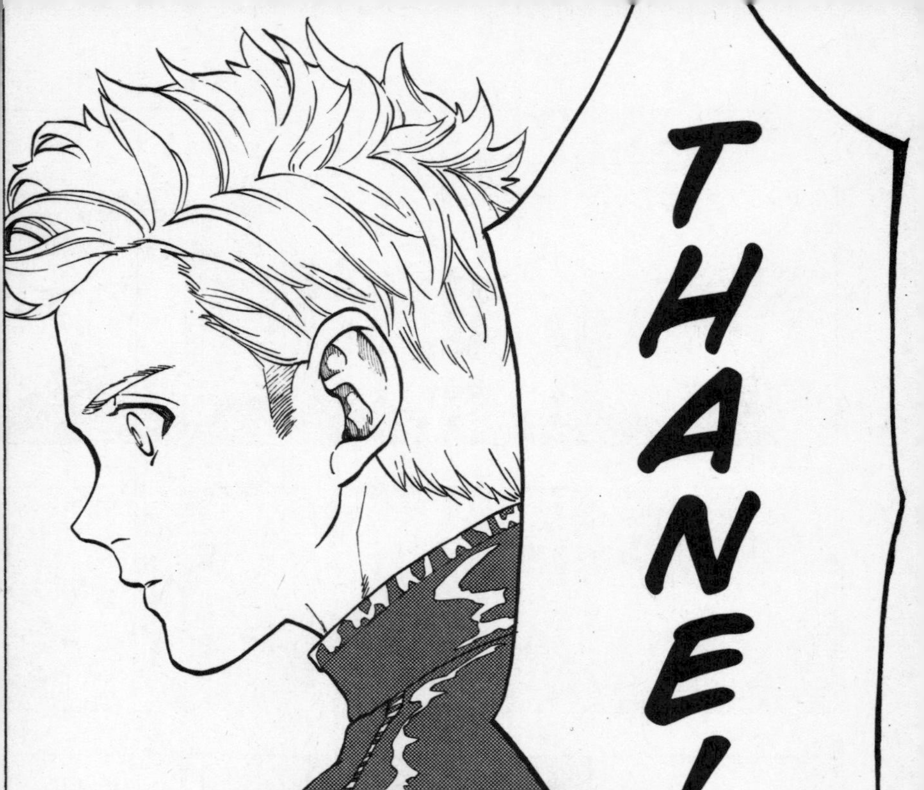
THANE!
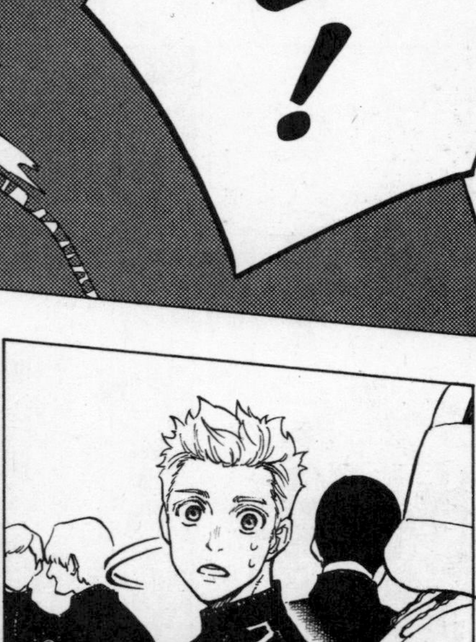
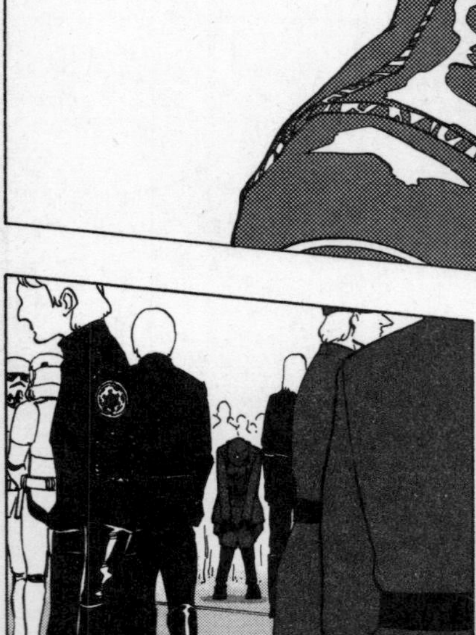

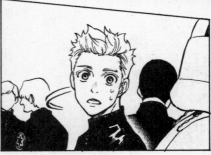

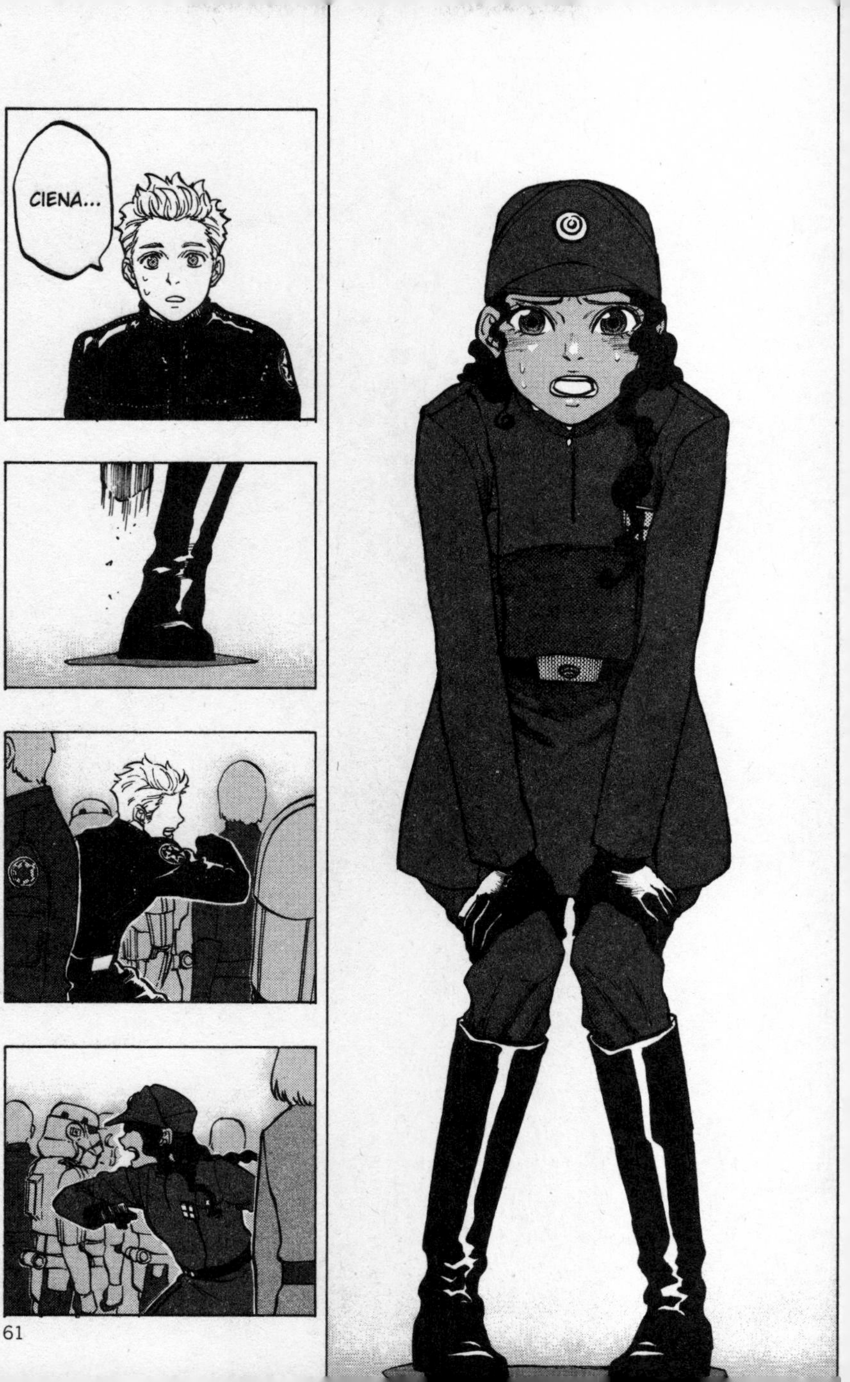
CIENA...

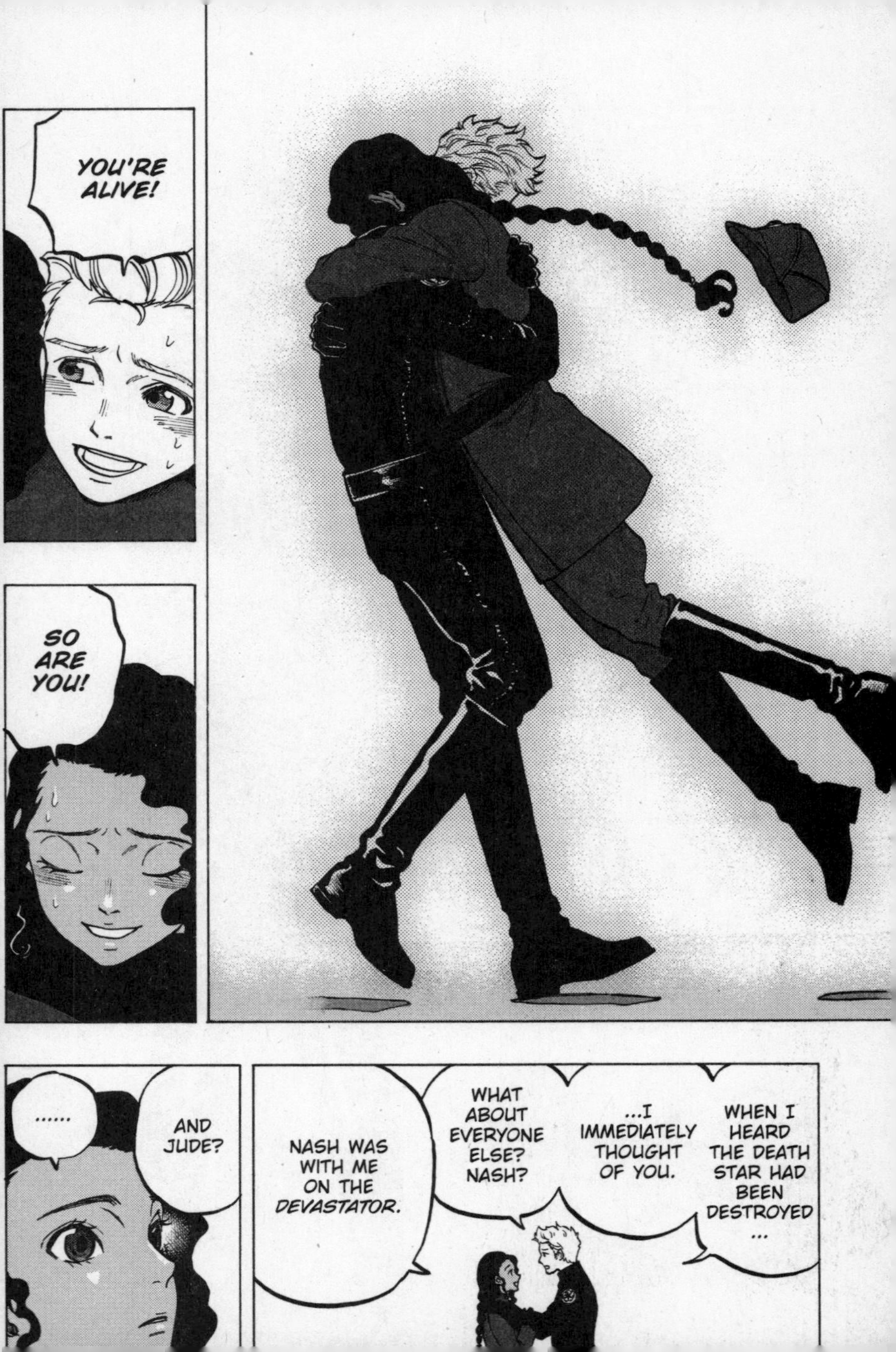
YOU'RE ALIVE!
SO ARE YOU!
WHEN I HEARD THE DEATH STAR HAD BEEN DESTROYED ...
...I IMMEDIATELY THOUGHT OF YOU.
WHAT ABOUT EVERYONE ELSE? NASH?
NASH WAS WITH ME ON THE *DEVASTATOR.*
AND JUDE?
......

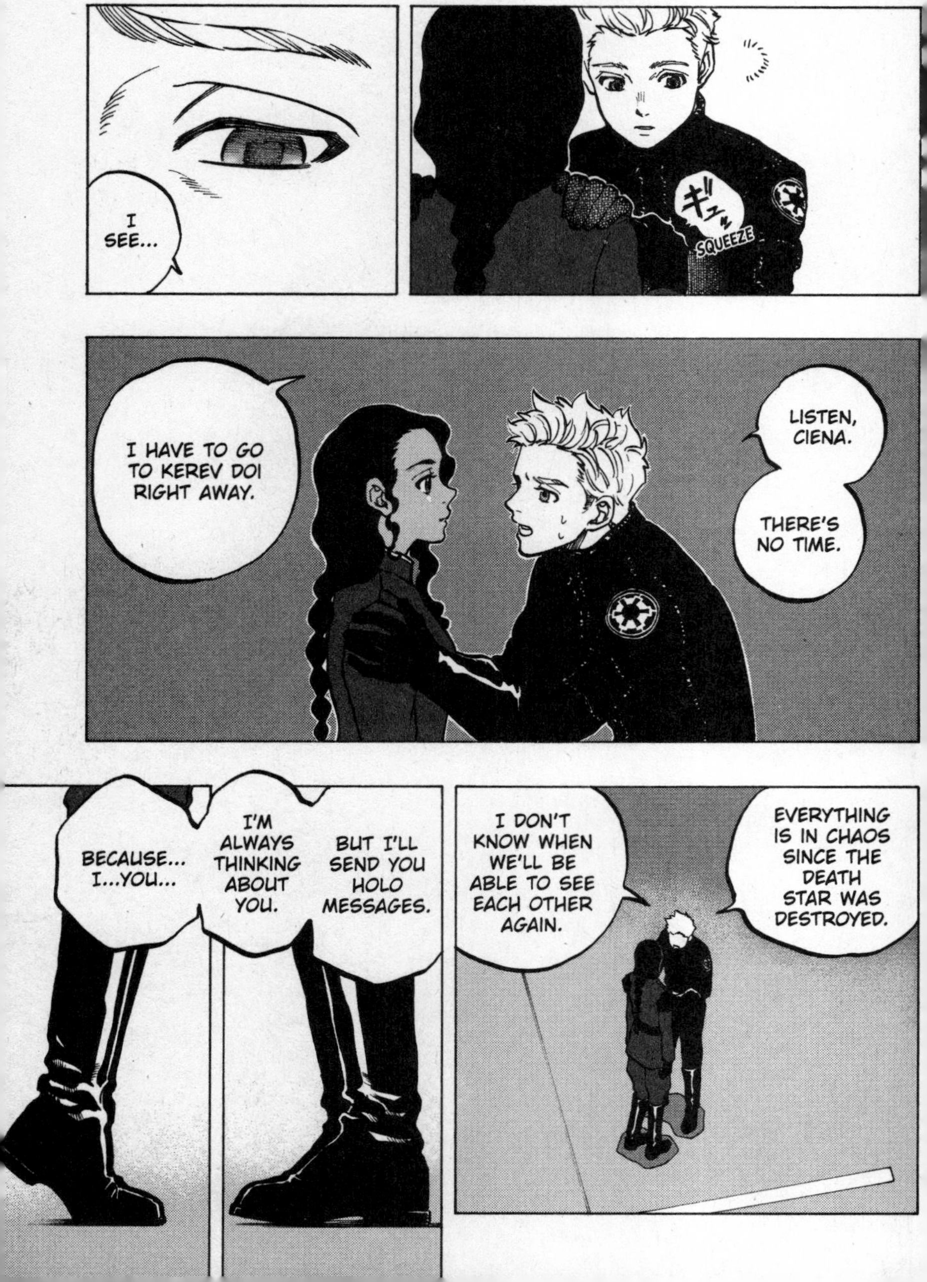
ギュ
SQUEEZE
I SEE...
LISTEN, CIENA.
THERE'S NO TIME.
I HAVE TO GO TO KEREV DOI RIGHT AWAY.
EVERYTHING IS IN CHAOS SINCE THE DEATH STAR WAS DESTROYED.
I DON'T KNOW WHEN WE'LL BE ABLE TO SEE EACH OTHER AGAIN.
BUT I'LL SEND YOU HOLO MESSAGES.
I'M ALWAYS THINKING ABOUT YOU.
BECAUSE... I...YOU...

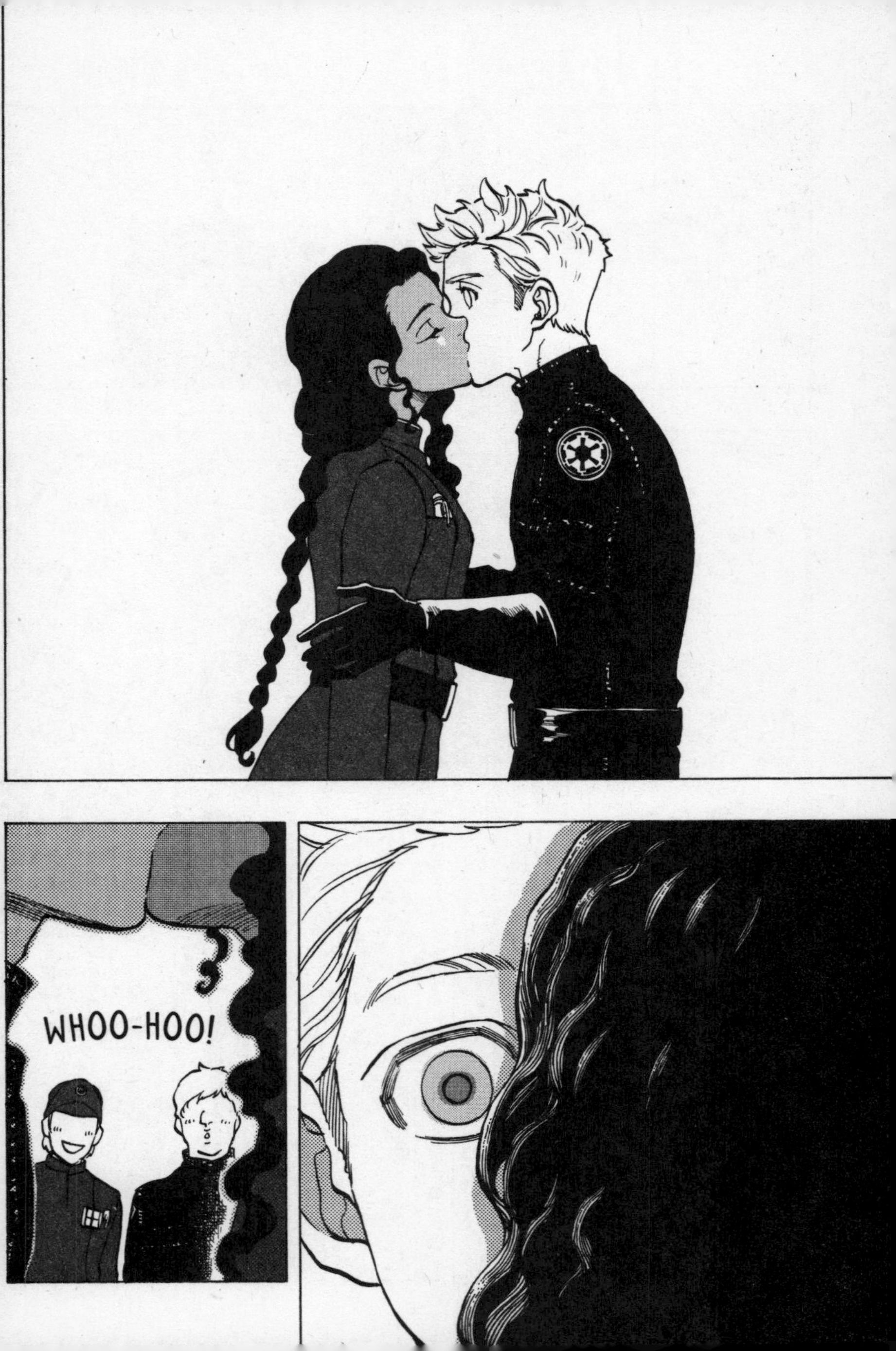
WHOO-HOO!

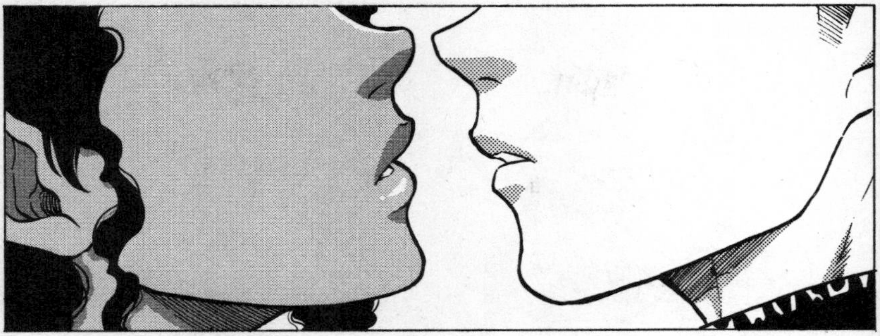

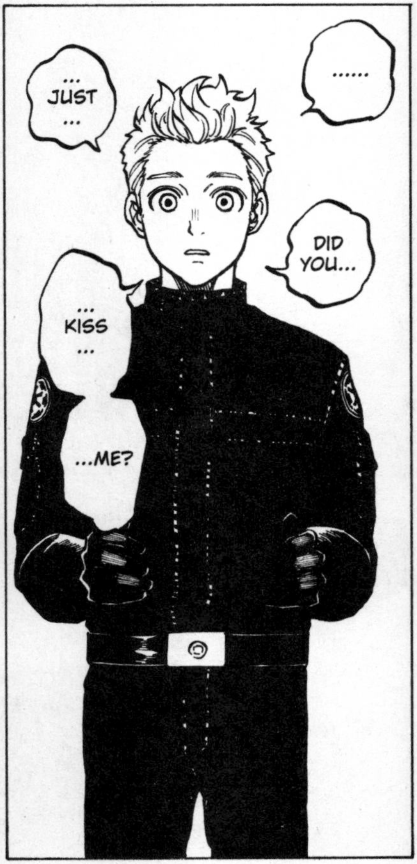
......
DID YOU...
...JUST...
...KISS...
...ME?

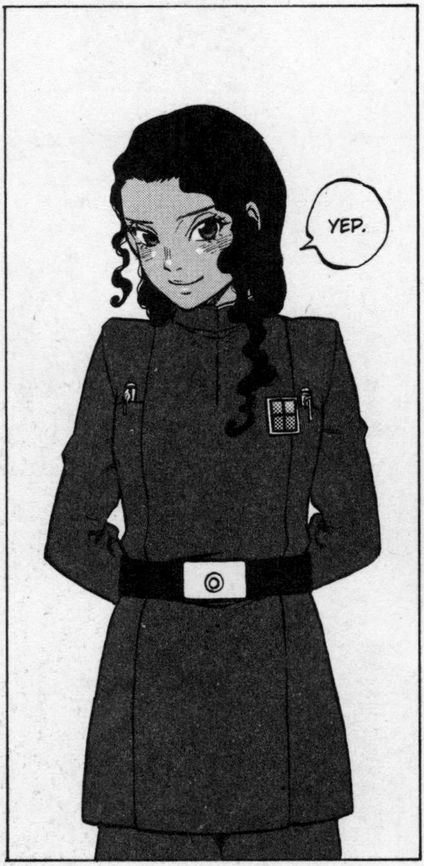
YEP.

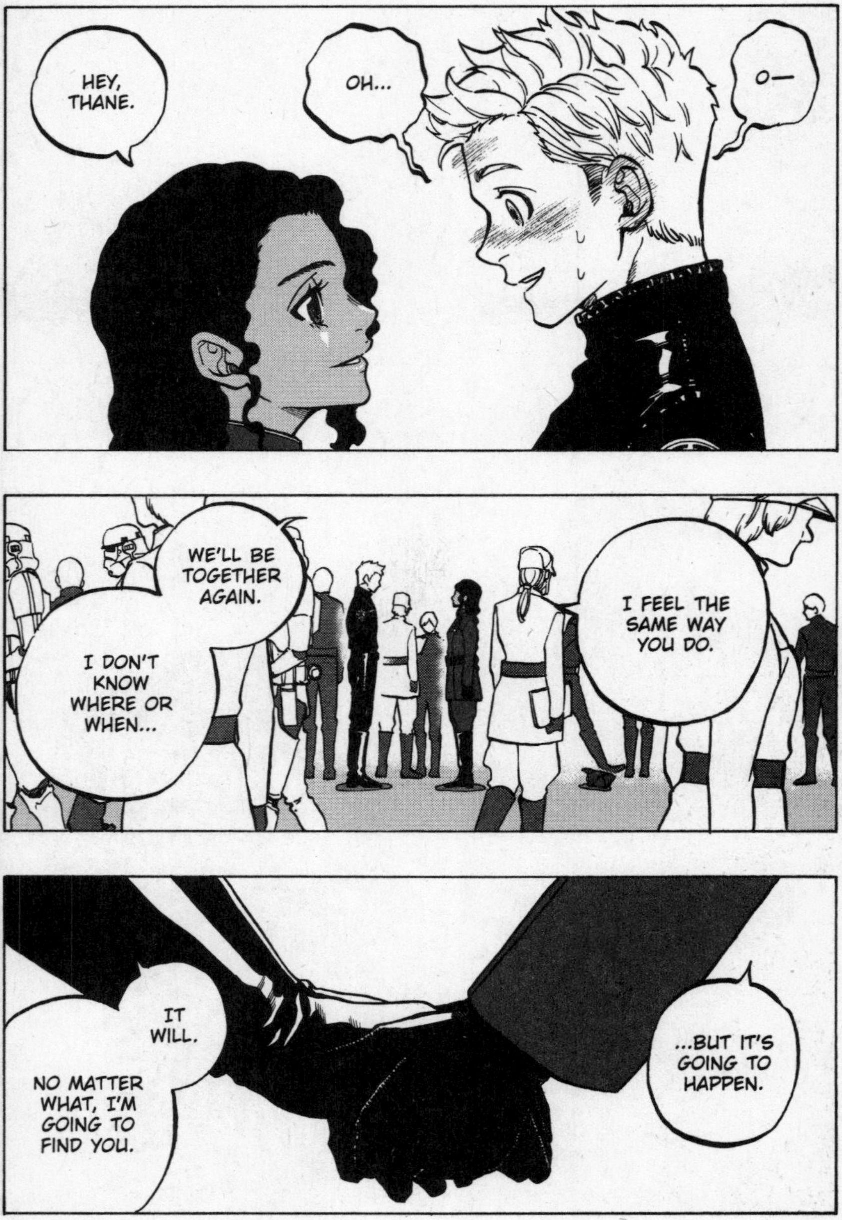
O—
OH...
HEY, THANE.
I FEEL THE SAME WAY YOU DO.
WE'LL BE TOGETHER AGAIN.
I DON'T KNOW WHERE OR WHEN...
...BUT IT'S GOING TO HAPPEN.
IT WILL.
NO MATTER WHAT, I'M GOING TO FIND YOU.

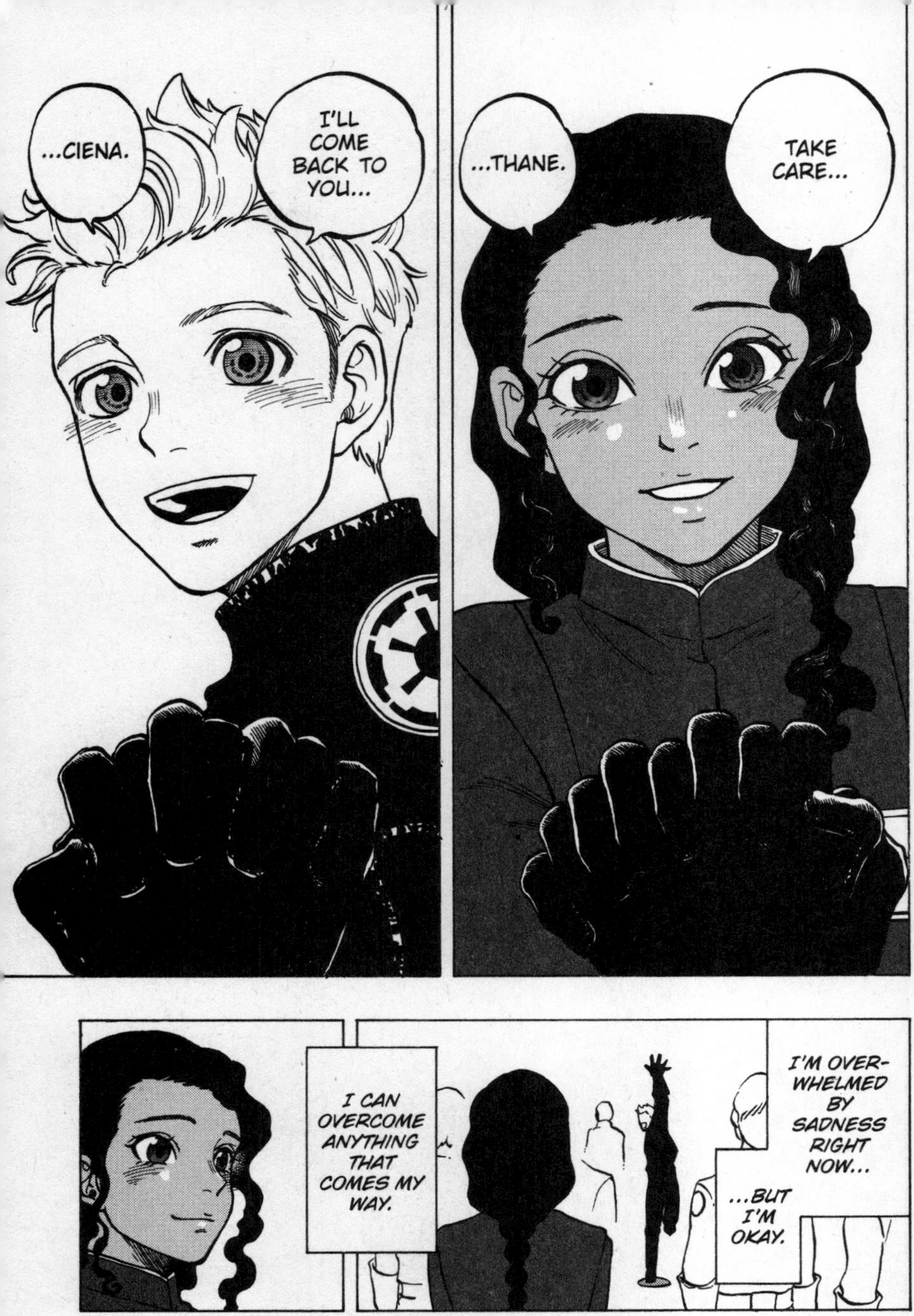
TAKE CARE...
...THANE.
I'LL COME BACK TO YOU...
...CIENA.
I'M OVER-WHELMED BY SADNESS RIGHT NOW...
...BUT I'M OKAY.
I CAN OVERCOME ANYTHING THAT COMES MY WAY.

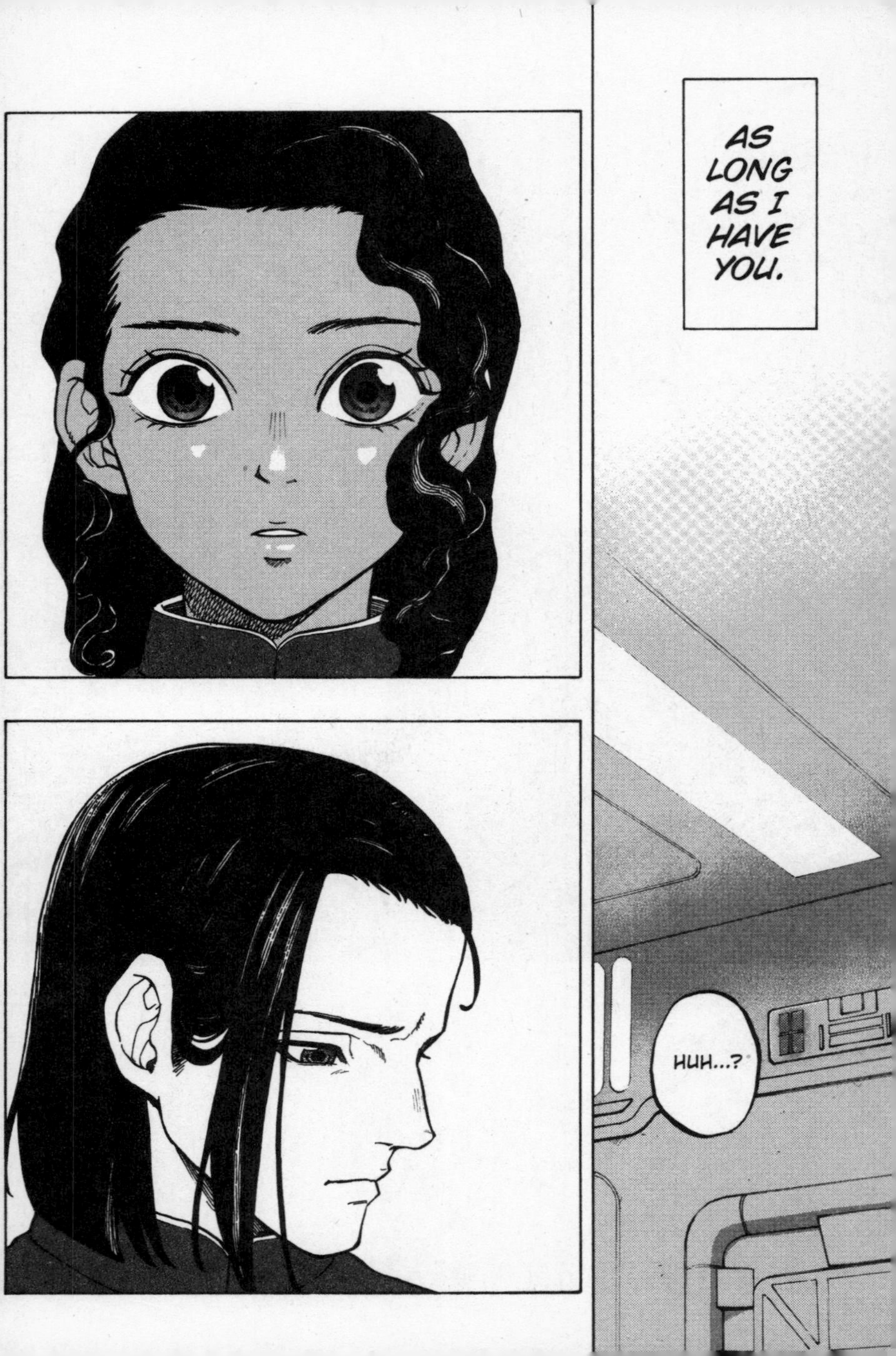
AS LONG AS I HAVE YOU.
HUH...?

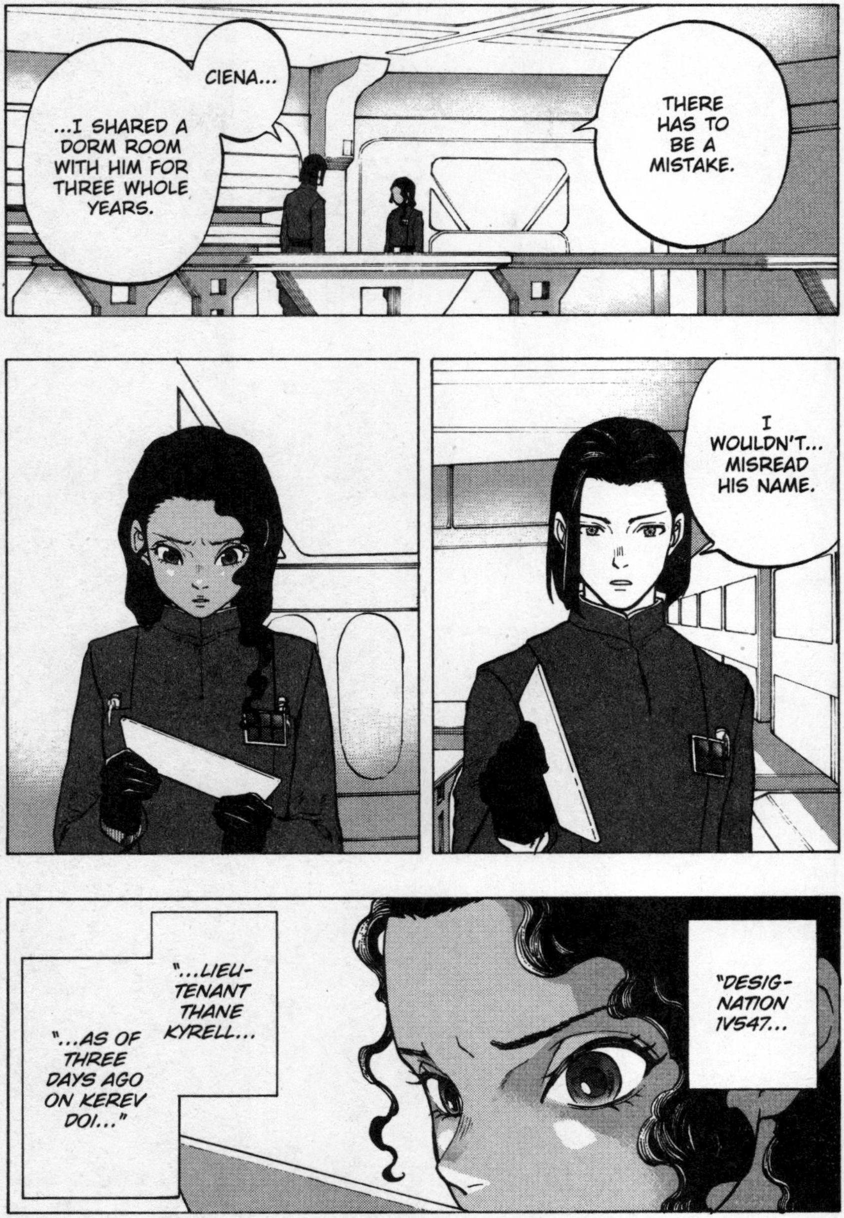
THERE HAS TO BE A MISTAKE.
CIENA...
...I SHARED A DORM ROOM WITH HIM FOR THREE WHOLE YEARS.
I WOULDN'T... MISREAD HIS NAME.
"DESIGNATION 1V547...
"...LIEUTENANT THANE KYRELL...
"...AS OF THREE DAYS AGO ON KEREV DOI..."

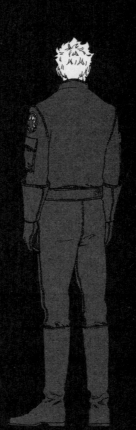

"...DESERTED
DUTY
AND FLED."

END

STAR WARS
LOST STARS
ロスト・スターズ

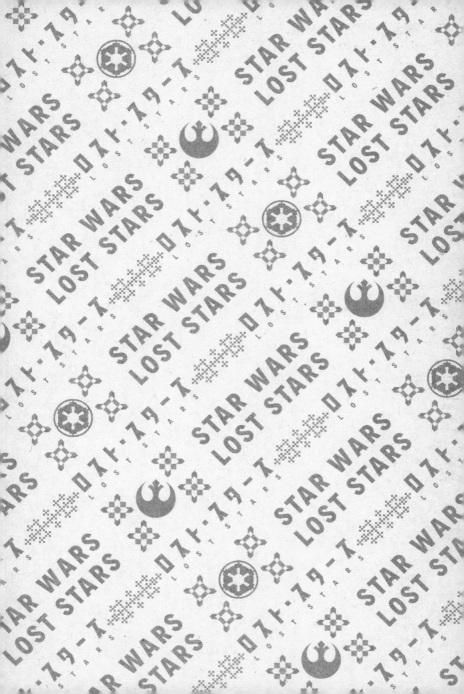

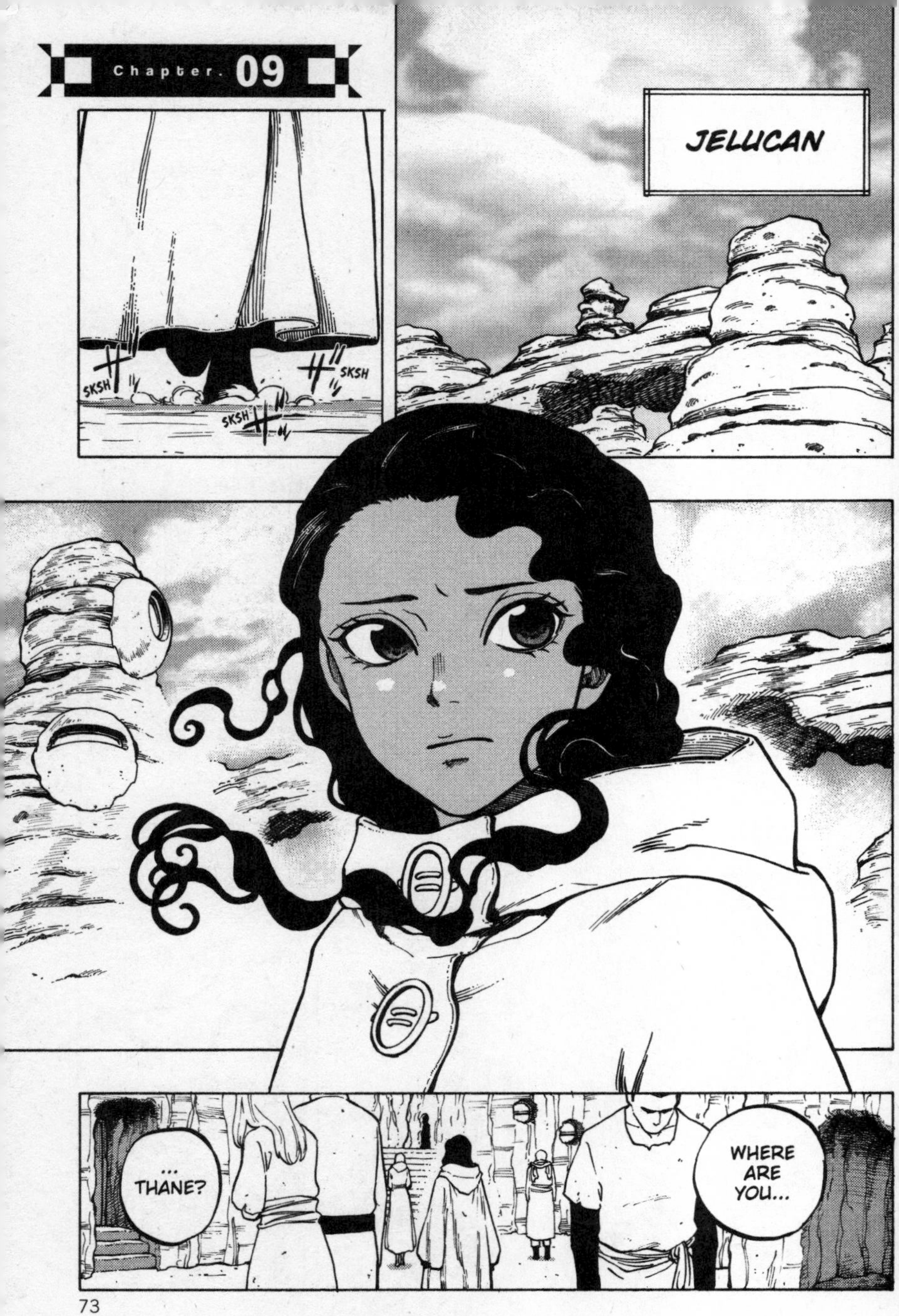
Chapter. 09
JELUCAN
SKSH
SKSH
SKSH
WHERE ARE YOU...
... THANE?

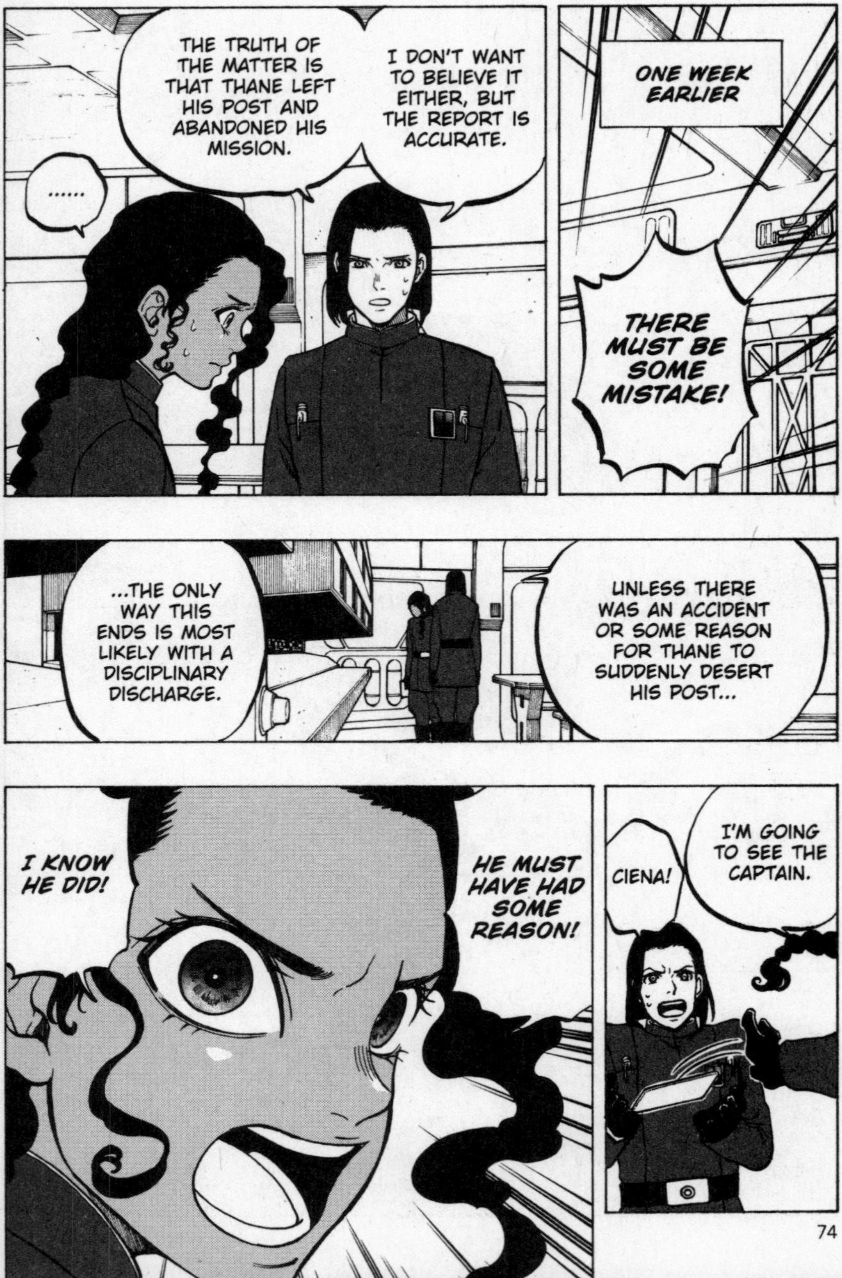
ONE WEEK EARLIER
THERE MUST BE SOME MISTAKE!
I DON'T WANT TO BELIEVE IT EITHER, BUT THE REPORT IS ACCURATE.
THE TRUTH OF THE MATTER IS THAT THANE LEFT HIS POST AND ABANDONED HIS MISSION.
......
UNLESS THERE WAS AN ACCIDENT OR SOME REASON FOR THANE TO SUDDENLY DESERT HIS POST...
...THE ONLY WAY THIS ENDS IS MOST LIKELY WITH A DISCIPLINARY DISCHARGE.
I'M GOING TO SEE THE CAPTAIN.
CIENA!
HE MUST HAVE HAD SOME REASON!
I KNOW HE DID!

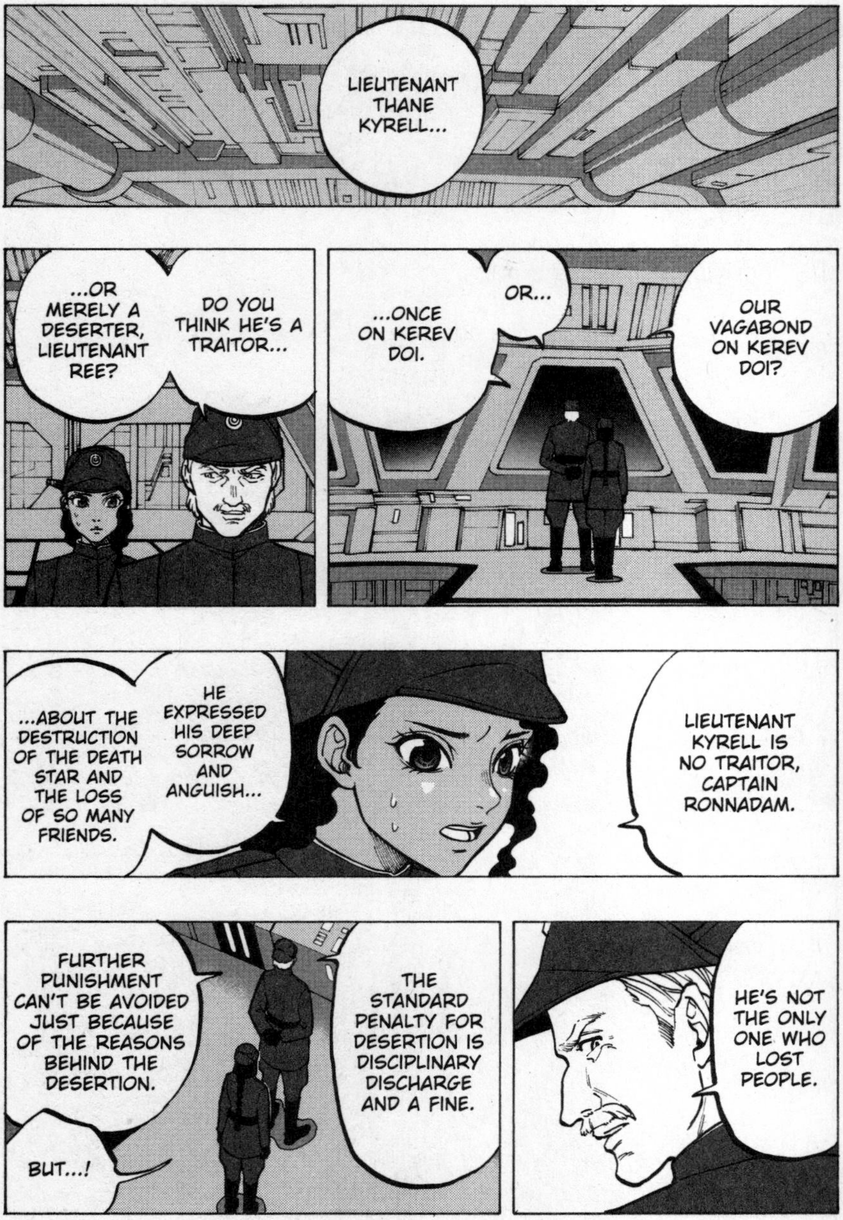
LIEUTENANT THANE KYRELL...
OUR VAGABOND ON KEREV DOI?
OR...
...ONCE ON KEREV DOI.
DO YOU THINK HE'S A TRAITOR...
...OR MERELY A DESERTER, LIEUTENANT REE?
LIEUTENANT KYRELL IS NO TRAITOR, CAPTAIN RONNADAM.
HE EXPRESSED HIS DEEP SORROW AND ANGUISH...
...ABOUT THE DESTRUCTION OF THE DEATH STAR AND THE LOSS OF SO MANY FRIENDS.
HE'S NOT THE ONLY ONE WHO LOST PEOPLE.
THE STANDARD PENALTY FOR DESERTION IS DISCIPLINARY DISCHARGE AND A FINE.
FURTHER PUNISHMENT CAN'T BE AVOIDED JUST BECAUSE OF THE REASONS BEHIND THE DESERTION.
BUT...!

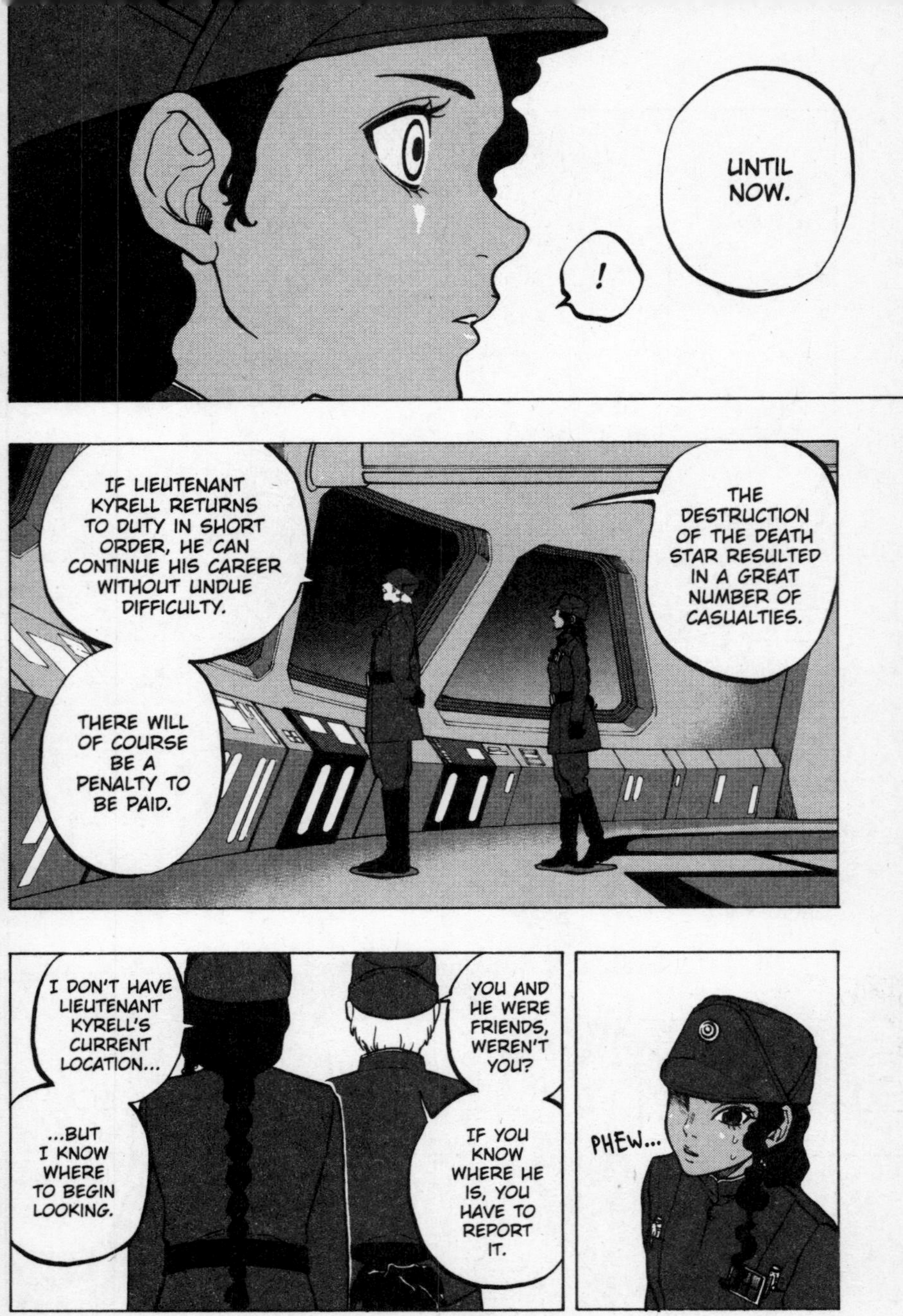
UNTIL NOW.
!
THE DESTRUCTION OF THE DEATH STAR RESULTED IN A GREAT NUMBER OF CASUALTIES.
IF LIEUTENANT KYRELL RETURNS TO DUTY IN SHORT ORDER, HE CAN CONTINUE HIS CAREER WITHOUT UNDUE DIFFICULTY.
THERE WILL OF COURSE BE A PENALTY TO BE PAID.
PHEW...
YOU AND HE WERE FRIENDS, WEREN'T YOU?
IF YOU KNOW WHERE HE IS, YOU HAVE TO REPORT IT.
I DON'T HAVE LIEUTENANT KYRELL'S CURRENT LOCATION...
...BUT I KNOW WHERE TO BEGIN LOOKING.

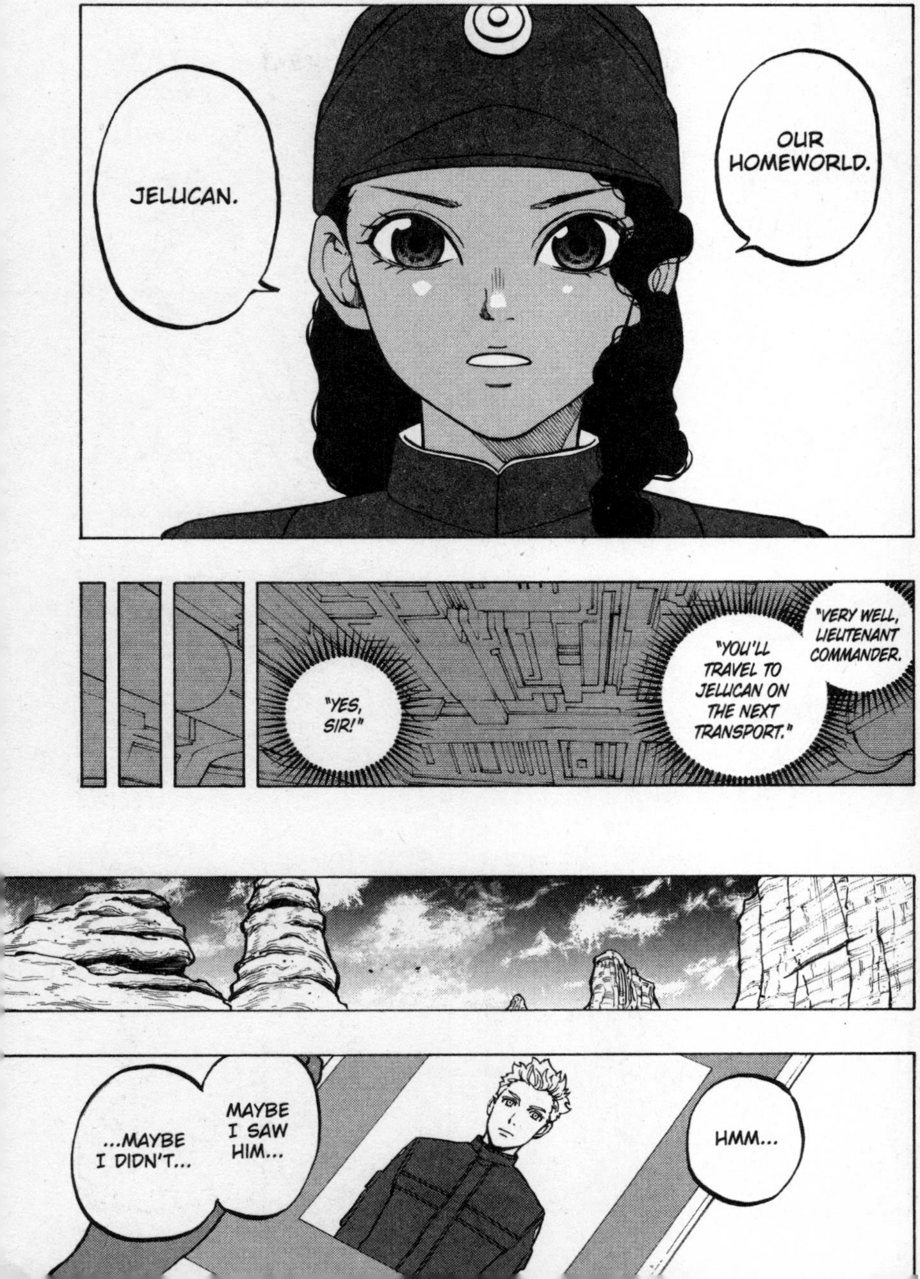
OUR HOMEWORLD.
JELUCAN.
"VERY WELL, LIEUTENANT COMMANDER.
"YOU'LL TRAVEL TO JELUCAN ON THE NEXT TRANSPORT."
"YES, SIR!"
HMM...
MAYBE I SAW HIM...
...MAYBE I DIDN'T...

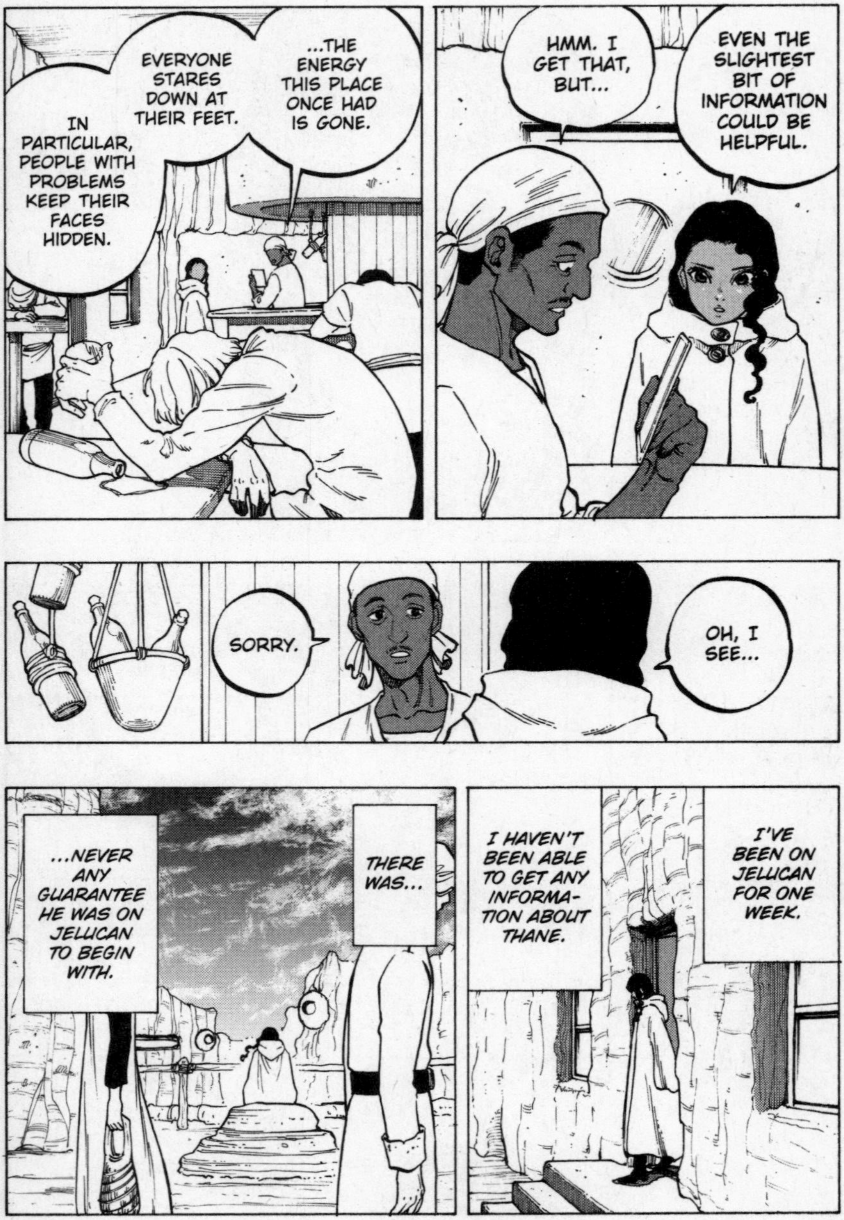
EVEN THE SLIGHTEST BIT OF INFORMATION COULD BE HELPFUL.
HMM. I GET THAT, BUT...
...THE ENERGY THIS PLACE ONCE HAD IS GONE.
EVERYONE STARES DOWN AT THEIR FEET.
IN PARTICULAR, PEOPLE WITH PROBLEMS KEEP THEIR FACES HIDDEN.
OH, I SEE...
SORRY.
I'VE BEEN ON JELICAN FOR ONE WEEK.
I HAVEN'T BEEN ABLE TO GET ANY INFORMATION ABOUT THANE.
THERE WAS...
...NEVER ANY GUARANTEE HE WAS ON JELICAN TO BEGIN WITH.

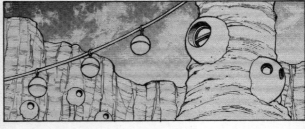

HE MUST
BE ON
ANOTHER
PLANET...

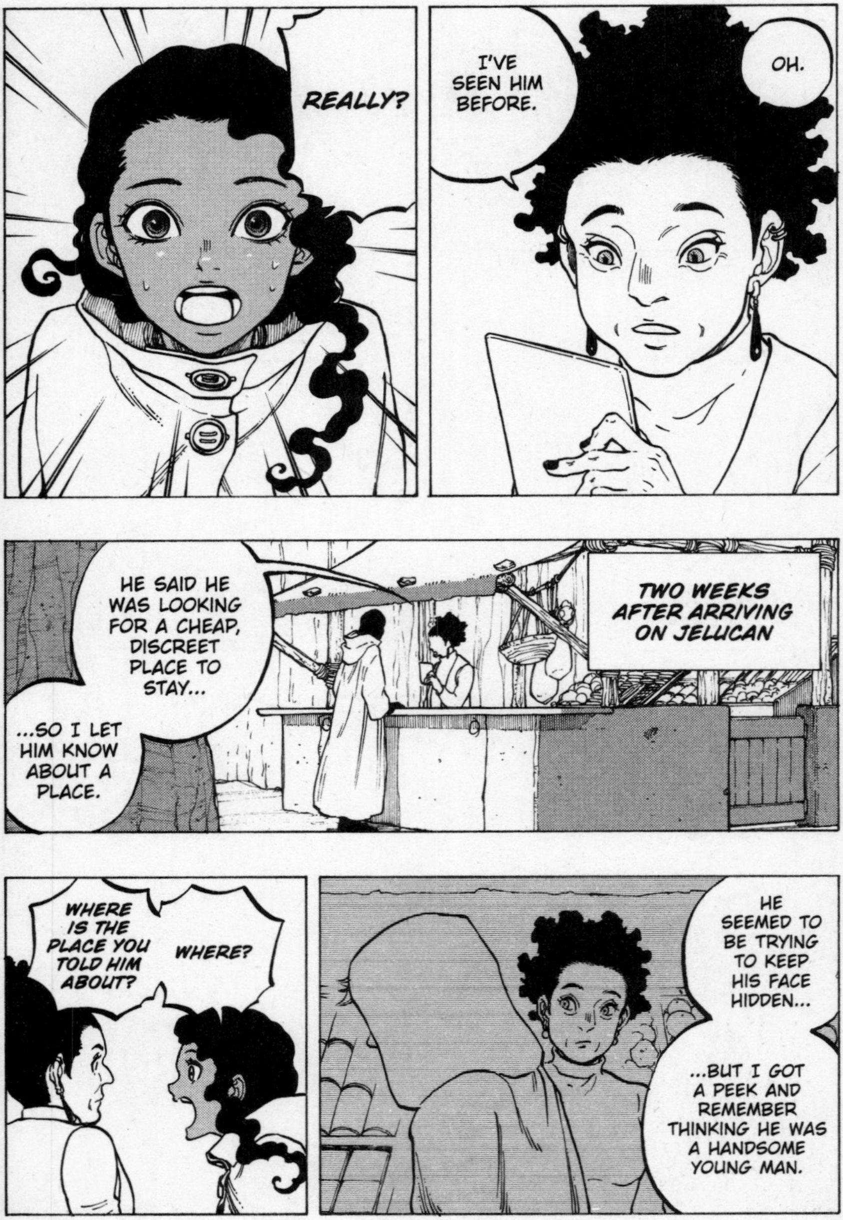
OH.
I'VE SEEN HIM BEFORE.
REALLY?
TWO WEEKS AFTER ARRIVING ON JELUCAN
HE SAID HE WAS LOOKING FOR A CHEAP, DISCREET PLACE TO STAY...
...SO I LET HIM KNOW ABOUT A PLACE.
HE SEEMED TO BE TRYING TO KEEP HIS FACE HIDDEN...
...BUT I GOT A PEEK AND REMEMBER THINKING HE WAS A HANDSOME YOUNG MAN.
WHERE?
WHERE IS THE PLACE YOU TOLD HIM ABOUT?

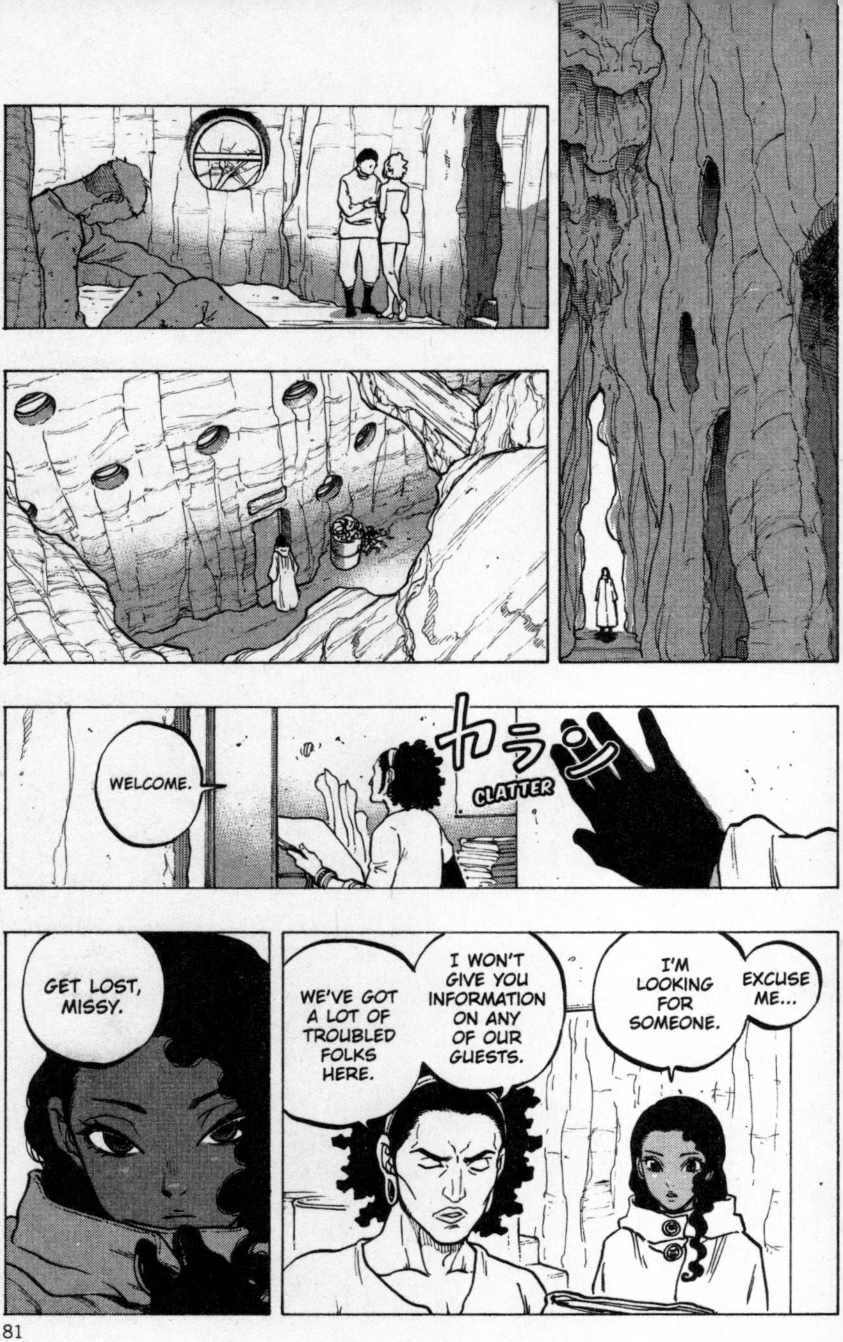
カラン
CLATTER
WELCOME.
EXCUSE ME...
I'M LOOKING FOR SOMEONE.
I WON'T GIVE YOU INFORMATION ON ANY OF OUR GUESTS.
WE'VE GOT A LOT OF TROUBLED FOLKS HERE.
GET LOST, MISSY.

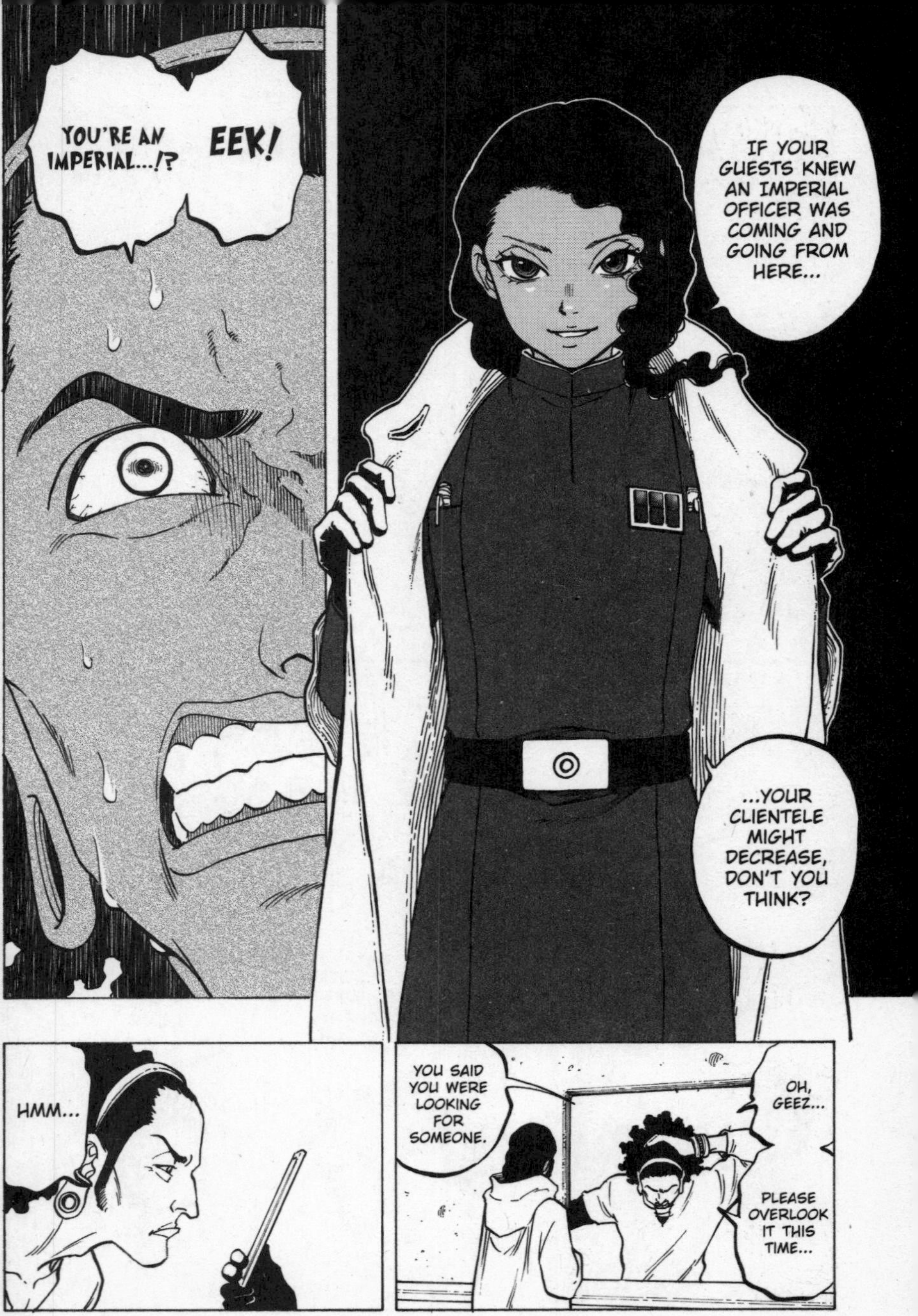
IF YOUR GUESTS KNEW AN IMPERIAL OFFICER WAS COMING AND GOING FROM HERE...
...YOUR CLIENTELE MIGHT DECREASE, DON'T YOU THINK?
EEK!
YOU'RE AN IMPERIAL...!?
OH, GEEZ...
PLEASE OVERLOOK IT THIS TIME...
YOU SAID YOU WERE LOOKING FOR SOMEONE.
HMM...

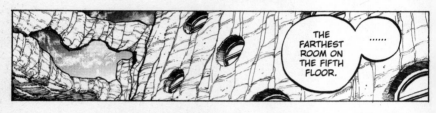

THE FARTHEST ROOM ON THE FIFTH FLOOR.

......

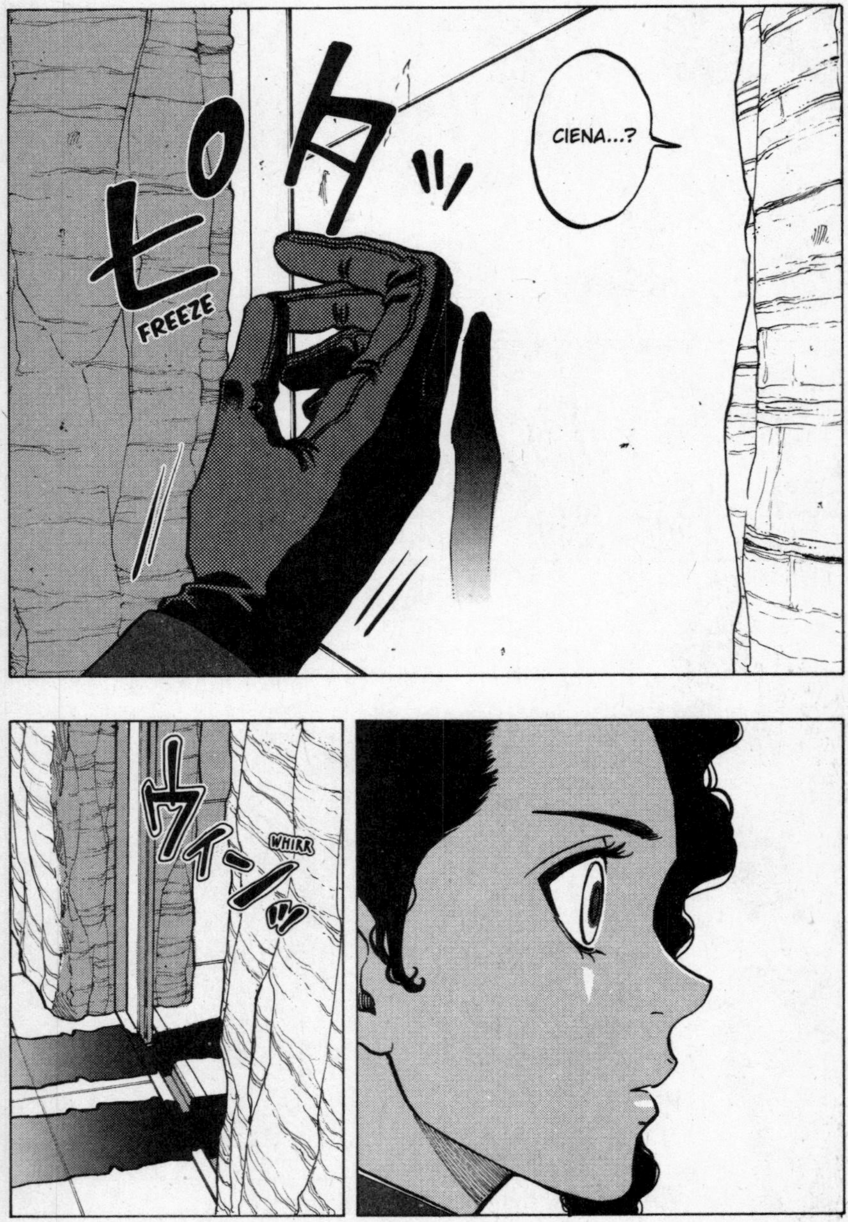
CIENA...?
ピタッ
FREEZE
ウィーンッ
WHIRR

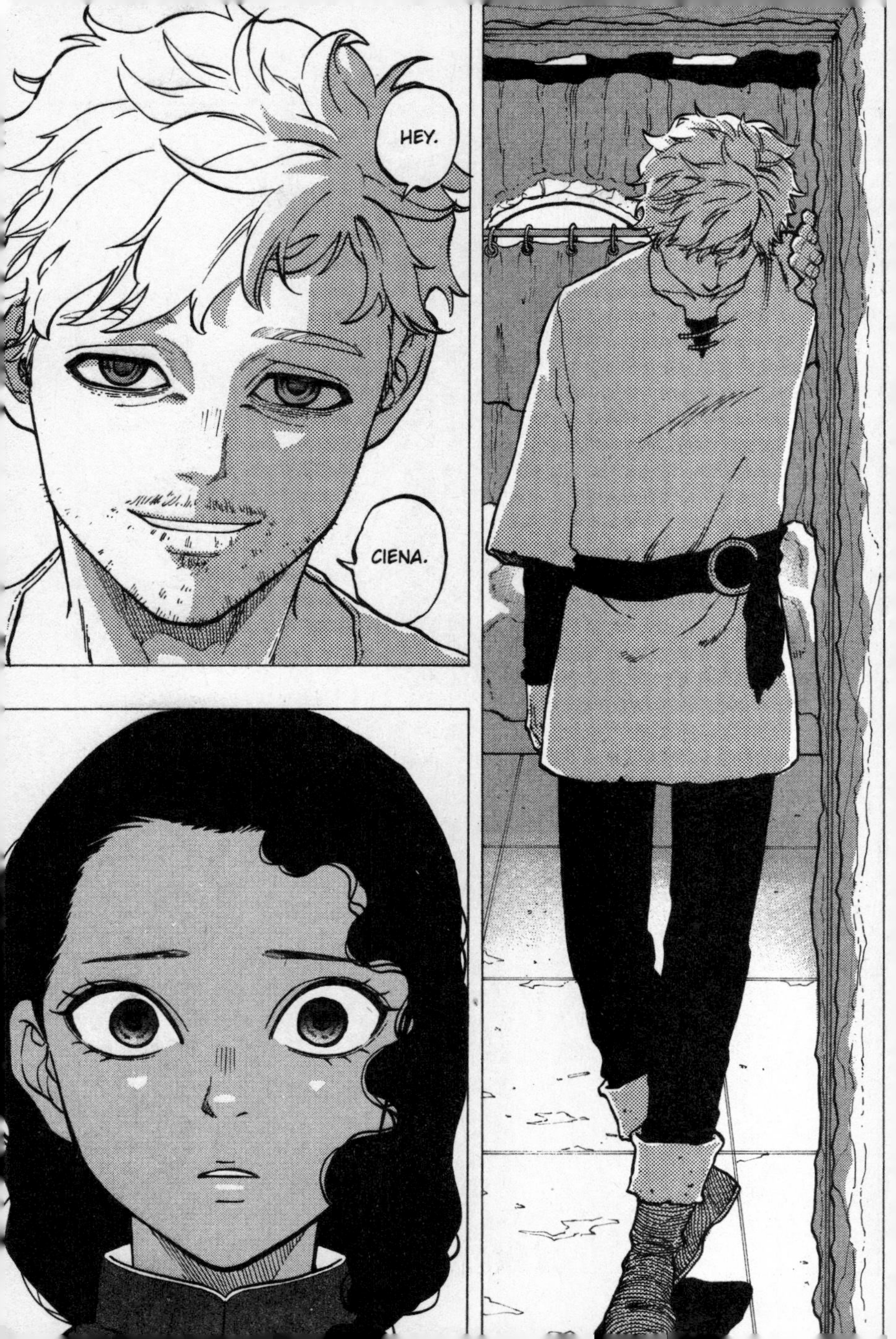
HEY.
CIENA.

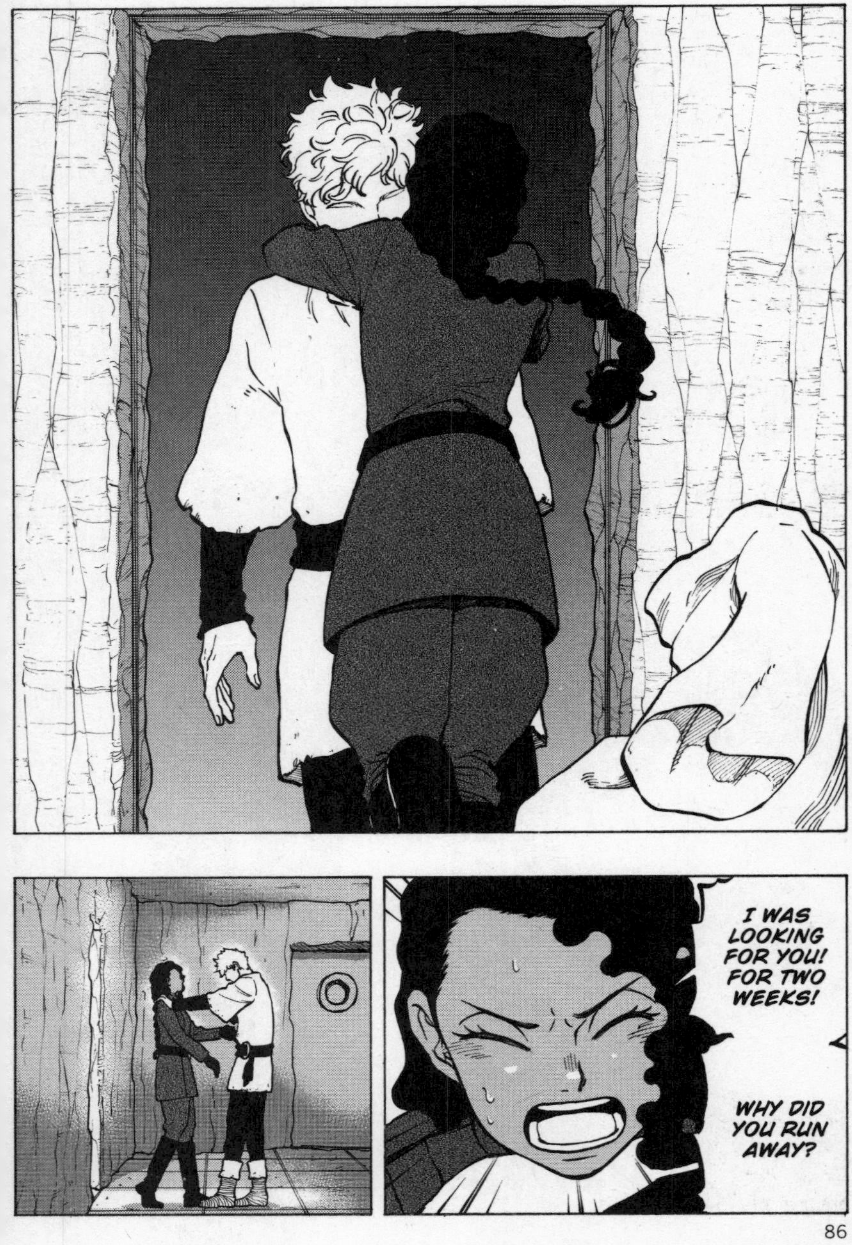
I WAS LOOKING FOR YOU! FOR TWO WEEKS!
WHY DID YOU RUN AWAY?

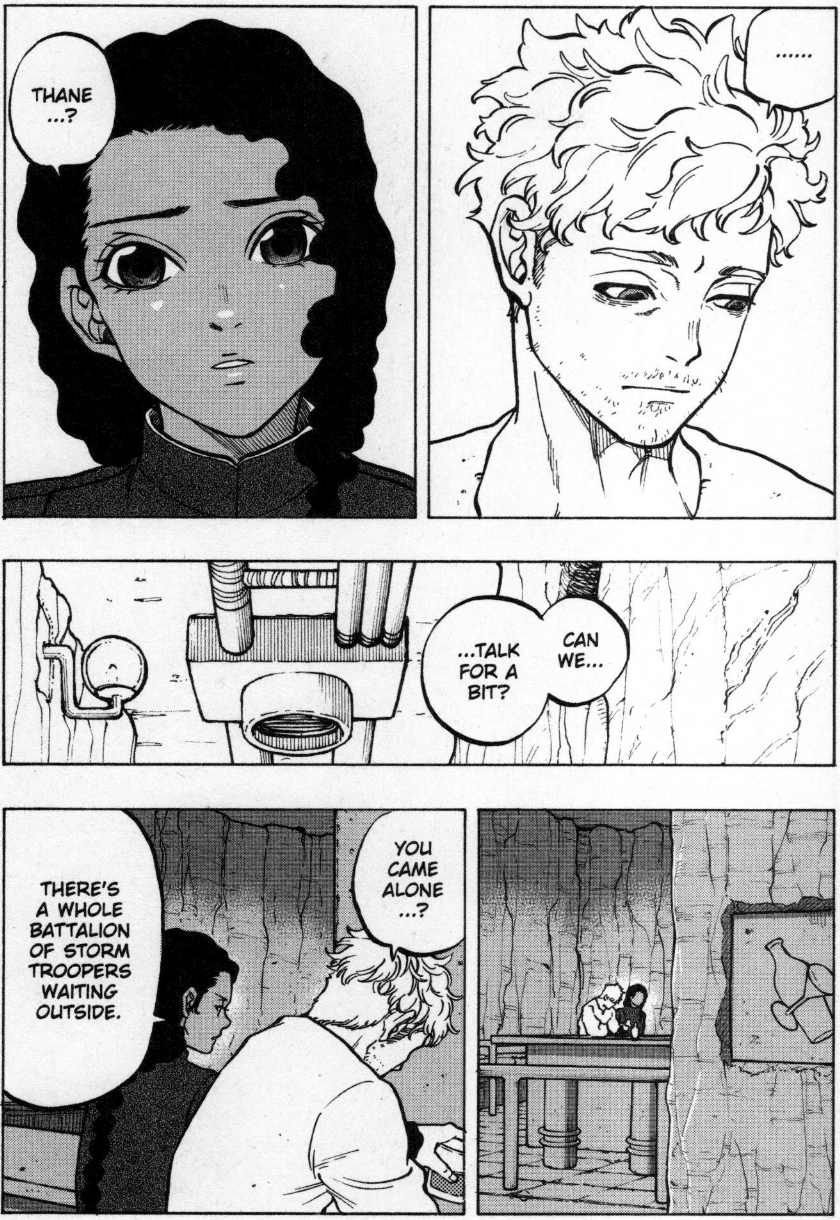
......
THANE ...?
CAN WE...
...TALK FOR A BIT?
YOU CAME ALONE ...?
THERE'S A WHOLE BATTALION OF STORM TROOPERS WAITING OUTSIDE.

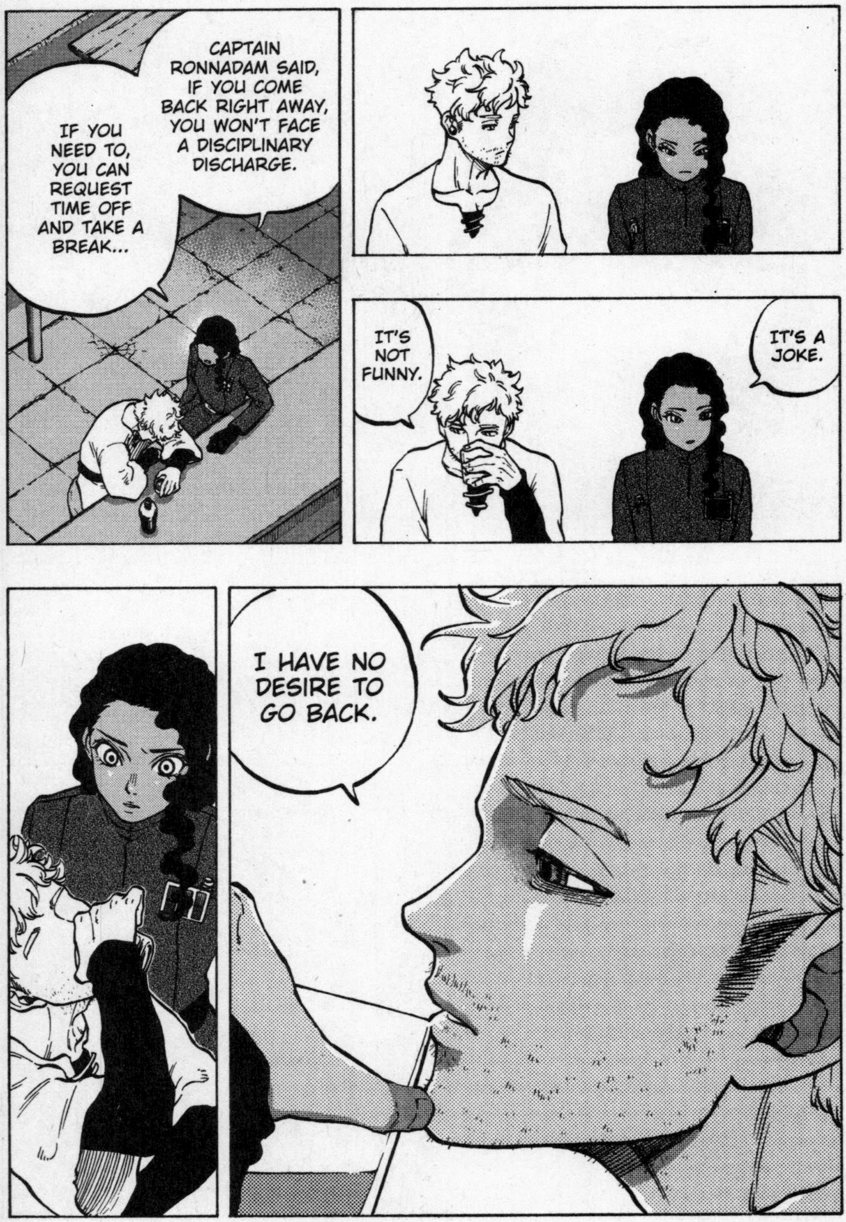
IT'S A JOKE.
IT'S NOT FUNNY.
CAPTAIN RONNADAM SAID, IF YOU COME BACK RIGHT AWAY, YOU WON'T FACE A DISCIPLINARY DISCHARGE.
IF YOU NEED TO, YOU CAN REQUEST TIME OFF AND TAKE A BREAK...
I HAVE NO DESIRE TO GO BACK.

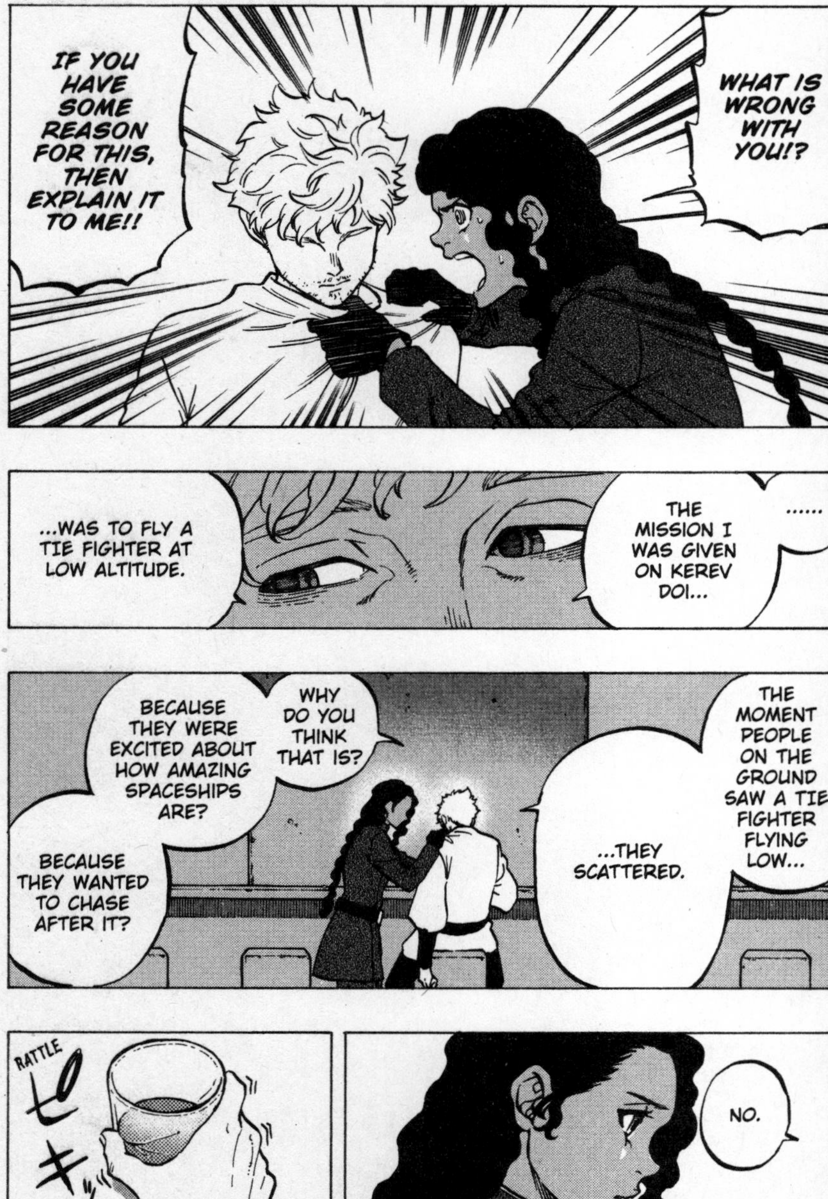
WHAT IS WRONG WITH YOU!?
IF YOU HAVE SOME REASON FOR THIS, THEN EXPLAIN IT TO ME!!
......
THE MISSION I WAS GIVEN ON KEREV DOI...
...WAS TO FLY A TIE FIGHTER AT LOW ALTITUDE.
THE MOMENT PEOPLE ON THE GROUND SAW A TIE FIGHTER FLYING LOW...
...THEY SCATTERED.
WHY DO YOU THINK THAT IS?
BECAUSE THEY WERE EXCITED ABOUT HOW AMAZING SPACESHIPS ARE?
BECAUSE THEY WANTED TO CHASE AFTER IT?
NO.
RATTLE

SEEING PEOPLE COWERING AND RUNNING FROM IMPERIAL SOLDIERS...

BEFORE THE DESTRUCTION OF ALDERAAN, I PROBABLY WOULD HAVE LAUGHED AT THAT.

IT SEEMS CRAZY...

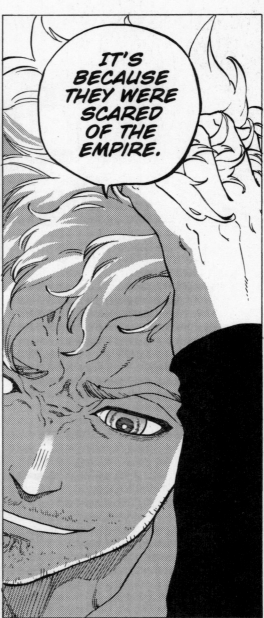

IT'S BECAUSE THEY WERE SCARED OF THE EMPIRE.

SO THAT'S THE REASON...?

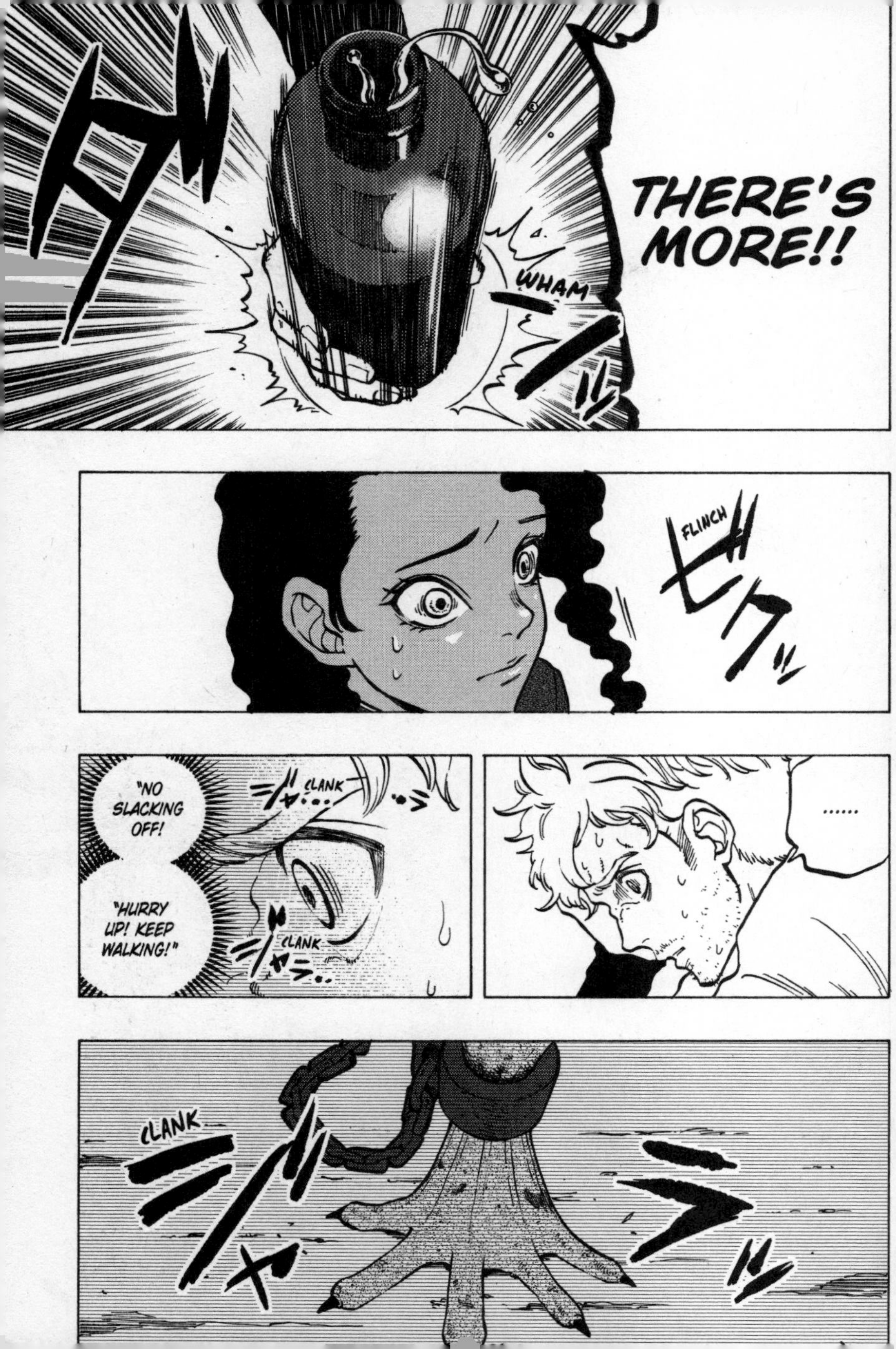
THERE'S MORE!!
WHAM
FLINCH
......
"NO SLACKING OFF!
CLANK
"HURRY UP! KEEP WALKING!"
CLANK
CLANK

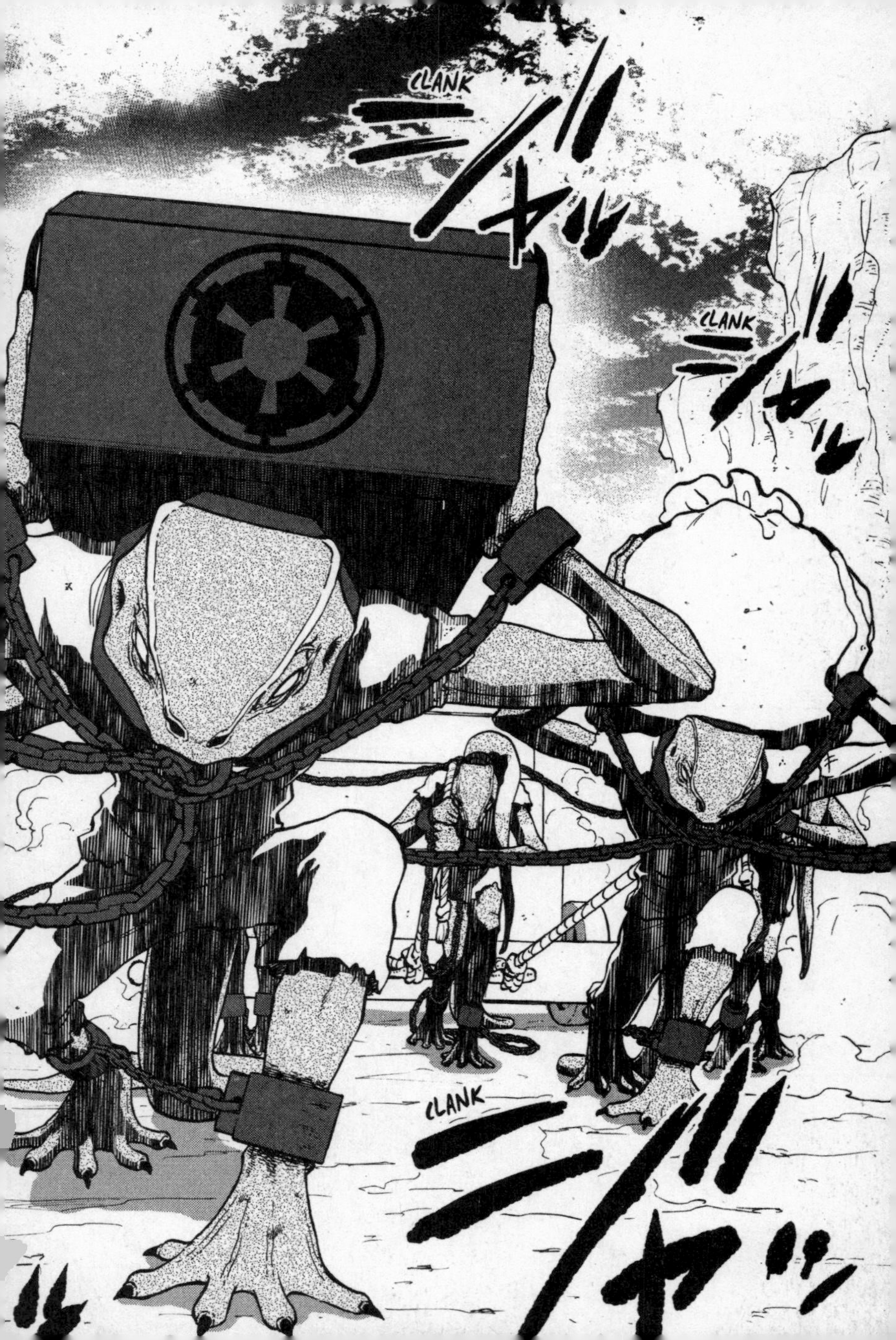
CLANK
ジャッ
CLANK
ジャッ
CLANK
ジャッ

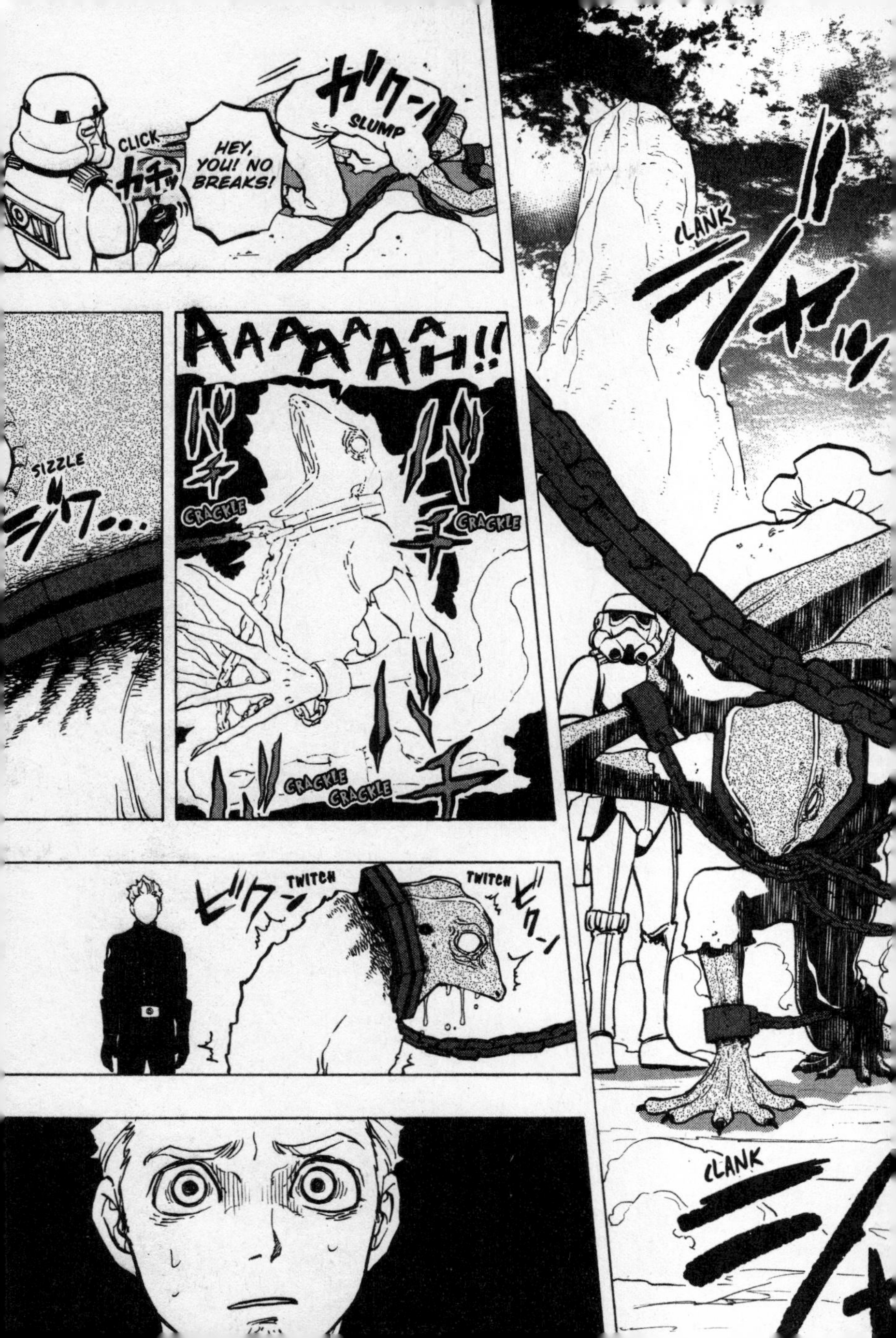
CLANK
CLANK
SLUMP
HEY, YOU! NO BREAKS!
CLICK
AAAAAAH!!
CRACKLE
CRACKLE
CRACKLE
CRACKLE
SIZZLE
TWITCH
TWITCH

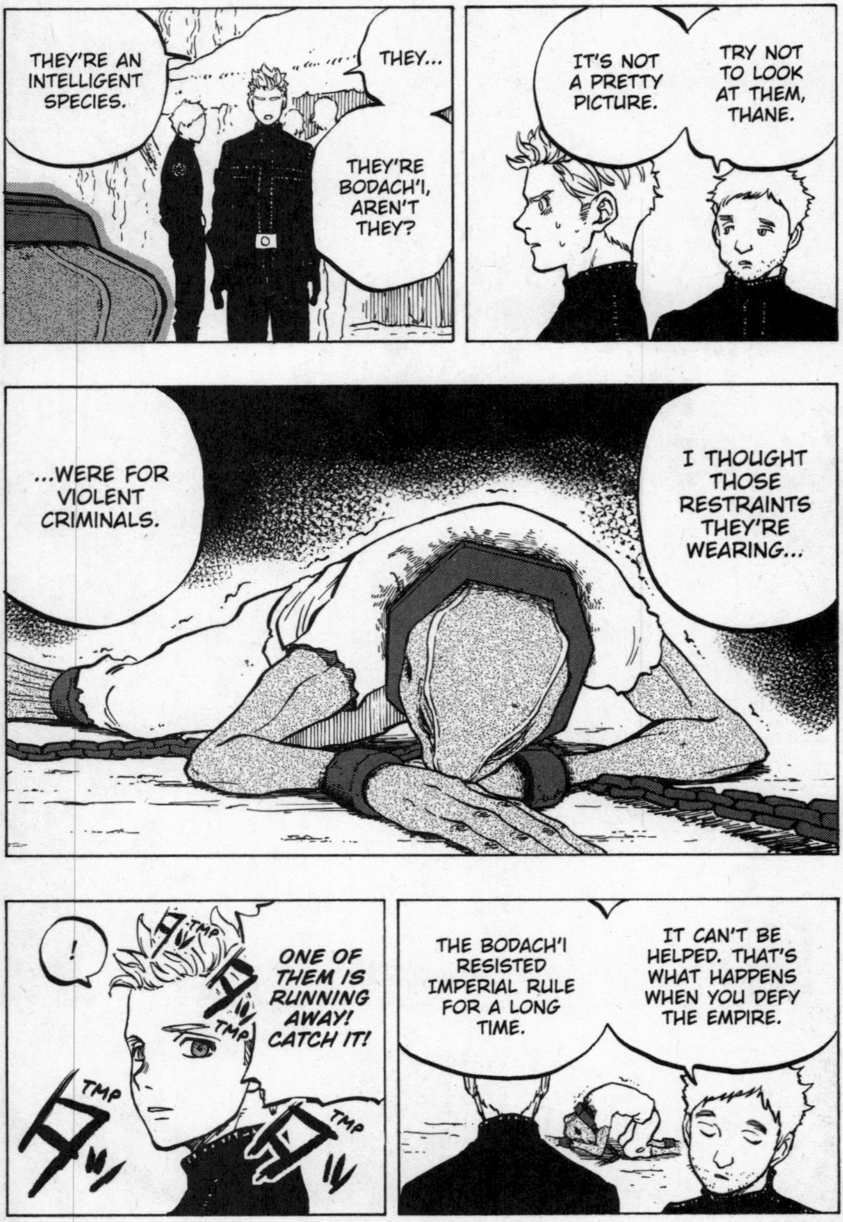
TRY NOT TO LOOK AT THEM, THANE.
IT'S NOT A PRETTY PICTURE.
THEY...
THEY'RE BODACH'I, AREN'T THEY?
THEY'RE AN INTELLIGENT SPECIES.
I THOUGHT THOSE RESTRAINTS THEY'RE WEARING...
...WERE FOR VIOLENT CRIMINALS.
IT CAN'T BE HELPED. THAT'S WHAT HAPPENS WHEN YOU DEFY THE EMPIRE.
THE BODACH'I RESISTED IMPERIAL RULE FOR A LONG TIME.
ONE OF THEM IS RUNNING AWAY! CATCH IT!
TMP
TMP
!
TMP
TMP

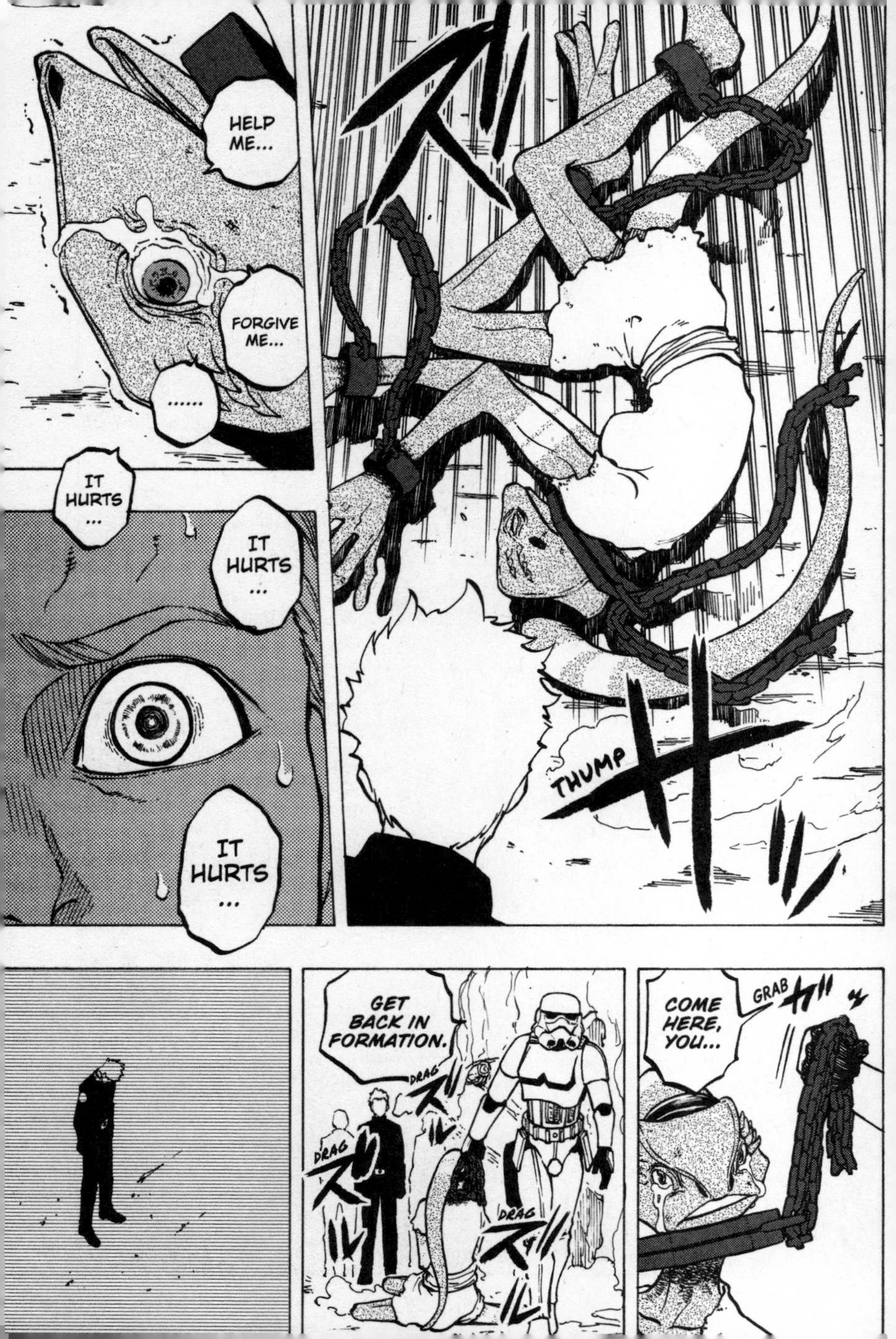
THUMP
HELP ME...
FORGIVE ME...
......
IT HURTS...
IT HURTS...
IT HURTS...
GRAB
COME HERE, YOU...
GET BACK IN FORMATION.
DRAG
DRAG
DRAG

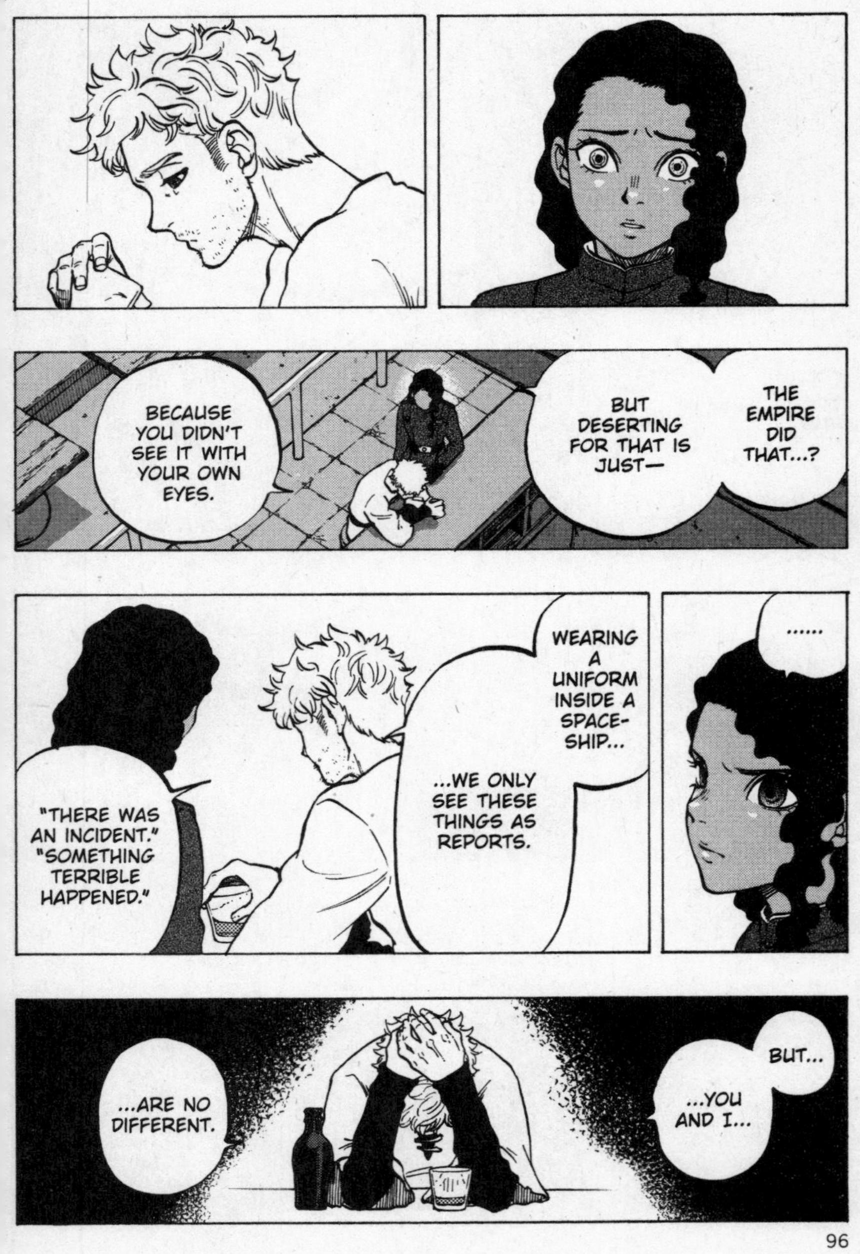
THE EMPIRE DID THAT...?
BUT DESERTING FOR THAT IS JUST—
BECAUSE YOU DIDN'T SEE IT WITH YOUR OWN EYES.
......
WEARING A UNIFORM INSIDE A SPACE-SHIP...
...WE ONLY SEE THESE THINGS AS REPORTS.
"THERE WAS AN INCIDENT." "SOMETHING TERRIBLE HAPPENED."
BUT...
...YOU AND I...
...ARE NO DIFFERENT.

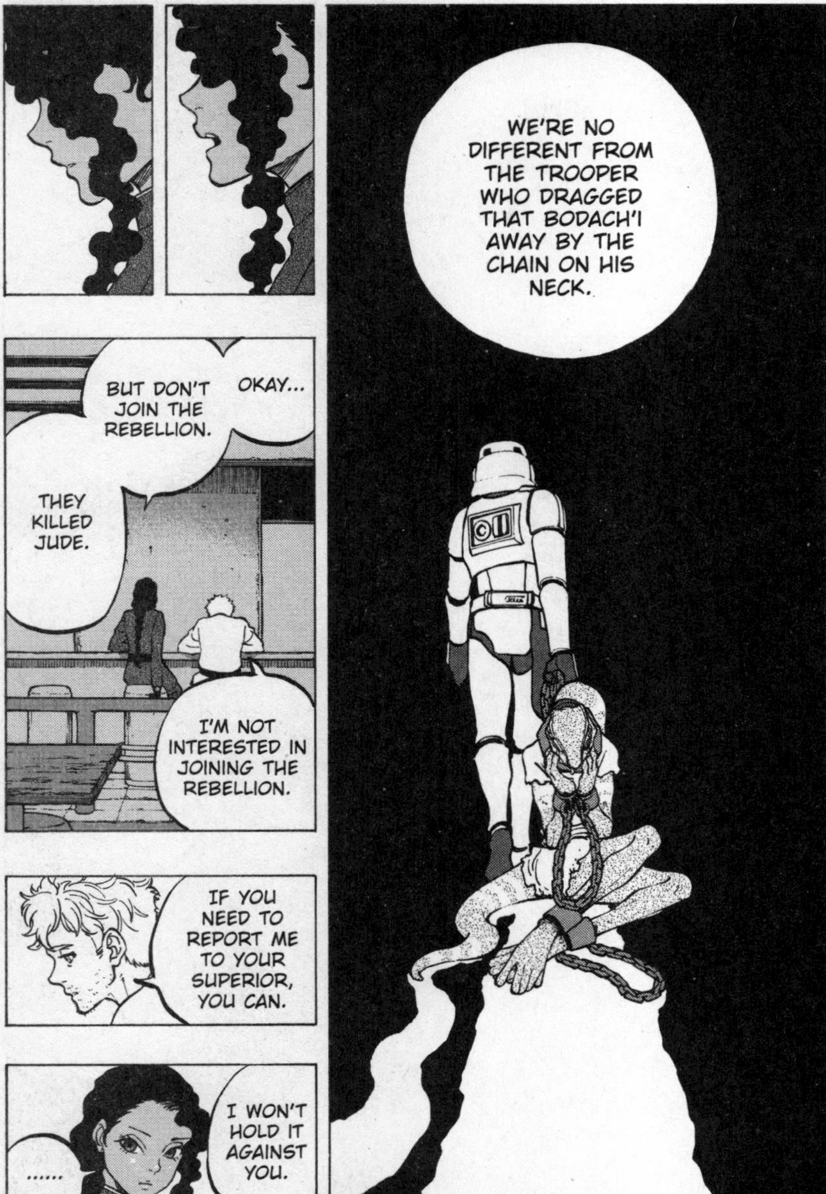
WE'RE NO DIFFERENT FROM THE TROOPER WHO DRAGGED THAT BODACH'I AWAY BY THE CHAIN ON HIS NECK.
OKAY...
BUT DON'T JOIN THE REBELLION.
THEY KILLED JUDE.
I'M NOT INTERESTED IN JOINING THE REBELLION.
IF YOU NEED TO REPORT ME TO YOUR SUPERIOR, YOU CAN.
I WON'T HOLD IT AGAINST YOU.
......

I AM LIEUTENANT COMMANDER CIENA REE OF THE IMPERIAL ARMY...

...BUT RIGHT NOW, I'M JUST PLAIN OLD CIENA REE.

YEAH.

YOU GOT PRO-MOTED?

......

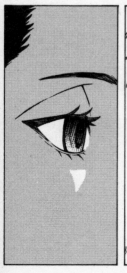

I SEE.

CONGRAT-ULATIONS...

THANKS.

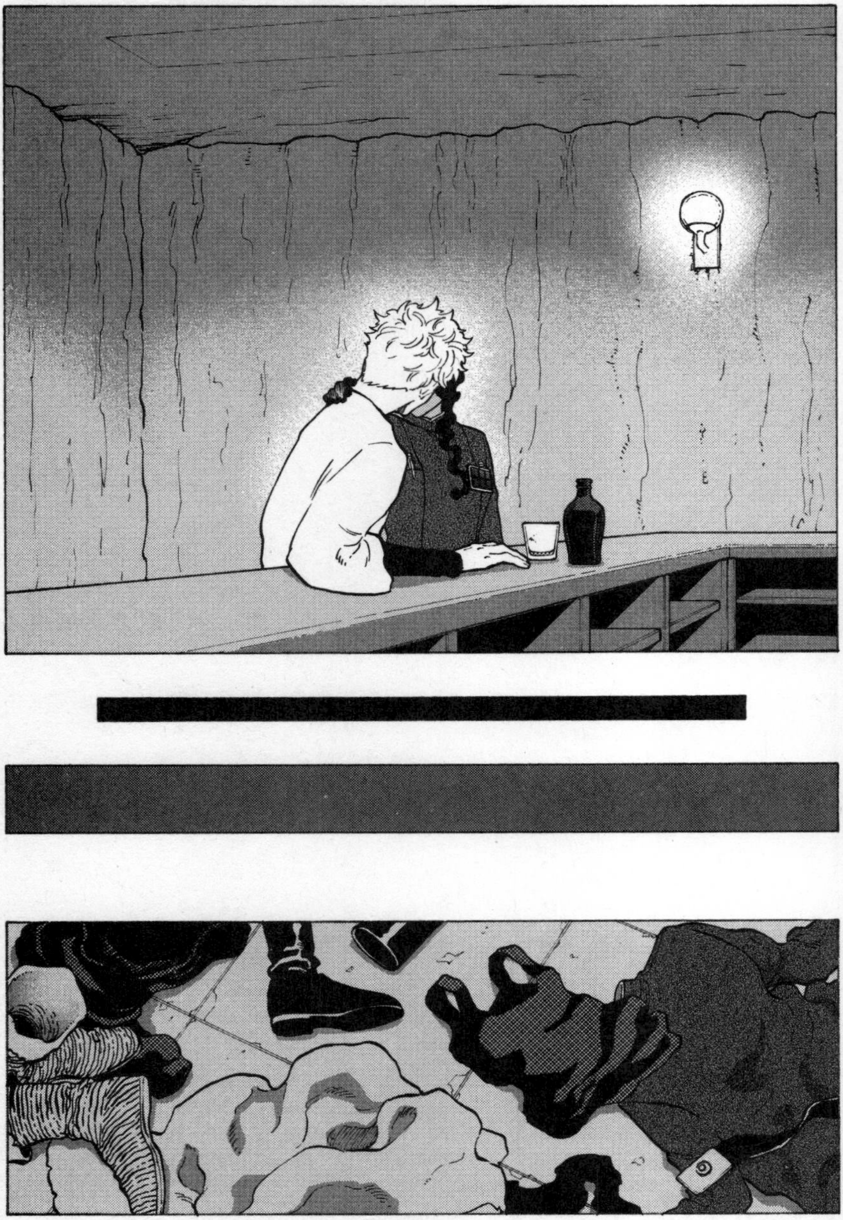

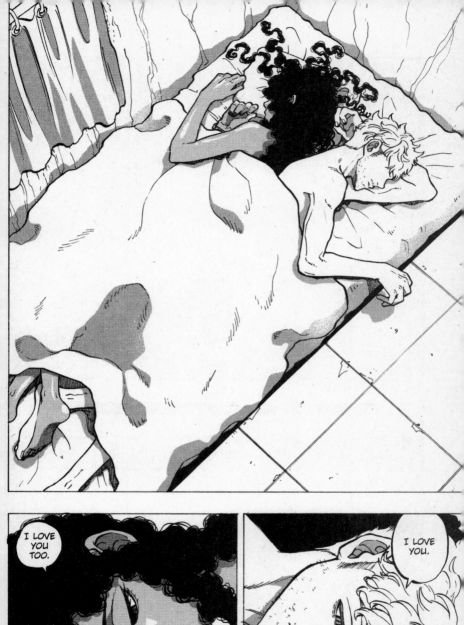

I LOVE
YOU
TOO.

I LOVE
YOU.

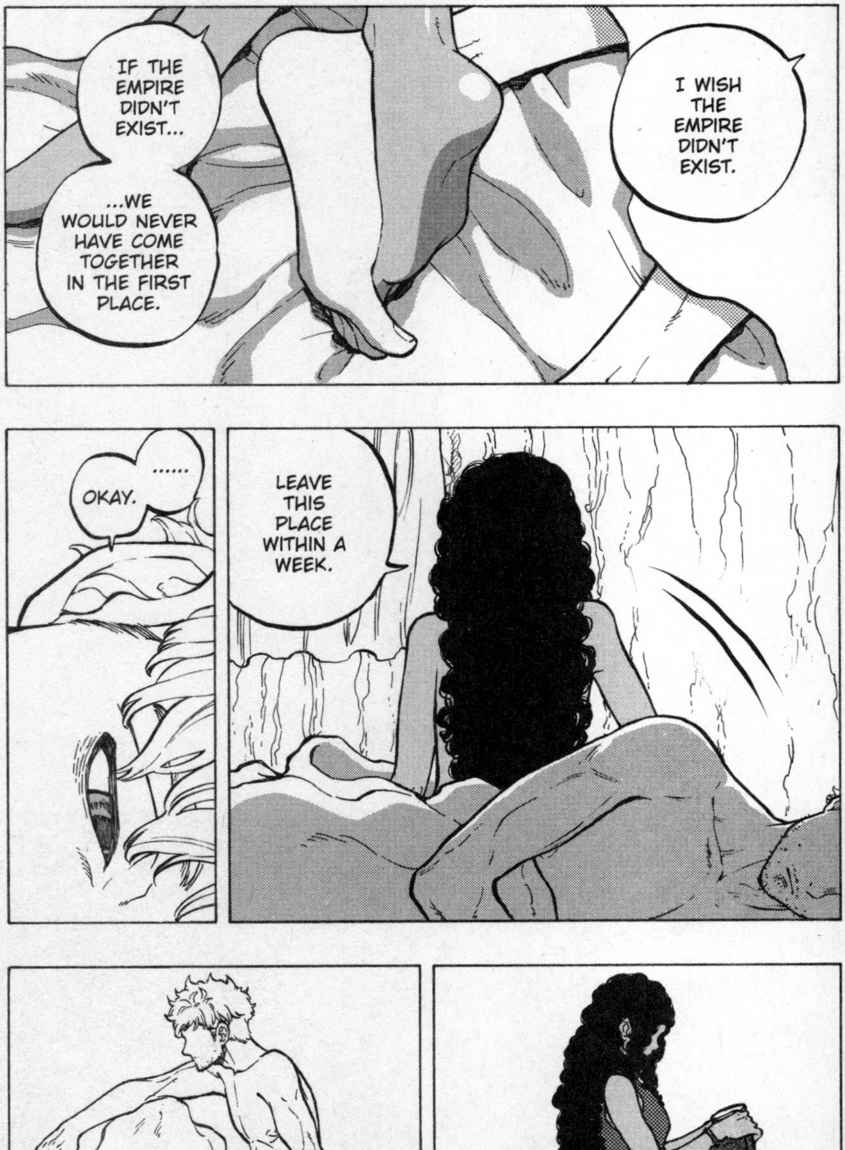
I WISH THE EMPIRE DIDN'T EXIST.
IF THE EMPIRE DIDN'T EXIST...
...WE WOULD NEVER HAVE COME TOGETHER IN THE FIRST PLACE.
LEAVE THIS PLACE WITHIN A WEEK.
...... OKAY.

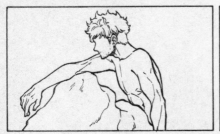

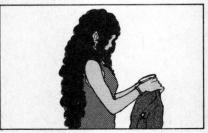

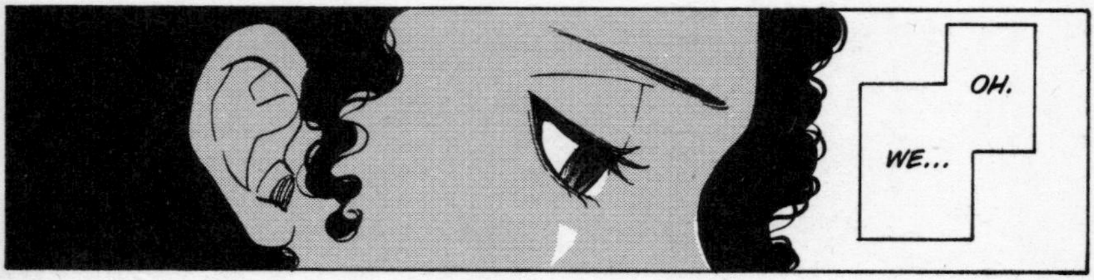
OH.
WE...

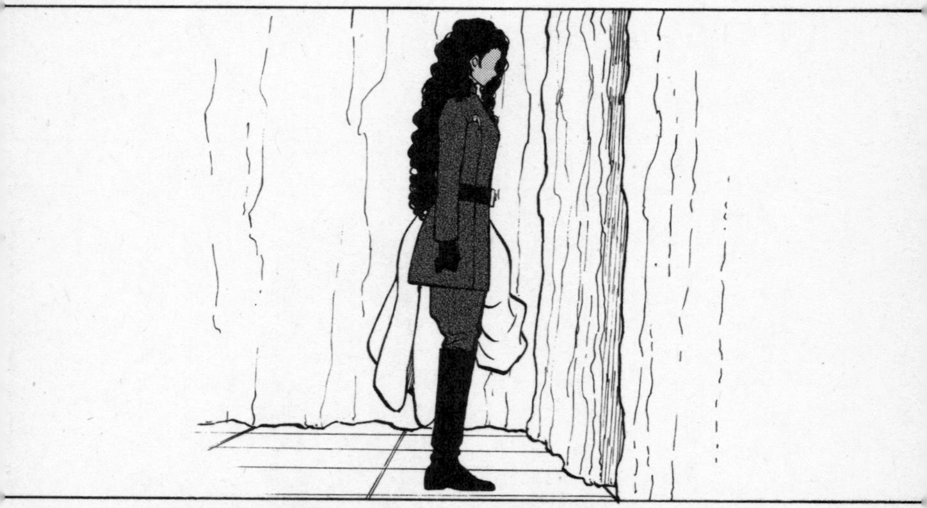

...WERE ALWAYS RUNNING AROUND TOGETHER...

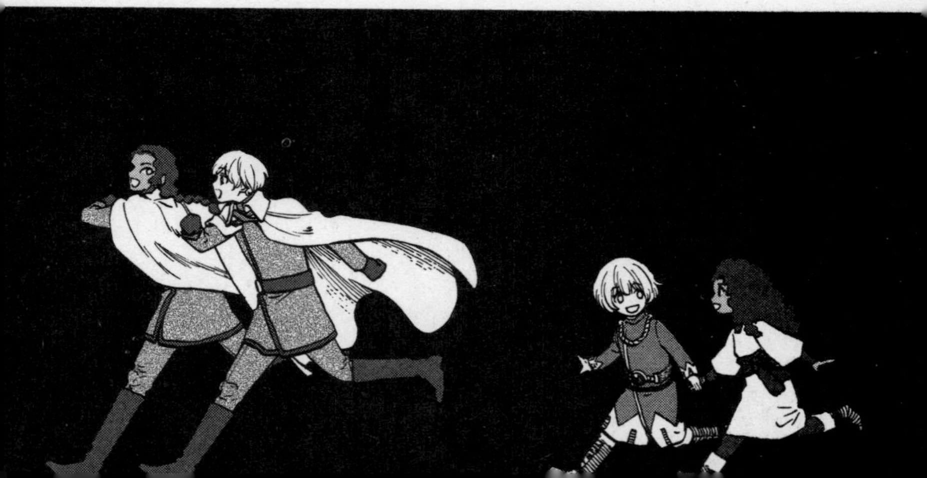

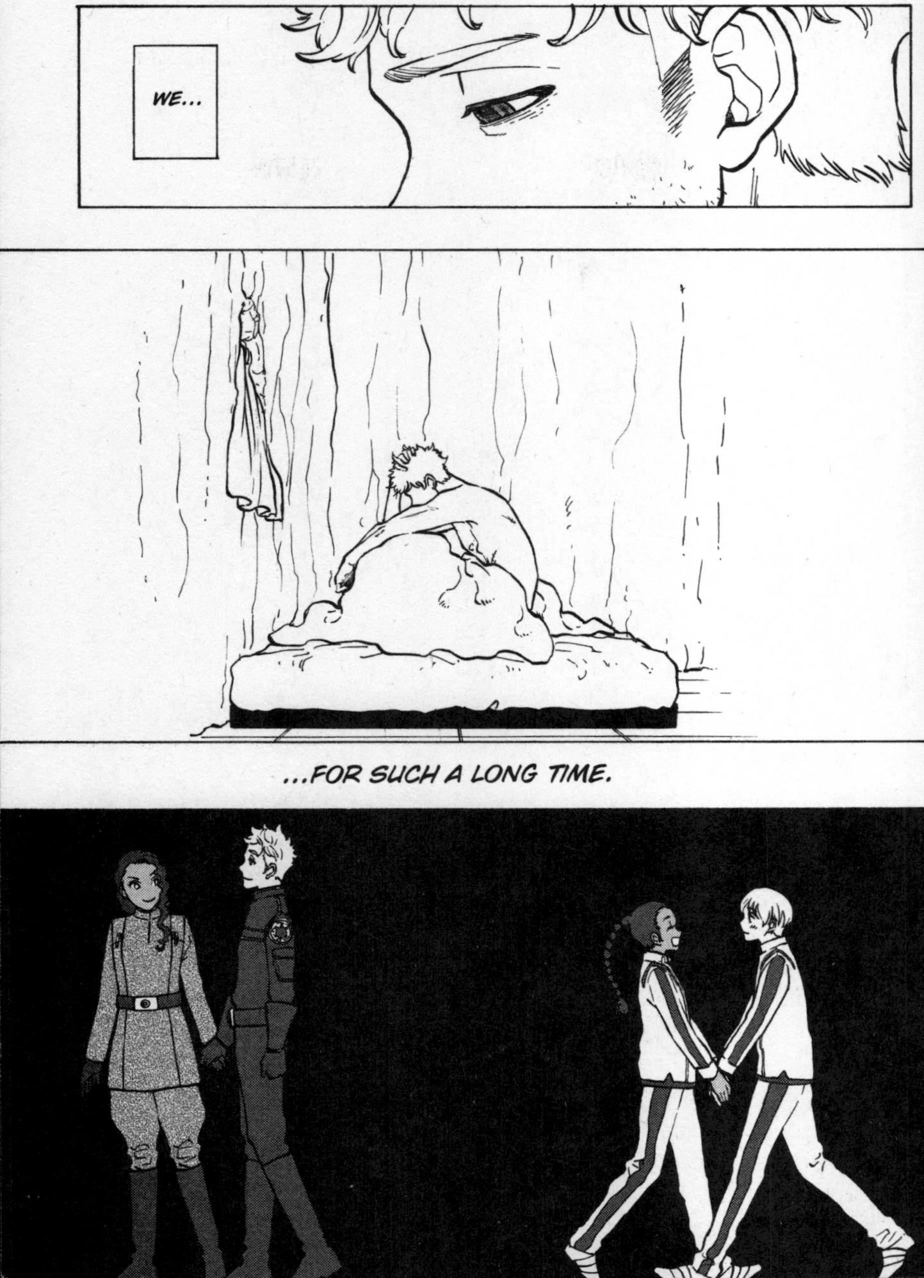
WE...
...FOR SUCH A LONG TIME.

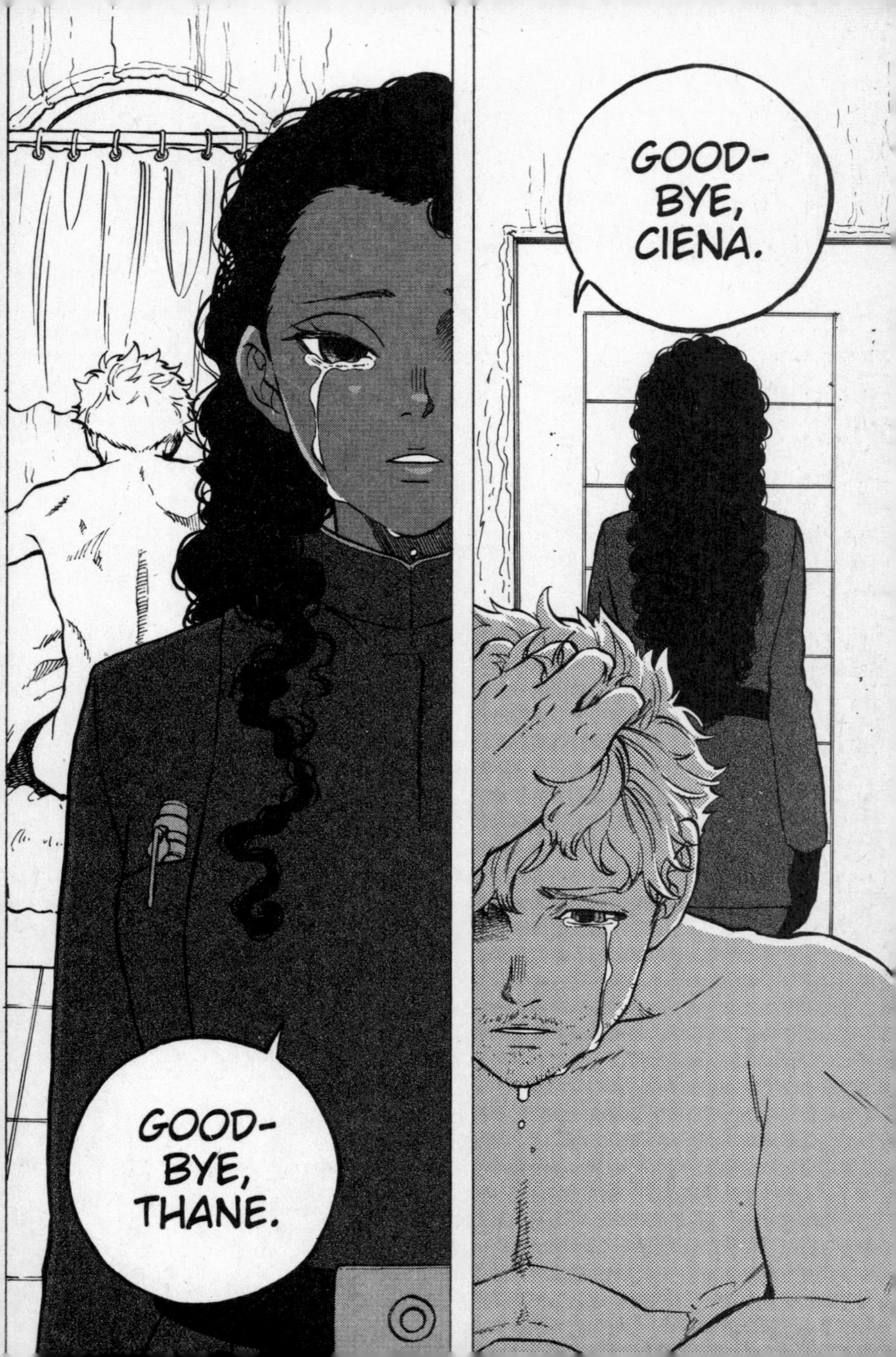
GOOD-BYE, CIENA.
GOOD-BYE, THANE.

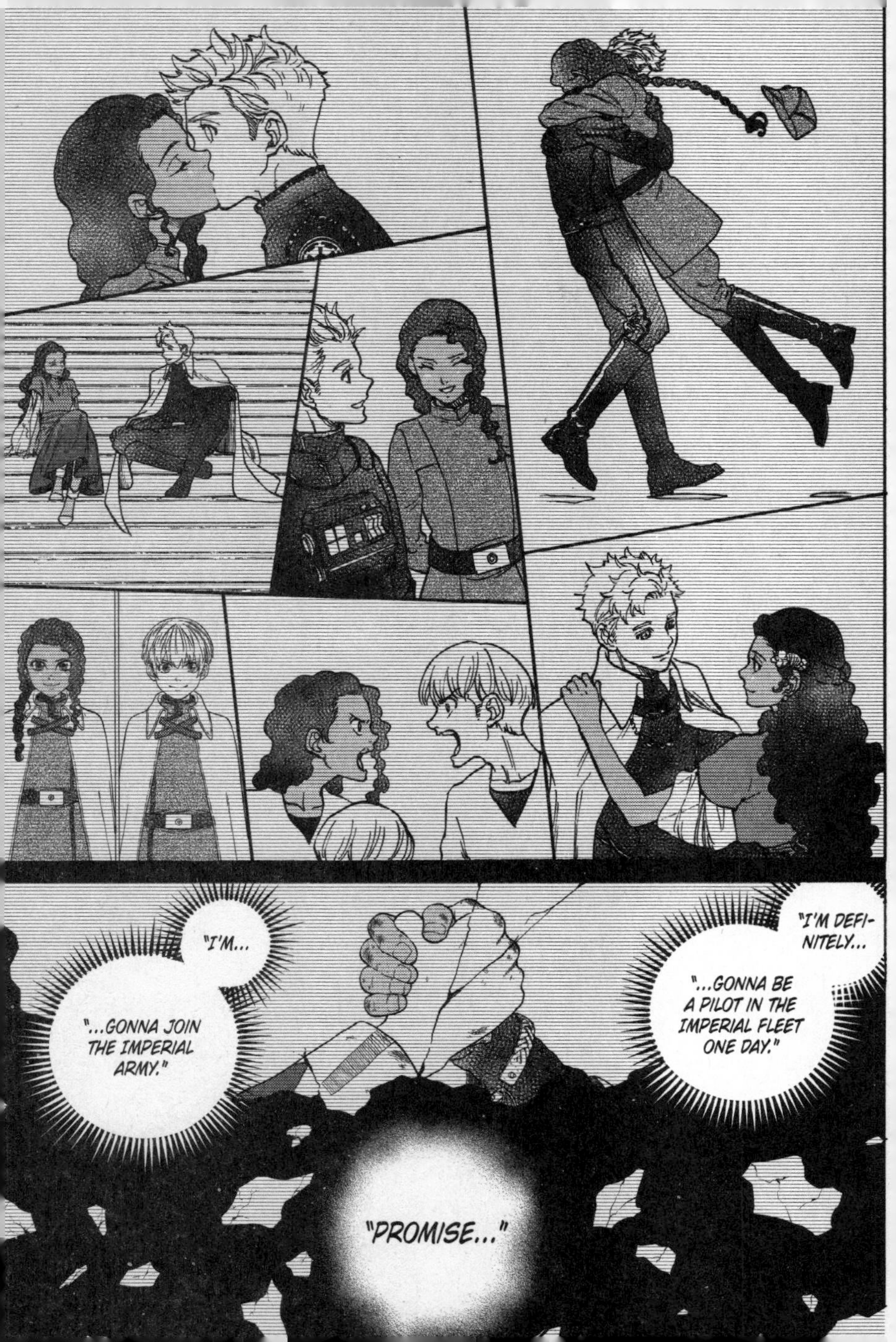
"I'M DEFI-
NITELY...
"...GONNA BE
A PILOT IN THE
IMPERIAL FLEET
ONE DAY."
"I'M...
"...GONNA JOIN
THE IMPERIAL
ARMY."
"PROMISE..."

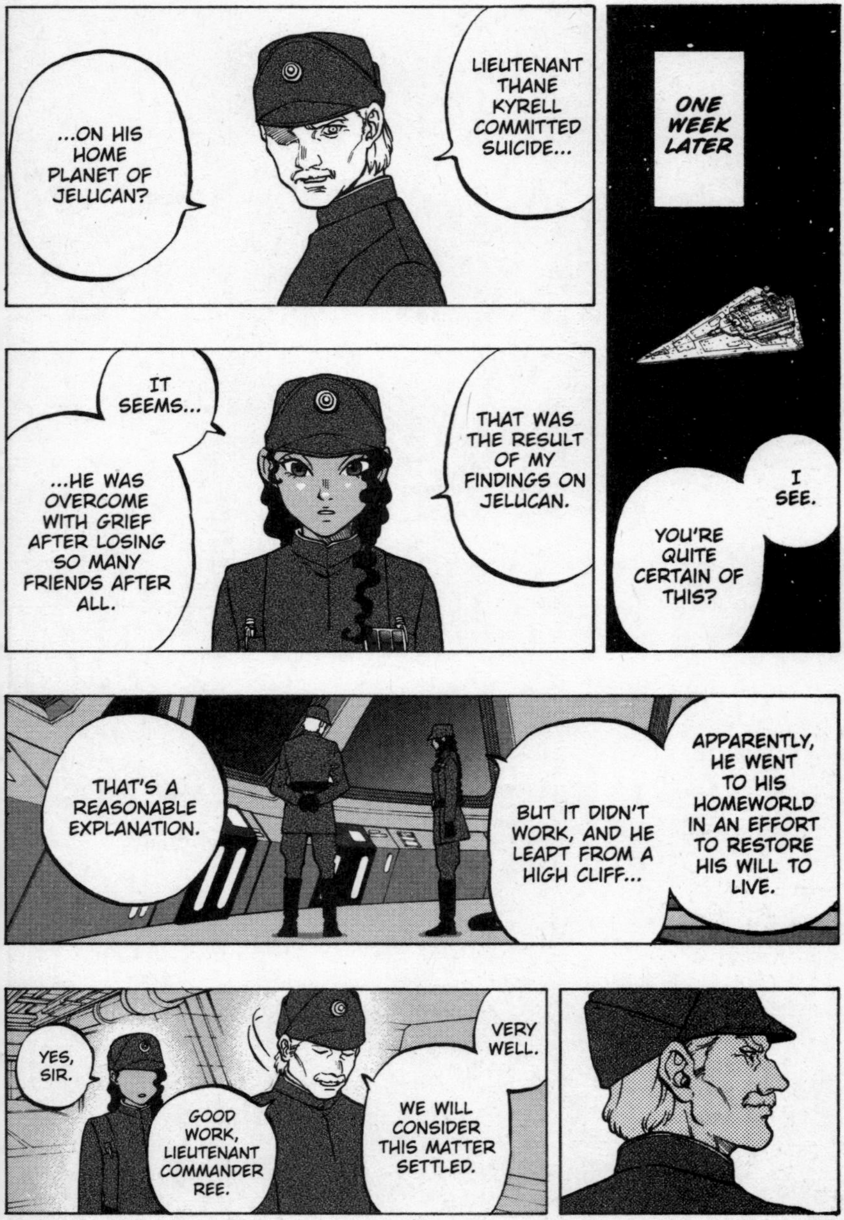
ONE WEEK LATER
I SEE.
YOU'RE QUITE CERTAIN OF THIS?
LIEUTENANT THANE KYRELL COMMITTED SUICIDE...
...ON HIS HOME PLANET OF JELUCAN?
THAT WAS THE RESULT OF MY FINDINGS ON JELUCAN.
IT SEEMS...
...HE WAS OVERCOME WITH GRIEF AFTER LOSING SO MANY FRIENDS AFTER ALL.
APPARENTLY, HE WENT TO HIS HOMEWORLD IN AN EFFORT TO RESTORE HIS WILL TO LIVE.
BUT IT DIDN'T WORK, AND HE LEAPT FROM A HIGH CLIFF...
THAT'S A REASONABLE EXPLANATION.
VERY WELL.
WE WILL CONSIDER THIS MATTER SETTLED.
GOOD WORK, LIEUTENANT COMMANDER REE.
YES, SIR.

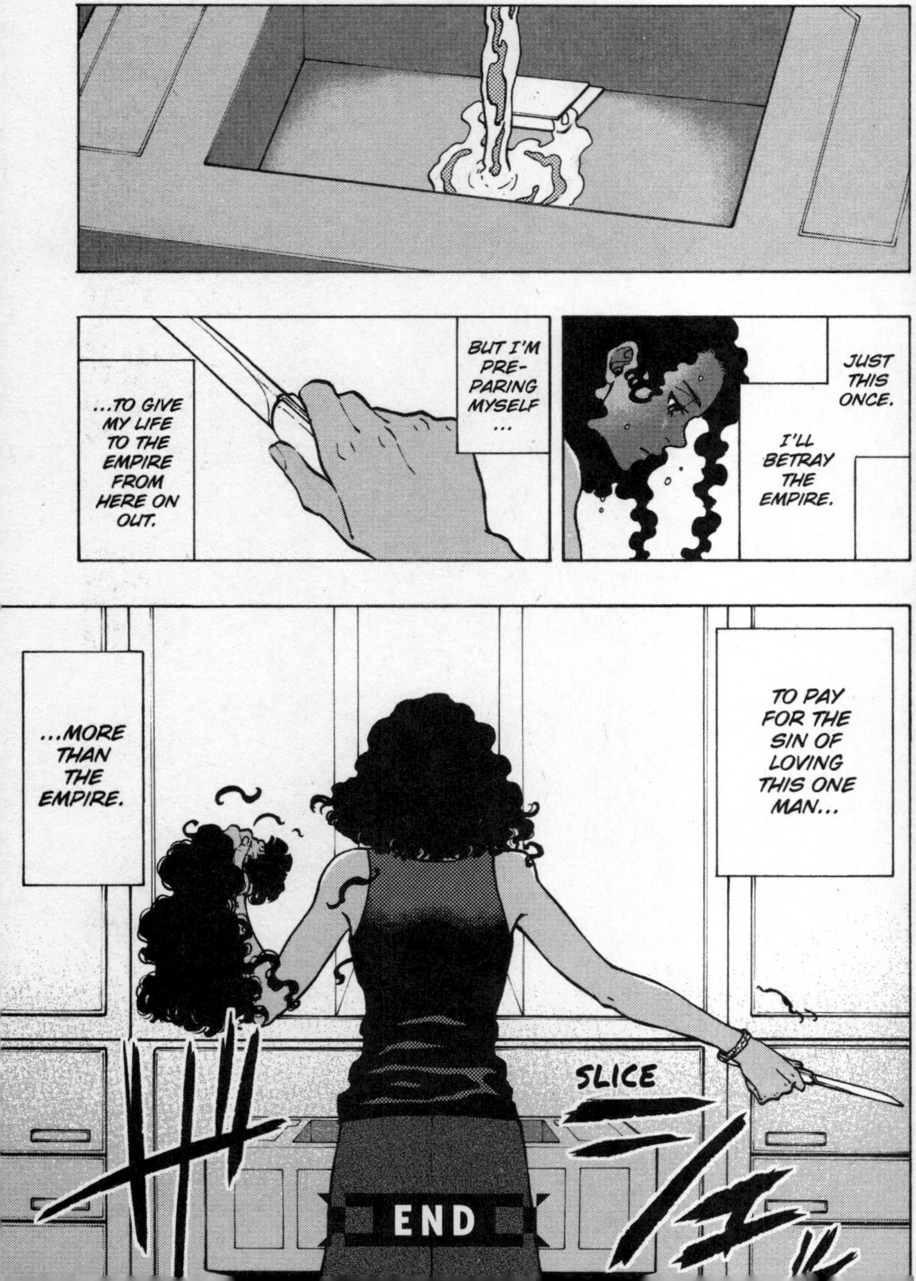
JUST THIS ONCE.
I'LL BETRAY THE EMPIRE.
BUT I'M PRE-PARING MYSELF...
...TO GIVE MY LIFE TO THE EMPIRE FROM HERE ON OUT.
TO PAY FOR THE SIN OF LOVING THIS ONE MAN...
...MORE THAN THE EMPIRE.
SLICE
END

STAR WARS
LOST STARS
ロスト・スターズ

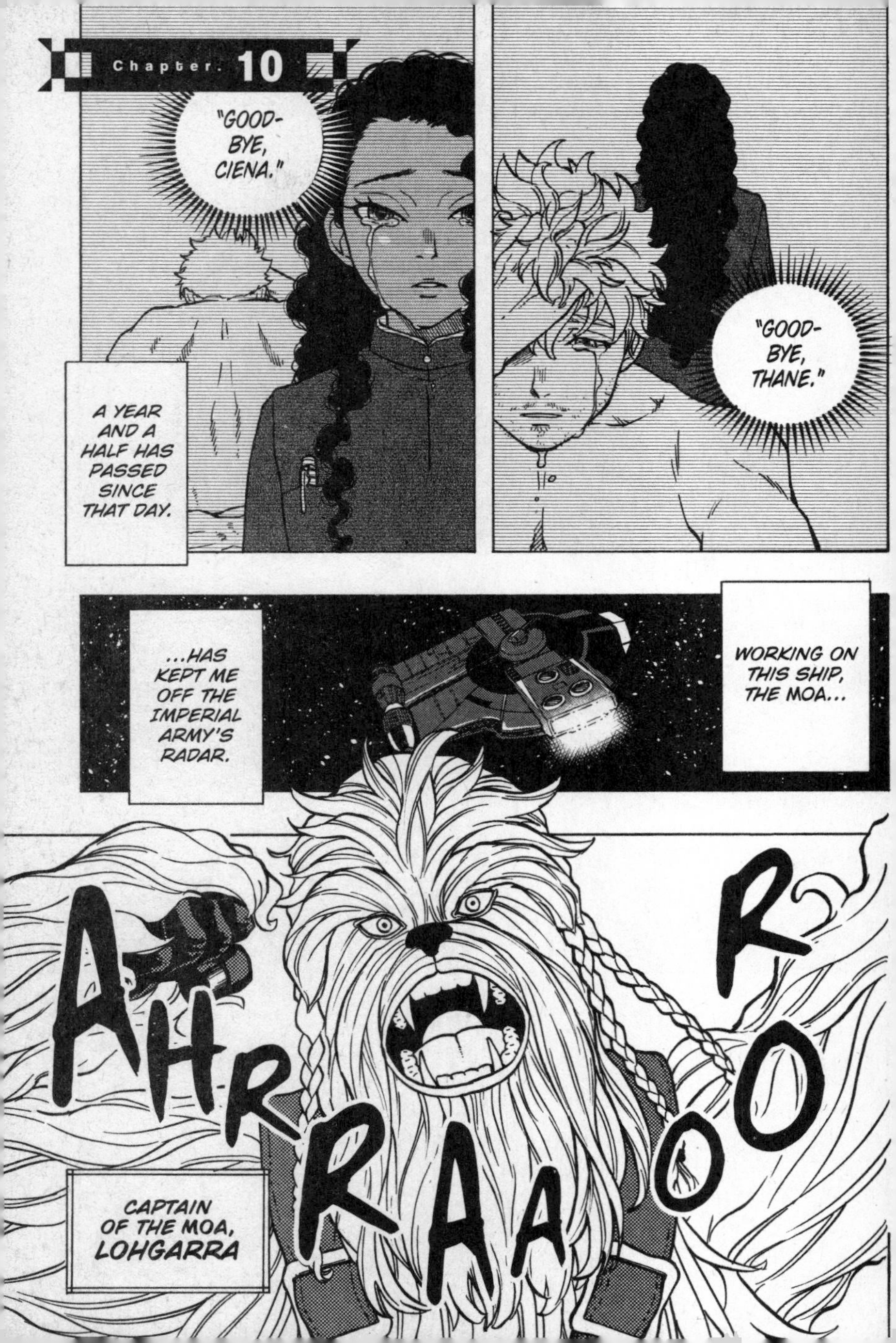
Chapter. 10
"GOOD-BYE, THANE."
"GOOD-BYE, CIENA."
A YEAR AND A HALF HAS PASSED SINCE THAT DAY.
WORKING ON THIS SHIP, THE MOA...
...HAS KEPT ME OFF THE IMPERIAL ARMY'S RADAR.
AHRRRAAOOOR
CAPTAIN OF THE MOA, LOHGARRA

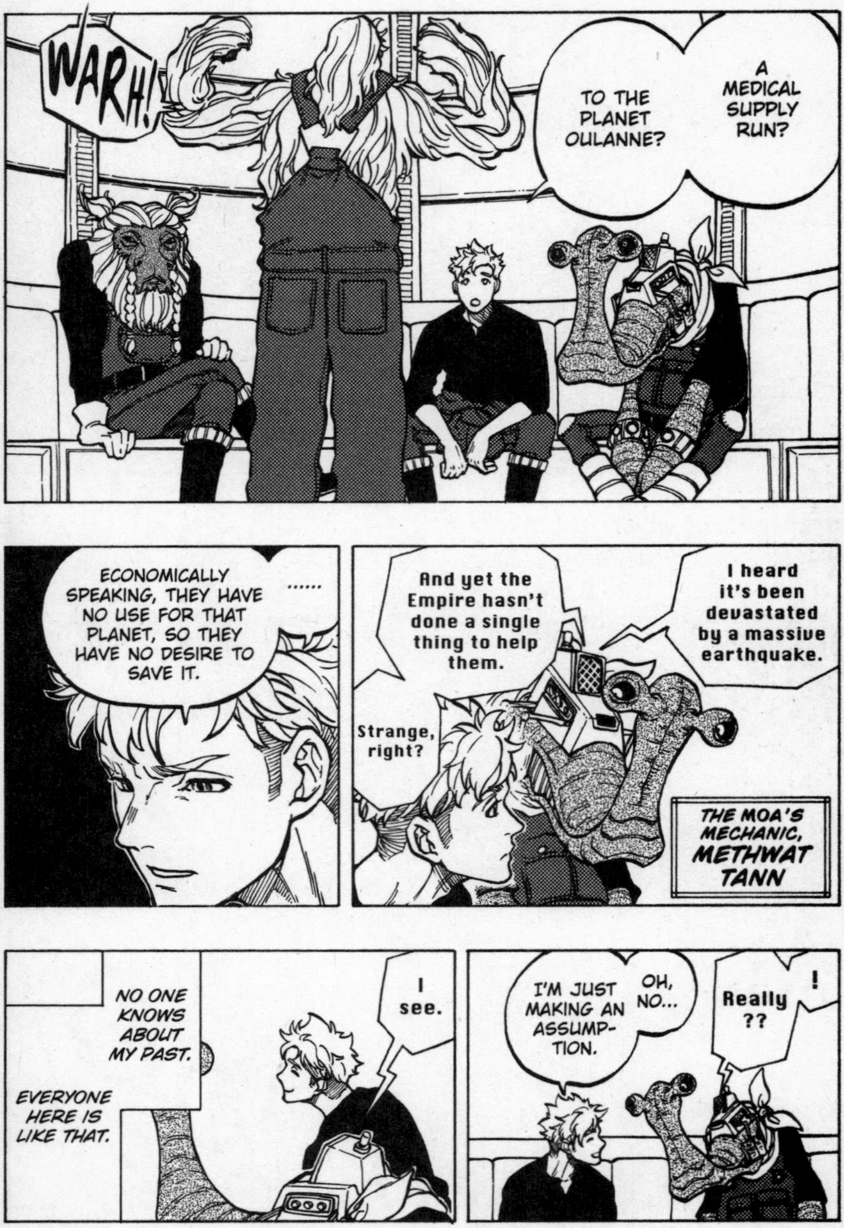
A MEDICAL SUPPLY RUN?
TO THE PLANET OULANNE?
WARH!
I heard it's been devastated by a massive earthquake.
And yet the Empire hasn't done a single thing to help them.
Strange, right?
THE MOA'S MECHANIC, METHWAT TANN
......
ECONOMICALLY SPEAKING, THEY HAVE NO USE FOR THAT PLANET, SO THEY HAVE NO DESIRE TO SAVE IT.
!
Really ??
OH, NO...
I'M JUST MAKING AN ASSUMPTION.
I see.
NO ONE KNOWS ABOUT MY PAST.
EVERYONE HERE IS LIKE THAT.

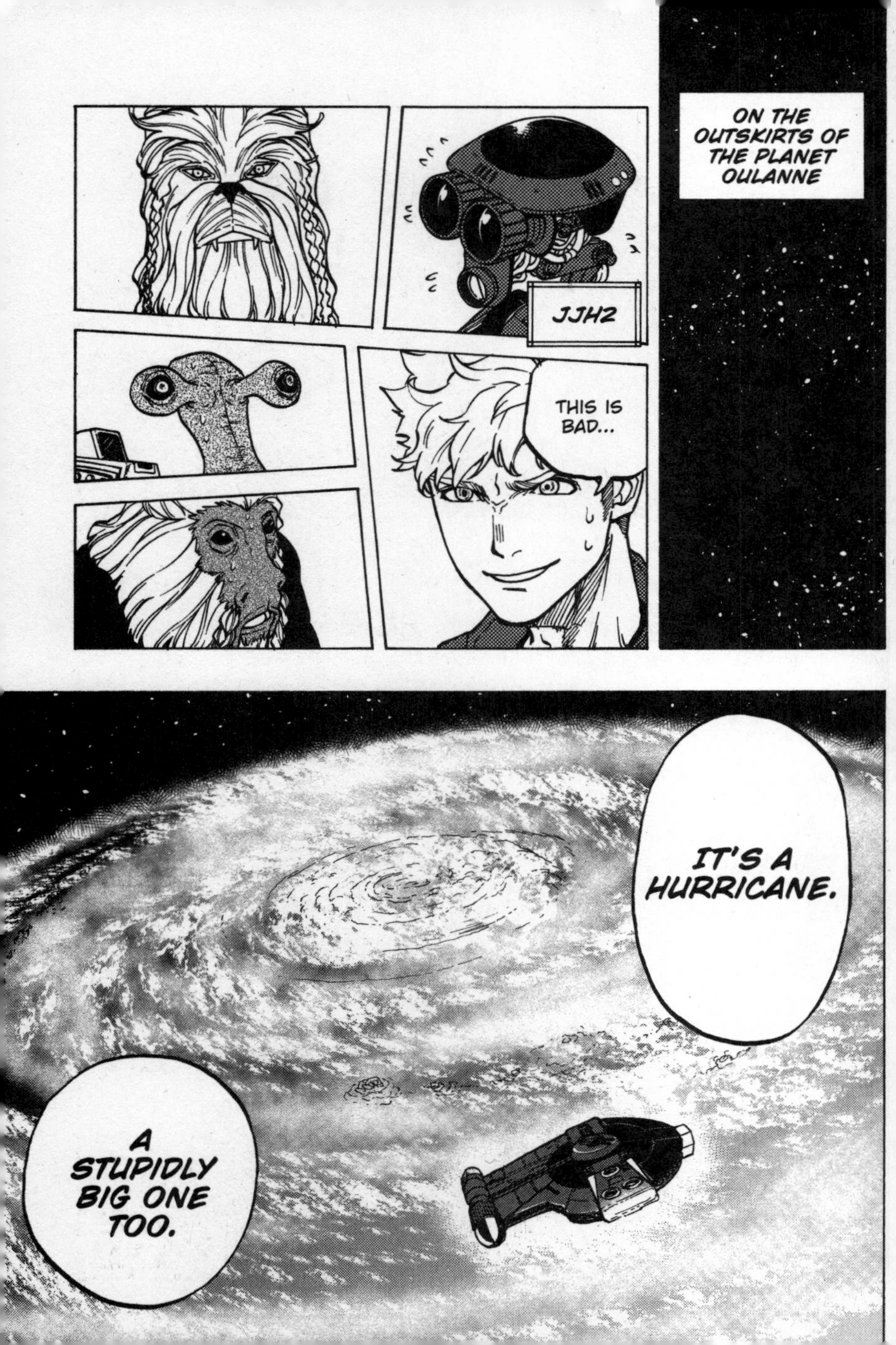
ON THE OUTSKIRTS OF THE PLANET OULANNE
JJH2
THIS IS BAD...
IT'S A HURRICANE.
A STUPIDLY BIG ONE TOO.

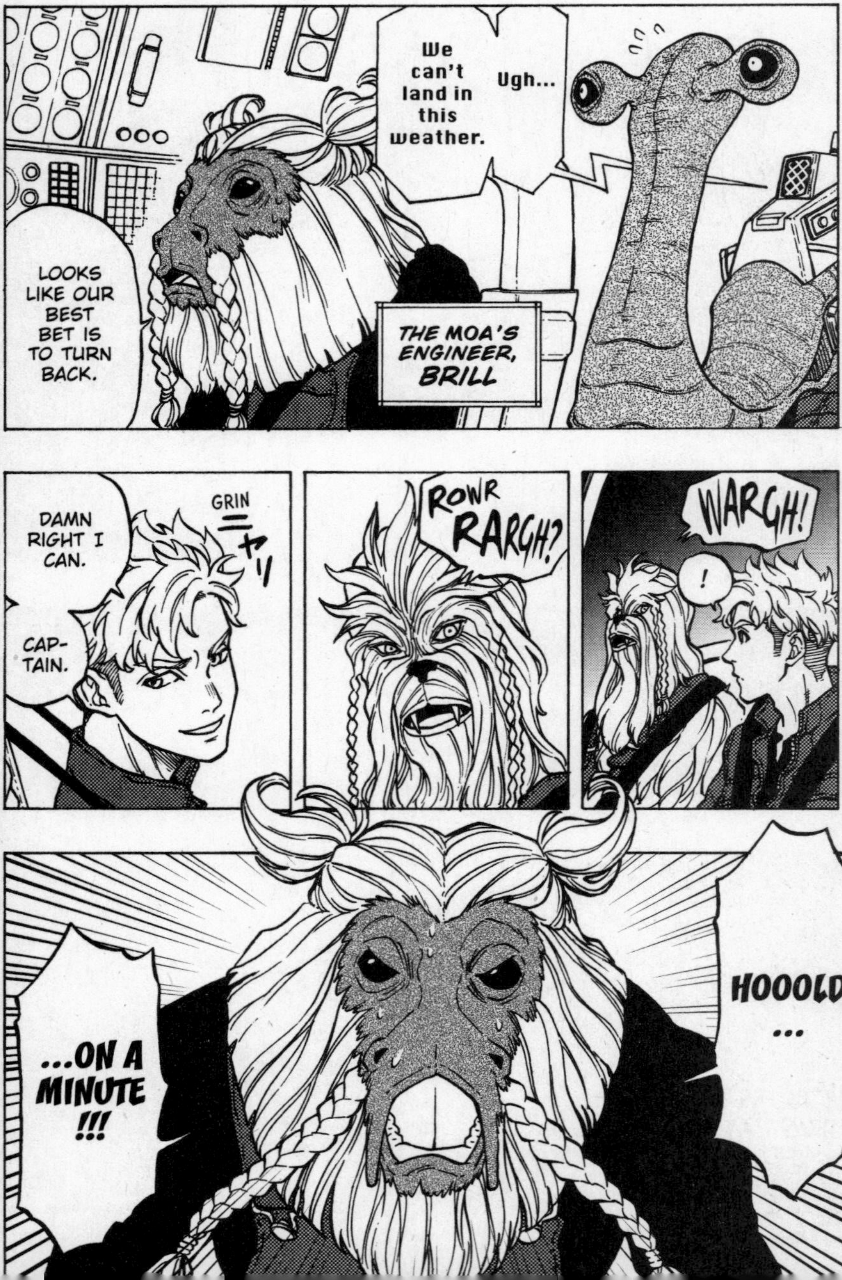
Ugh...
We can't land in this weather.
THE MOA'S ENGINEER, BRILL
LOOKS LIKE OUR BEST BET IS TO TURN BACK.
WARGH!
!
ROWR RARGH?
GRIN
ニヤリ
DAMN RIGHT I CAN.
CAP-TAIN.
HOOOLD ...
...ON A MINUTE !!!

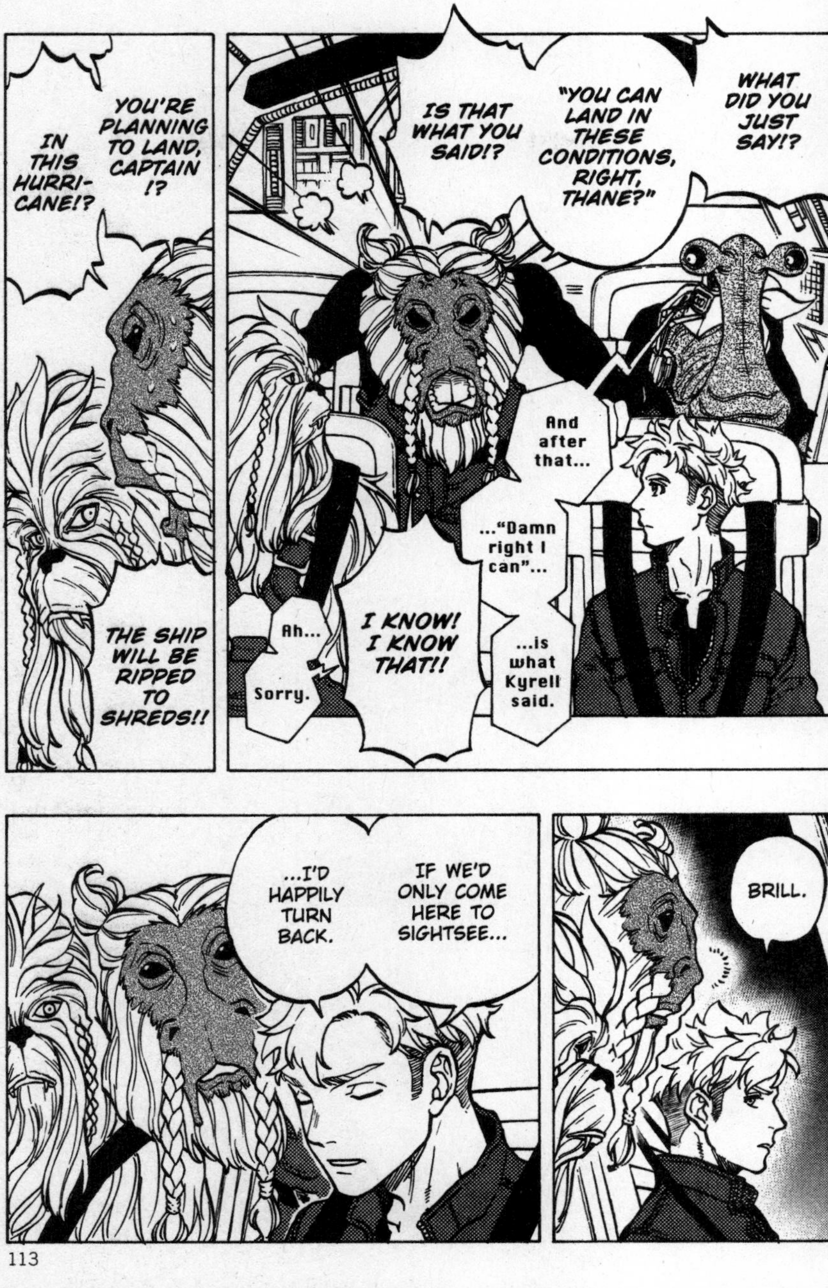
WHAT DID YOU JUST SAY!?
"YOU CAN LAND IN THESE CONDITIONS, RIGHT, THANE?"
IS THAT WHAT YOU SAID!?
And after that...
..."Damn right I can"...
...is what Kyrell said.
I KNOW! I KNOW THAT!!
Ah...
Sorry.
YOU'RE PLANNING TO LAND, CAPTAIN!?
IN THIS HURRI-CANE!?
THE SHIP WILL BE RIPPED TO SHREDS!!
BRILL.
IF WE'D ONLY COME HERE TO SIGHTSEE...
...I'D HAPPILY TURN BACK.

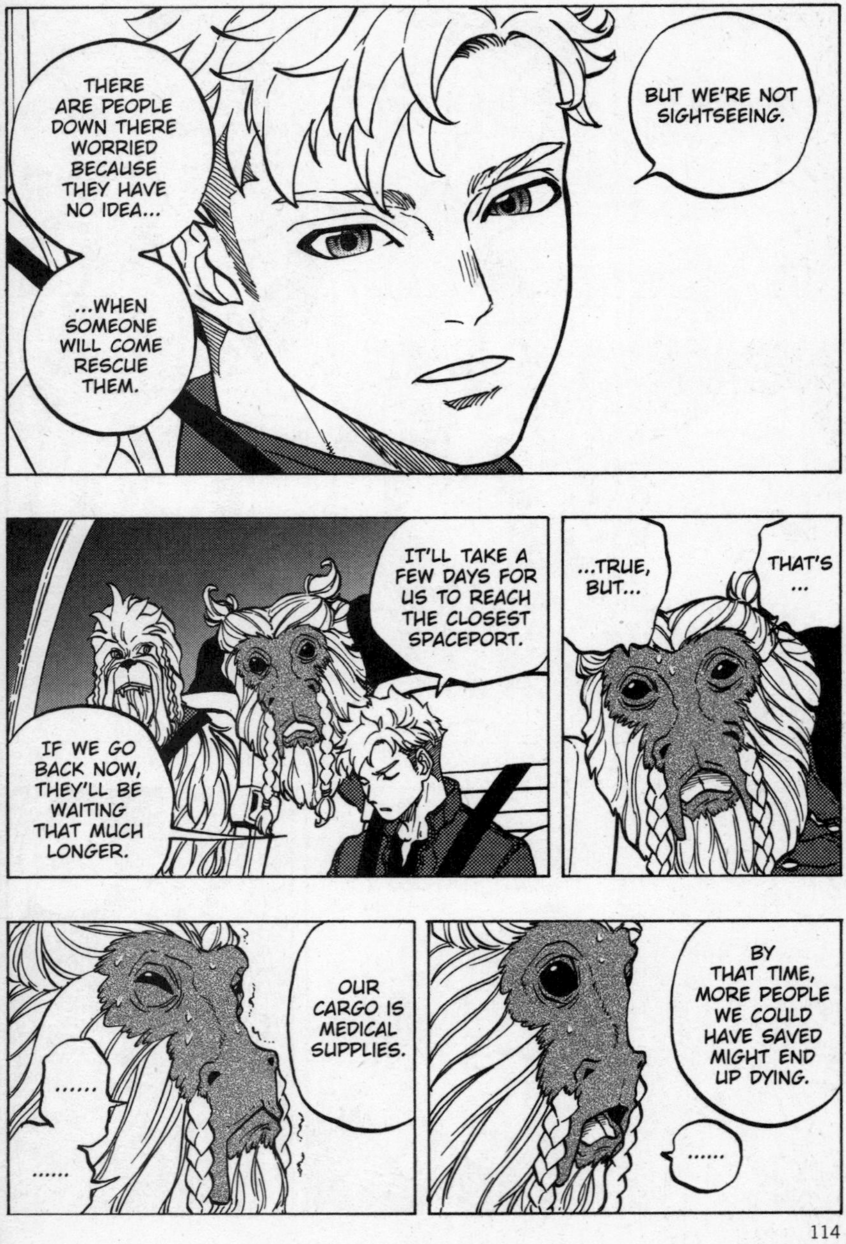
BUT WE'RE NOT SIGHTSEEING.
THERE ARE PEOPLE DOWN THERE WORRIED BECAUSE THEY HAVE NO IDEA...
...WHEN SOMEONE WILL COME RESCUE THEM.
IT'LL TAKE A FEW DAYS FOR US TO REACH THE CLOSEST SPACEPORT.
IF WE GO BACK NOW, THEY'LL BE WAITING THAT MUCH LONGER.
THAT'S ...
...TRUE, BUT...
BY THAT TIME, MORE PEOPLE WE COULD HAVE SAVED MIGHT END UP DYING.
......
OUR CARGO IS MEDICAL SUPPLIES.
......
......

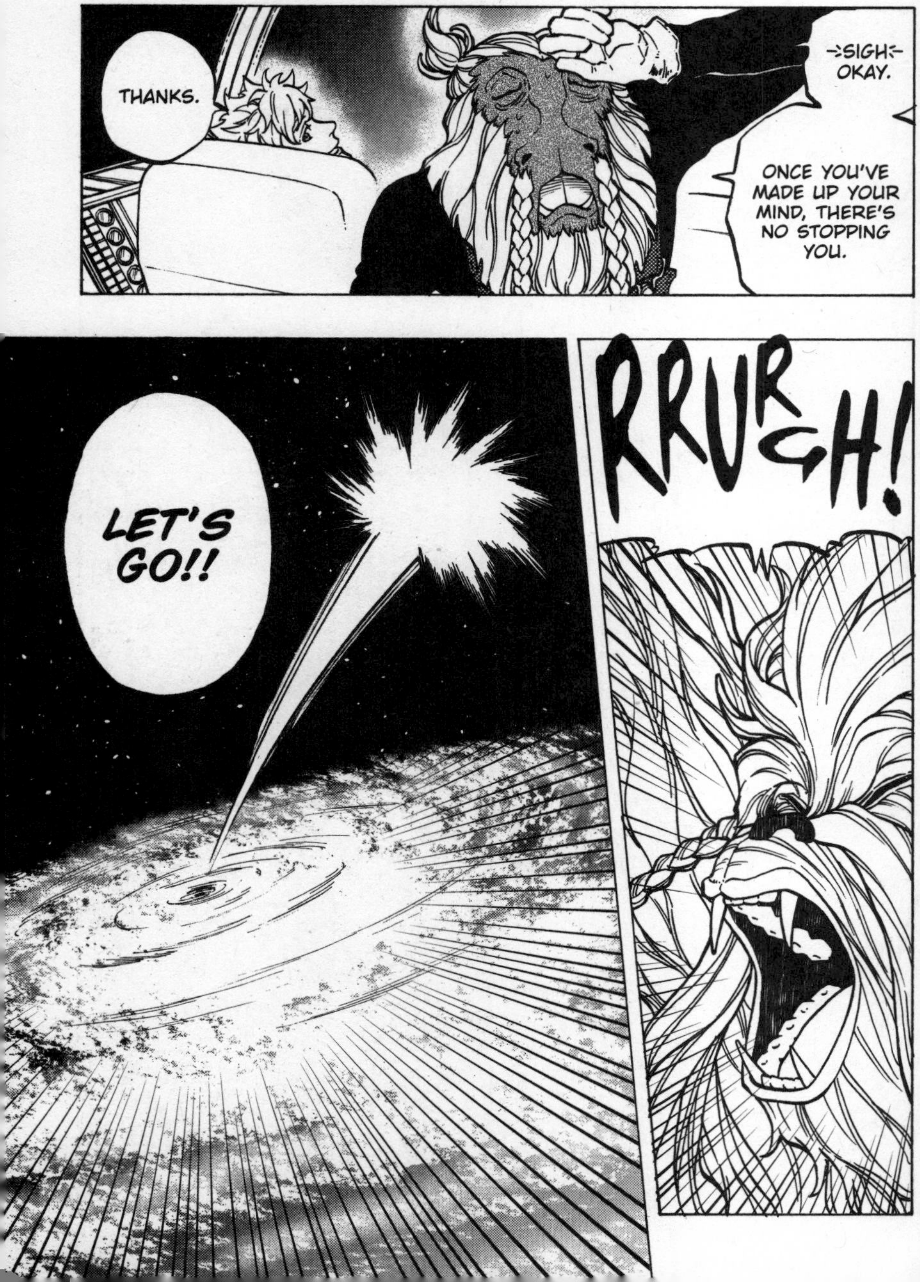
-SIGH- OKAY.
ONCE YOU'VE MADE UP YOUR MIND, THERE'S NO STOPPING YOU.
THANKS.
RRURGH!
LET'S GO!!

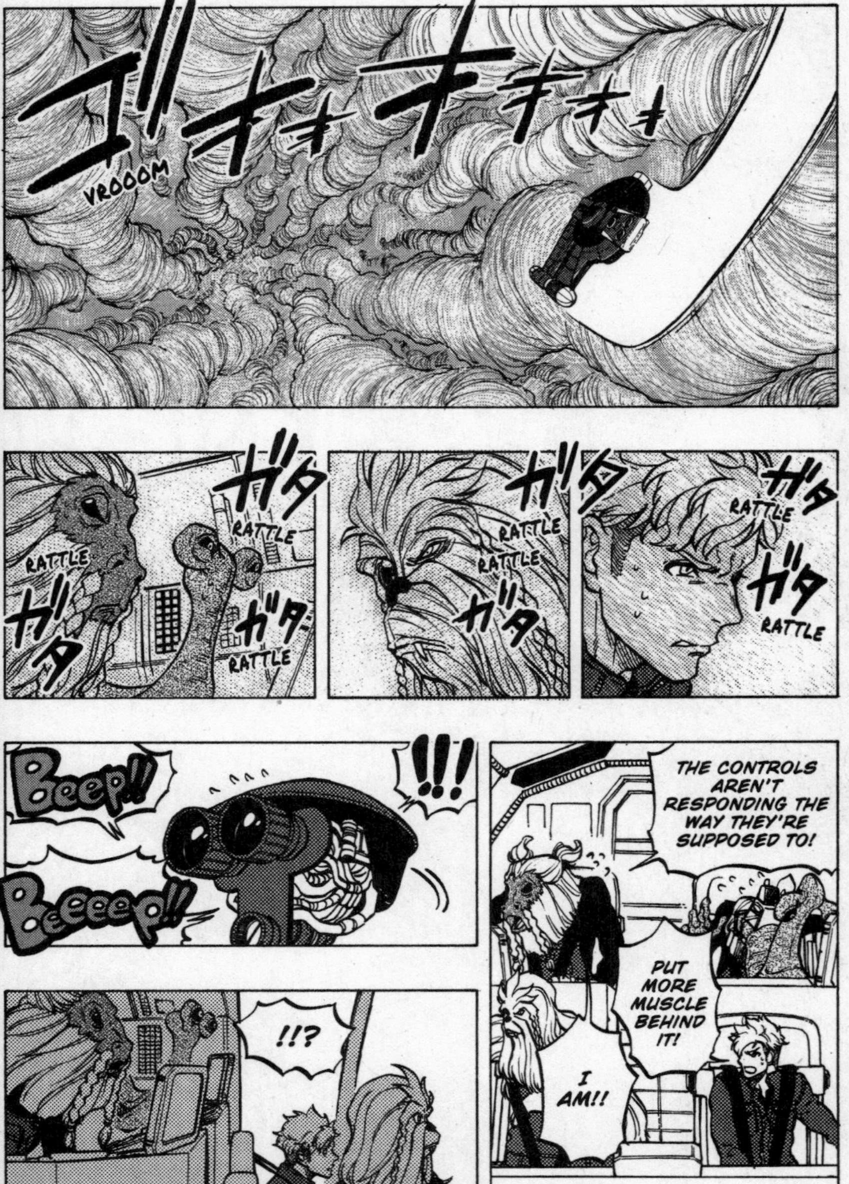
ゴォォォォォォ
VROOOM
ガタ
RATTLE
ガタ
RATTLE
ガタ
RATTLE
RATTLE
ガタ
ガタ
RATTLE
RATTLE
ガタ
ガタ
RATTLE
THE CONTROLS AREN'T RESPONDING THE WAY THEY'RE SUPPOSED TO!
PUT MORE MUSCLE BEHIND IT!
I AM!!
!!!
Beep!!
Beeeep!!
!!?

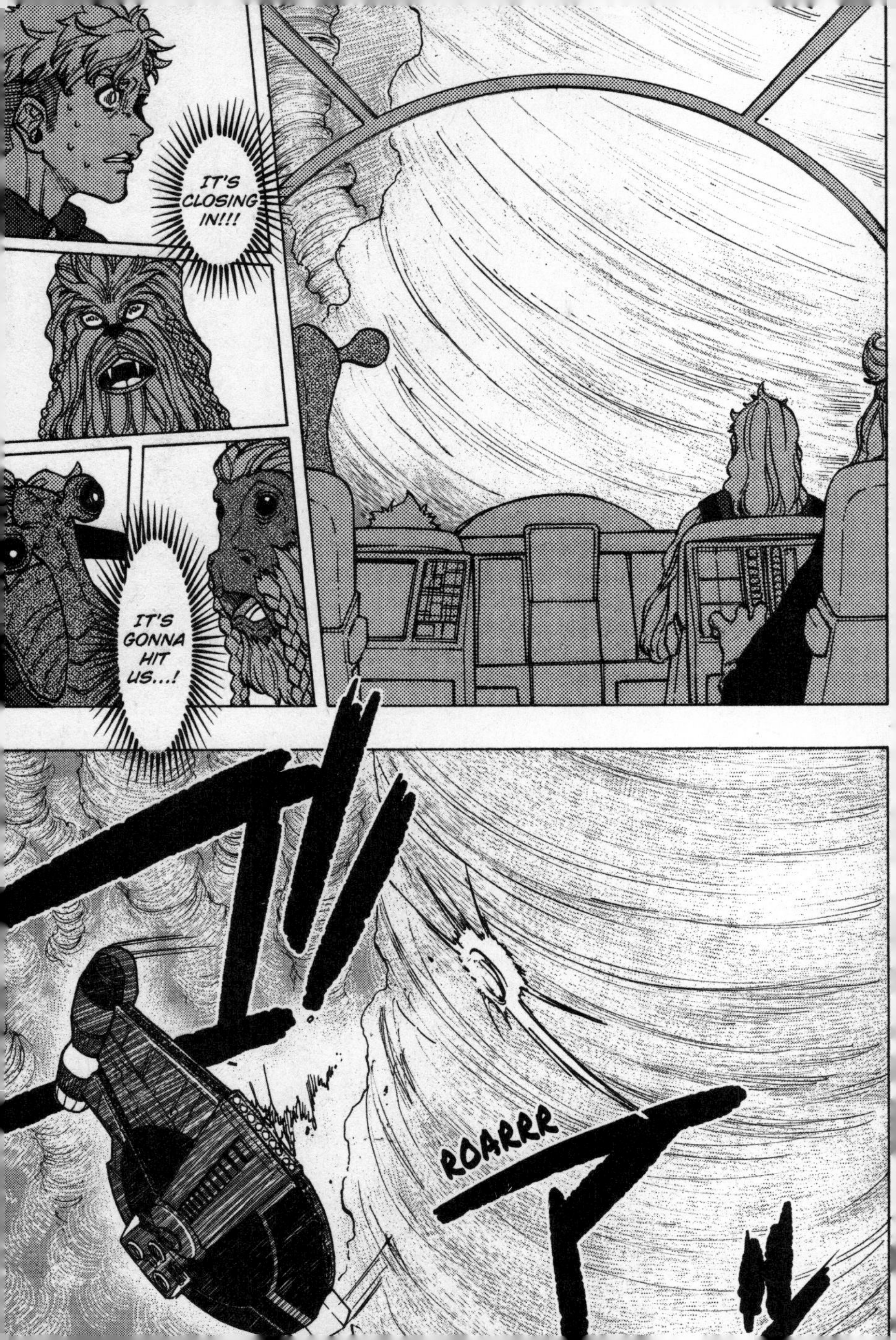
IT'S CLOSING IN!!!
IT'S GONNA HIT US...!
ROARRR

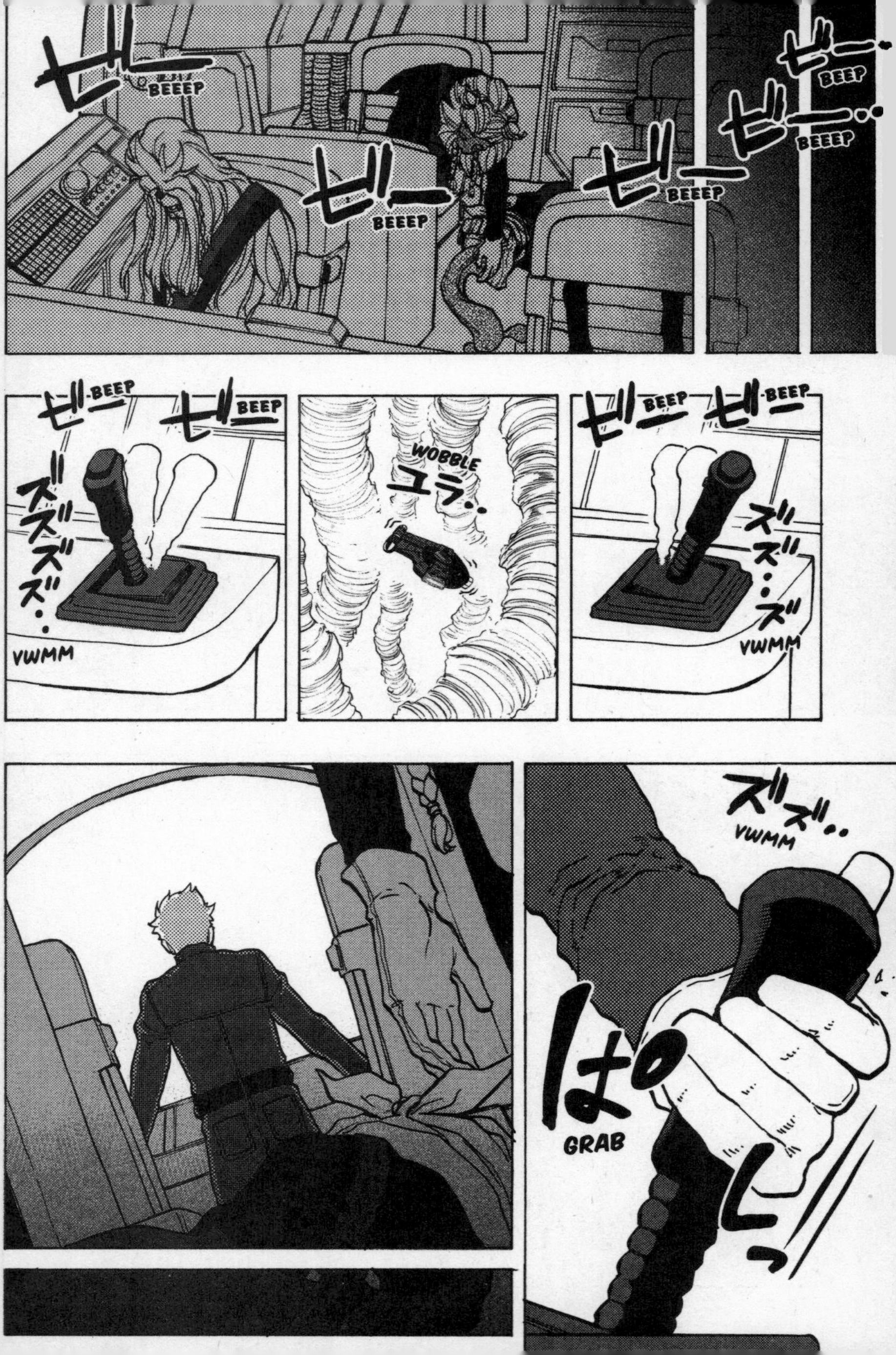
ビー…
BEEP
ビー…
BEEEP
ビー
BEEEP
ビー
BEEEP
ビー
BEEEP
ビー BEEP ビー BEEP
ズズ…ズ
VWMM
WOBBLE
ユラ…
ビー BEEP ビー BEEP
ズズズズ…
VWMM
ズズ…
VWMM
はっ
GRAB

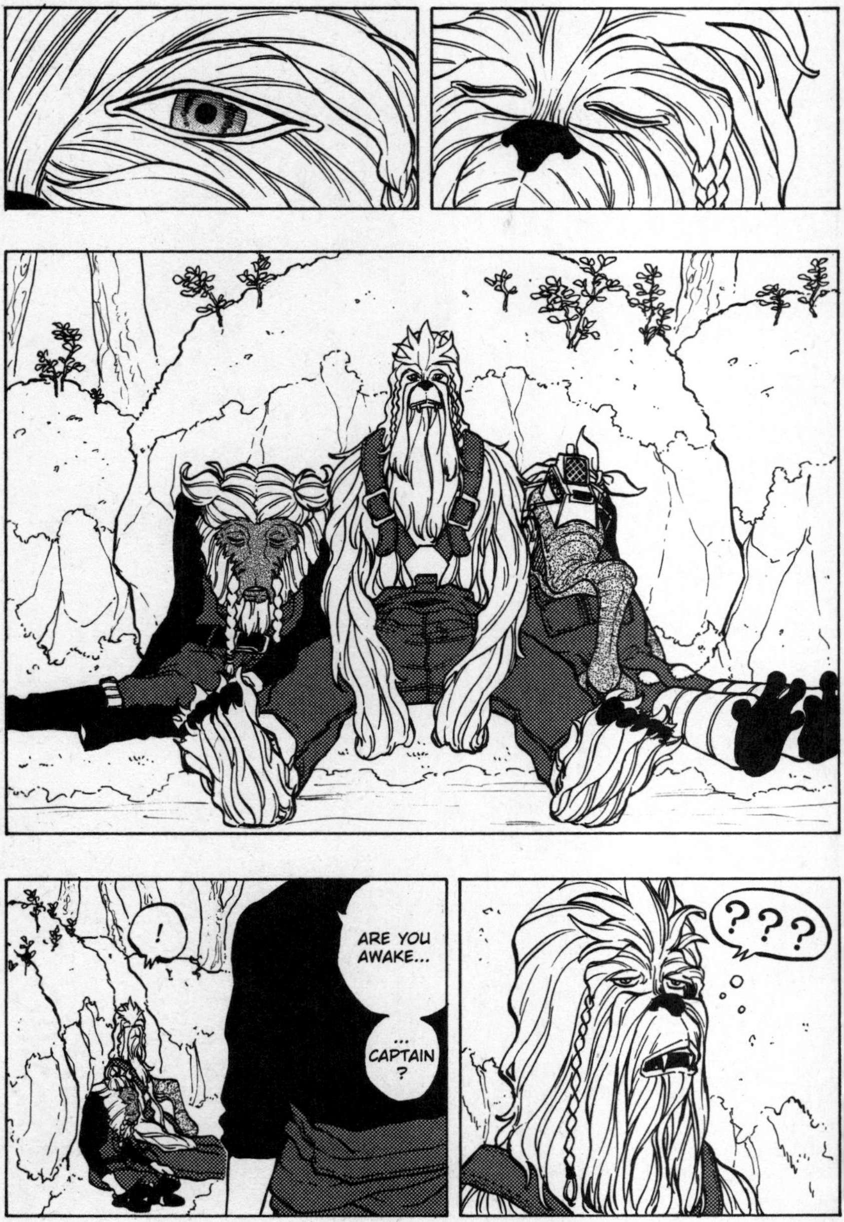
???
ARE YOU AWAKE...
... CAPTAIN ?
!

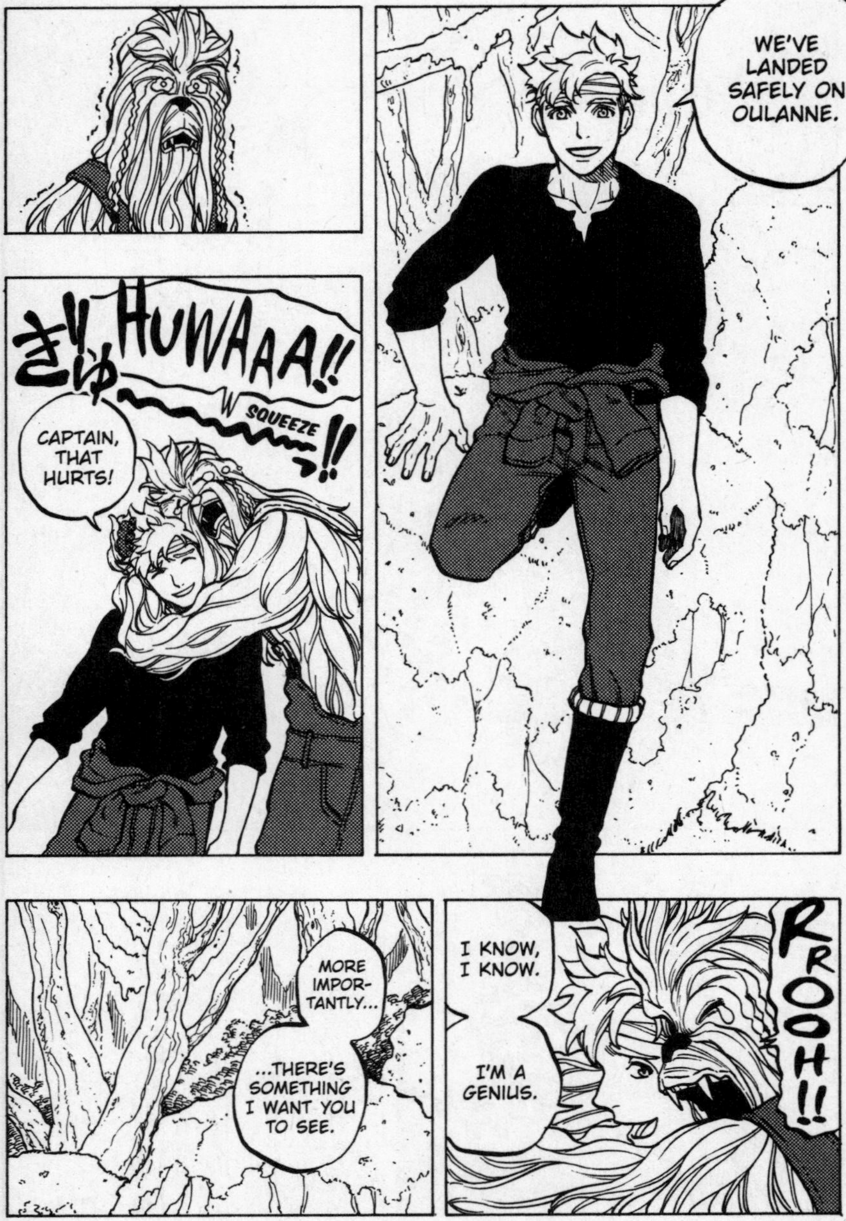

WE'VE LANDED SAFELY ON OULANNE.
HUWAAA!!
きゅ
SQUEEZE
CAPTAIN, THAT HURTS!
RROOOH!!
I KNOW, I KNOW.
I'M A GENIUS.
MORE IMPOR-TANTLY...
...THERE'S SOMETHING I WANT YOU TO SEE.

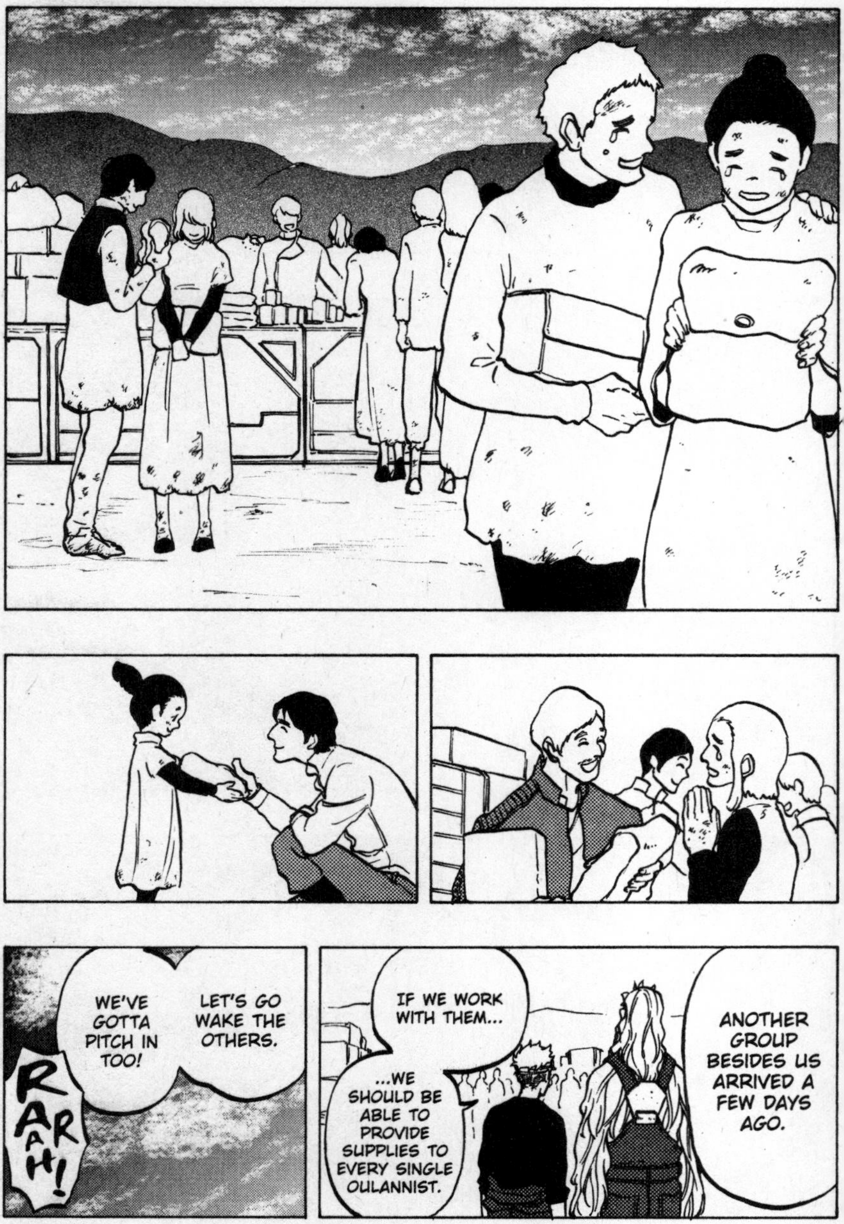
ANOTHER GROUP BESIDES US ARRIVED A FEW DAYS AGO.
IF WE WORK WITH THEM...
...WE SHOULD BE ABLE TO PROVIDE SUPPLIES TO EVERY SINGLE OULANNIST.
LET'S GO WAKE THE OTHERS.
WE'VE GOTTA PITCH IN TOO!
RARAH!

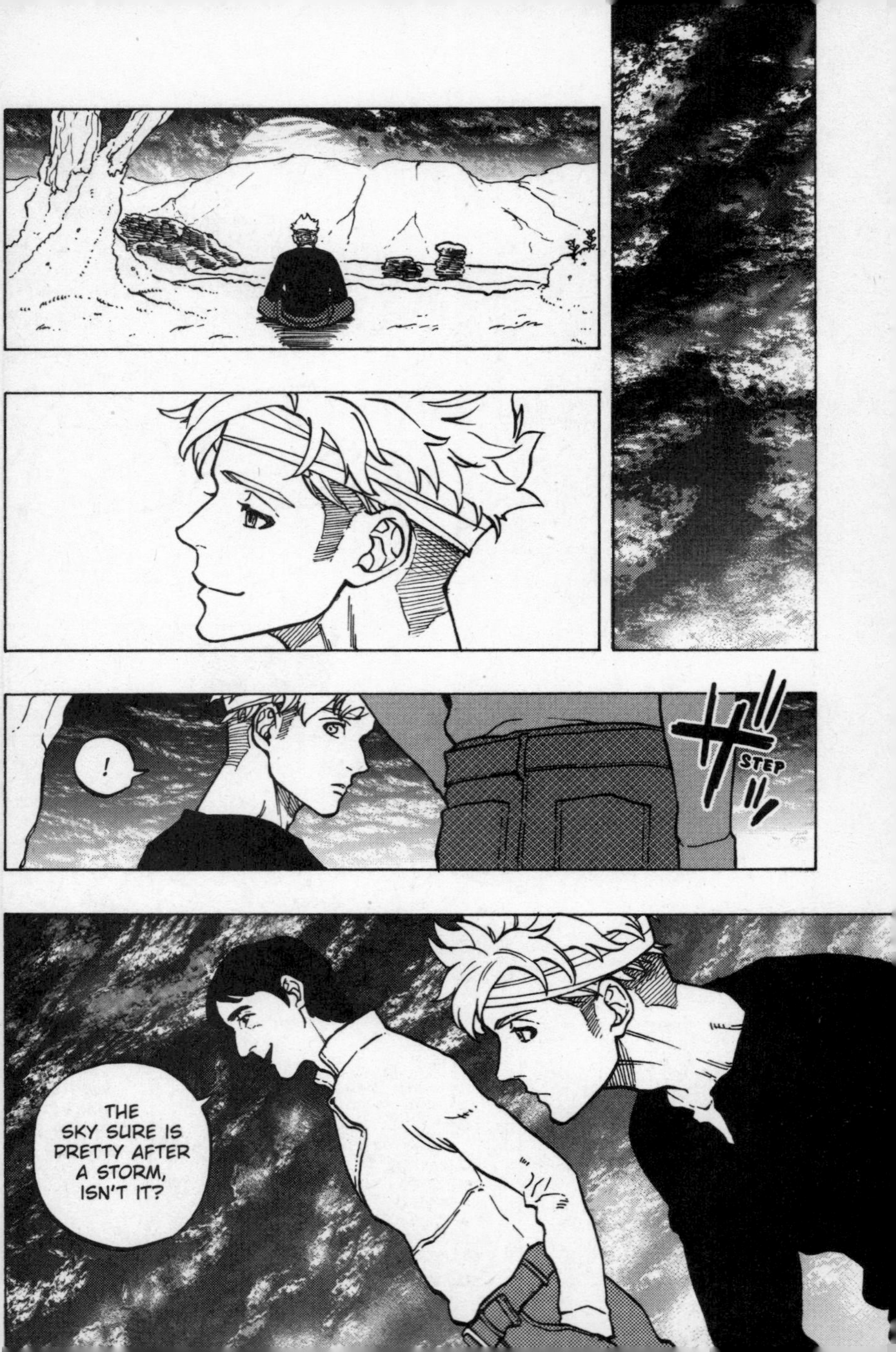
!
STEP
THE SKY SURE IS PRETTY AFTER A STORM, ISN'T IT?

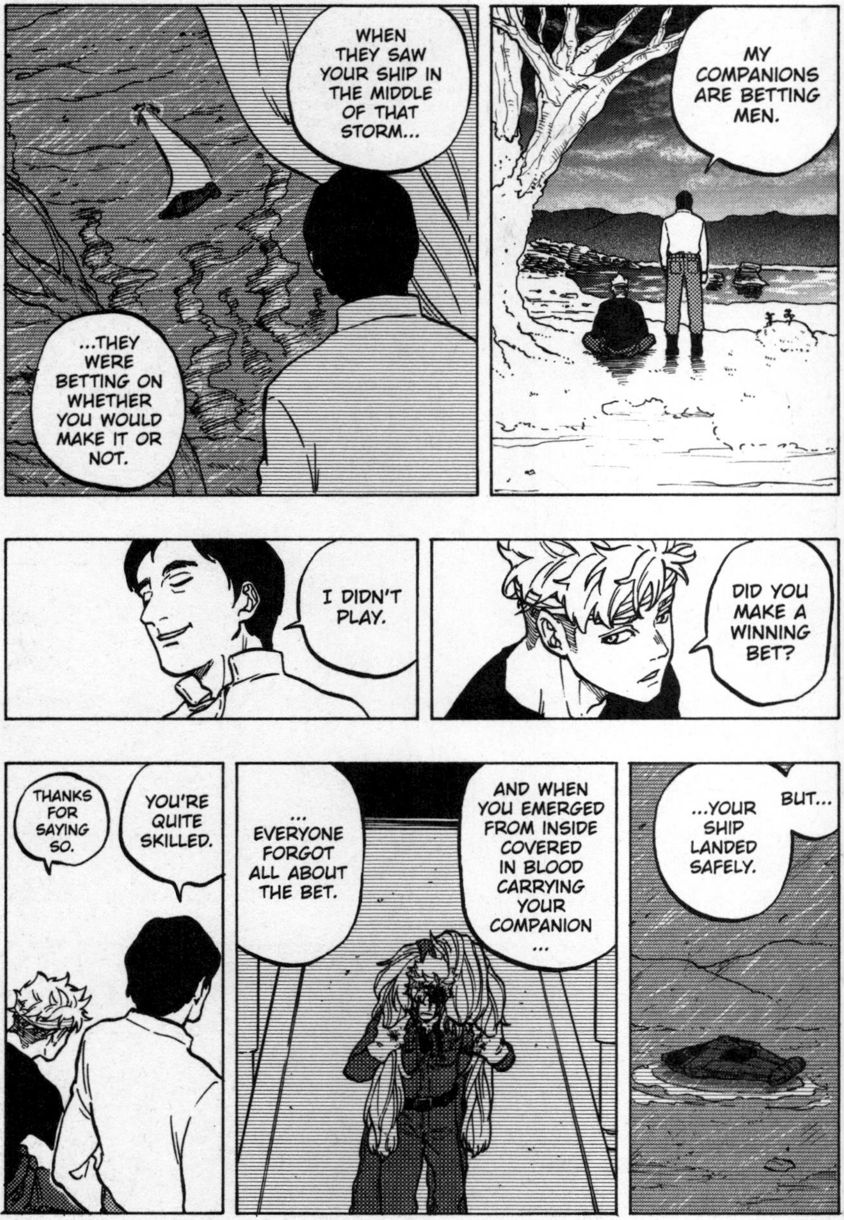
MY COMPANIONS ARE BETTING MEN.
WHEN THEY SAW YOUR SHIP IN THE MIDDLE OF THAT STORM...
...THEY WERE BETTING ON WHETHER YOU WOULD MAKE IT OR NOT.
DID YOU MAKE A WINNING BET?
I DIDN'T PLAY.
BUT...
...YOUR SHIP LANDED SAFELY.
AND WHEN YOU EMERGED FROM INSIDE COVERED IN BLOOD CARRYING YOUR COMPANION ...
... EVERYONE FORGOT ALL ABOUT THE BET.
YOU'RE QUITE SKILLED.
THANKS FOR SAYING SO.

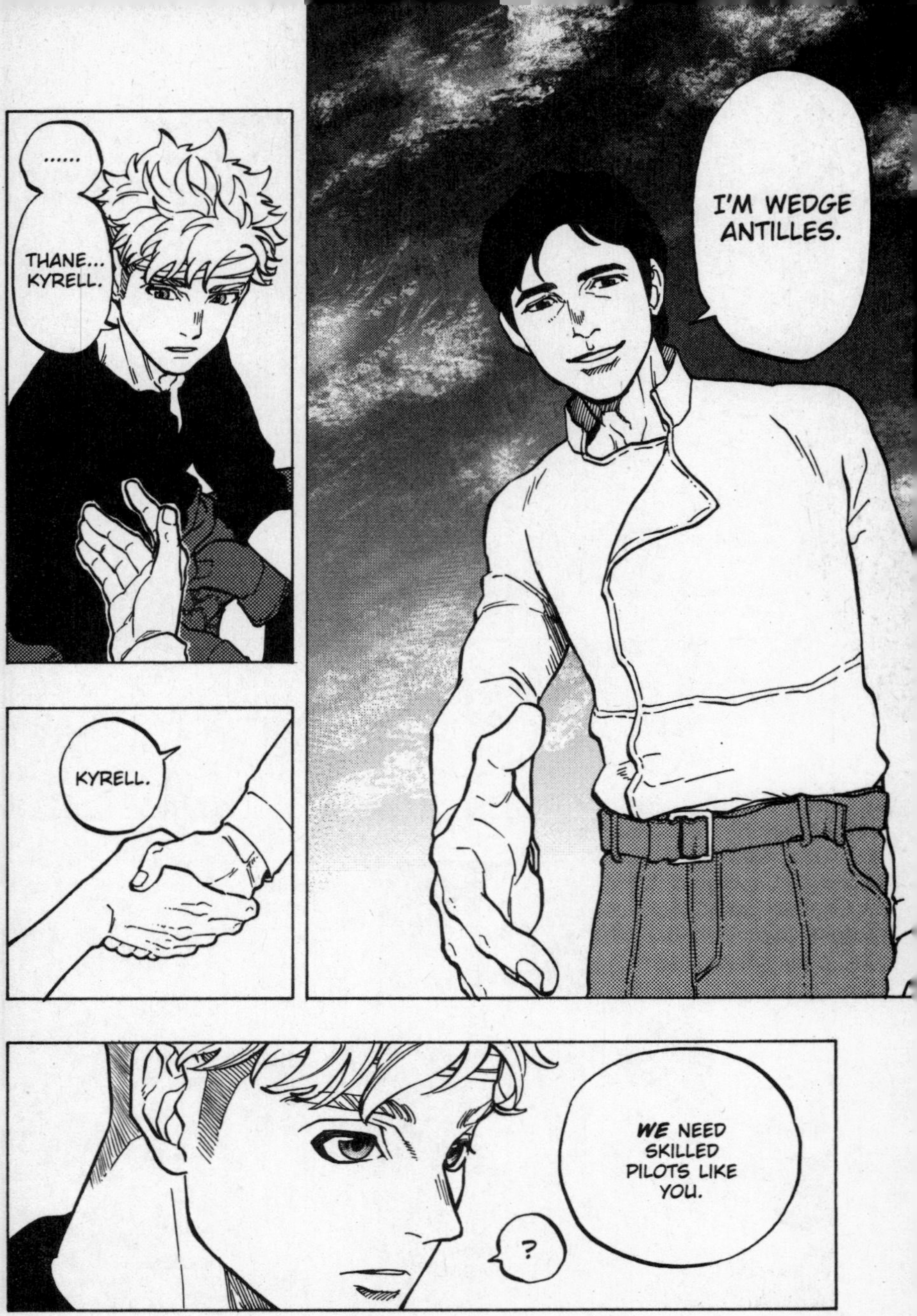
I'M WEDGE ANTILLES.
......
THANE... KYRELL.
KYRELL.
WE NEED SKILLED PILOTS LIKE YOU.
?

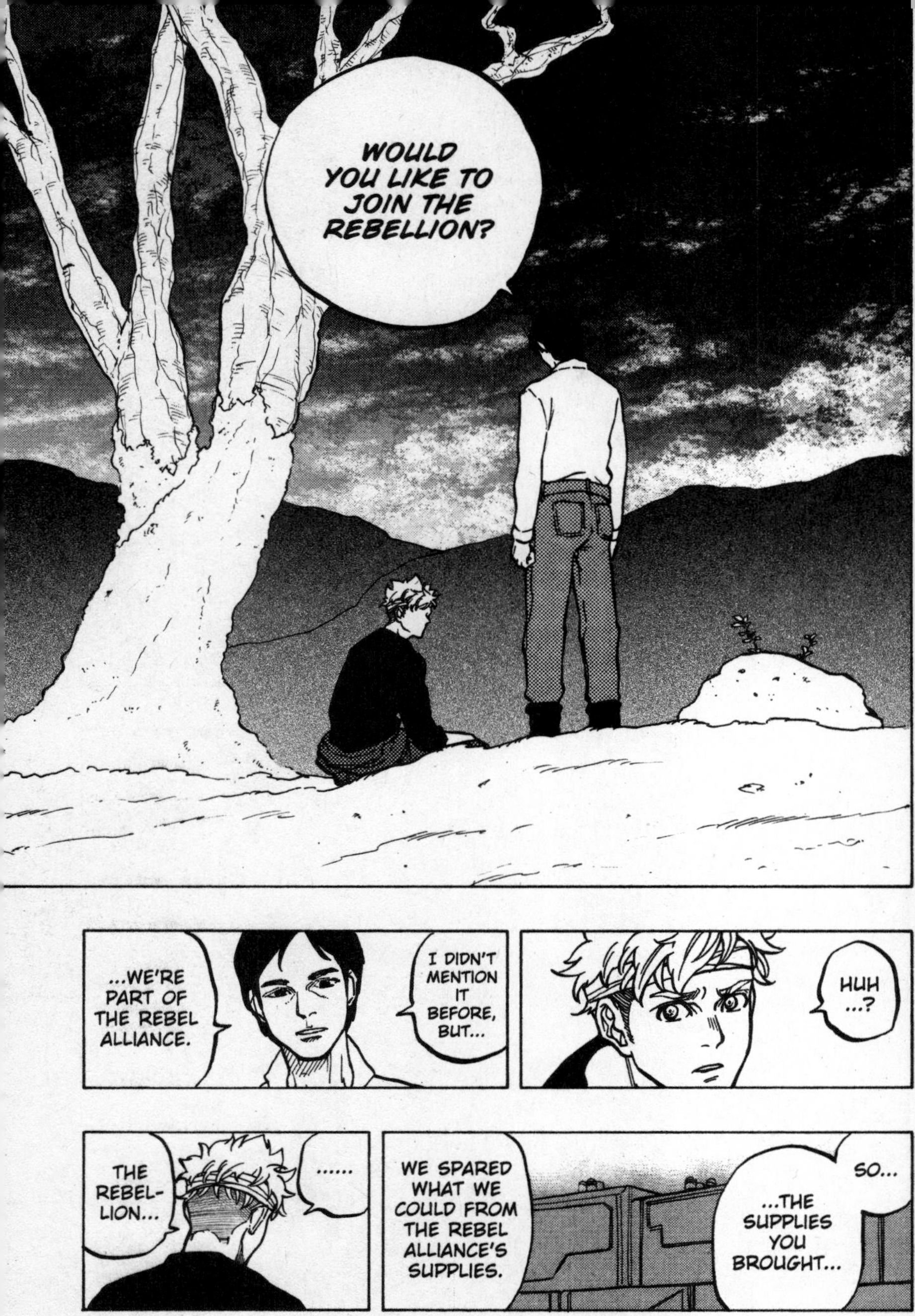
WOULD YOU LIKE TO JOIN THE REBELLION?
HUH ...?
I DIDN'T MENTION IT BEFORE, BUT...
...WE'RE PART OF THE REBEL ALLIANCE.
SO...
...THE SUPPLIES YOU BROUGHT...
WE SPARED WHAT WE COULD FROM THE REBEL ALLIANCE'S SUPPLIES.
......
THE REBEL-LION...

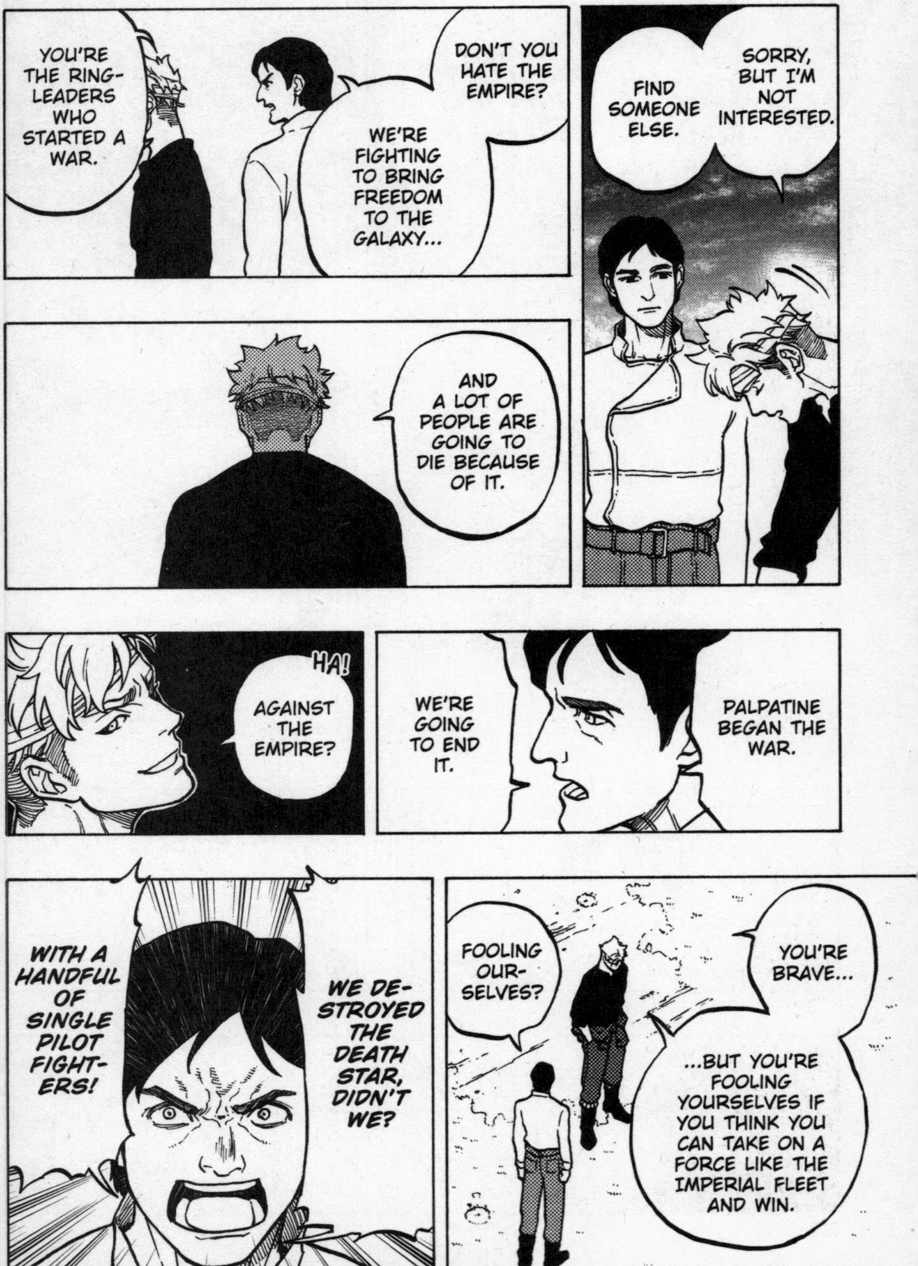
SORRY, BUT I'M NOT INTERESTED.
FIND SOMEONE ELSE.
DON'T YOU HATE THE EMPIRE?
WE'RE FIGHTING TO BRING FREEDOM TO THE GALAXY...
YOU'RE THE RING-LEADERS WHO STARTED A WAR.
AND A LOT OF PEOPLE ARE GOING TO DIE BECAUSE OF IT.
PALPATINE BEGAN THE WAR.
WE'RE GOING TO END IT.
HA!
AGAINST THE EMPIRE?
YOU'RE BRAVE...
...BUT YOU'RE FOOLING YOURSELVES IF YOU THINK YOU CAN TAKE ON A FORCE LIKE THE IMPERIAL FLEET AND WIN.
FOOLING OUR-SELVES?
WE DE-STROYED THE DEATH STAR, DIDN'T WE?
WITH A HANDFUL OF SINGLE PILOT FIGHT-ERS!

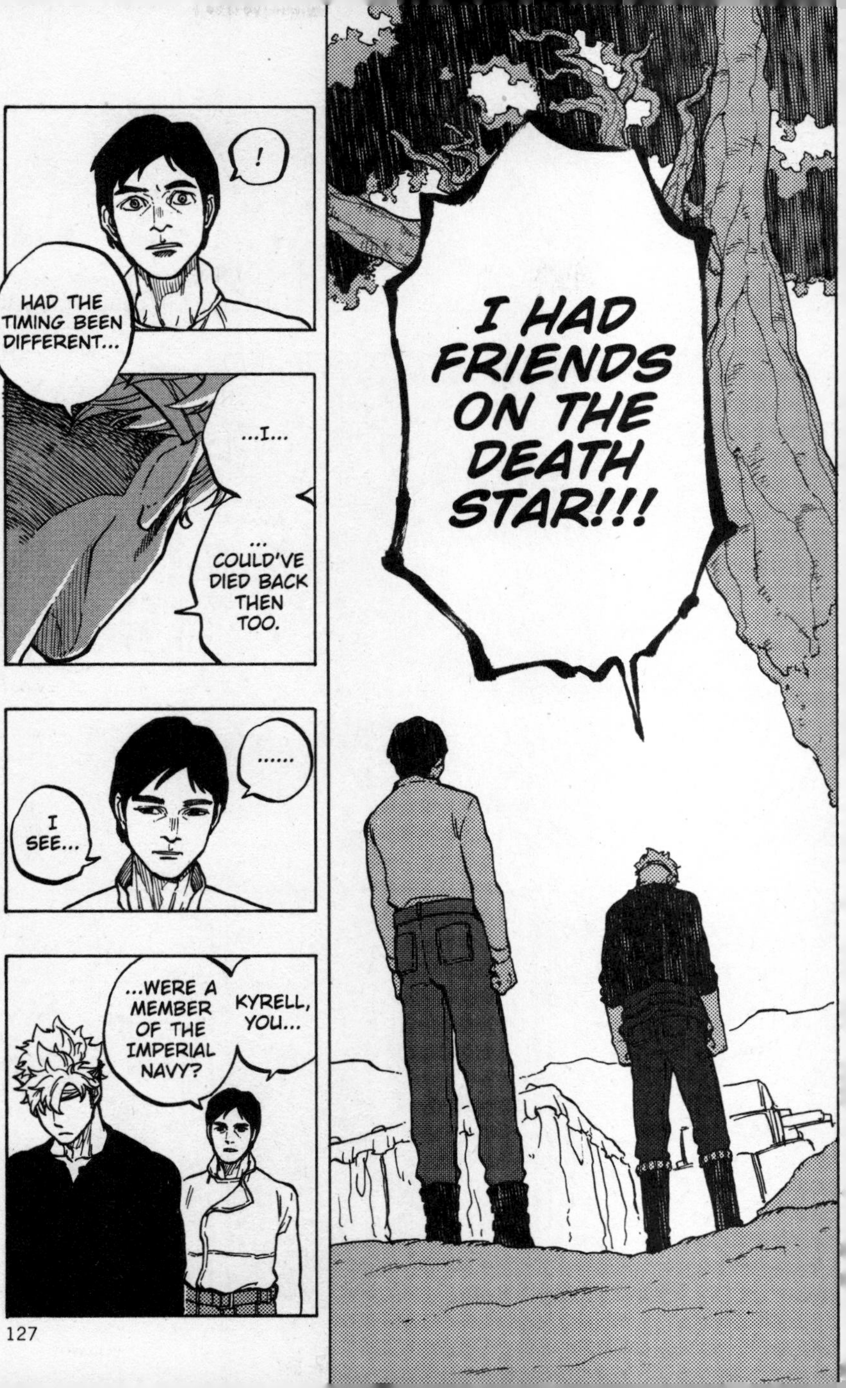

I HAD FRIENDS ON THE DEATH STAR!!!
!
HAD THE TIMING BEEN DIFFERENT...
...I...
...COULD'VE DIED BACK THEN TOO.
......
I SEE...
KYRELL, YOU...
...WERE A MEMBER OF THE IMPERIAL NAVY?

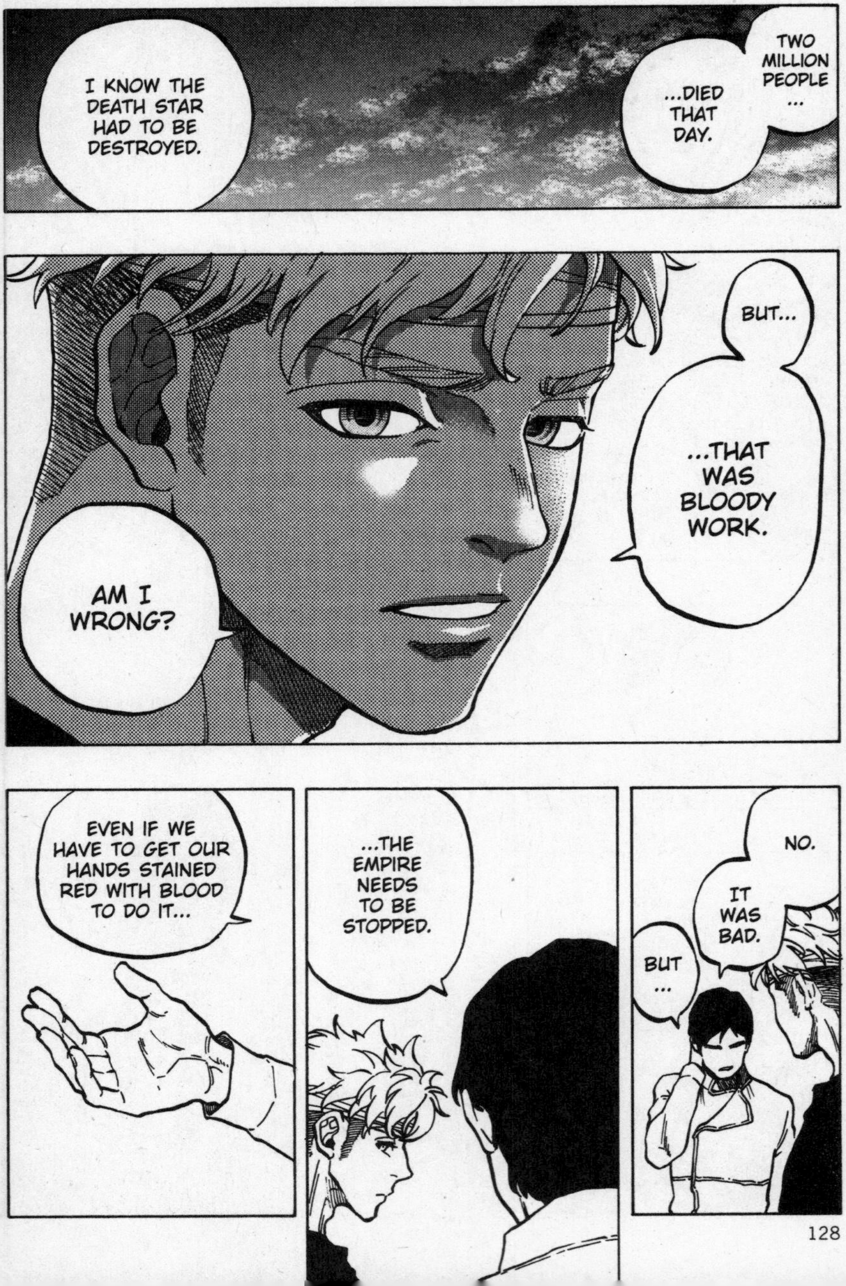
TWO MILLION PEOPLE ...
...DIED THAT DAY.
I KNOW THE DEATH STAR HAD TO BE DESTROYED.
BUT...
...THAT WAS BLOODY WORK.
AM I WRONG?
NO.
IT WAS BAD.
BUT ...
...THE EMPIRE NEEDS TO BE STOPPED.
EVEN IF WE HAVE TO GET OUR HANDS STAINED RED WITH BLOOD TO DO IT...

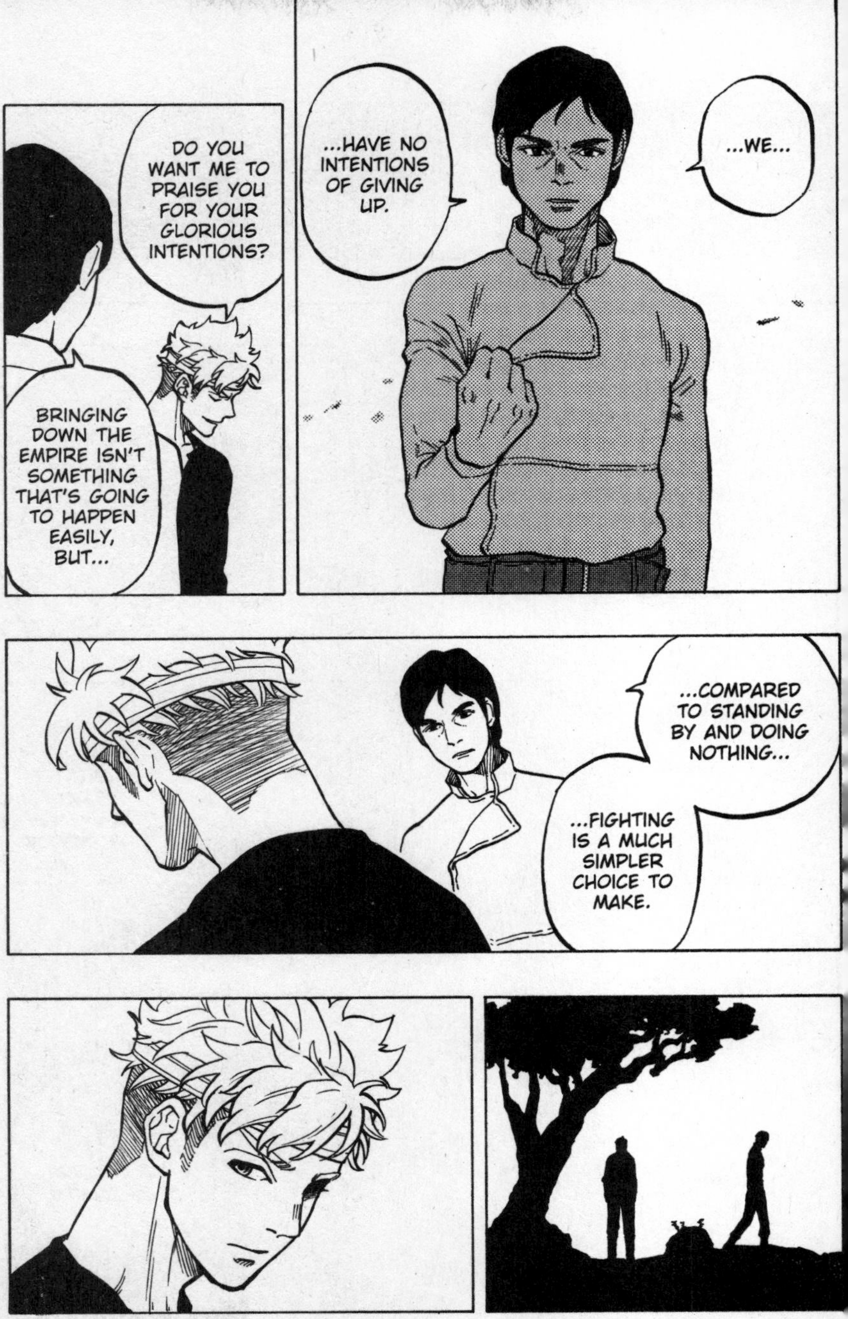
...WE...
...HAVE NO INTENTIONS OF GIVING UP.
DO YOU WANT ME TO PRAISE YOU FOR YOUR GLORIOUS INTENTIONS?
BRINGING DOWN THE EMPIRE ISN'T SOMETHING THAT'S GOING TO HAPPEN EASILY, BUT...
...COMPARED TO STANDING BY AND DOING NOTHING...
...FIGHTING IS A MUCH SIMPLER CHOICE TO MAKE.

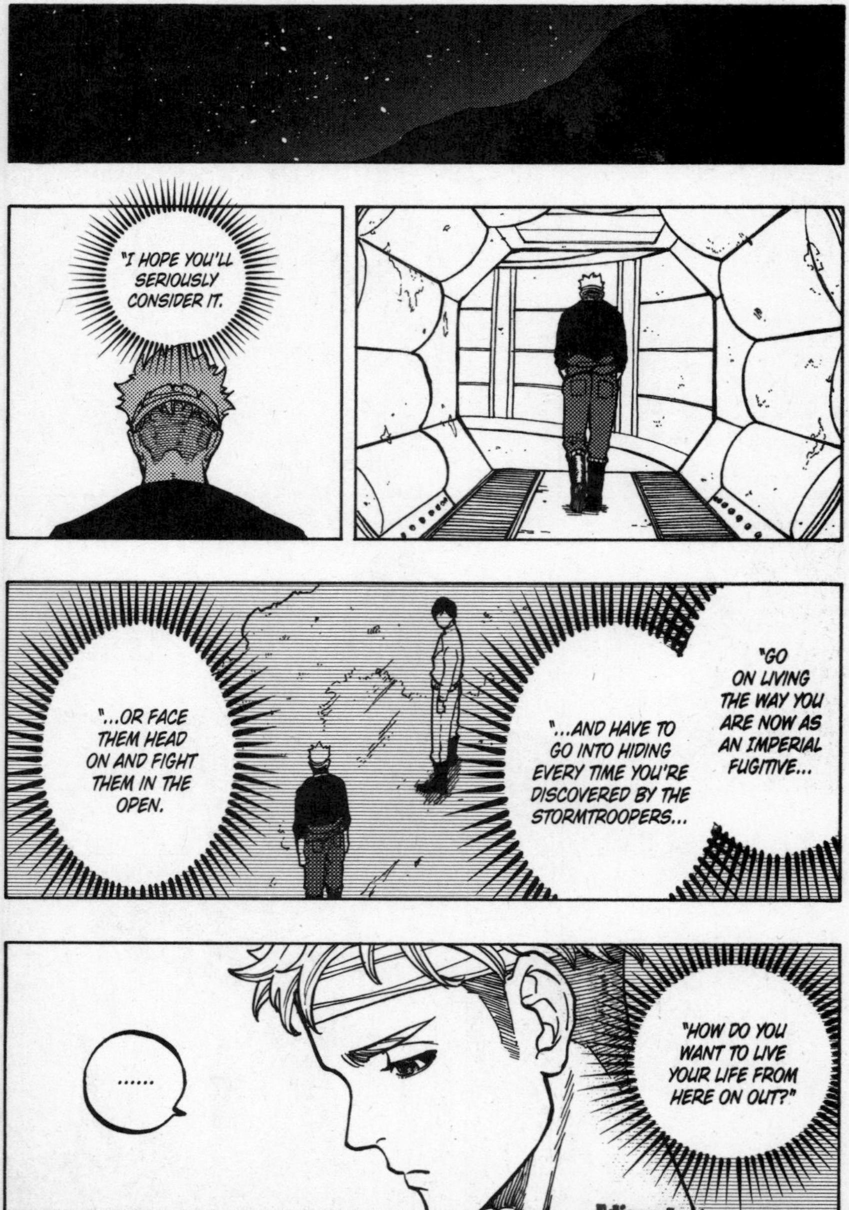
"I HOPE YOU'LL SERIOUSLY CONSIDER IT.
"GO ON LIVING THE WAY YOU ARE NOW AS AN IMPERIAL FUGITIVE...
"...AND HAVE TO GO INTO HIDING EVERY TIME YOU'RE DISCOVERED BY THE STORMTROOPERS...
"...OR FACE THEM HEAD ON AND FIGHT THEM IN THE OPEN.
"HOW DO YOU WANT TO LIVE YOUR LIFE FROM HERE ON OUT?"
......

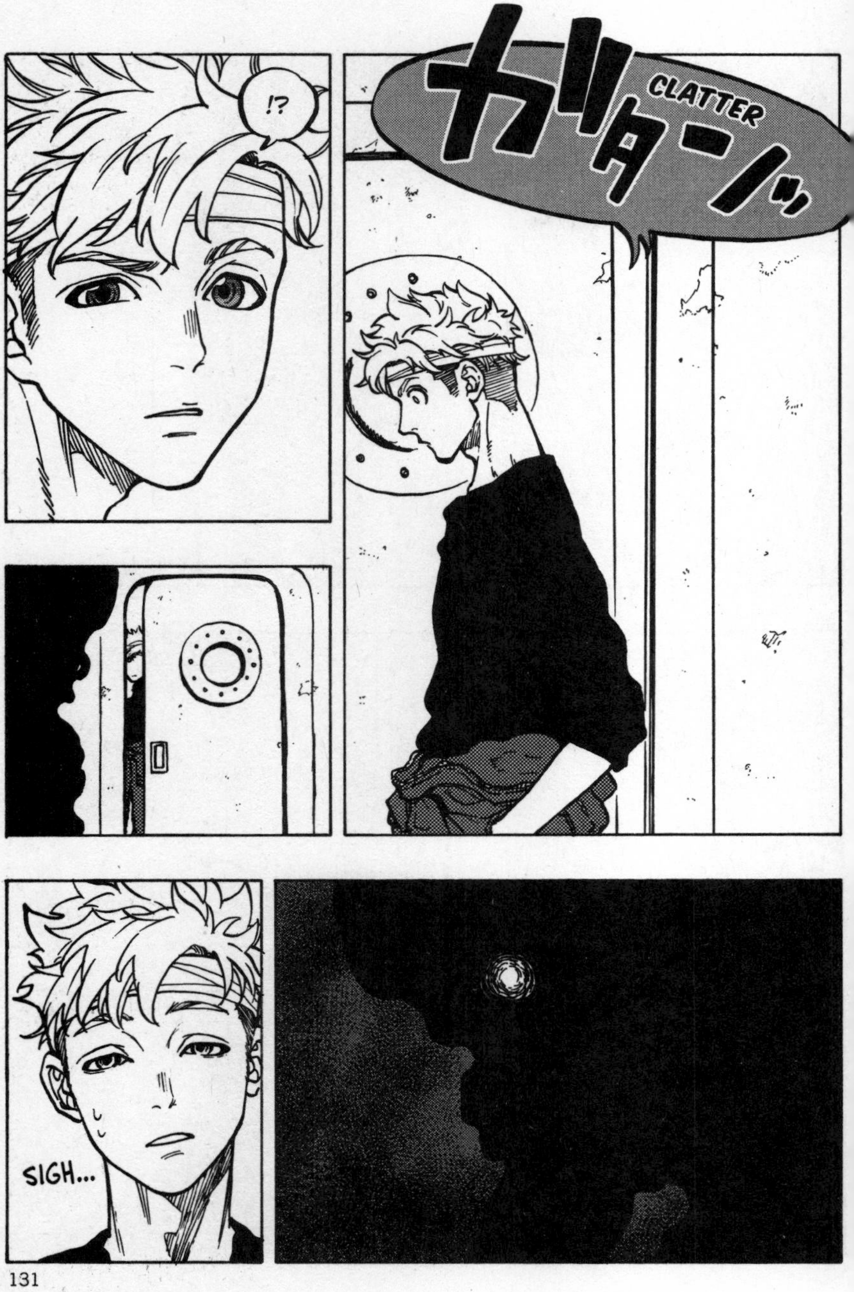
CLATTER
!?
SIGH...

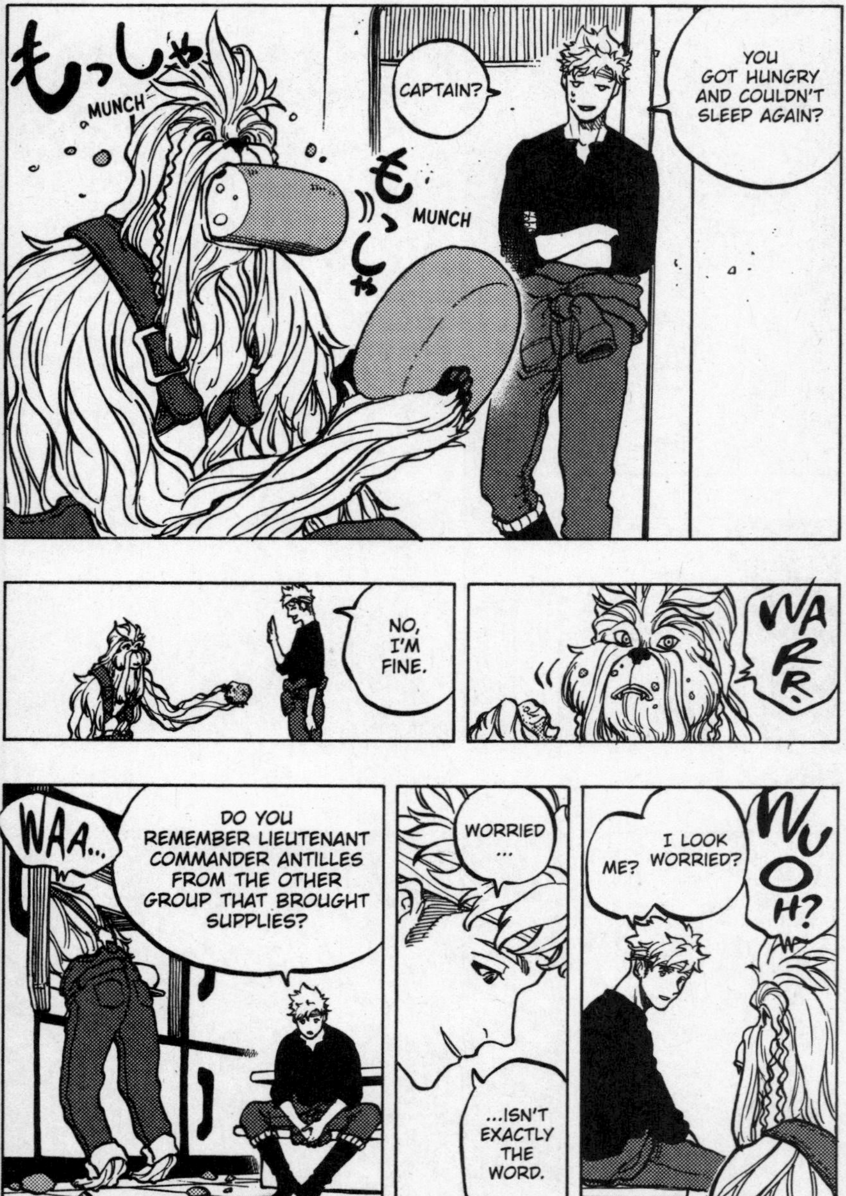
YOU GOT HUNGRY AND COULDN'T SLEEP AGAIN?
CAPTAIN?
もっしゃ
MUNCH
もっしゃ
MUNCH
WARR.
NO, I'M FINE.
WUOH?
I LOOK WORRIED?
ME?
WORRIED ...
...ISN'T EXACTLY THE WORD.
DO YOU REMEMBER LIEUTENANT COMMANDER ANTILLES FROM THE OTHER GROUP THAT BROUGHT SUPPLIES?
WAA...

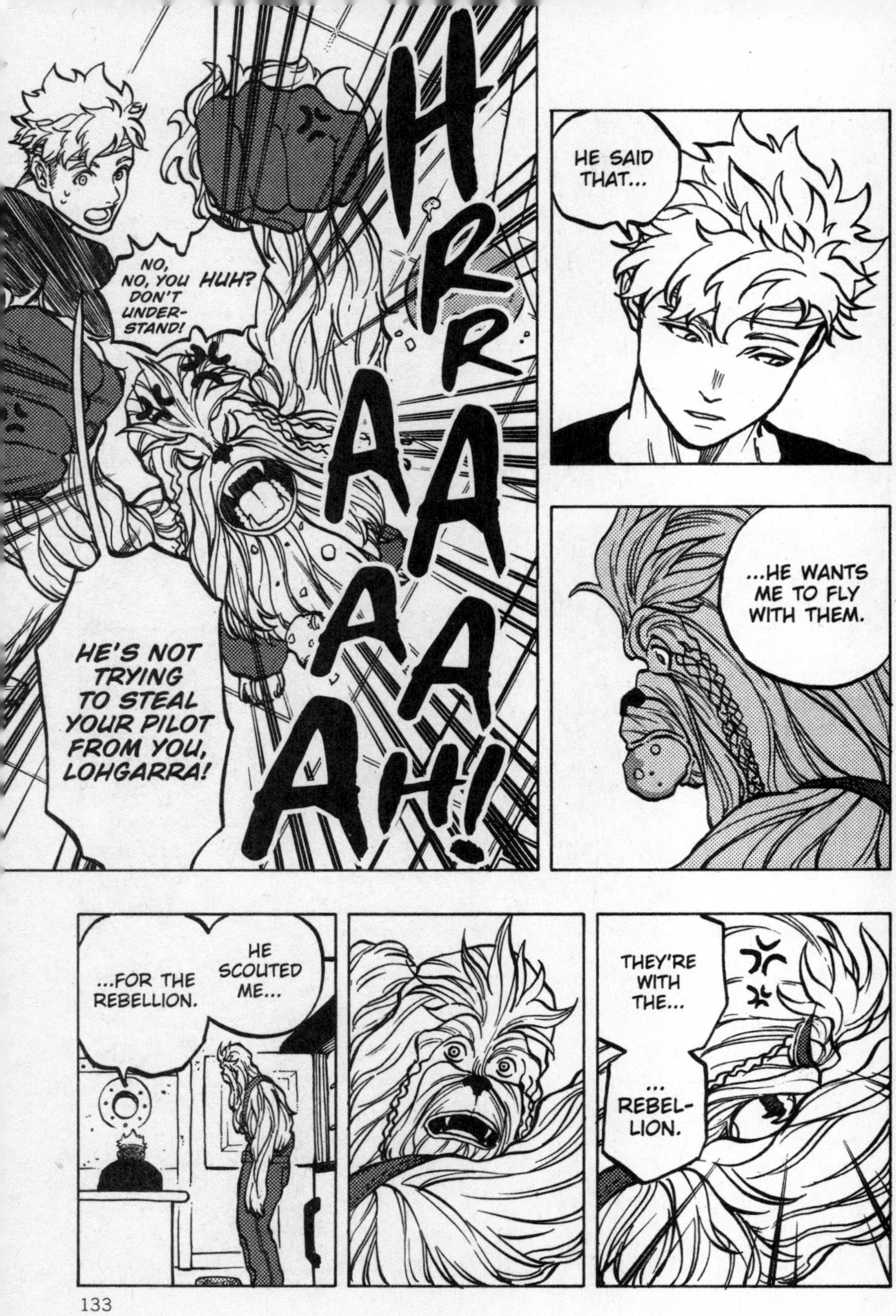
HE SAID THAT...
...HE WANTS ME TO FLY WITH THEM.
HRRAAAAAH!
HUH?
NO, NO, YOU DON'T UNDER-STAND!
HE'S NOT TRYING TO STEAL YOUR PILOT FROM YOU, LOHGARRA!
THEY'RE WITH THE...
...REBEL-LION.
HE SCOUTED ME...
...FOR THE REBELLION.

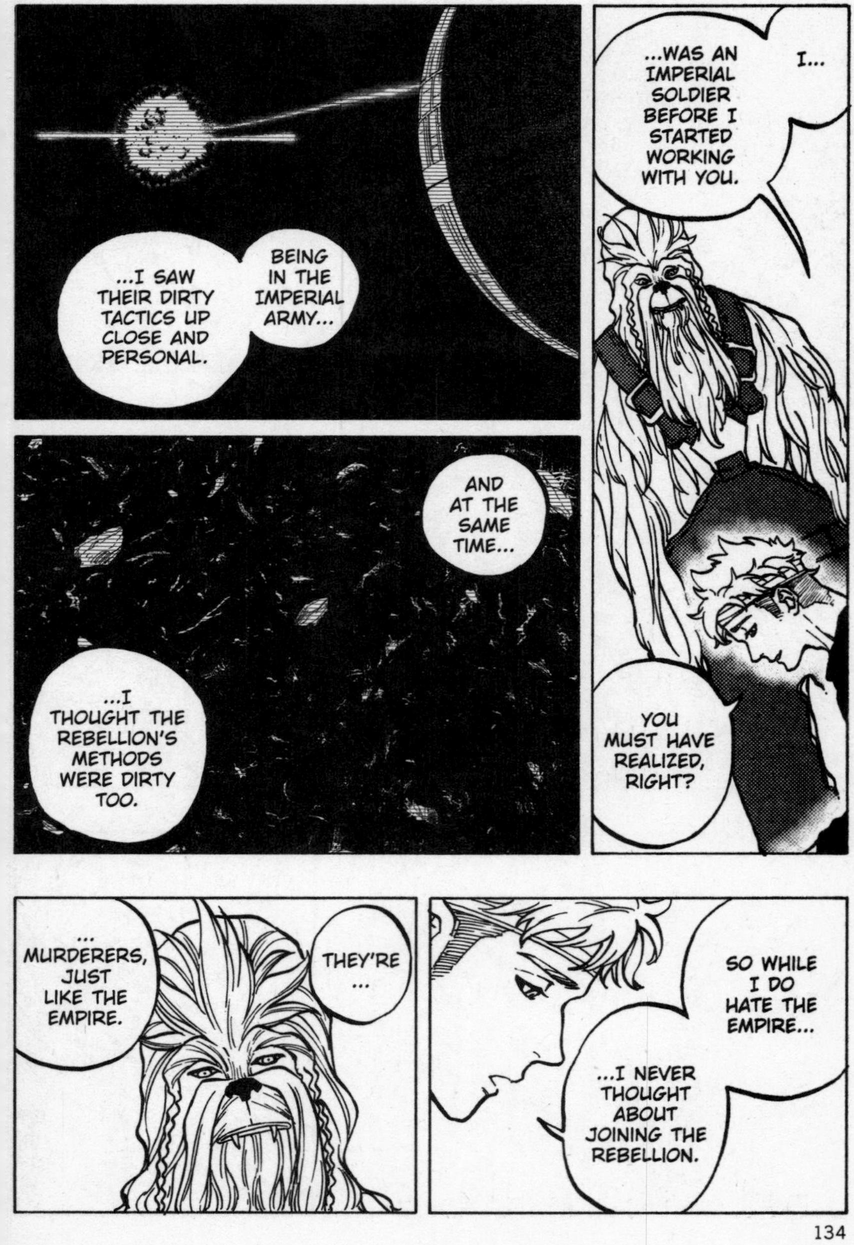
I...
...WAS AN IMPERIAL SOLDIER BEFORE I STARTED WORKING WITH YOU.
BEING IN THE IMPERIAL ARMY...
...I SAW THEIR DIRTY TACTICS UP CLOSE AND PERSONAL.
AND AT THE SAME TIME...
...I THOUGHT THE REBELLION'S METHODS WERE DIRTY TOO.
YOU MUST HAVE REALIZED, RIGHT?
SO WHILE I DO HATE THE EMPIRE...
...I NEVER THOUGHT ABOUT JOINING THE REBELLION.
THEY'RE ...
... MURDERERS, JUST LIKE THE EMPIRE.

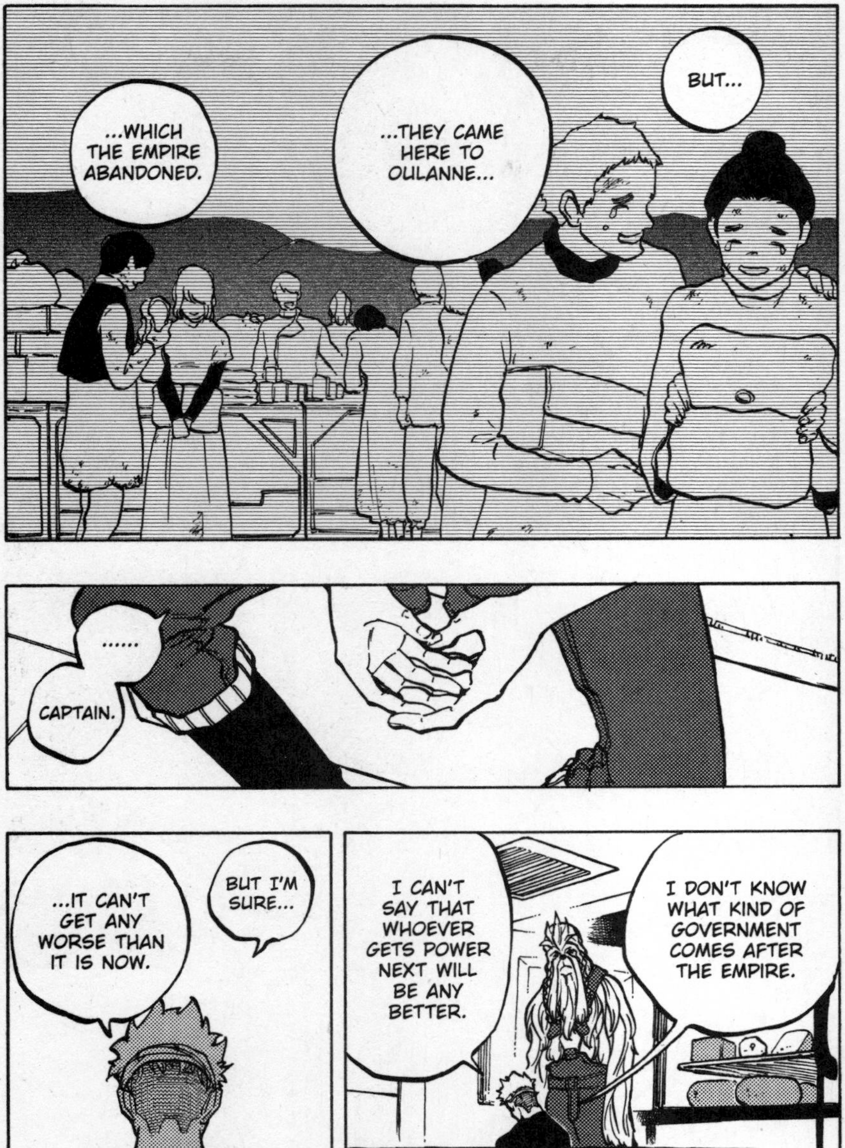
BUT...
...THEY CAME HERE TO OULANNE...
...WHICH THE EMPIRE ABANDONED.
......
CAPTAIN.
I DON'T KNOW WHAT KIND OF GOVERNMENT COMES AFTER THE EMPIRE.
I CAN'T SAY THAT WHOEVER GETS POWER NEXT WILL BE ANY BETTER.
BUT I'M SURE...
...IT CAN'T GET ANY WORSE THAN IT IS NOW.

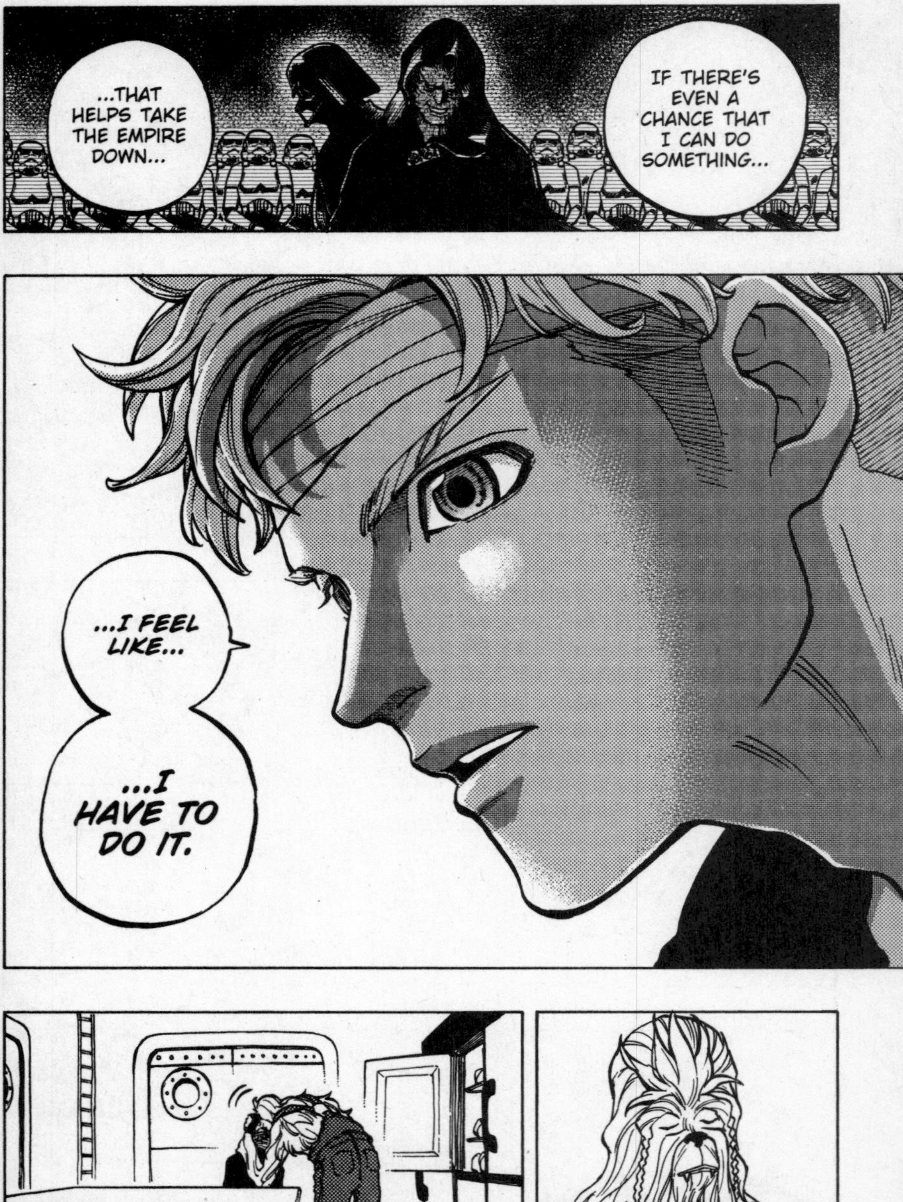
IF THERE'S EVEN A CHANCE THAT I CAN DO SOMETHING...
...THAT HELPS TAKE THE EMPIRE DOWN...
...I FEEL LIKE...
...I HAVE TO DO IT.

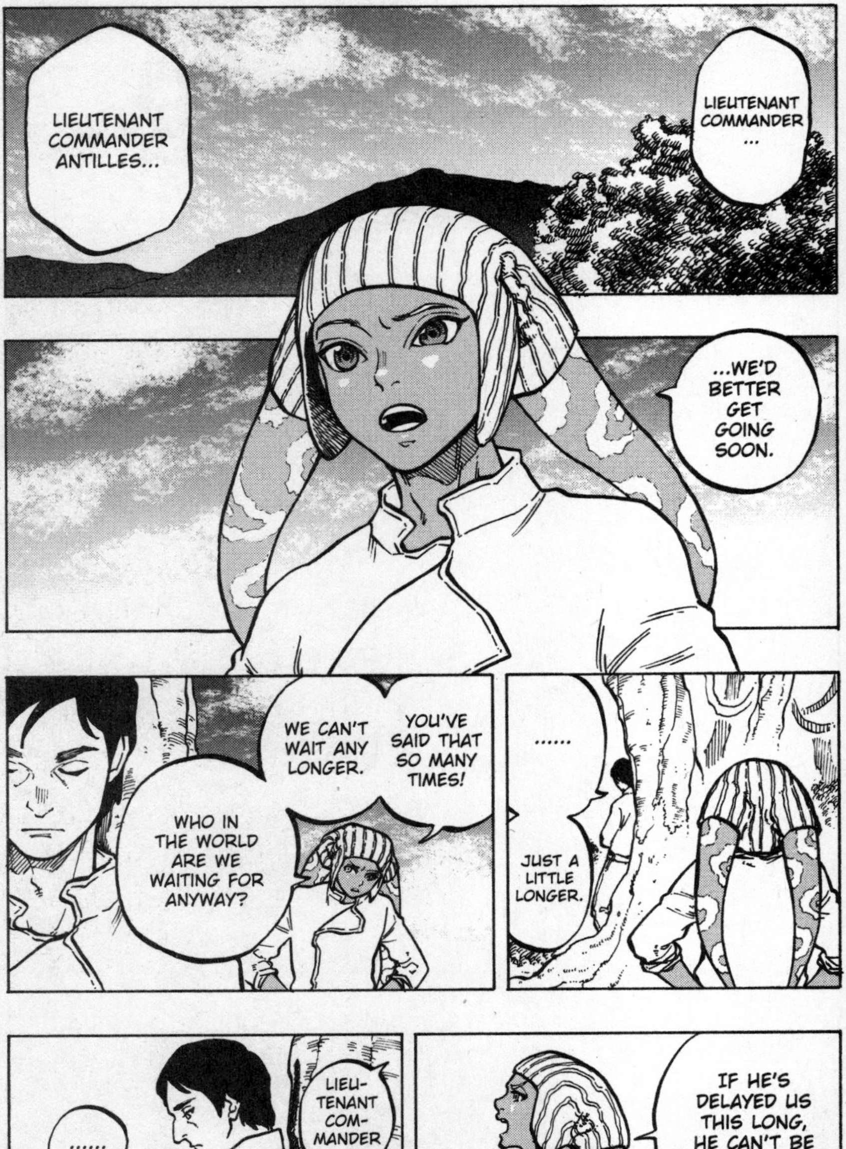
LIEUTENANT COMMANDER ...
LIEUTENANT COMMANDER ANTILLES...
...WE'D BETTER GET GOING SOON.
......
JUST A LITTLE LONGER.
YOU'VE SAID THAT SO MANY TIMES!
WE CAN'T WAIT ANY LONGER.
WHO IN THE WORLD ARE WE WAITING FOR ANYWAY?
IF HE'S DELAYED US THIS LONG, HE CAN'T BE MUCH GOOD.
LIEU-TENANT COM-MANDER ?
......

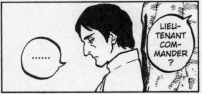

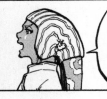

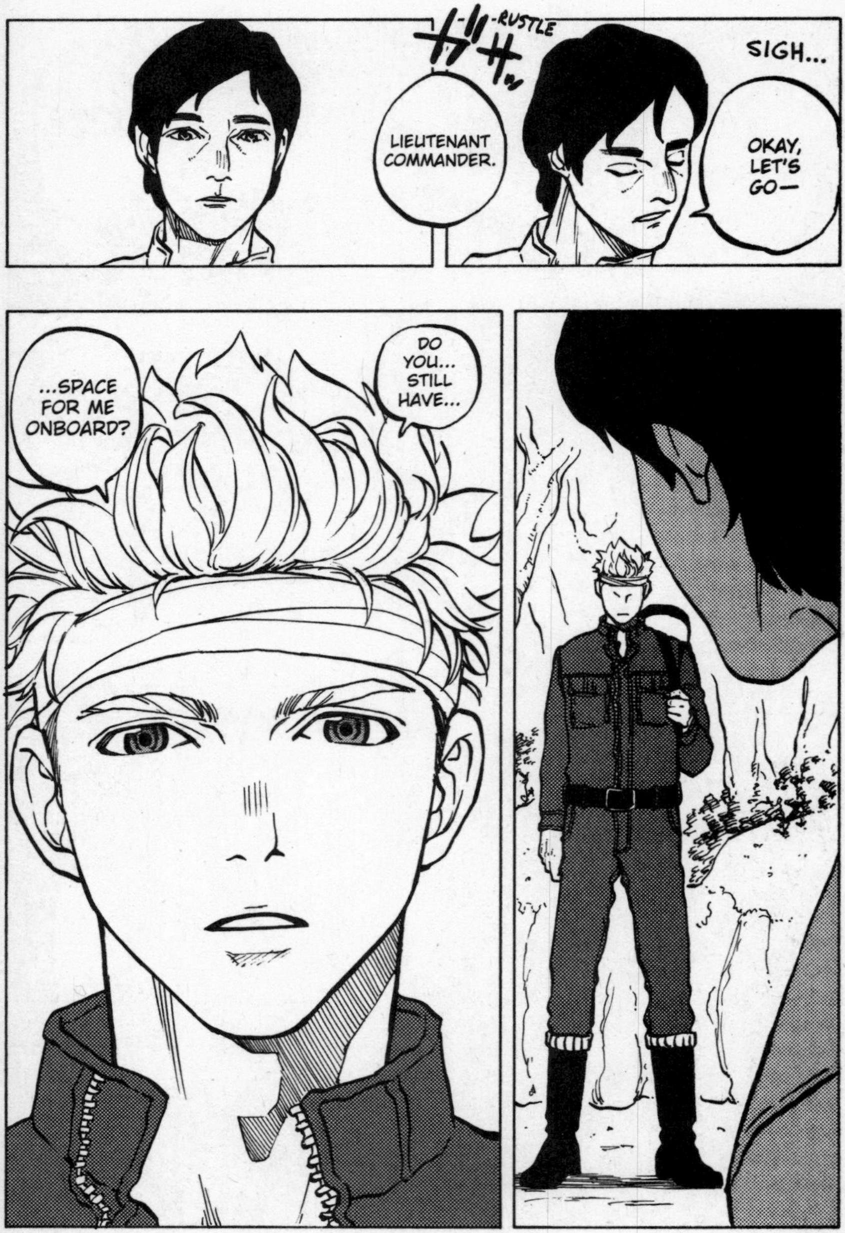
SIGH...
OKAY, LET'S GO—
-RUSTLE
LIEUTENANT COMMANDER.
DO YOU... STILL HAVE...
...SPACE FOR ME ONBOARD?

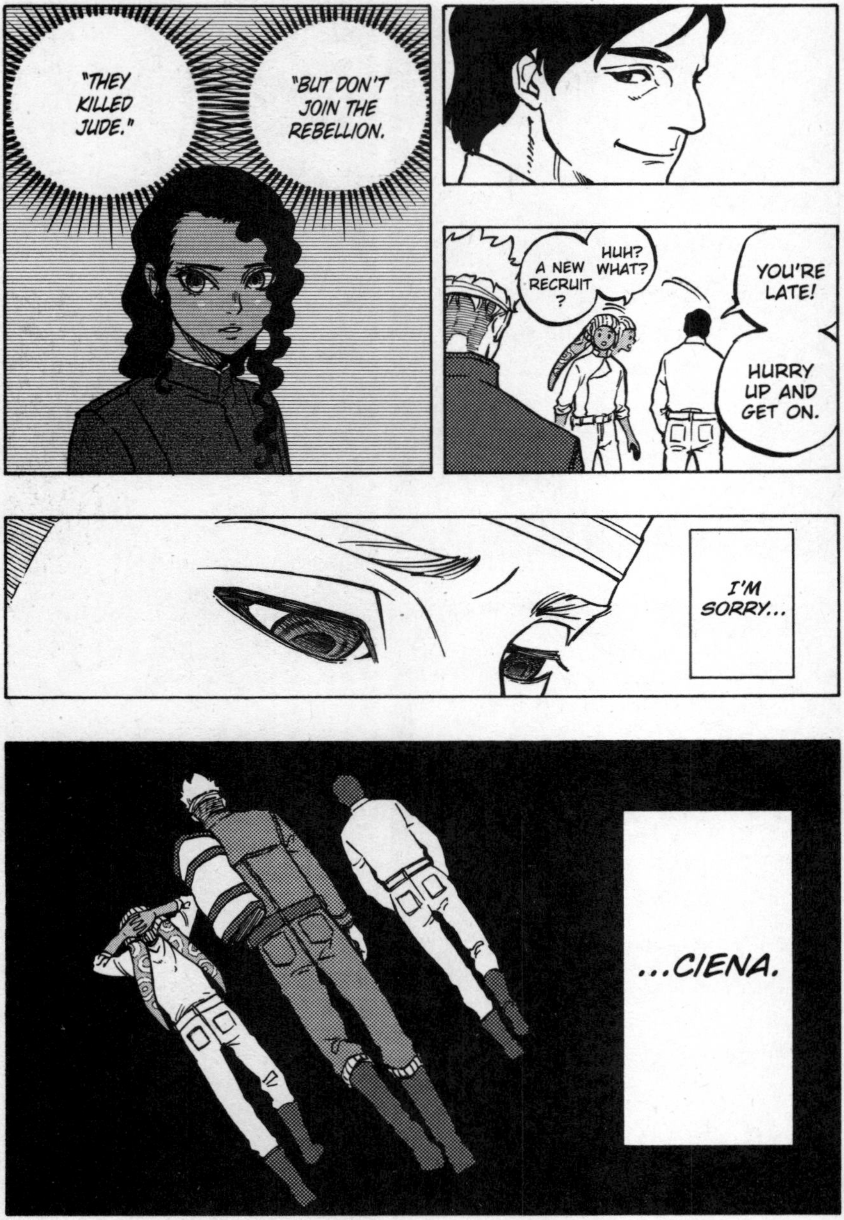
YOU'RE LATE!
HURRY UP AND GET ON.
HUH? WHAT?
A NEW RECRUIT?
"BUT DON'T JOIN THE REBELLION.
"THEY KILLED JUDE."
I'M SORRY...
...CIENA.

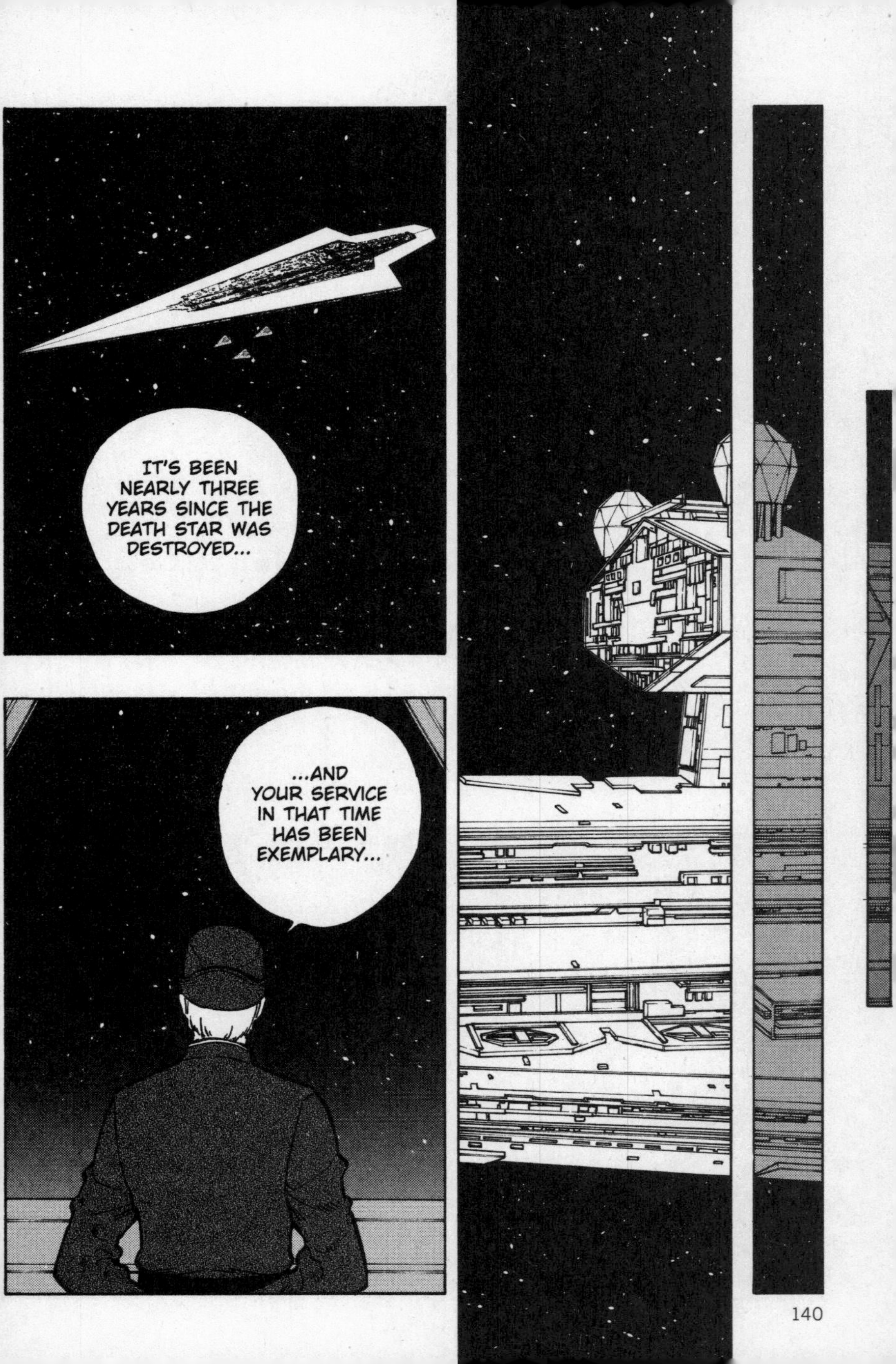
IT'S BEEN NEARLY THREE YEARS SINCE THE DEATH STAR WAS DESTROYED...
...AND YOUR SERVICE IN THAT TIME HAS BEEN EXEMPLARY...

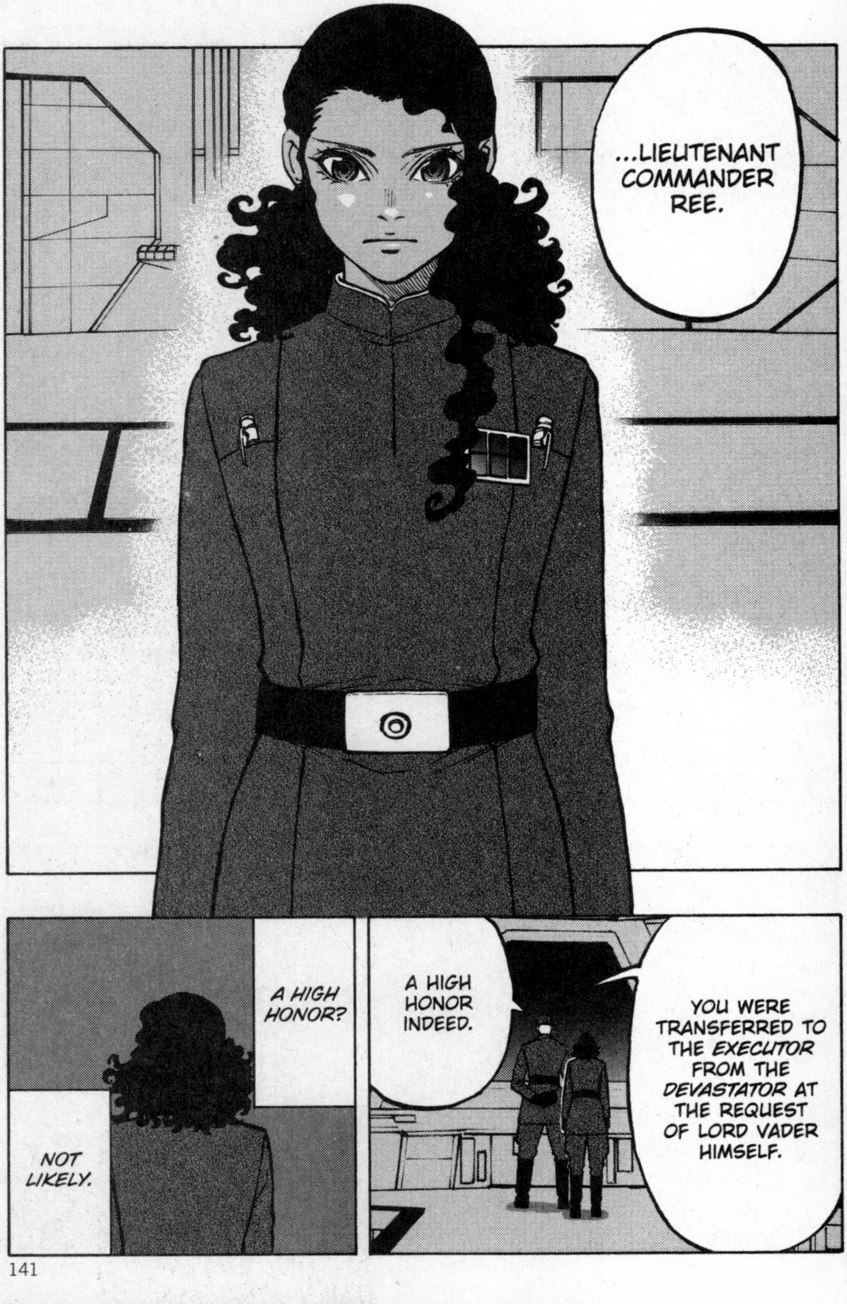
...LIEUTENANT COMMANDER REE.
YOU WERE TRANSFERRED TO THE *EXECUTOR* FROM THE *DEVASTATOR* AT THE REQUEST OF LORD VADER HIMSELF.
A HIGH HONOR INDEED.
A HIGH HONOR?
NOT LIKELY.

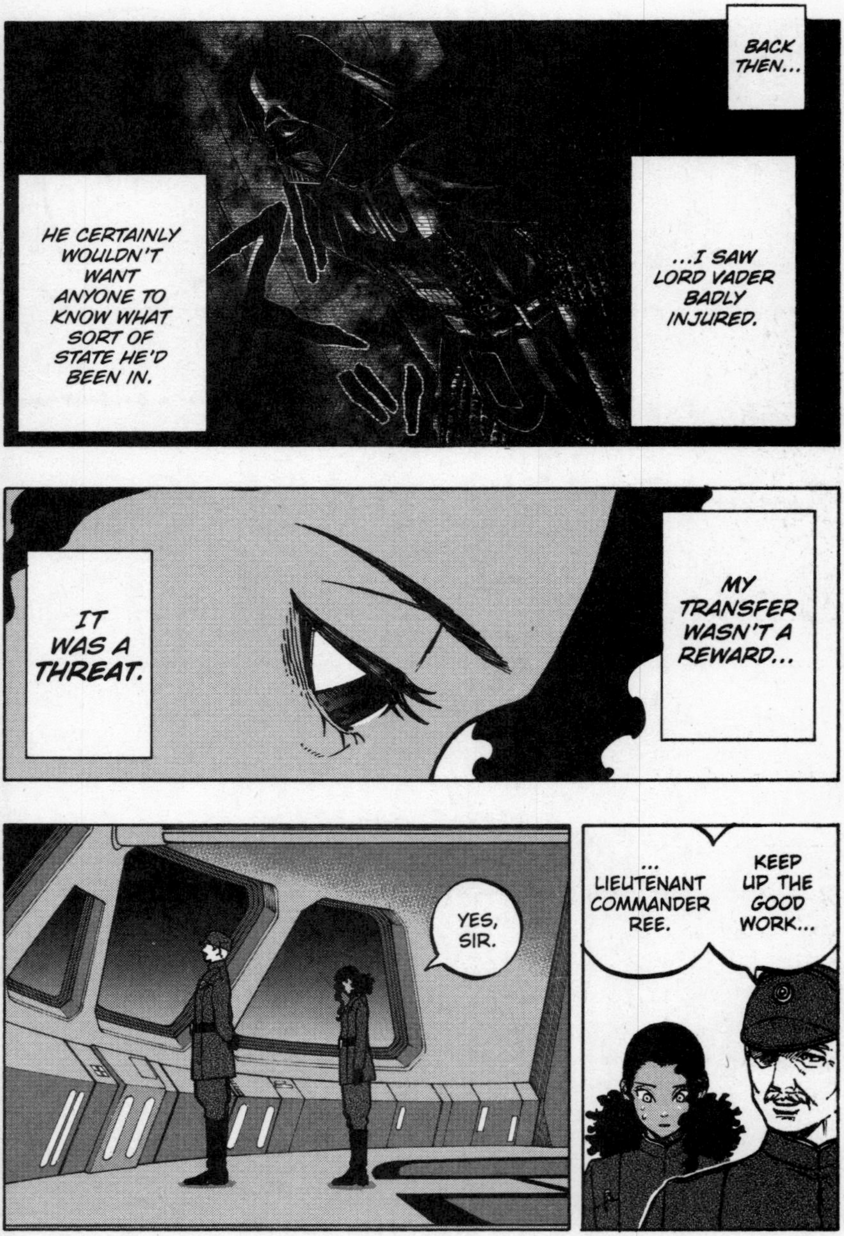
BACK THEN...
...I SAW LORD VADER BADLY INJURED.
HE CERTAINLY WOULDN'T WANT ANYONE TO KNOW WHAT SORT OF STATE HE'D BEEN IN.
MY TRANSFER WASN'T A REWARD...
IT WAS A THREAT.
KEEP UP THE GOOD WORK...
... LIEUTENANT COMMANDER REE.
YES, SIR.

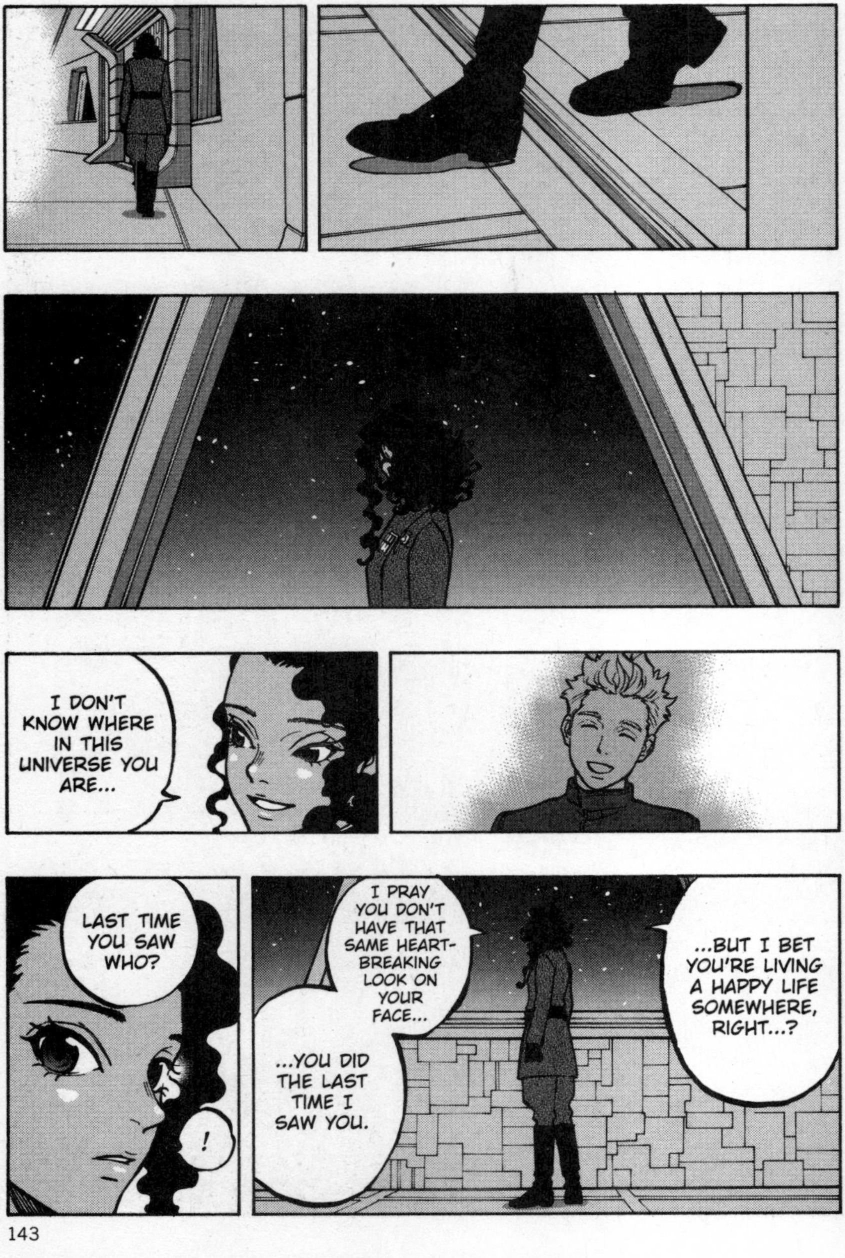
I DON'T KNOW WHERE IN THIS UNIVERSE YOU ARE...
...BUT I BET YOU'RE LIVING A HAPPY LIFE SOMEWHERE, RIGHT...?
I PRAY YOU DON'T HAVE THAT SAME HEART-BREAKING LOOK ON YOUR FACE...
...YOU DID THE LAST TIME I SAW YOU.
LAST TIME YOU SAW WHO?
!

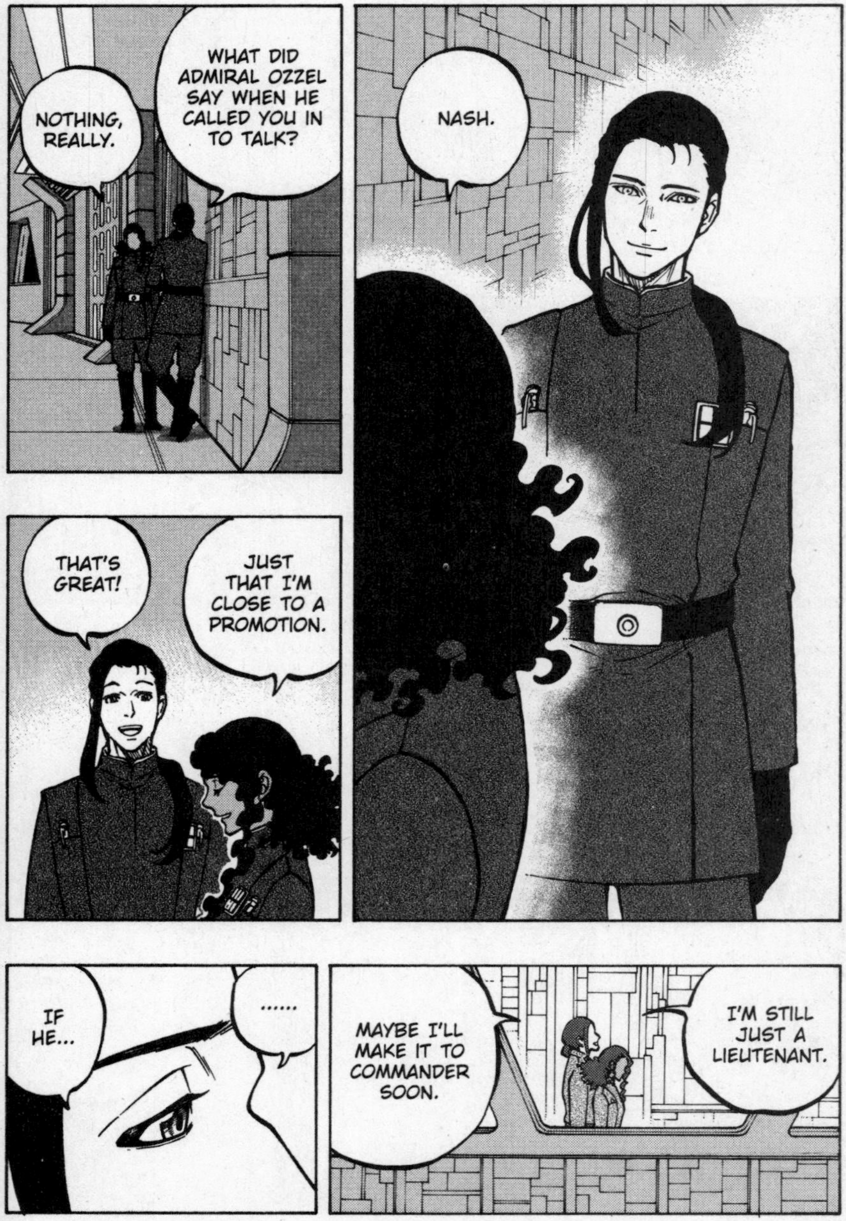
NASH.
WHAT DID ADMIRAL OZZEL SAY WHEN HE CALLED YOU IN TO TALK?
NOTHING, REALLY.
JUST THAT I'M CLOSE TO A PROMOTION.
THAT'S GREAT!
I'M STILL JUST A LIEUTENANT.
MAYBE I'LL MAKE IT TO COMMANDER SOON.
......
IF HE...

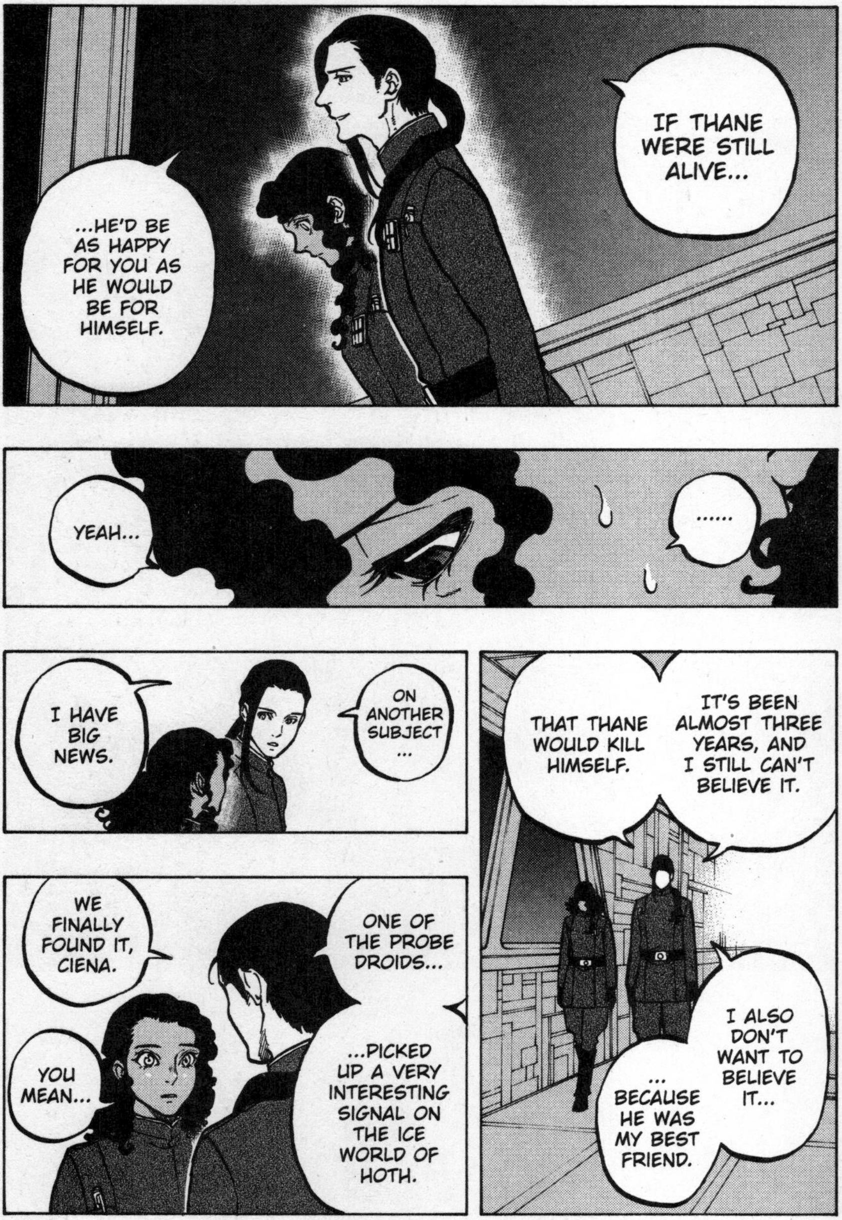
IF THANE WERE STILL ALIVE...
...HE'D BE AS HAPPY FOR YOU AS HE WOULD BE FOR HIMSELF.
......
YEAH...
IT'S BEEN ALMOST THREE YEARS, AND I STILL CAN'T BELIEVE IT.
THAT THANE WOULD KILL HIMSELF.
I ALSO DON'T WANT TO BELIEVE IT...
...BECAUSE HE WAS MY BEST FRIEND.
ON ANOTHER SUBJECT...
I HAVE BIG NEWS.
ONE OF THE PROBE DROIDS...
WE FINALLY FOUND IT, CIENA.
...PICKED UP A VERY INTERESTING SIGNAL ON THE ICE WORLD OF HOTH.
YOU MEAN...

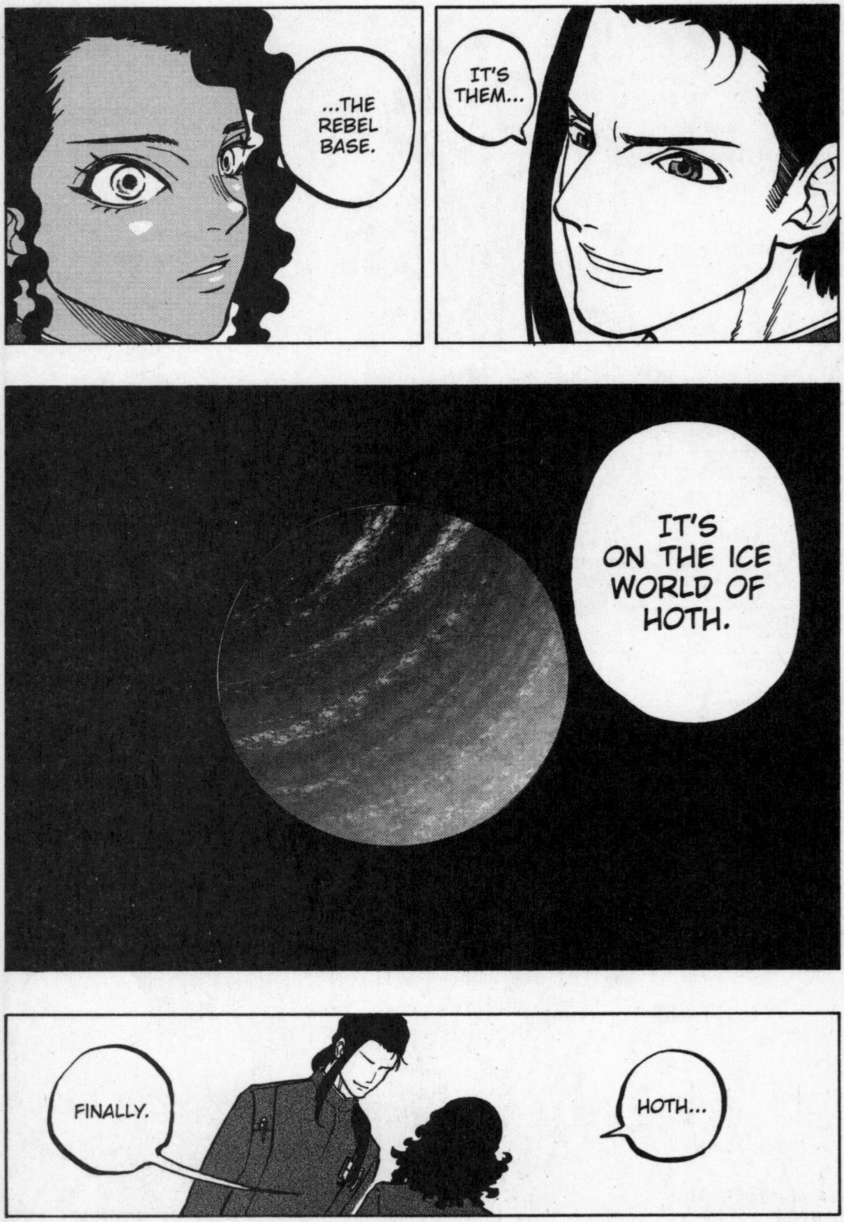
IT'S THEM...
...THE REBEL BASE.
IT'S ON THE ICE WORLD OF HOTH.
HOTH...
FINALLY.

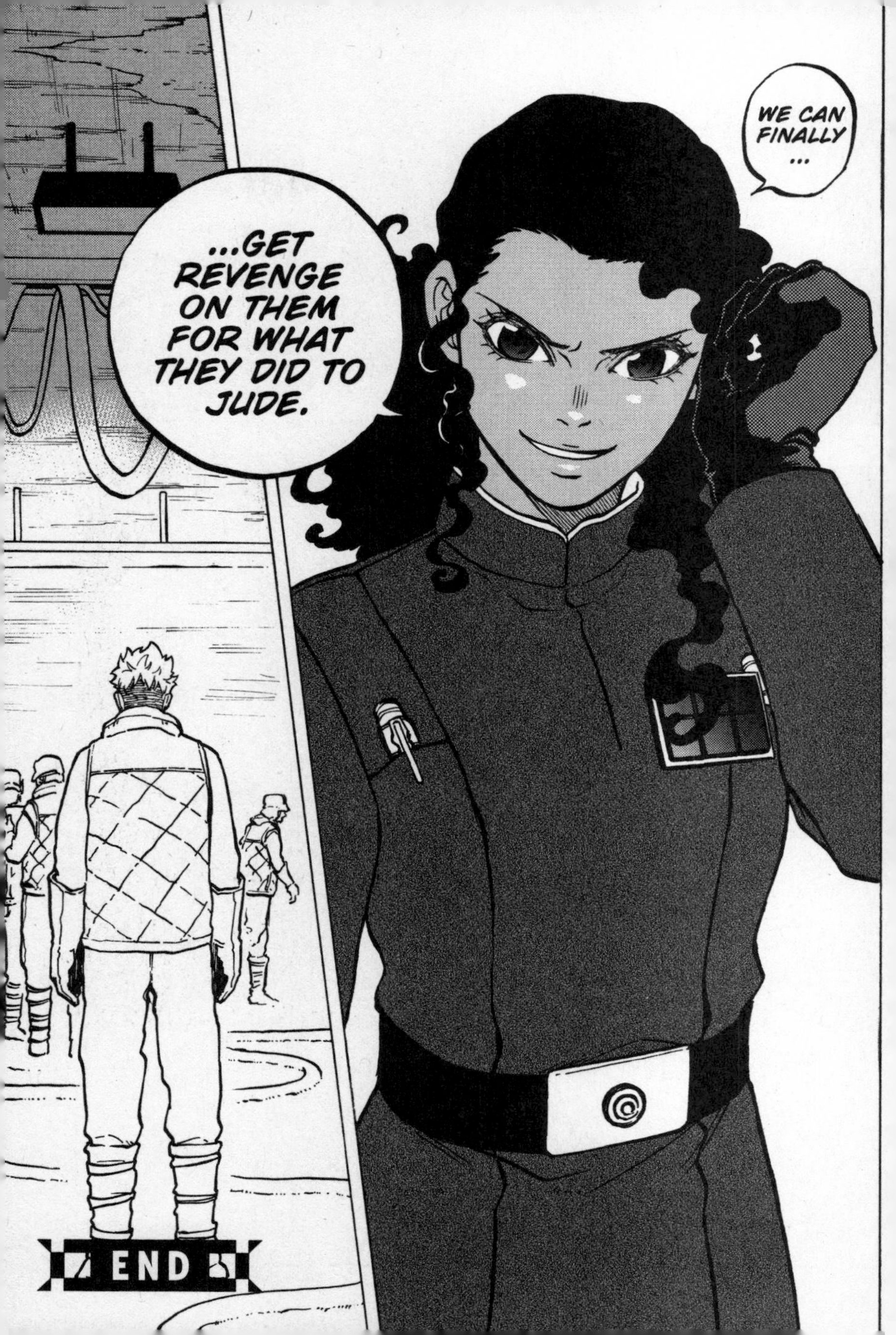
WE CAN FINALLY ...
...GET REVENGE ON THEM FOR WHAT THEY DID TO JUDE.
END

STAR WARS
LOST STARS
ロスト・スター

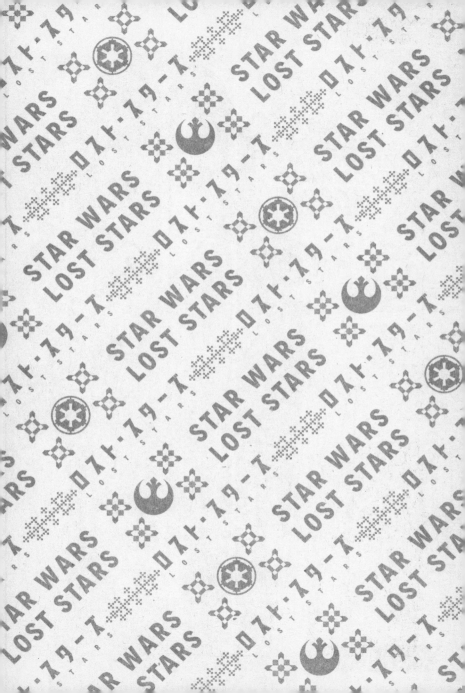

Chapter. 11

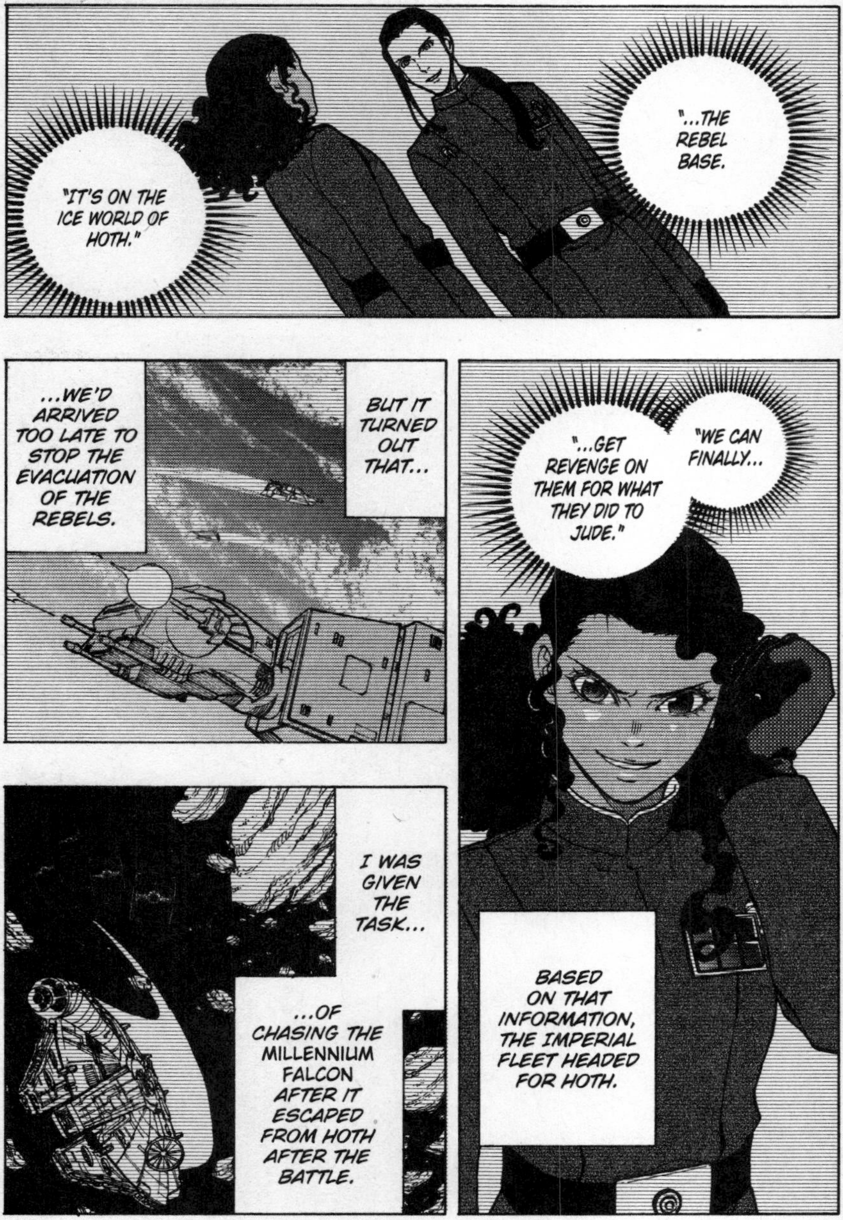
"...THE REBEL BASE.
"IT'S ON THE ICE WORLD OF HOTH."
"WE CAN FINALLY...
"...GET REVENGE ON THEM FOR WHAT THEY DID TO JUDE."
BASED ON THAT INFORMATION, THE IMPERIAL FLEET HEADED FOR HOTH.
BUT IT TURNED OUT THAT...
...WE'D ARRIVED TOO LATE TO STOP THE EVACUATION OF THE REBELS.
I WAS GIVEN THE TASK...
...OF CHASING THE MILLENNIUM FALCON AFTER IT ESCAPED FROM HOTH AFTER THE BATTLE.

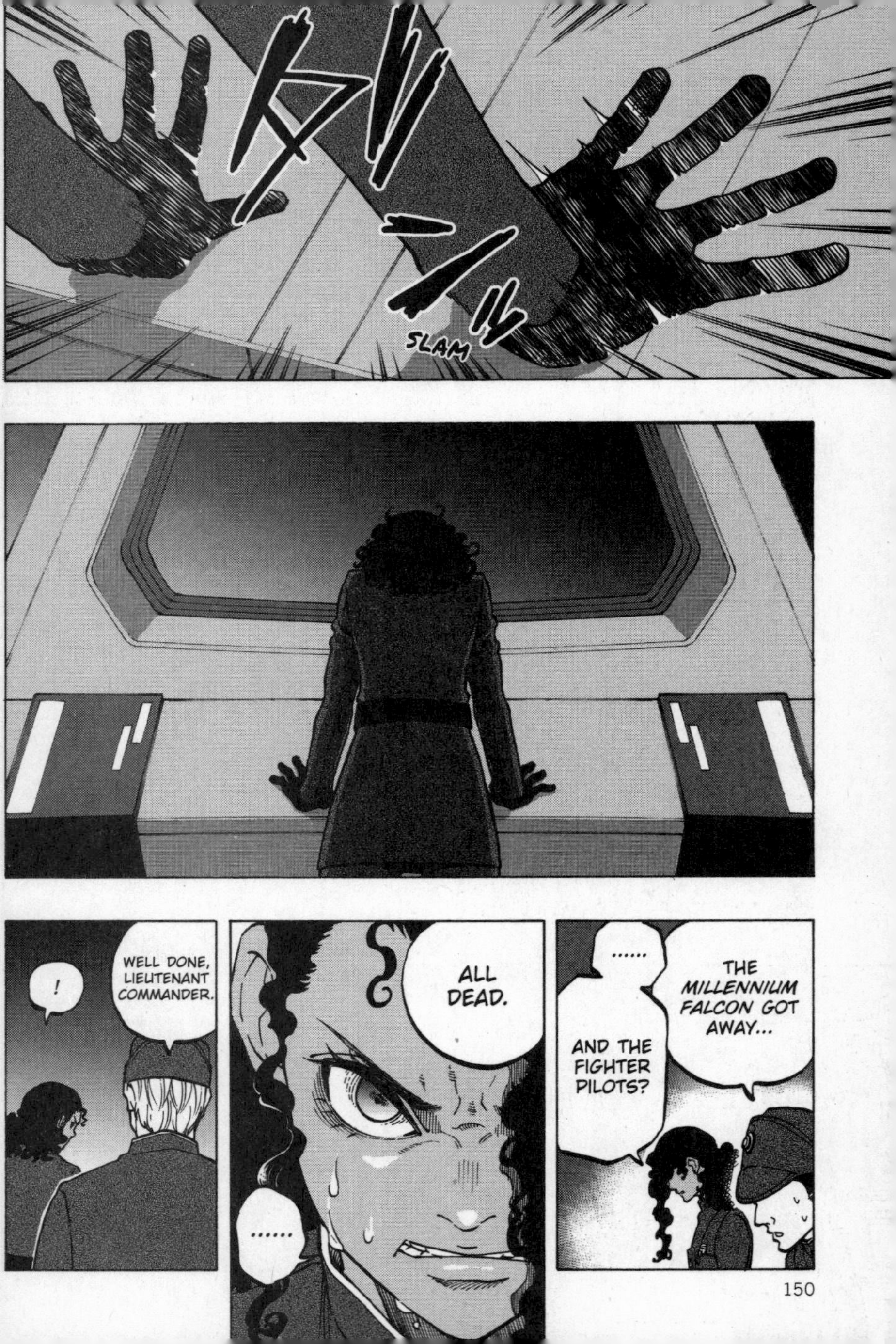
SLAM
THE *MILLENNIUM FALCON* GOT AWAY...
......
AND THE FIGHTER PILOTS?
ALL DEAD.
......
WELL DONE, LIEUTENANT COMMANDER.
!

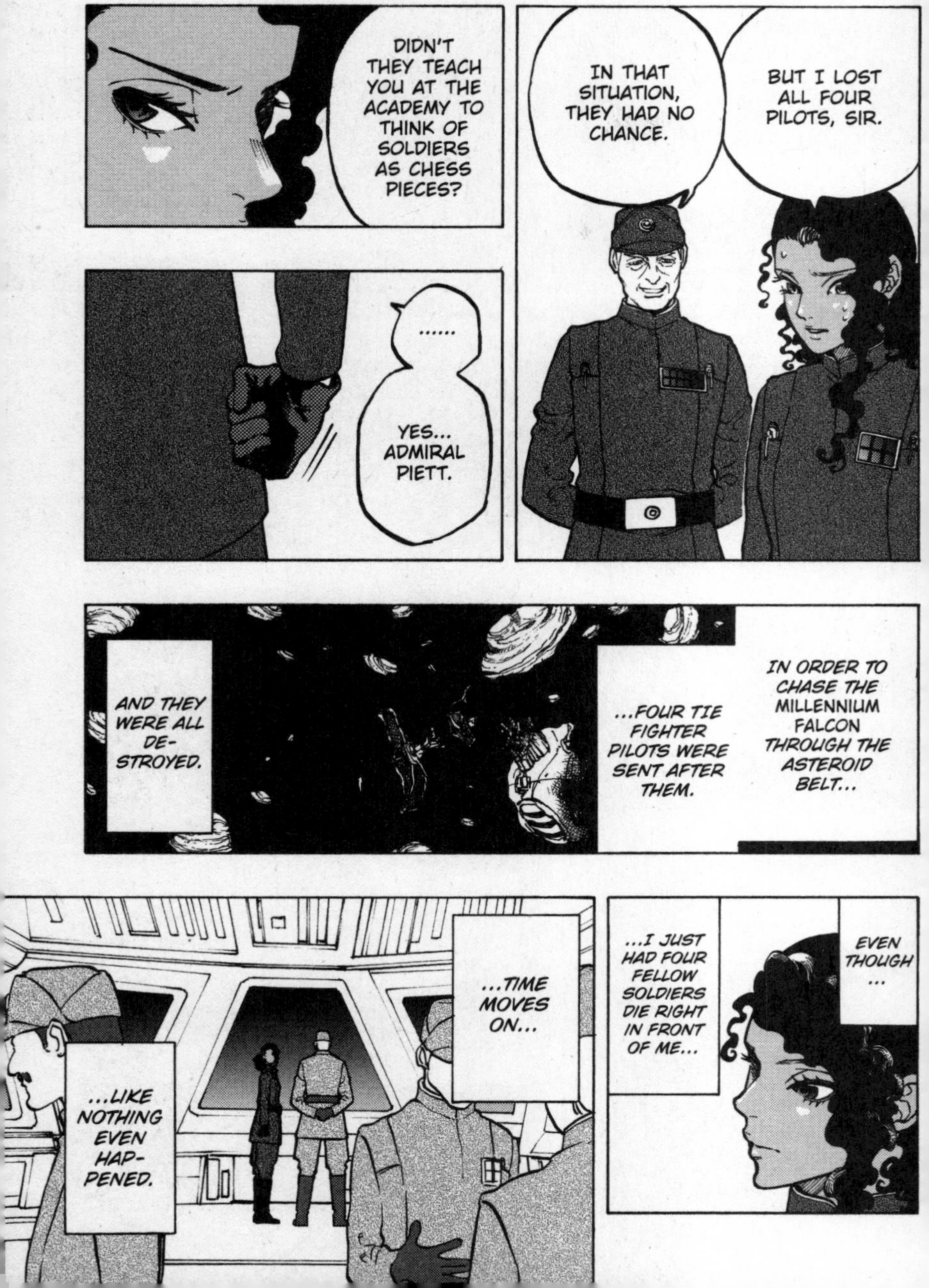
BUT I LOST ALL FOUR PILOTS, SIR.
IN THAT SITUATION, THEY HAD NO CHANCE.
DIDN'T THEY TEACH YOU AT THE ACADEMY TO THINK OF SOLDIERS AS CHESS PIECES?
...... YES... ADMIRAL PIETT.
IN ORDER TO CHASE THE MILLENNIUM FALCON THROUGH THE ASTEROID BELT...
...FOUR TIE FIGHTER PILOTS WERE SENT AFTER THEM.
AND THEY WERE ALL DE-STROYED.
EVEN THOUGH...
...I JUST HAD FOUR FELLOW SOLDIERS DIE RIGHT IN FRONT OF ME...
...TIME MOVES ON...
...LIKE NOTHING EVEN HAP-PENED.

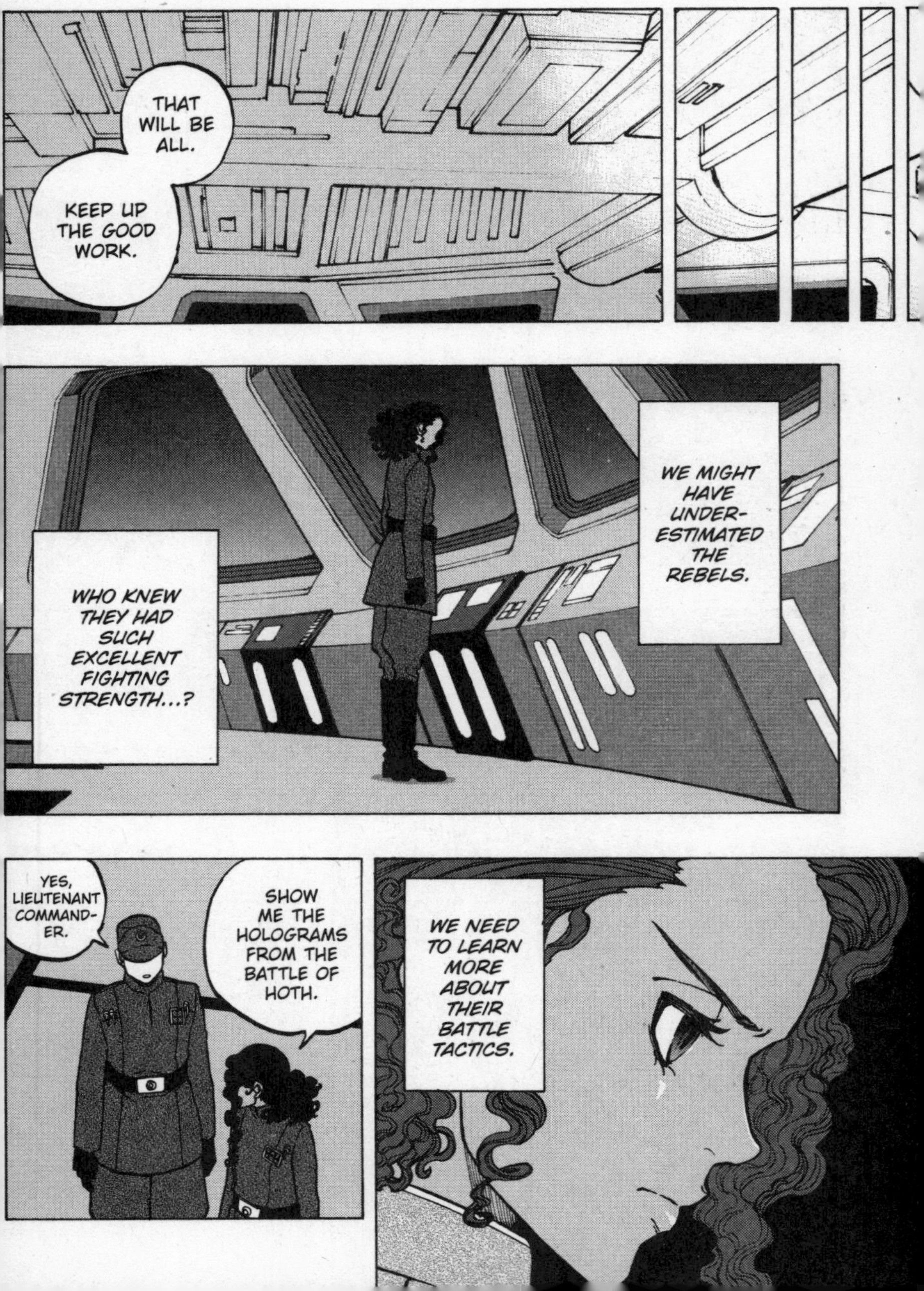
THAT WILL BE ALL.
KEEP UP THE GOOD WORK.
WE MIGHT HAVE UNDER-ESTIMATED THE REBELS.
WHO KNEW THEY HAD SUCH EXCELLENT FIGHTING STRENGTH...?
WE NEED TO LEARN MORE ABOUT THEIR BATTLE TACTICS.
SHOW ME THE HOLOGRAMS FROM THE BATTLE OF HOTH.
YES, LIEUTENANT COMMANDER.

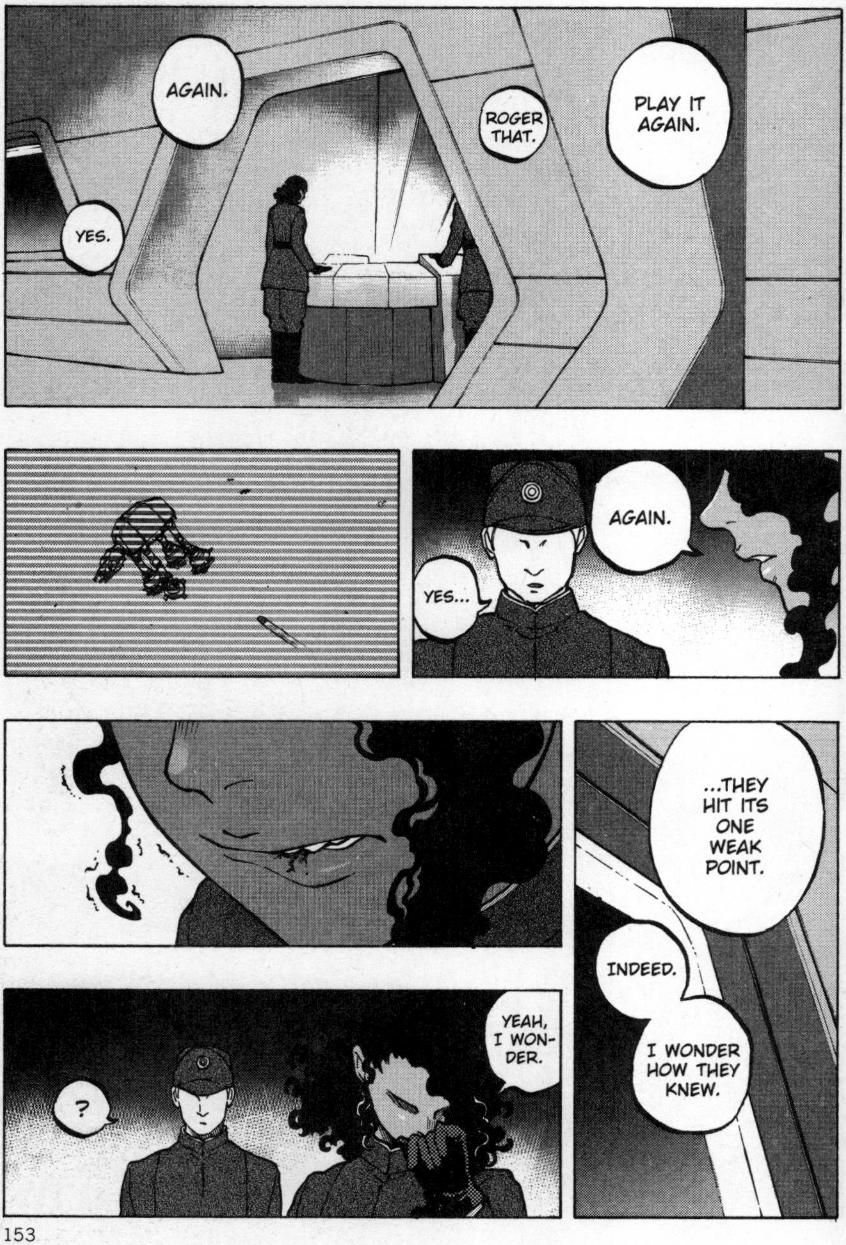

PLAY IT AGAIN.
ROGER THAT.
AGAIN.
YES.
AGAIN.
YES...
...THEY HIT ITS ONE WEAK POINT.
INDEED.
I WONDER HOW THEY KNEW.
YEAH, I WON-DER.
?

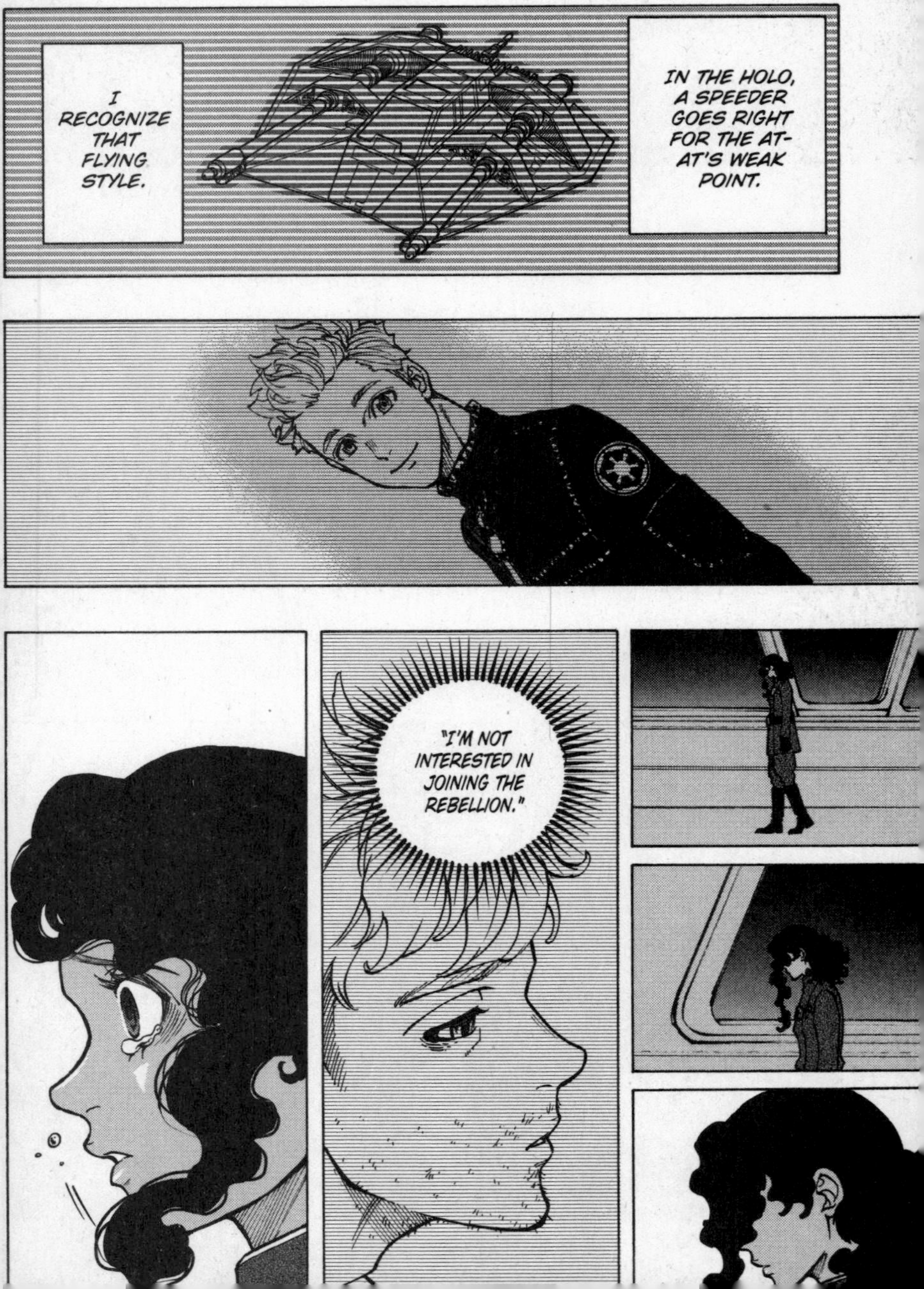
IN THE HOLO, A SPEEDER GOES RIGHT FOR THE AT-AT'S WEAK POINT.
I RECOGNIZE THAT FLYING STYLE.
"I'M NOT INTERESTED IN JOINING THE REBELLION."

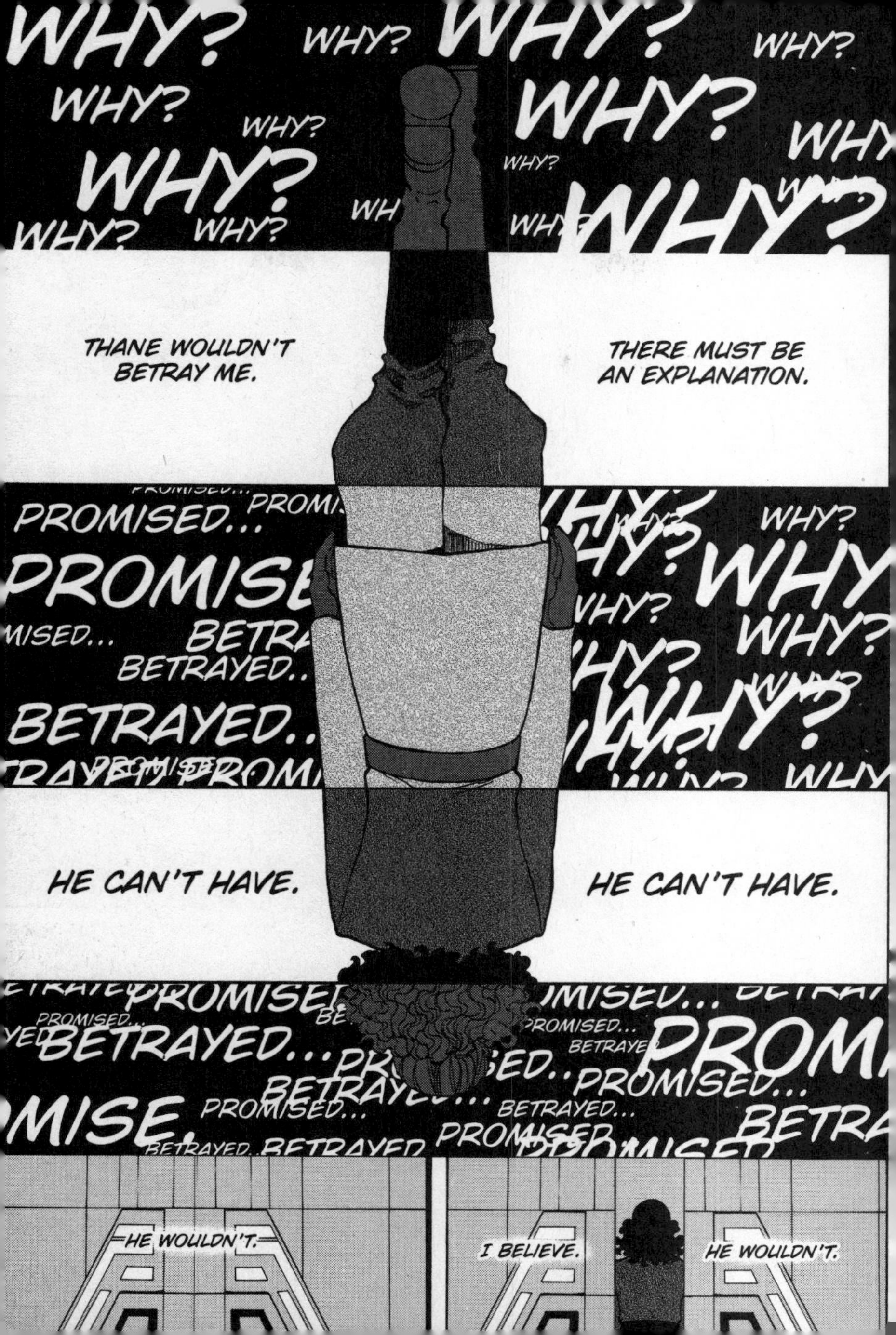
WHY? WHY? WHY? WHY?
WHY? WHY? WHY?
WHY? WHY?
WHY? WHY?
THANE WOULDN'T BETRAY ME.
THERE MUST BE AN EXPLANATION.
PROMISED... WHY?
PROMISED... WHY? WHY? WHY?
BETRAYED... WHY?
BETRAYED...
HE CAN'T HAVE.
HE CAN'T HAVE.
PROMISED... BETRAYED... PROMISED... BETRAYED...
PROMISED... BETRAYED... PROMISED... BETRAYED...
HE WOULDN'T.
I BELIEVE.
HE WOULDN'T.

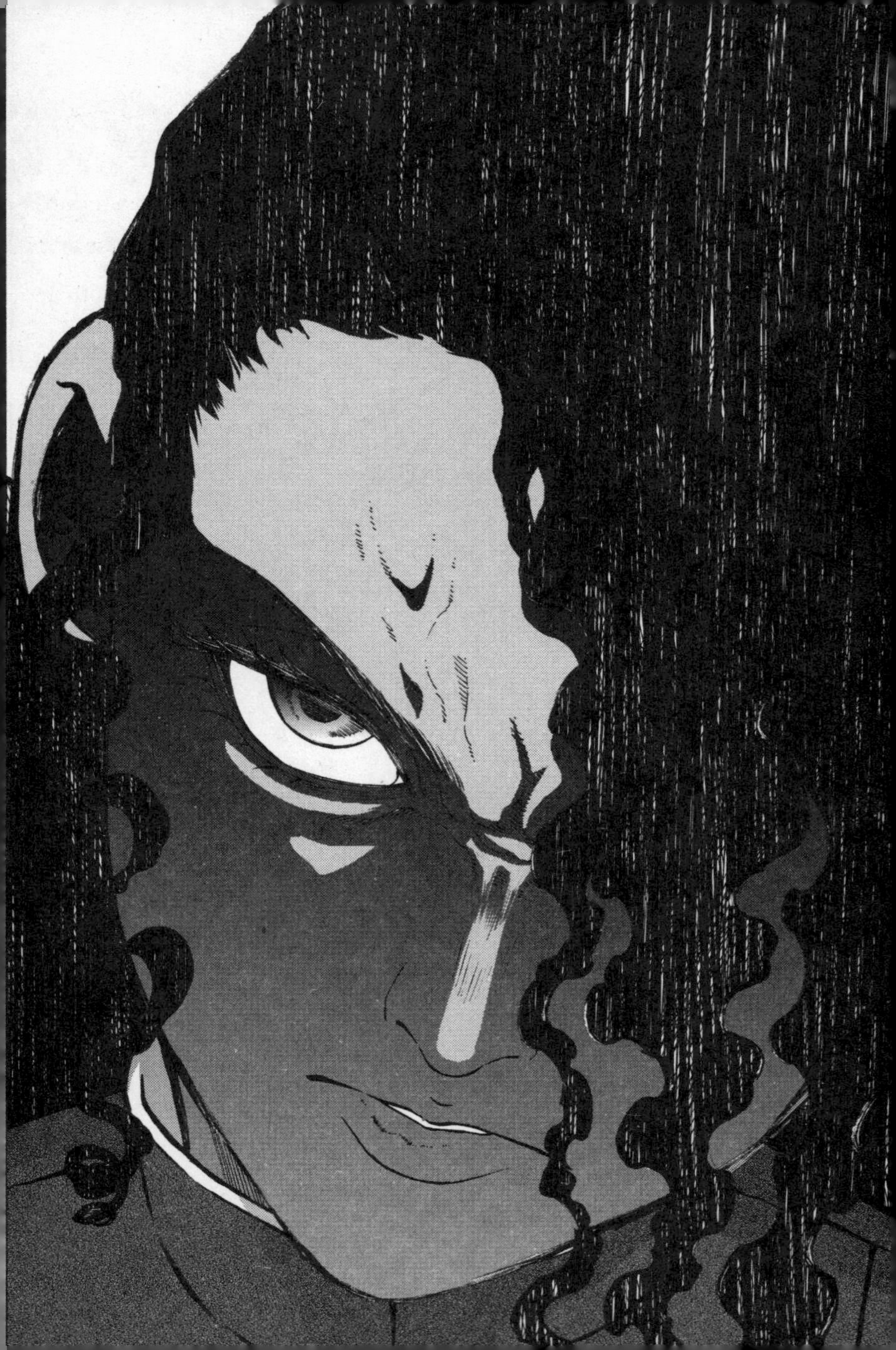

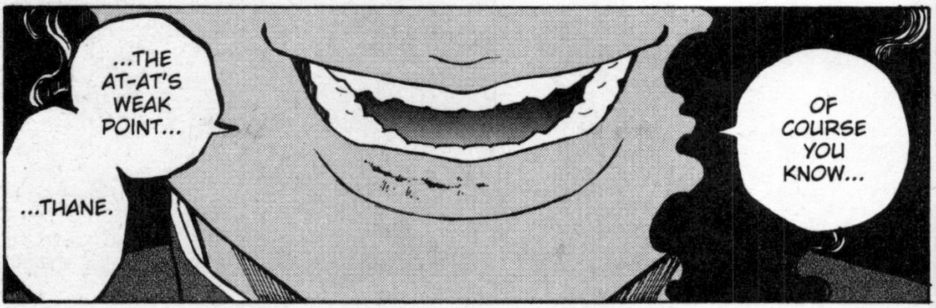
OF COURSE YOU KNOW...
...THE AT-AT'S WEAK POINT...
...THANE.

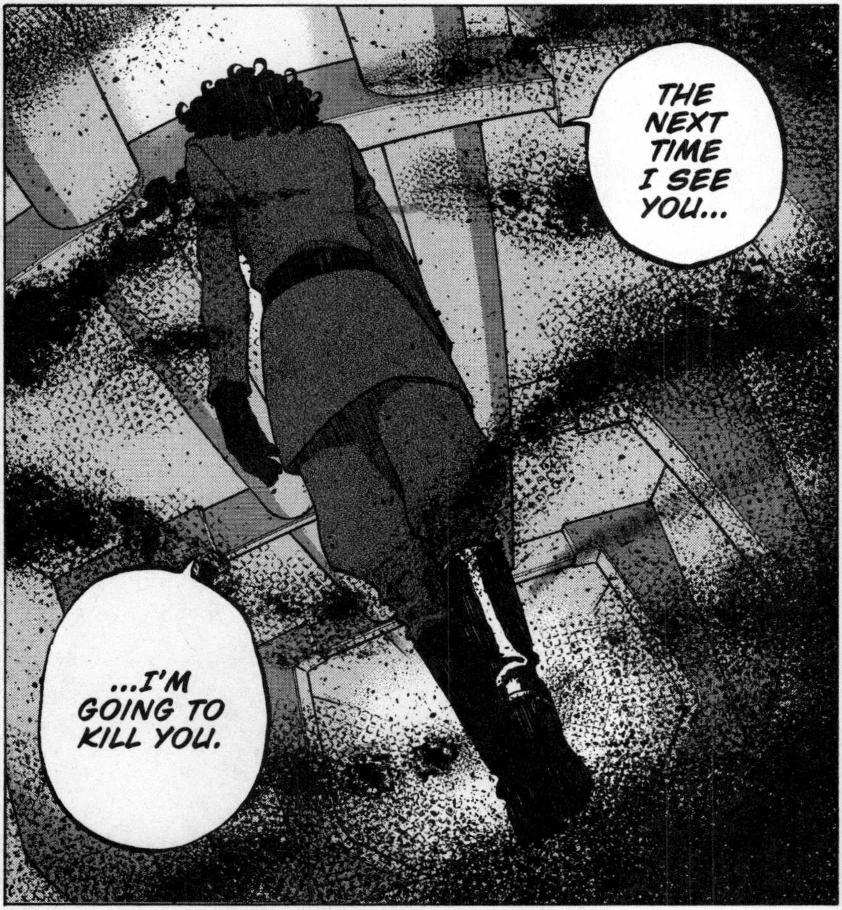
THE NEXT TIME I SEE YOU...
...I'M GOING TO KILL YOU.

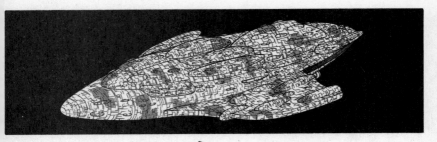

THANE KYRELL!!!

FWUMP

WHAM

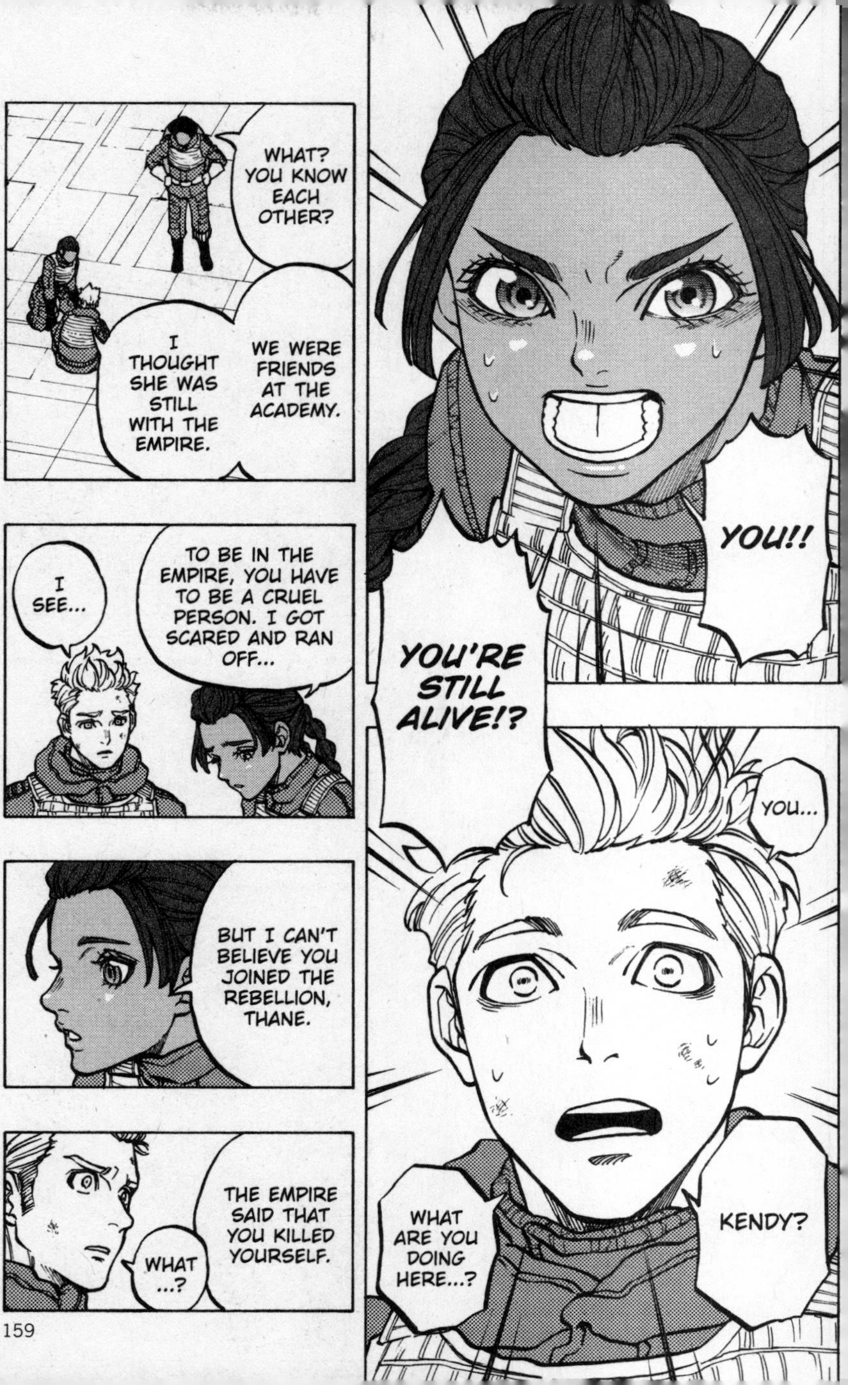
YOU!!
YOU'RE STILL ALIVE!?
YOU...
KENDY?
WHAT ARE YOU DOING HERE...?
WHAT? YOU KNOW EACH OTHER?
WE WERE FRIENDS AT THE ACADEMY.
I THOUGHT SHE WAS STILL WITH THE EMPIRE.
TO BE IN THE EMPIRE, YOU HAVE TO BE A CRUEL PERSON. I GOT SCARED AND RAN OFF...
I SEE...
BUT I CAN'T BELIEVE YOU JOINED THE REBELLION, THANE.
THE EMPIRE SAID THAT YOU KILLED YOURSELF.
WHAT ...?

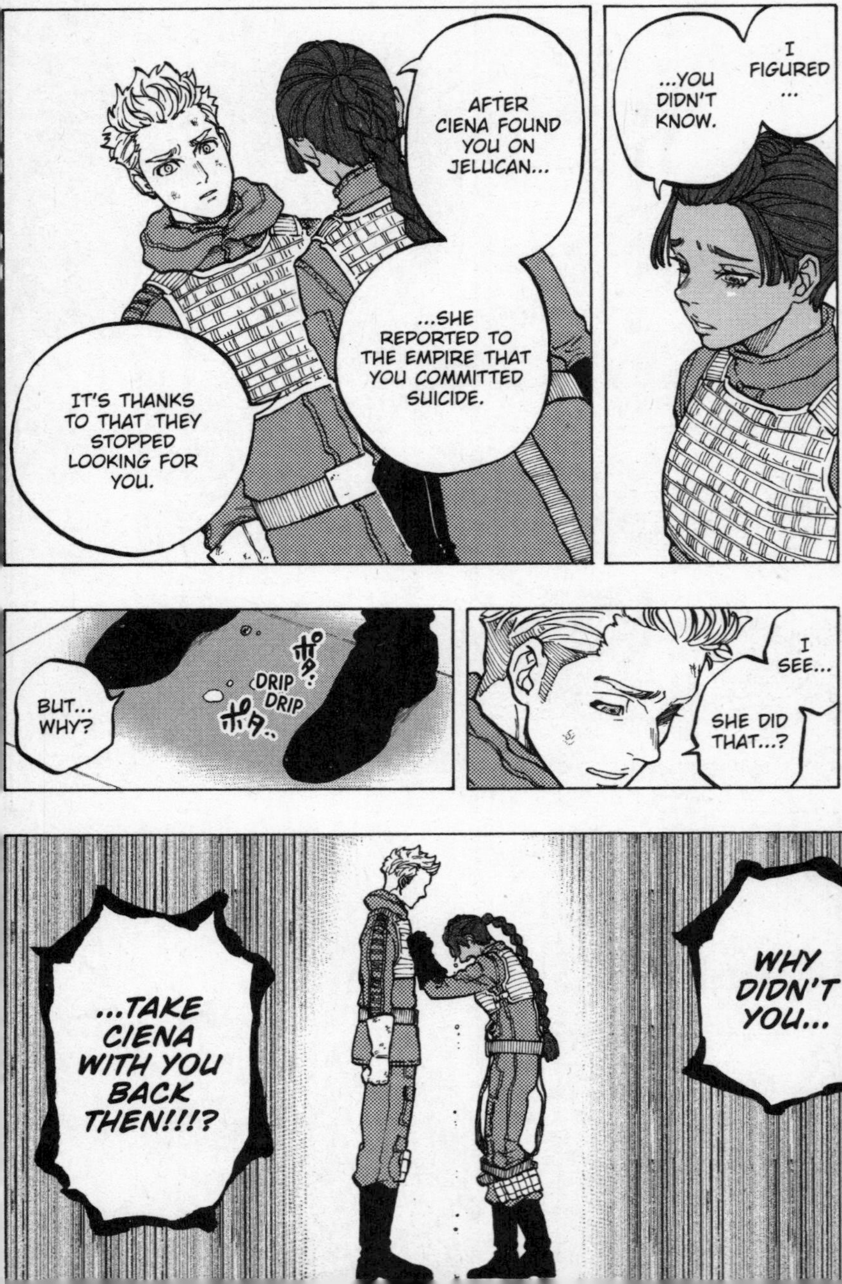
I FIGURED...
...YOU DIDN'T KNOW.
AFTER CIENA FOUND YOU ON JELUCAN...
...SHE REPORTED TO THE EMPIRE THAT YOU COMMITTED SUICIDE.
IT'S THANKS TO THAT THEY STOPPED LOOKING FOR YOU.
I SEE...
SHE DID THAT...?
ポタ.
DRIP DRIP
ポタ..
BUT... WHY?
WHY DIDN'T YOU...
...TAKE CIENA WITH YOU BACK THEN!!!?

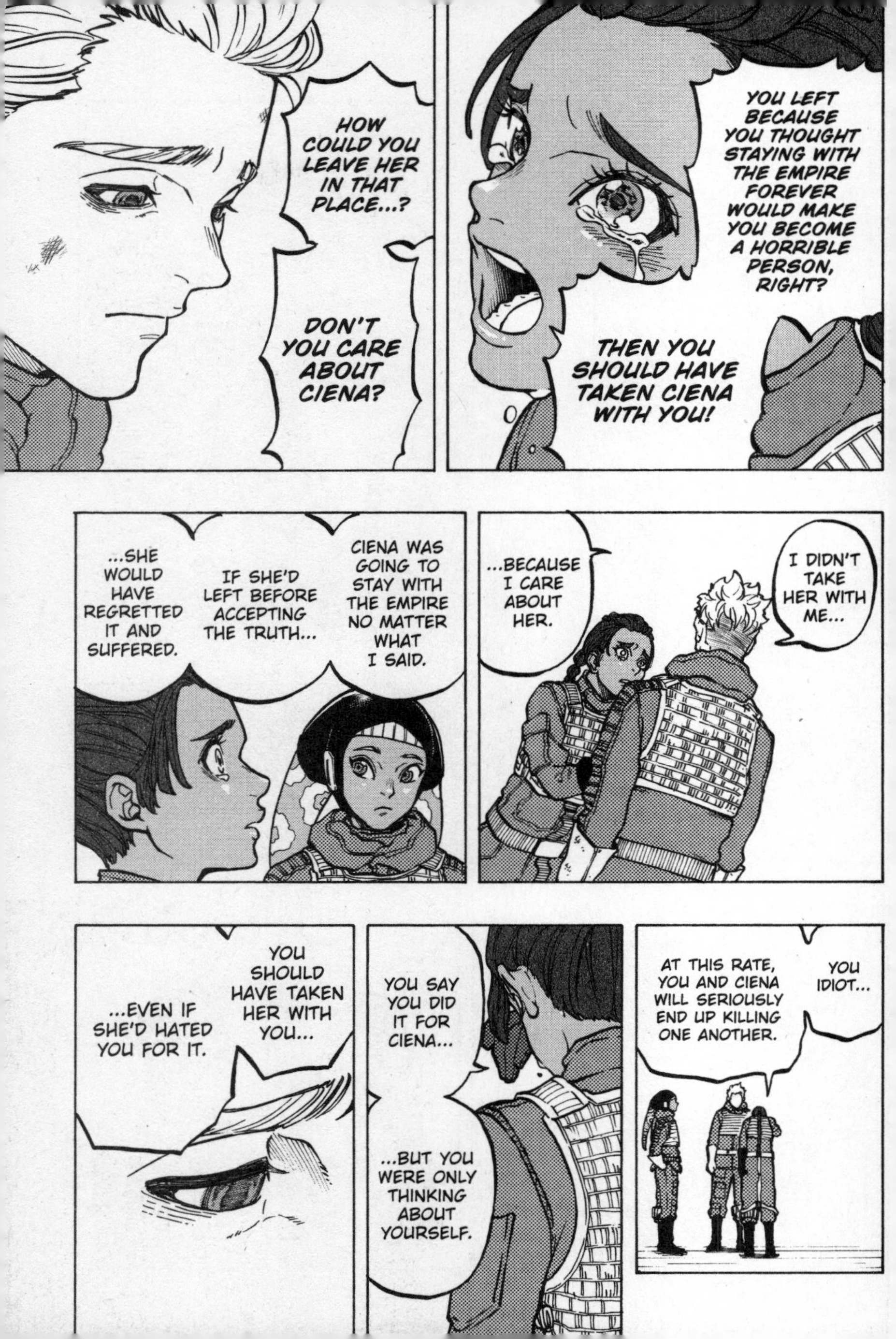
YOU LEFT BECAUSE YOU THOUGHT STAYING WITH THE EMPIRE FOREVER WOULD MAKE YOU BECOME A HORRIBLE PERSON, RIGHT?
THEN YOU SHOULD HAVE TAKEN CIENA WITH YOU!
HOW COULD YOU LEAVE HER IN THAT PLACE...?
DON'T YOU CARE ABOUT CIENA?
I DIDN'T TAKE HER WITH ME...
...BECAUSE I CARE ABOUT HER.
CIENA WAS GOING TO STAY WITH THE EMPIRE NO MATTER WHAT I SAID.
IF SHE'D LEFT BEFORE ACCEPTING THE TRUTH...
...SHE WOULD HAVE REGRETTED IT AND SUFFERED.
YOU IDIOT...
AT THIS RATE, YOU AND CIENA WILL SERIOUSLY END UP KILLING ONE ANOTHER.
YOU SAY YOU DID IT FOR CIENA...
...BUT YOU WERE ONLY THINKING ABOUT YOURSELF.
YOU SHOULD HAVE TAKEN HER WITH YOU...
...EVEN IF SHE'D HATED YOU FOR IT.

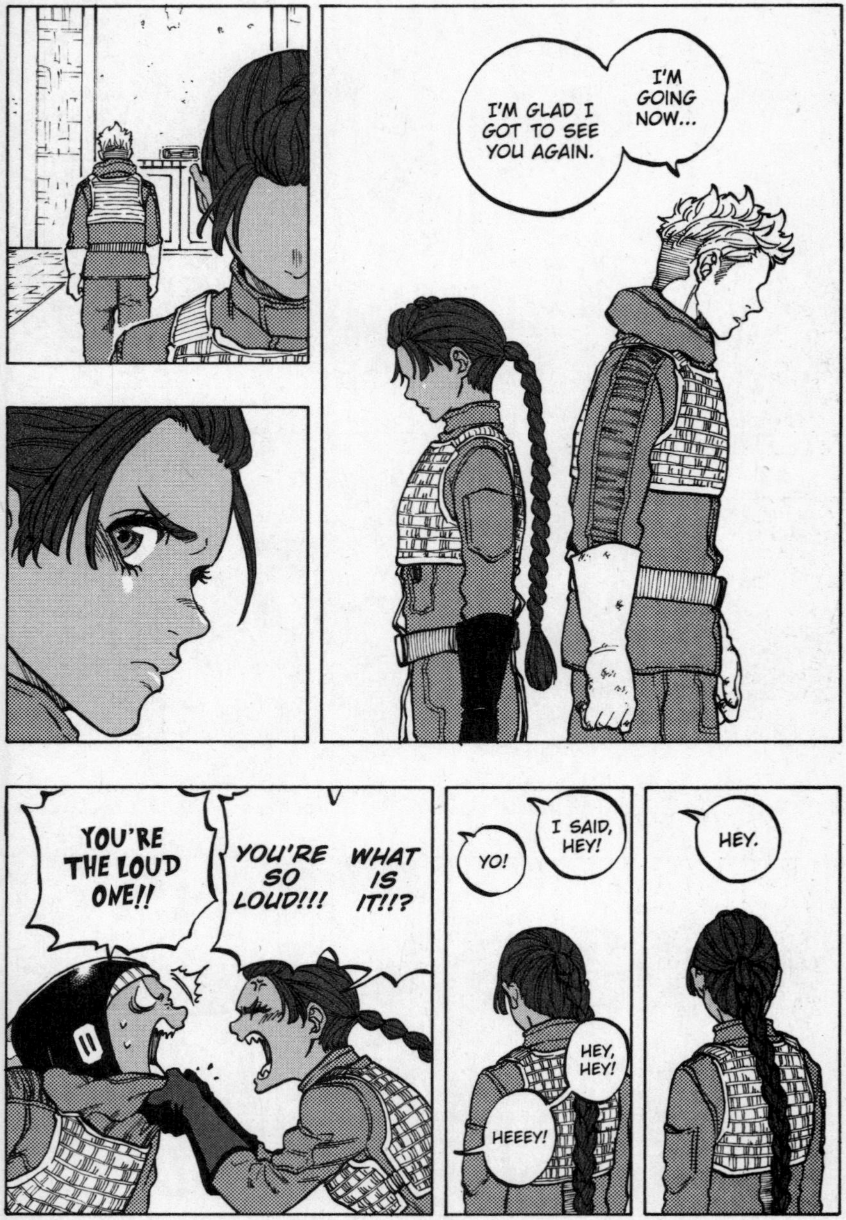
I'M GOING NOW...
I'M GLAD I GOT TO SEE YOU AGAIN.
HEY.
I SAID, HEY!
YO!
HEY, HEY!
HEEEY!
WHAT IS IT!!?
YOU'RE SO LOUD!!!
YOU'RE THE LOUD ONE!!

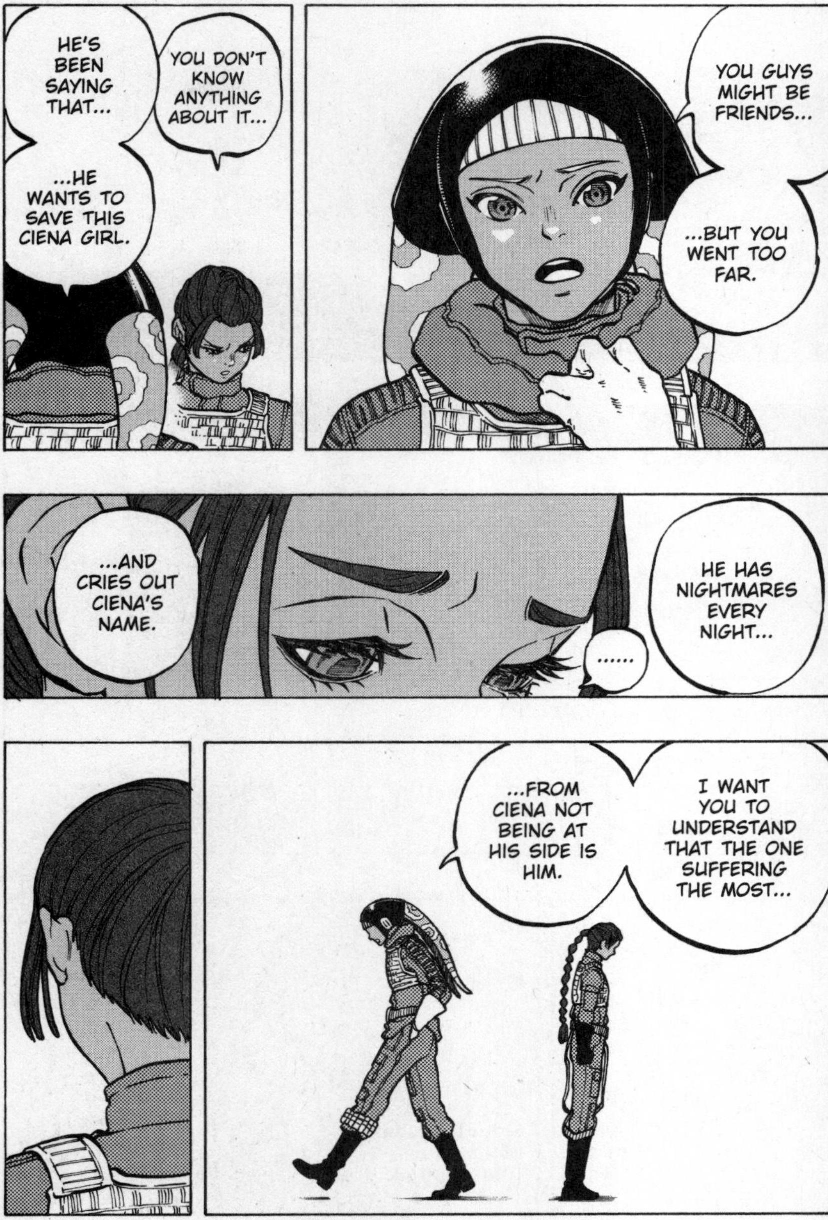
YOU GUYS MIGHT BE FRIENDS...
...BUT YOU WENT TOO FAR.
YOU DON'T KNOW ANYTHING ABOUT IT...
HE'S BEEN SAYING THAT...
...HE WANTS TO SAVE THIS CIENA GIRL.
HE HAS NIGHTMARES EVERY NIGHT...
......
...AND CRIES OUT CIENA'S NAME.
I WANT YOU TO UNDERSTAND THAT THE ONE SUFFERING THE MOST...
...FROM CIENA NOT BEING AT HIS SIDE IS HIM.

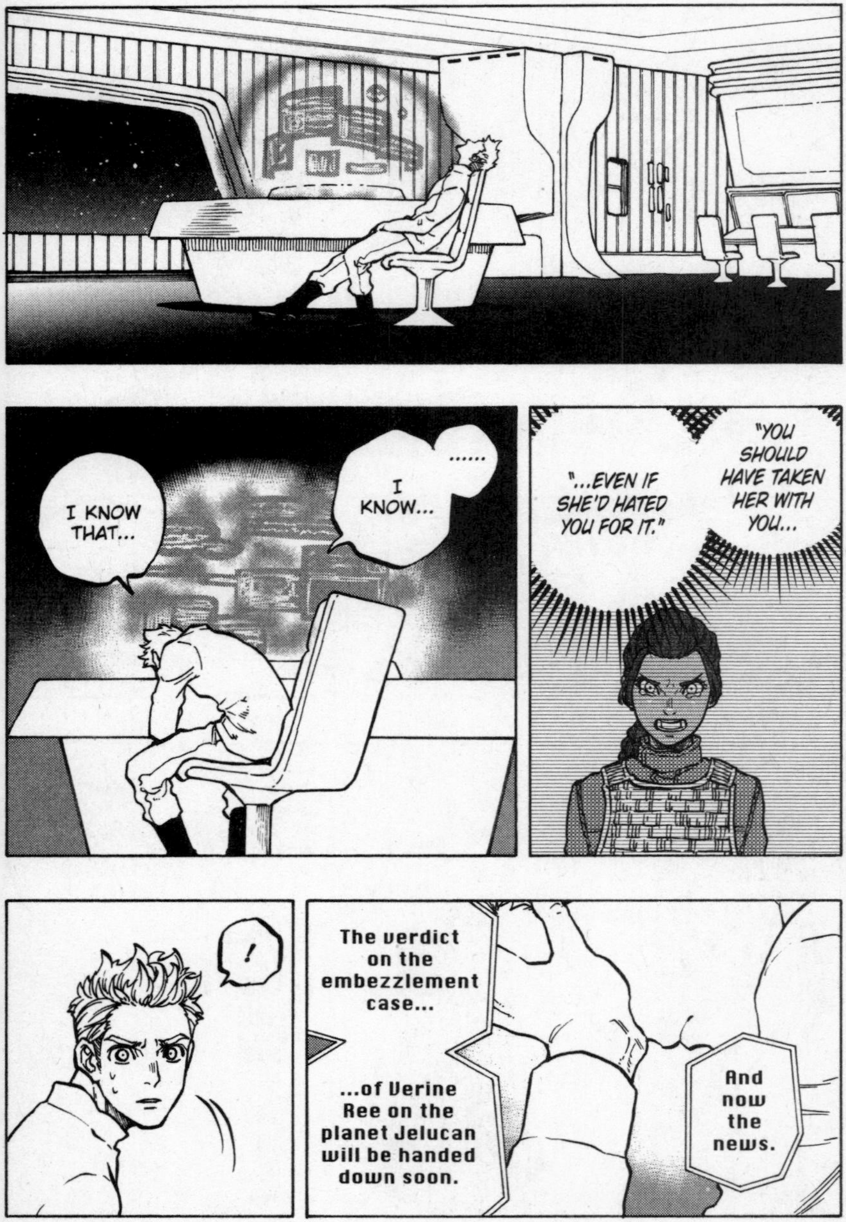
"YOU SHOULD HAVE TAKEN HER WITH YOU...
...EVEN IF SHE'D HATED YOU FOR IT."
......
I KNOW...
I KNOW THAT...
And now the news.
The verdict on the embezzlement case...
...of Verine Ree on the planet Jelucan will be handed down soon.
!

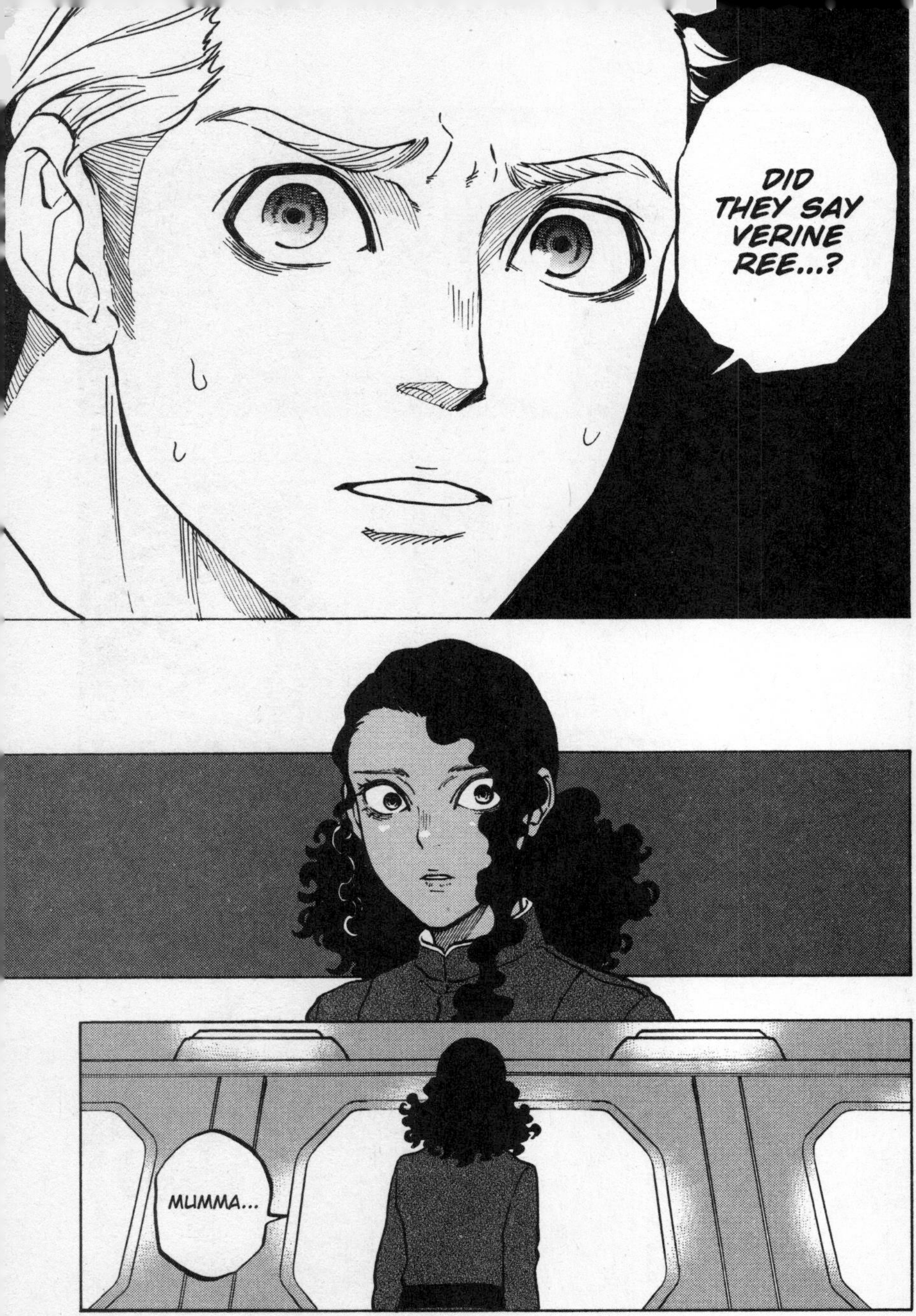
DID THEY SAY VERINE REE...?
MUMMA...

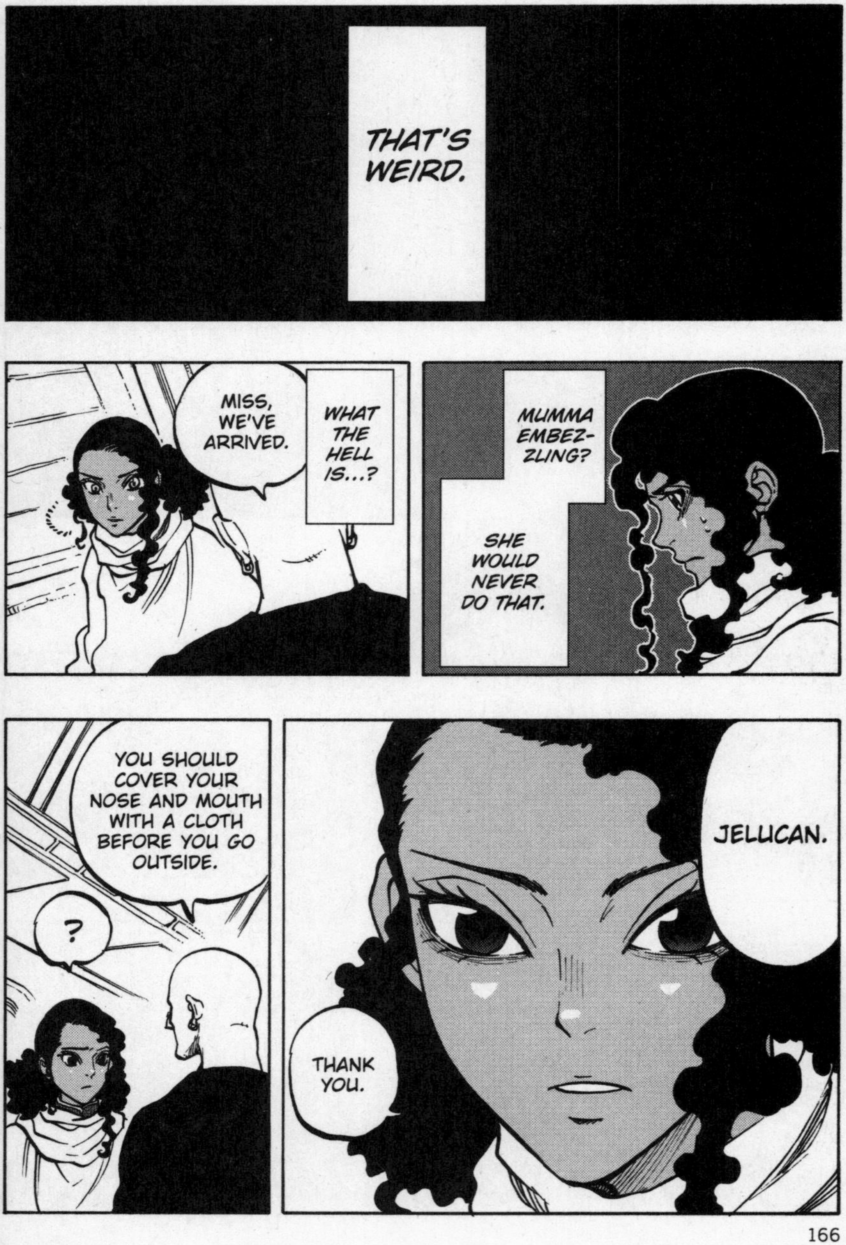
THAT'S WEIRD.
MUMMA EMBEZZLING?
SHE WOULD NEVER DO THAT.
WHAT THE HELL IS...?
MISS, WE'VE ARRIVED.
JELUCAN.
THANK YOU.
YOU SHOULD COVER YOUR NOSE AND MOUTH WITH A CLOTH BEFORE YOU GO OUTSIDE.
?

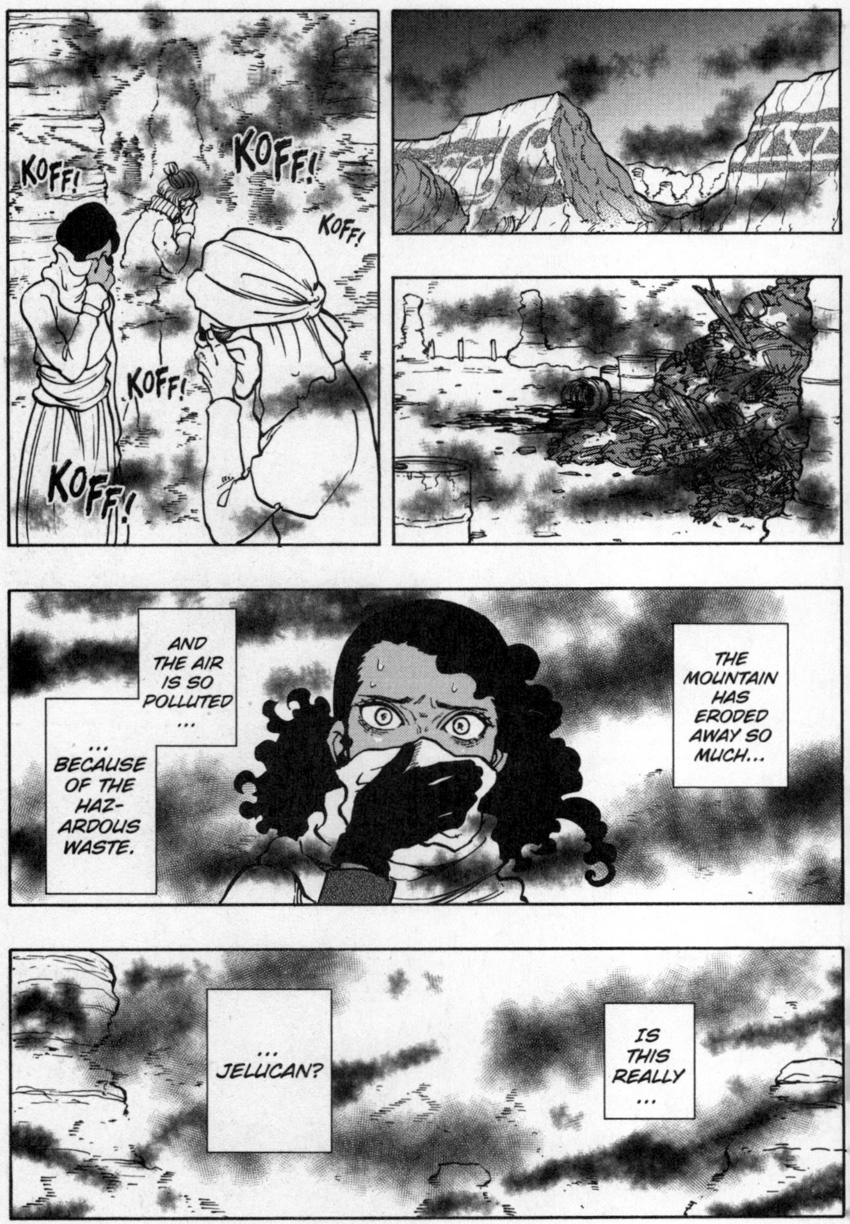
KOFF!
KOFF!
KOFF!
KOFF!
KOFF!
THE MOUNTAIN HAS ERODED AWAY SO MUCH...
AND THE AIR IS SO POLLUTED ...
... BECAUSE OF THE HAZ-ARDOUS WASTE.
IS THIS REALLY ...
... JELUCAN?

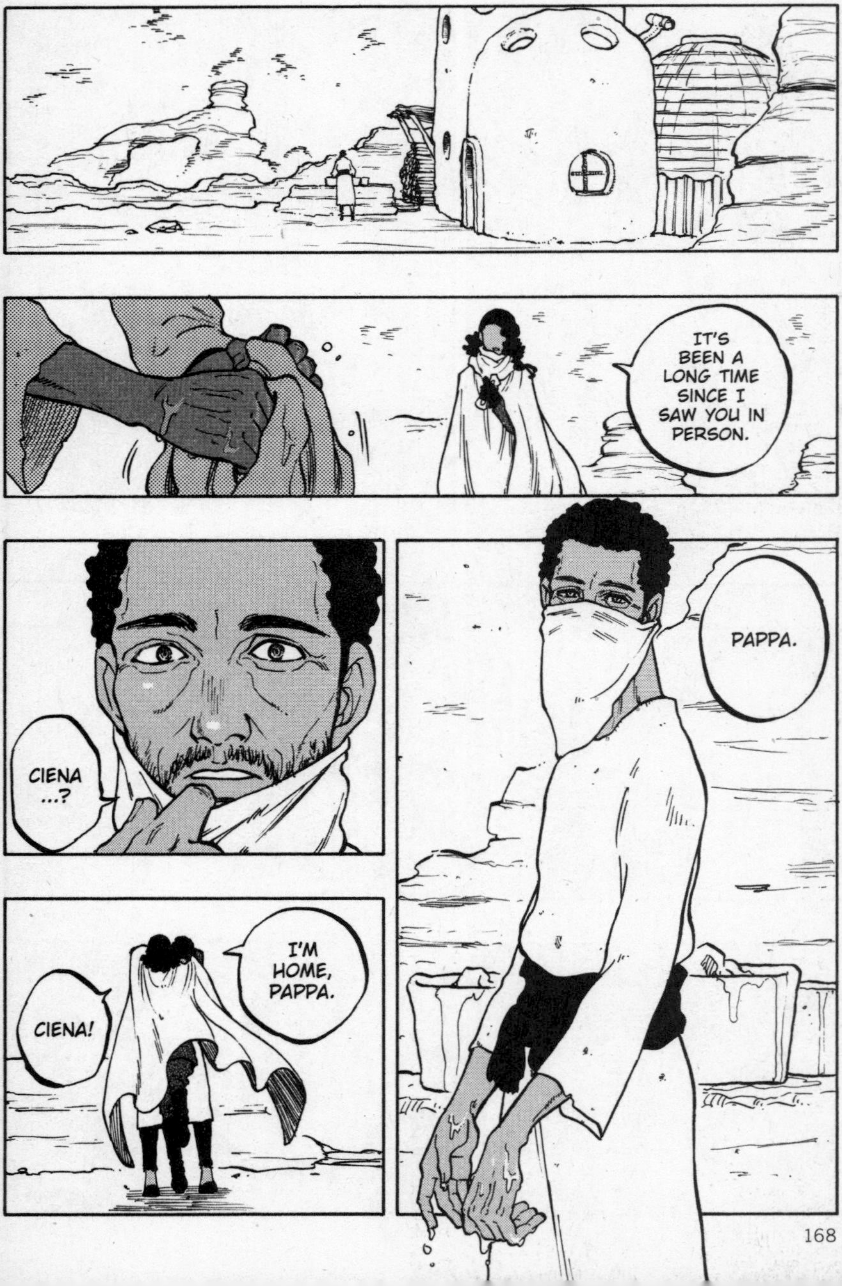
IT'S BEEN A LONG TIME SINCE I SAW YOU IN PERSON.
PAPPA.
CIENA ...?
I'M HOME, PAPPA.
CIENA!

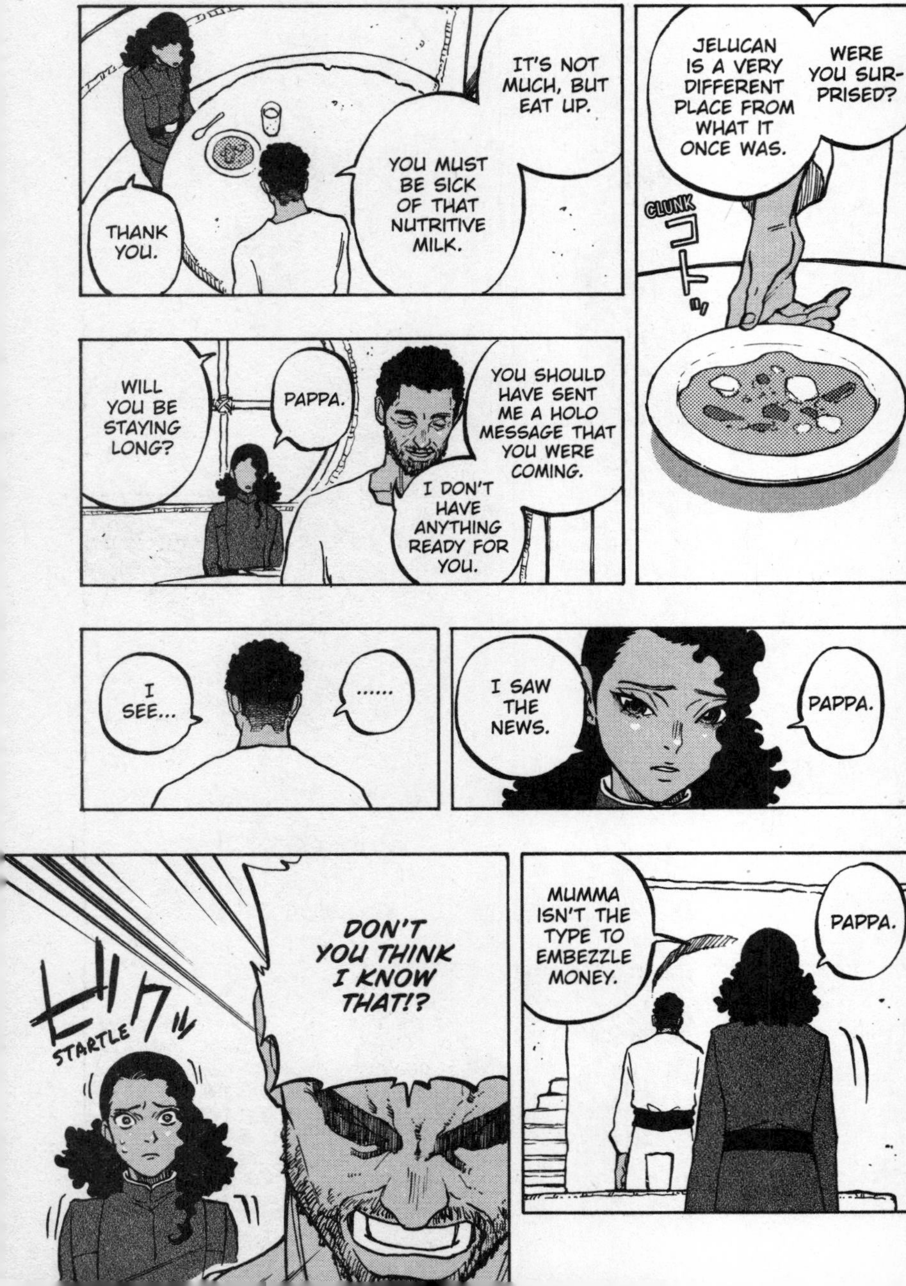
WERE YOU SURPRISED?
JELUCAN IS A VERY DIFFERENT PLACE FROM WHAT IT ONCE WAS.
CLUNK
IT'S NOT MUCH, BUT EAT UP.
YOU MUST BE SICK OF THAT NUTRITIVE MILK.
THANK YOU.
YOU SHOULD HAVE SENT ME A HOLO MESSAGE THAT YOU WERE COMING.
I DON'T HAVE ANYTHING READY FOR YOU.
PAPPA.
WILL YOU BE STAYING LONG?
PAPPA.
I SAW THE NEWS.
......
I SEE...
PAPPA.
MUMMA ISN'T THE TYPE TO EMBEZZLE MONEY.
DON'T YOU THINK I KNOW THAT!?
STARTLE

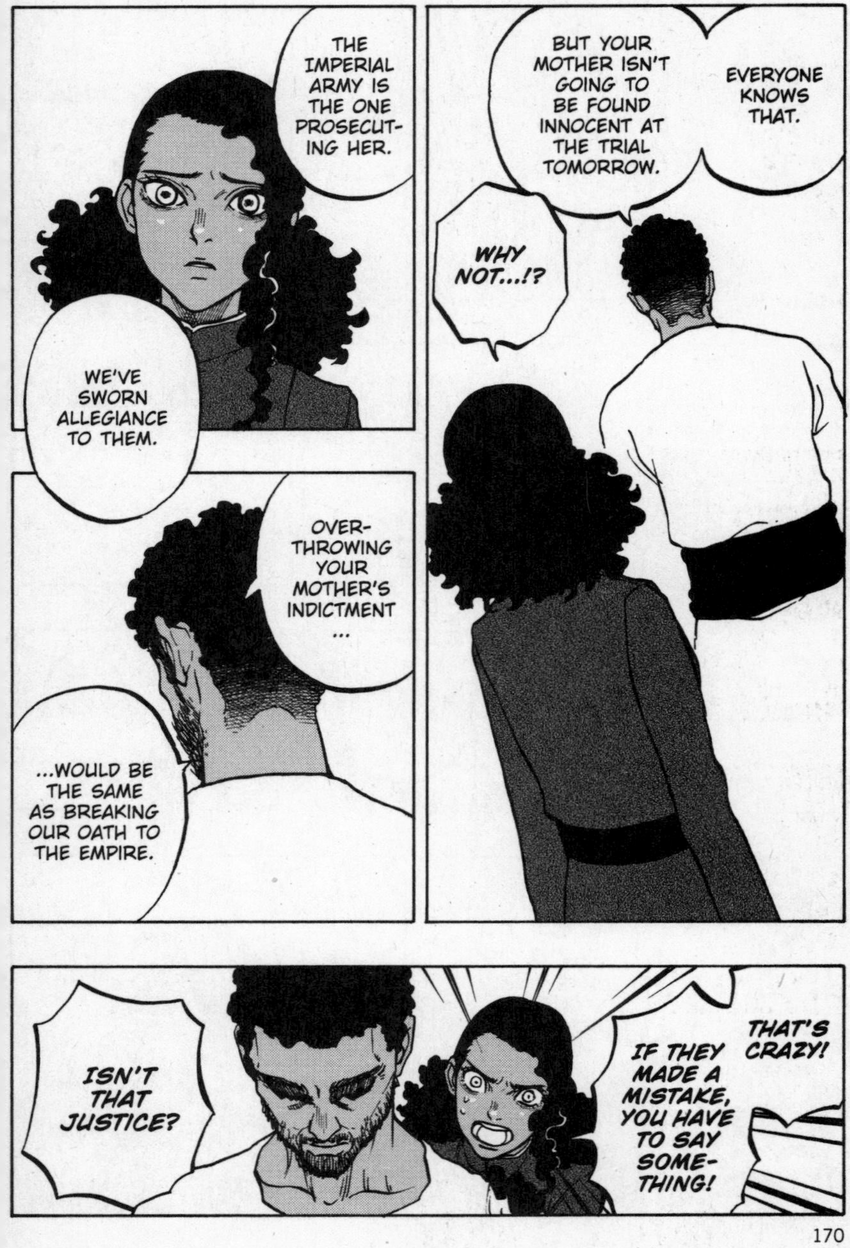
BUT YOUR MOTHER ISN'T GOING TO BE FOUND INNOCENT AT THE TRIAL TOMORROW.
EVERYONE KNOWS THAT.
WHY NOT...!?
THE IMPERIAL ARMY IS THE ONE PROSECUT-ING HER.
WE'VE SWORN ALLEGIANCE TO THEM.
OVER-THROWING YOUR MOTHER'S INDICTMENT ...
...WOULD BE THE SAME AS BREAKING OUR OATH TO THE EMPIRE.
THAT'S CRAZY!
IF THEY MADE A MISTAKE, YOU HAVE TO SAY SOME-THING!
ISN'T THAT JUSTICE?

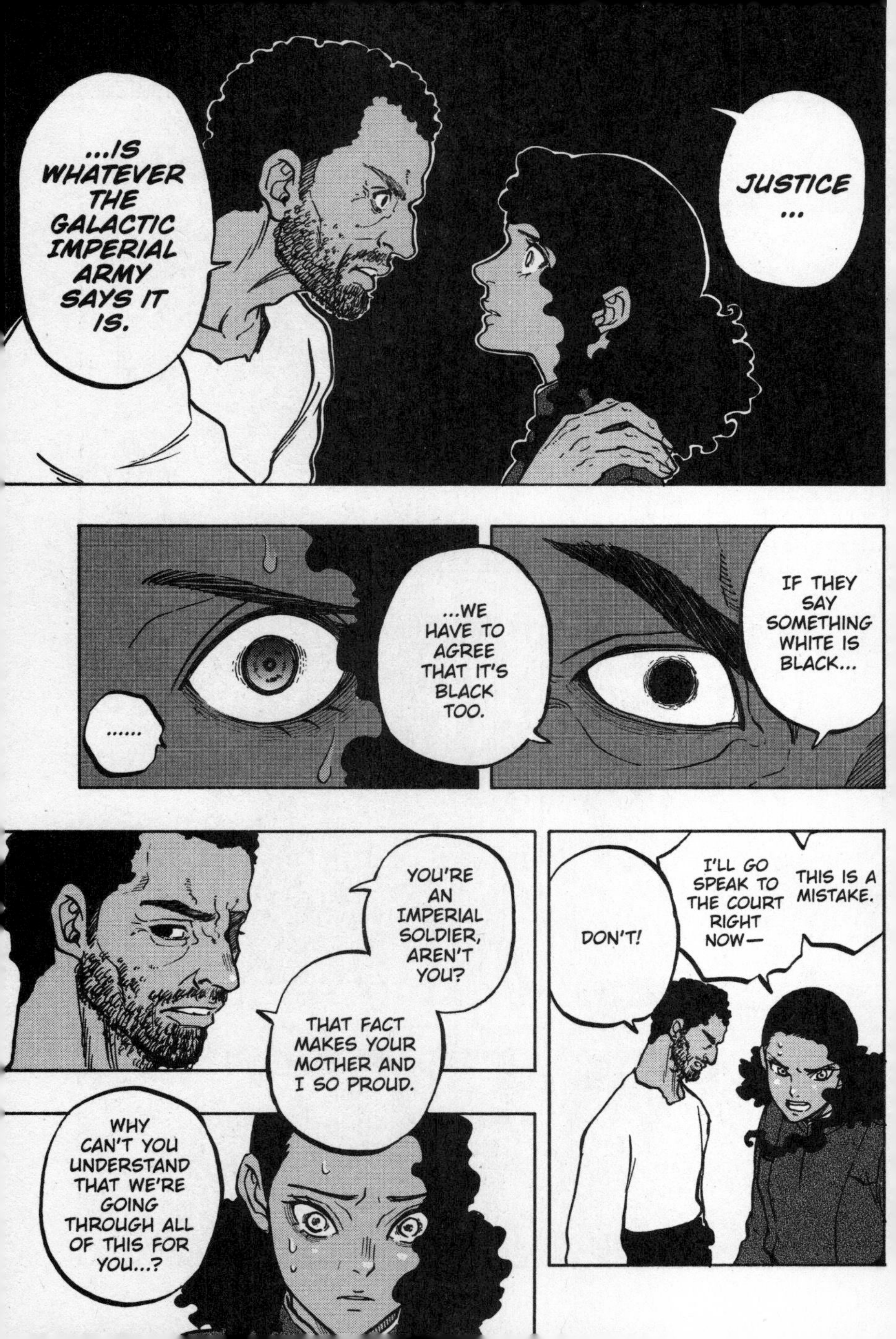
JUSTICE ...
...IS WHATEVER THE GALACTIC IMPERIAL ARMY SAYS IT IS.
IF THEY SAY SOMETHING WHITE IS BLACK...
...WE HAVE TO AGREE THAT IT'S BLACK TOO.
......
THIS IS A MISTAKE.
I'LL GO SPEAK TO THE COURT RIGHT NOW—
DON'T!
YOU'RE AN IMPERIAL SOLDIER, AREN'T YOU?
THAT FACT MAKES YOUR MOTHER AND I SO PROUD.
WHY CAN'T YOU UNDERSTAND THAT WE'RE GOING THROUGH ALL OF THIS FOR YOU...?

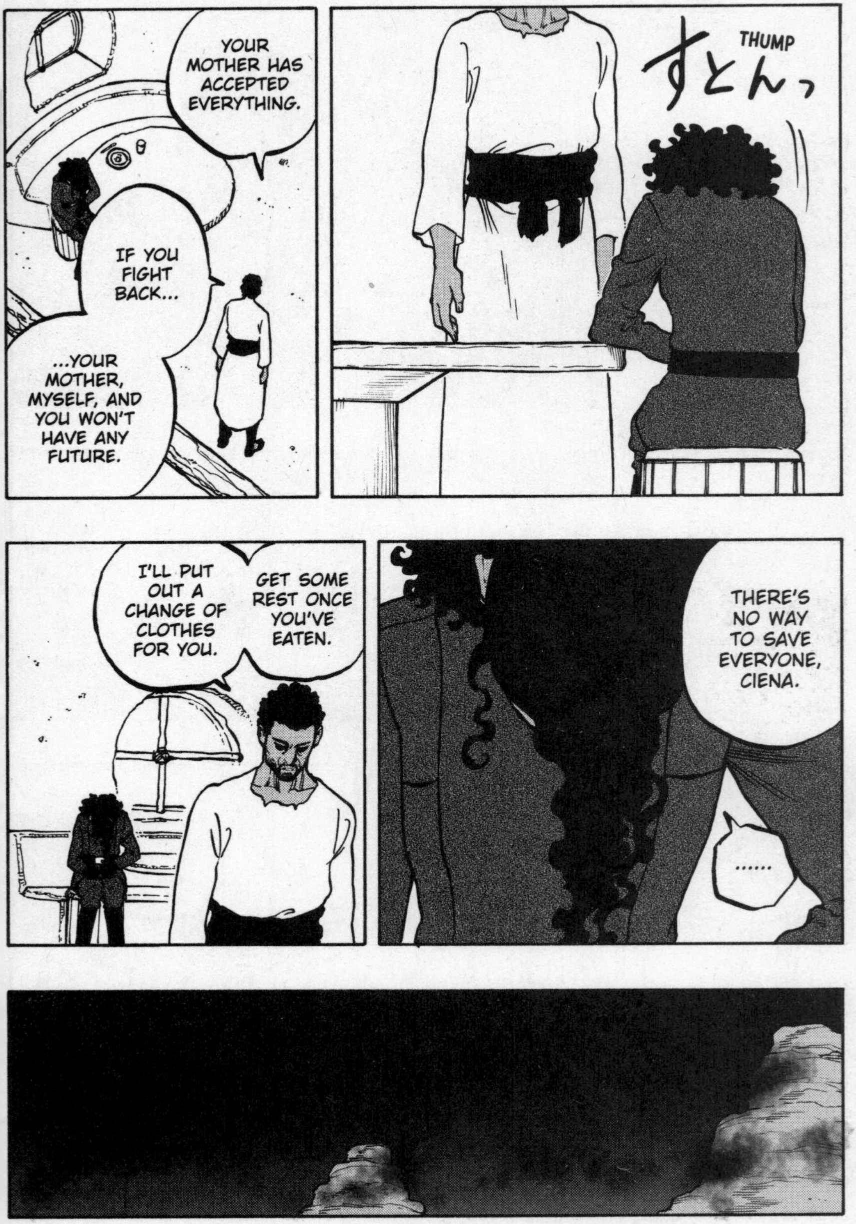

THUMP
すとんっ
YOUR MOTHER HAS ACCEPTED EVERYTHING.
IF YOU FIGHT BACK...
...YOUR MOTHER, MYSELF, AND YOU WON'T HAVE ANY FUTURE.
THERE'S NO WAY TO SAVE EVERYONE, CIENA.
......
GET SOME REST ONCE YOU'VE EATEN.
I'LL PUT OUT A CHANGE OF CLOTHES FOR YOU.

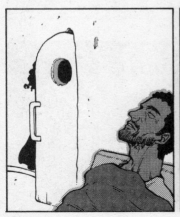

PAPPA.

HE'S LOST WEIGHT ...

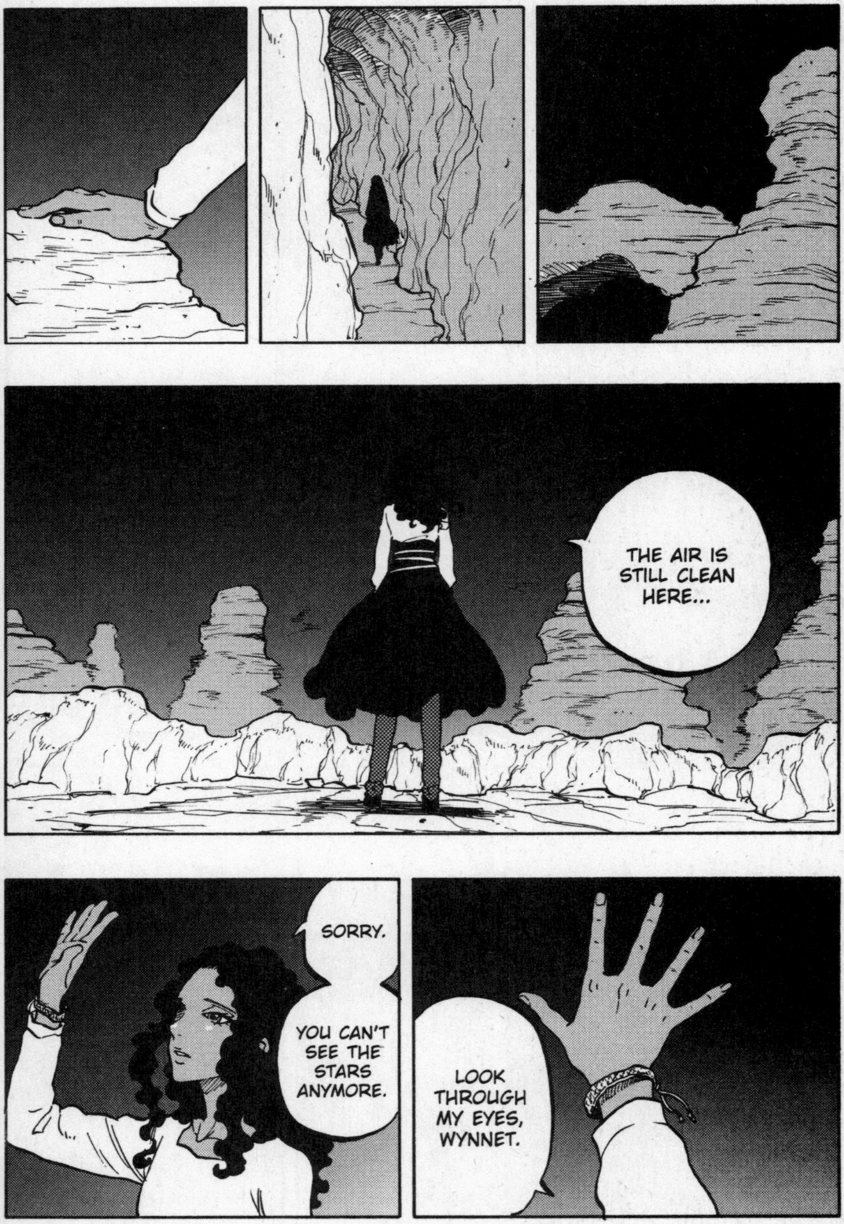
THE AIR IS STILL CLEAN HERE...
LOOK THROUGH MY EYES, WYNNET.
SORRY.
YOU CAN'T SEE THE STARS ANYMORE.

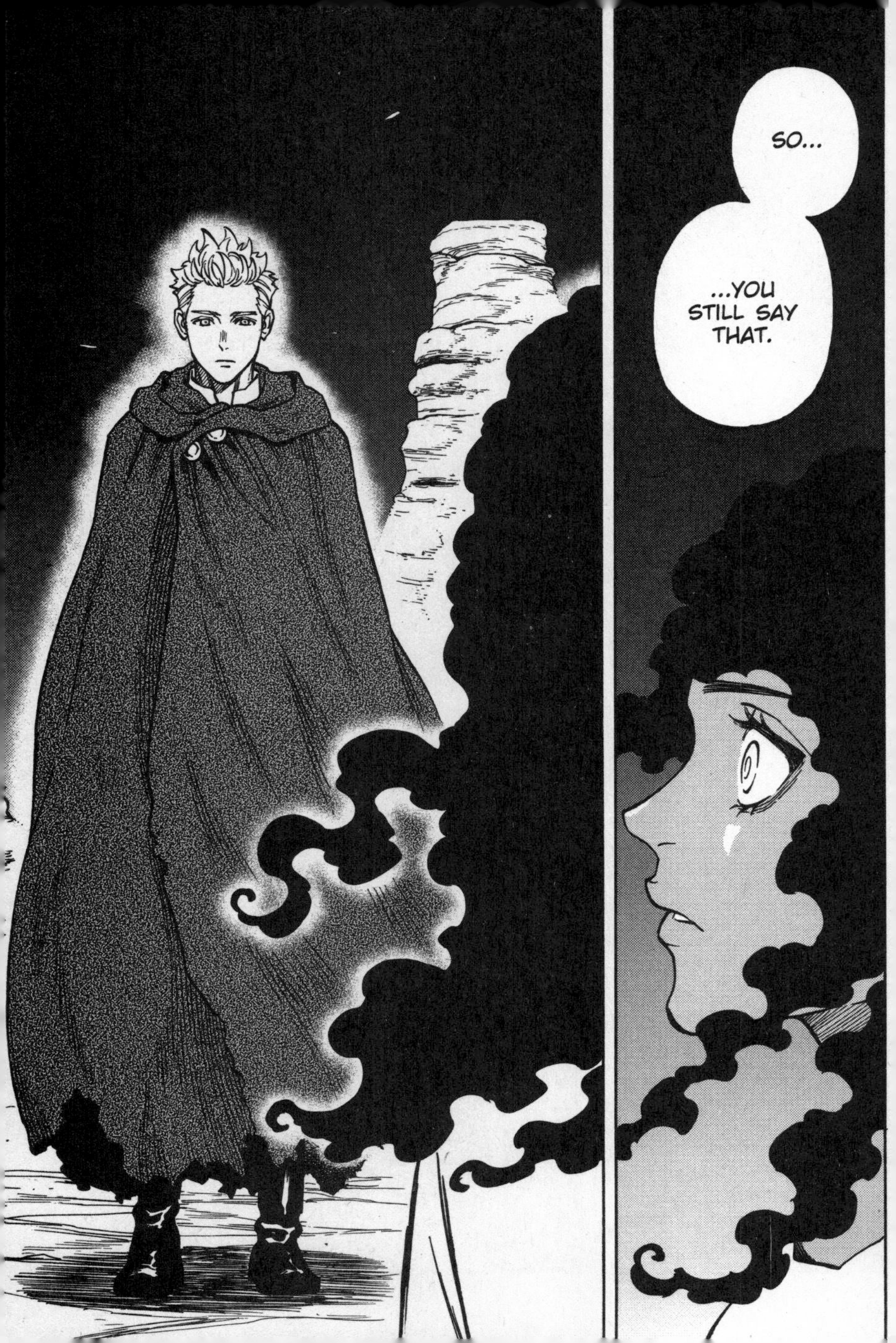
SO...
...YOU STILL SAY THAT.

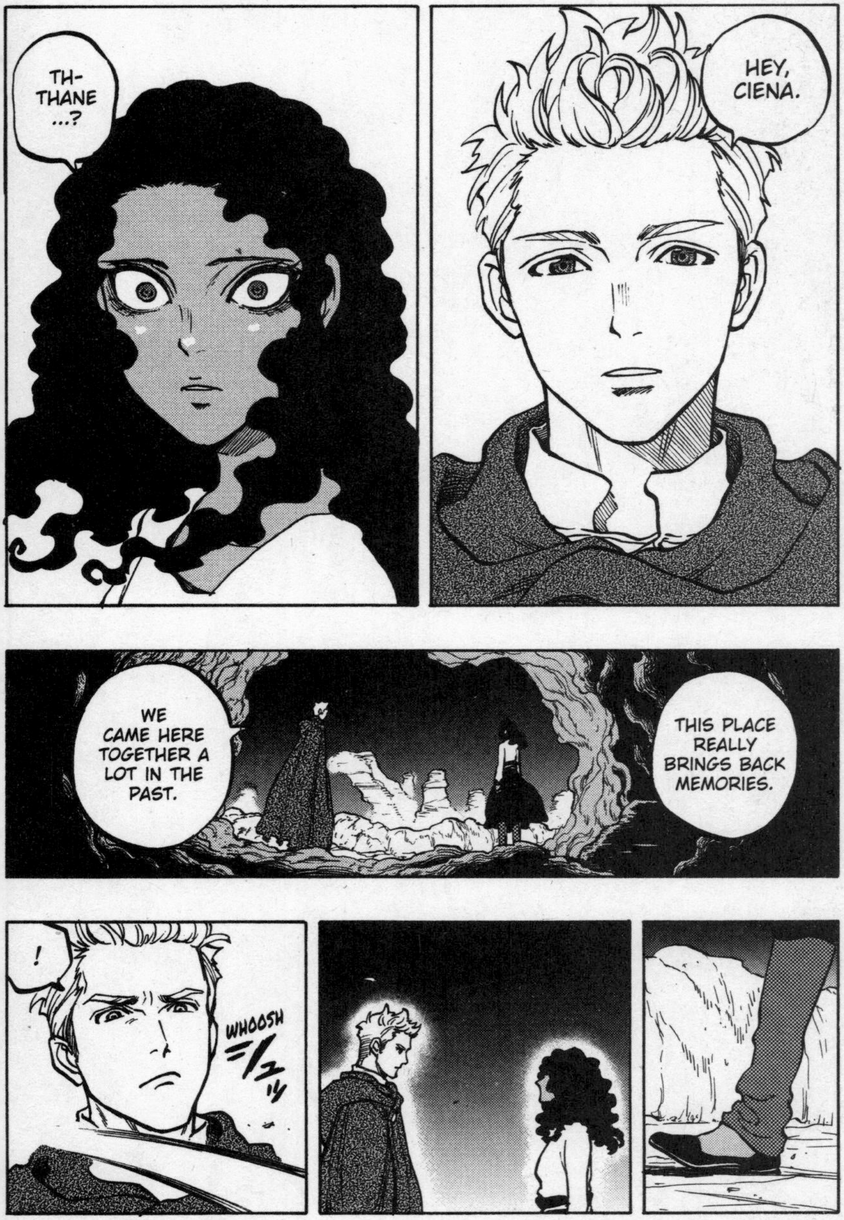
HEY, CIENA.
TH- THANE ...?
THIS PLACE REALLY BRINGS BACK MEMORIES.
WE CAME HERE TOGETHER A LOT IN THE PAST.
!
WHOOSH

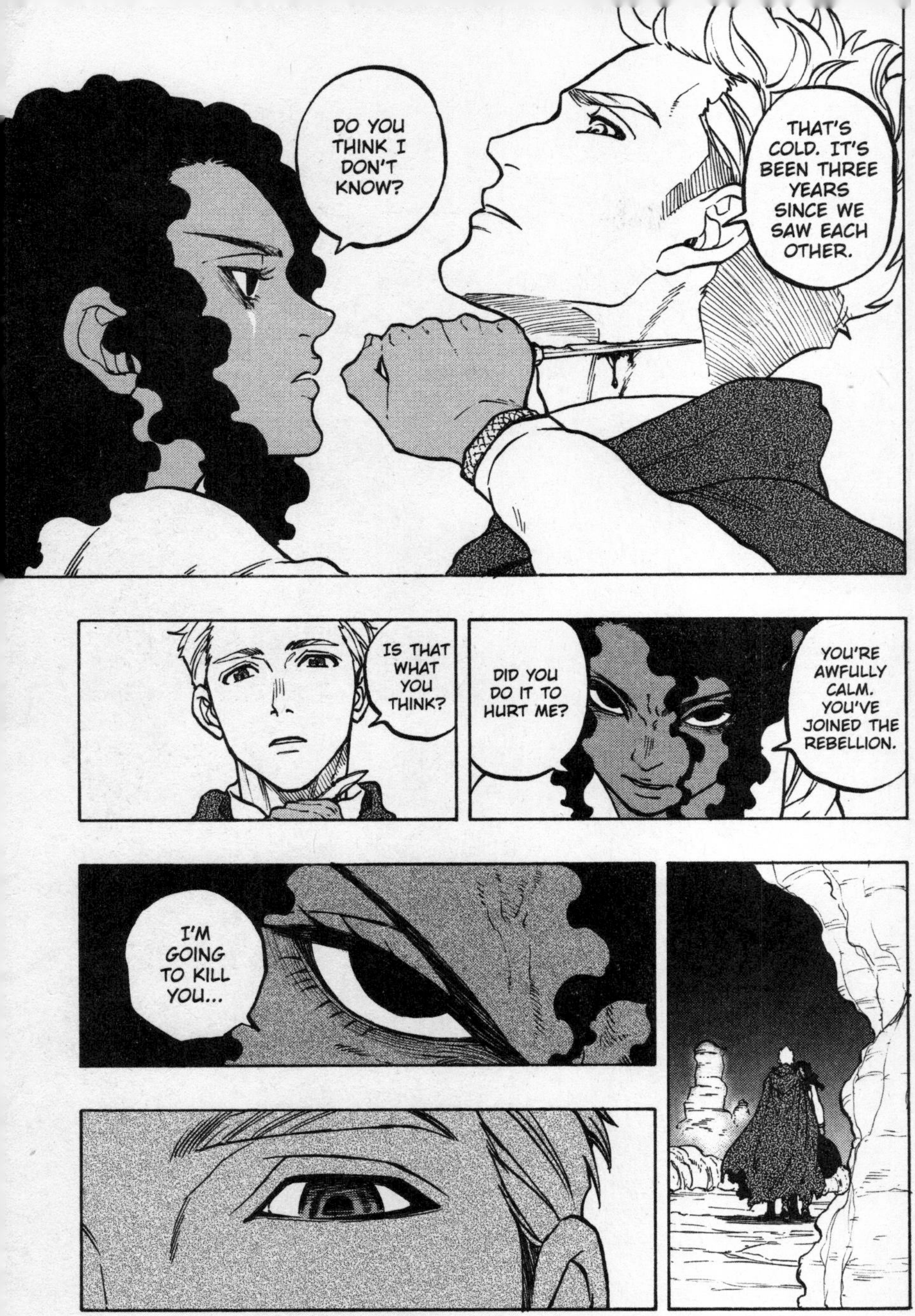
THAT'S COLD. IT'S BEEN THREE YEARS SINCE WE SAW EACH OTHER.
DO YOU THINK I DON'T KNOW?
YOU'RE AWFULLY CALM. YOU'VE JOINED THE REBELLION.
DID YOU DO IT TO HURT ME?
IS THAT WHAT YOU THINK?
I'M GOING TO KILL YOU...

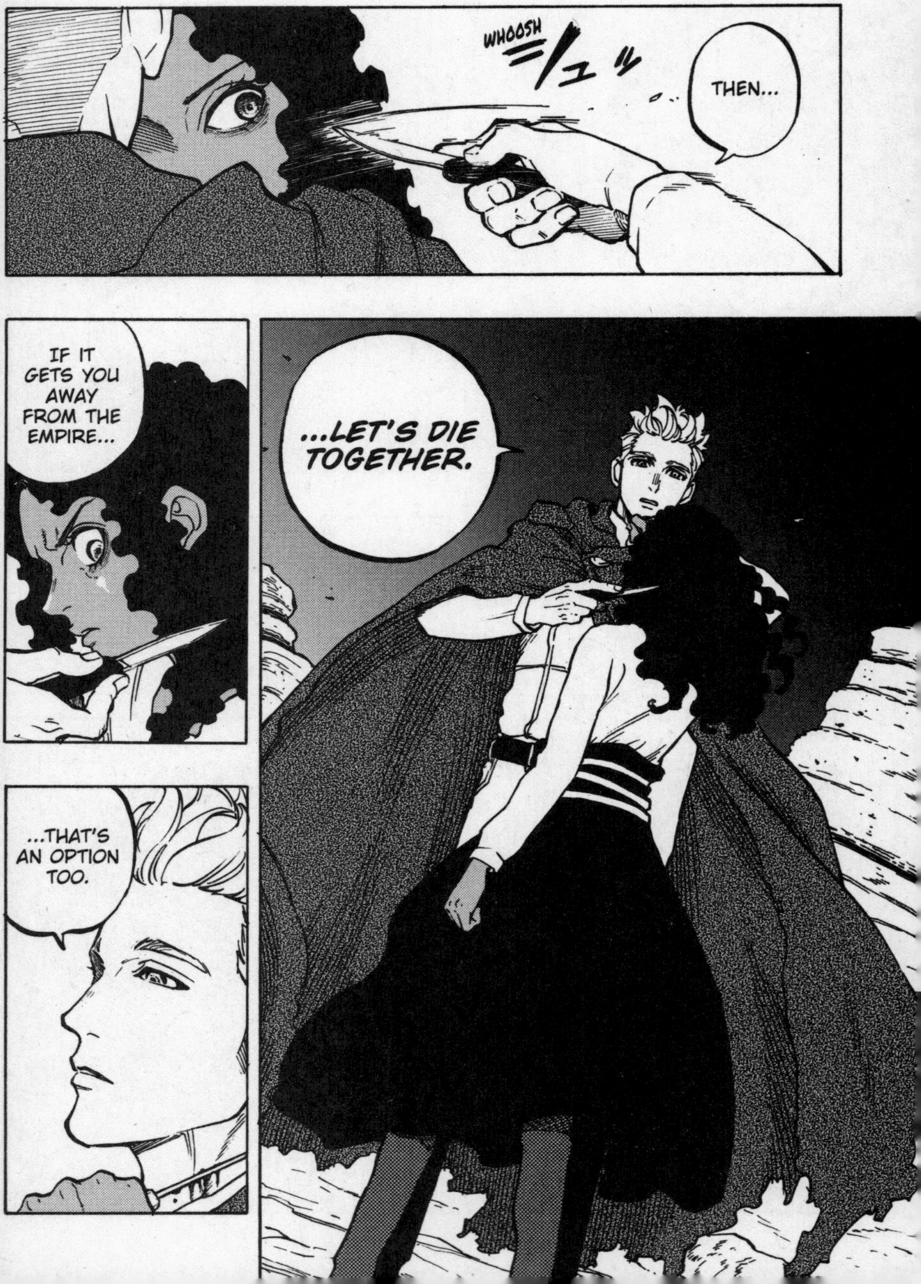
WHOOSH
THEN...
...LET'S DIE TOGETHER.
IF IT GETS YOU AWAY FROM THE EMPIRE...
...THAT'S AN OPTION TOO.

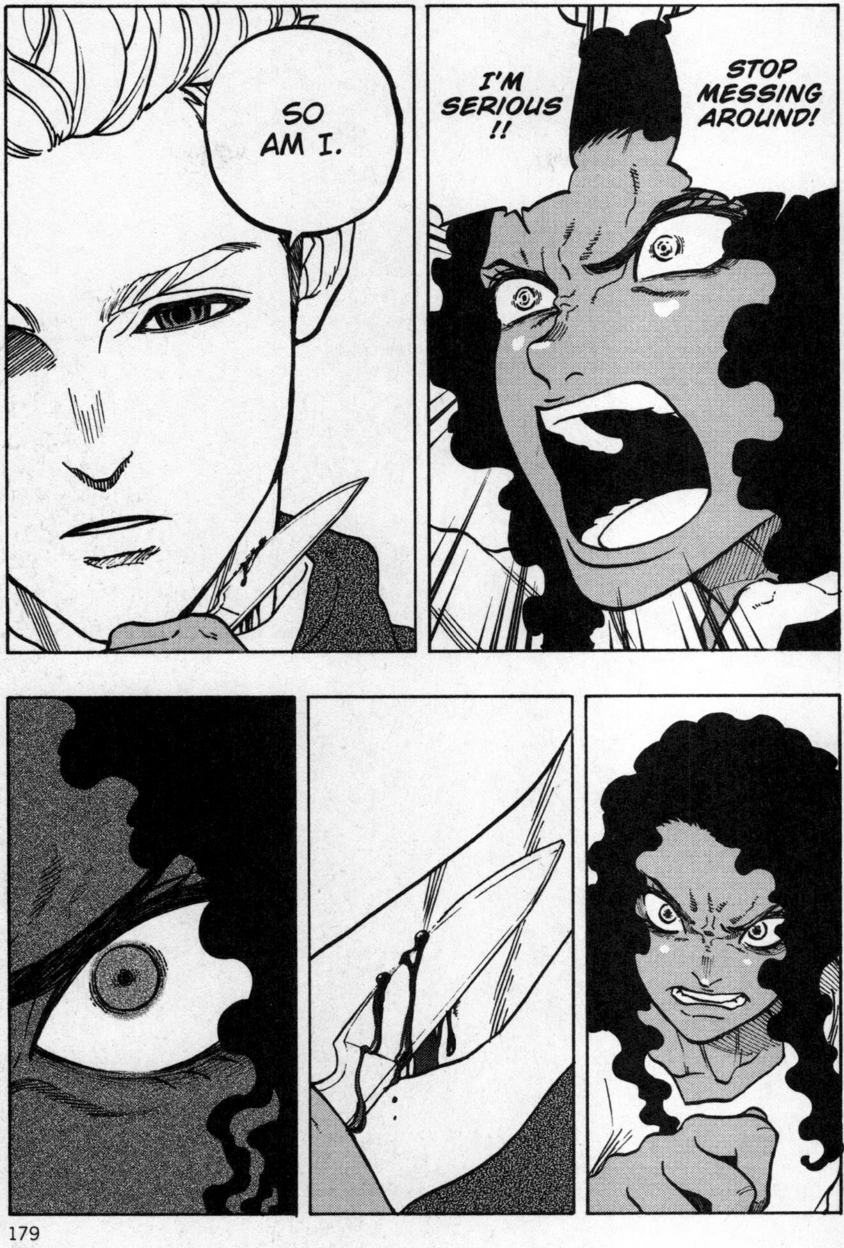
STOP MESSING AROUND!
I'M SERIOUS !!
SO AM I.

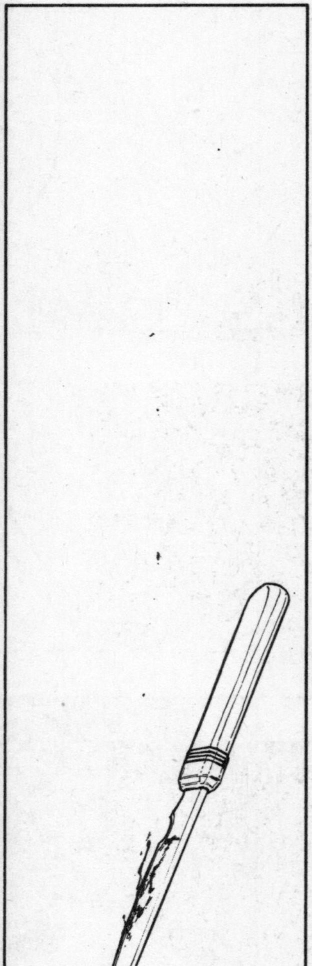
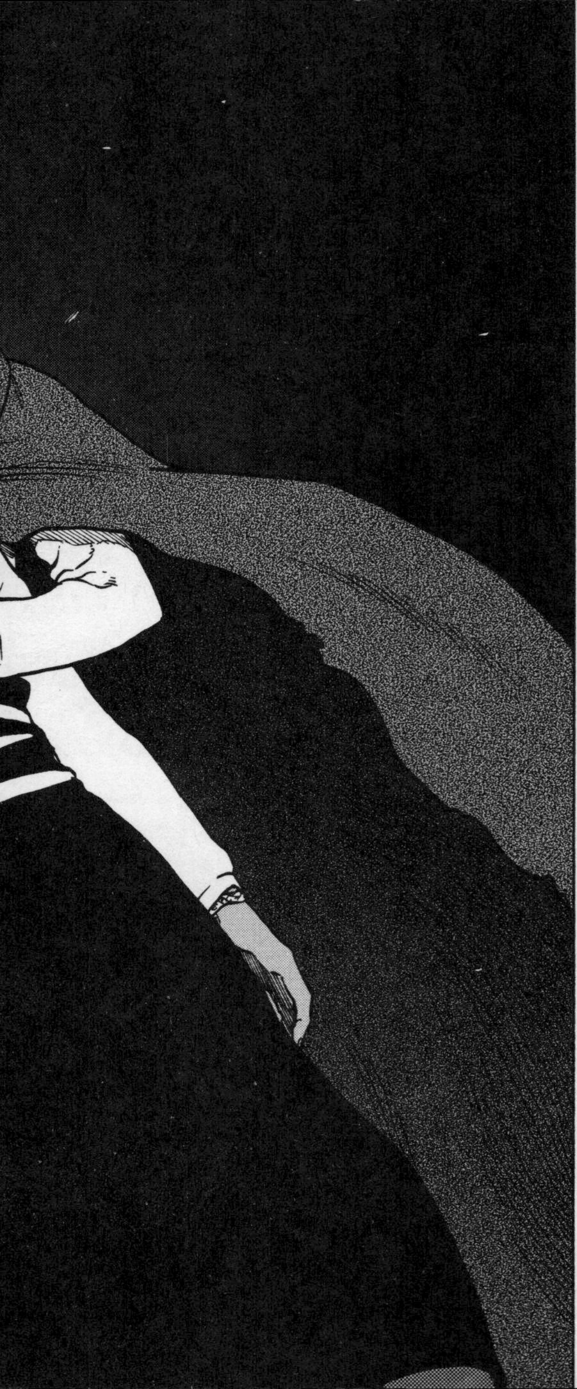

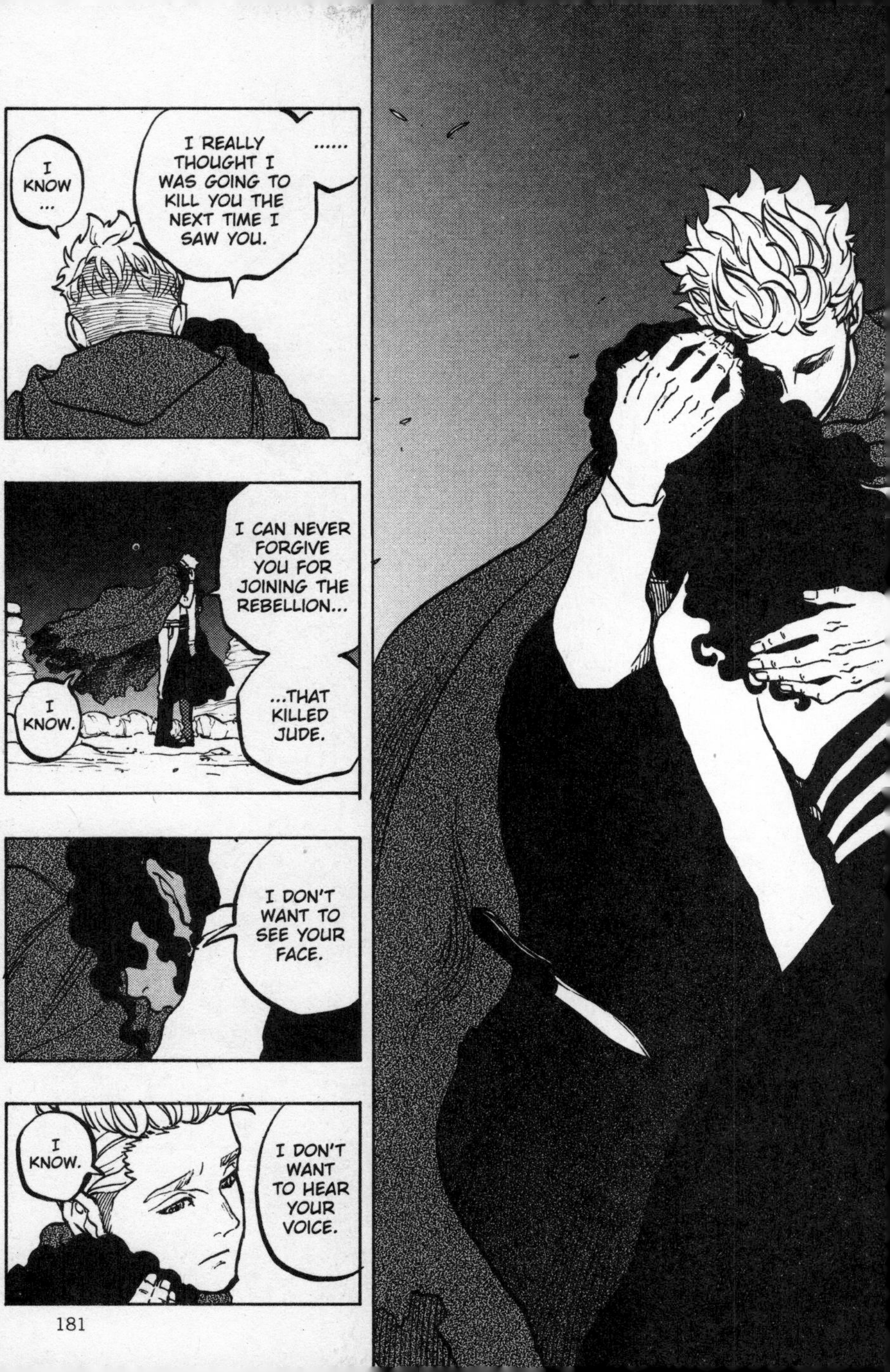
......
I REALLY THOUGHT I WAS GOING TO KILL YOU THE NEXT TIME I SAW YOU.
I KNOW ...
I CAN NEVER FORGIVE YOU FOR JOINING THE REBELLION...
...THAT KILLED JUDE.
I KNOW.
I DON'T WANT TO SEE YOUR FACE.
I DON'T WANT TO HEAR YOUR VOICE.
I KNOW.

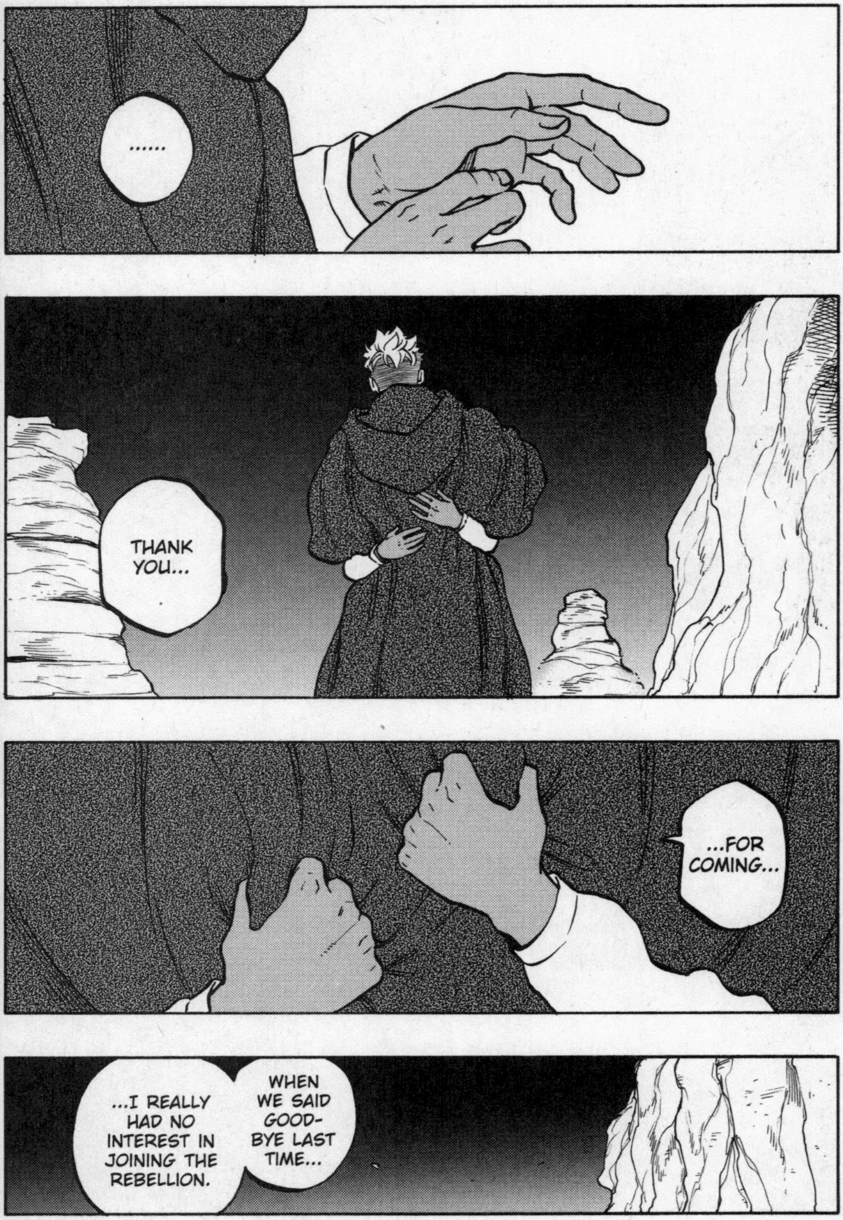
......
THANK YOU...
...FOR COMING...
WHEN WE SAID GOOD-BYE LAST TIME...
...I REALLY HAD NO INTEREST IN JOINING THE REBELLION.

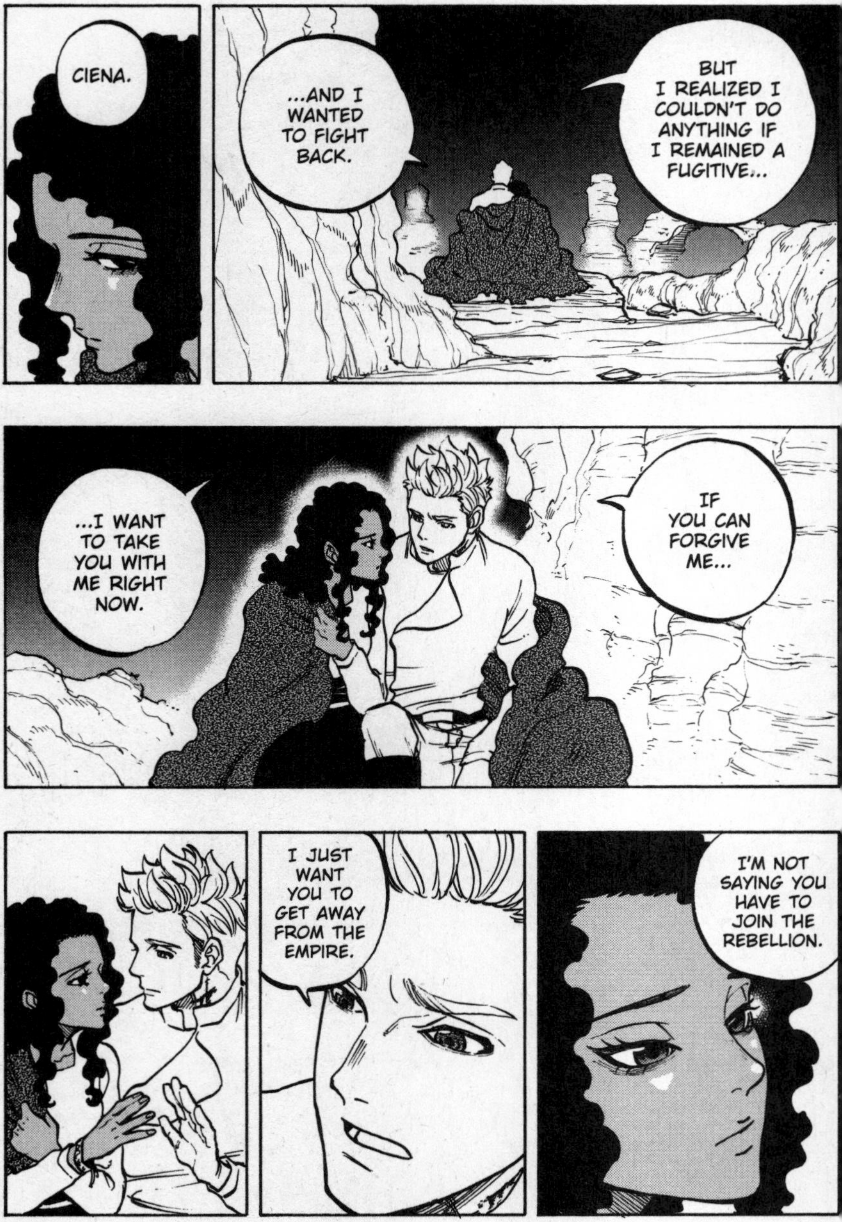
BUT I REALIZED I COULDN'T DO ANYTHING IF I REMAINED A FUGITIVE...
...AND I WANTED TO FIGHT BACK.
CIENA.
IF YOU CAN FORGIVE ME...
...I WANT TO TAKE YOU WITH ME RIGHT NOW.
I'M NOT SAYING YOU HAVE TO JOIN THE REBELLION.
I JUST WANT YOU TO GET AWAY FROM THE EMPIRE.

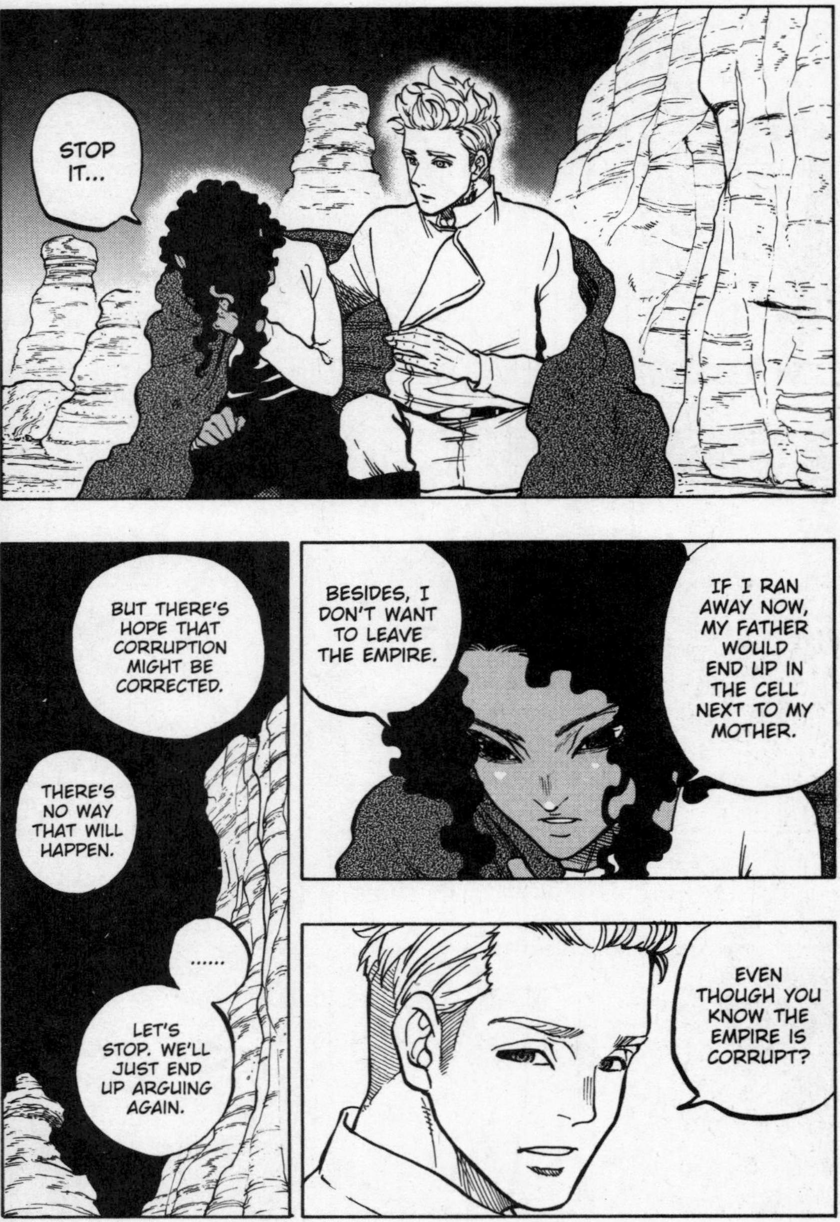
STOP IT...
IF I RAN AWAY NOW, MY FATHER WOULD END UP IN THE CELL NEXT TO MY MOTHER.
BESIDES, I DON'T WANT TO LEAVE THE EMPIRE.
EVEN THOUGH YOU KNOW THE EMPIRE IS CORRUPT?
BUT THERE'S HOPE THAT CORRUPTION MIGHT BE CORRECTED.
THERE'S NO WAY THAT WILL HAPPEN.
......
LET'S STOP. WE'LL JUST END UP ARGUING AGAIN.

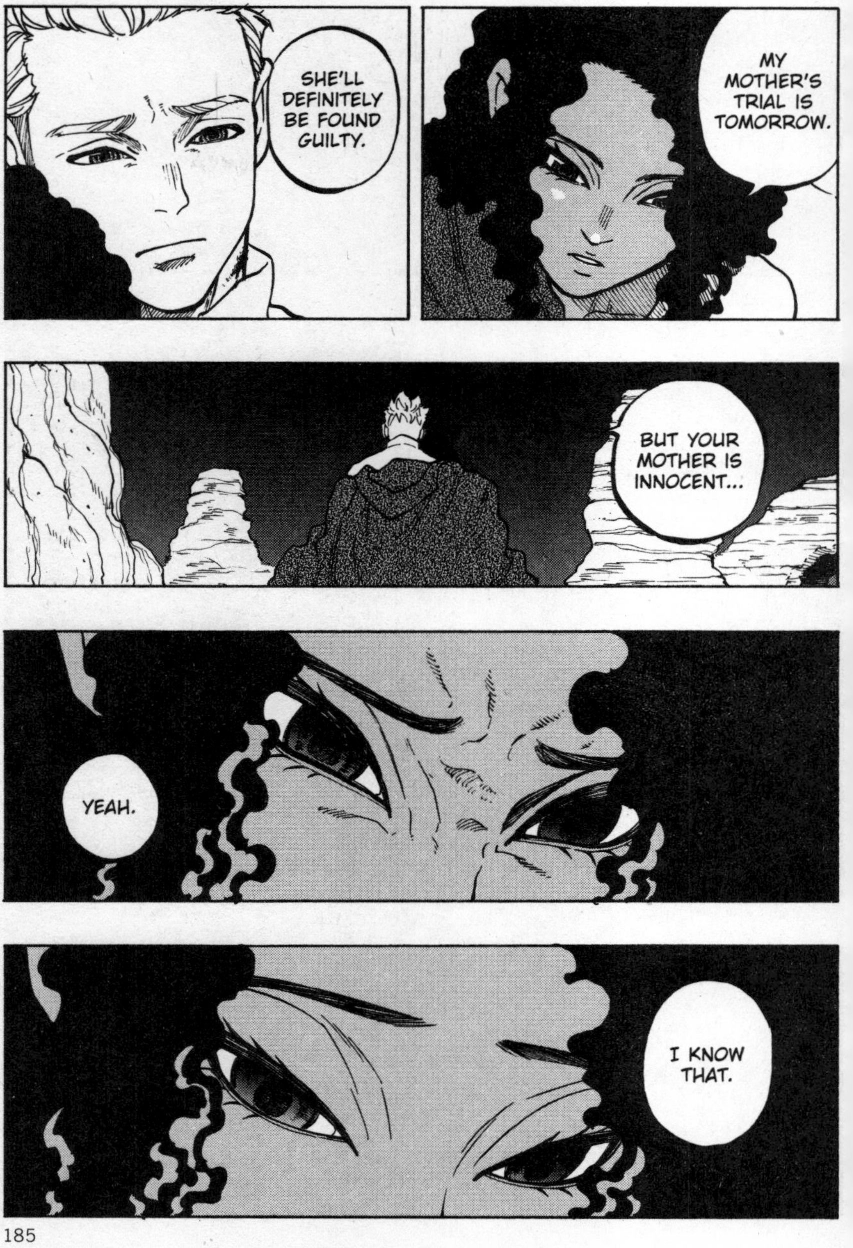
MY MOTHER'S TRIAL IS TOMORROW.
SHE'LL DEFINITELY BE FOUND GUILTY.
BUT YOUR MOTHER IS INNOCENT...
YEAH.
I KNOW THAT.

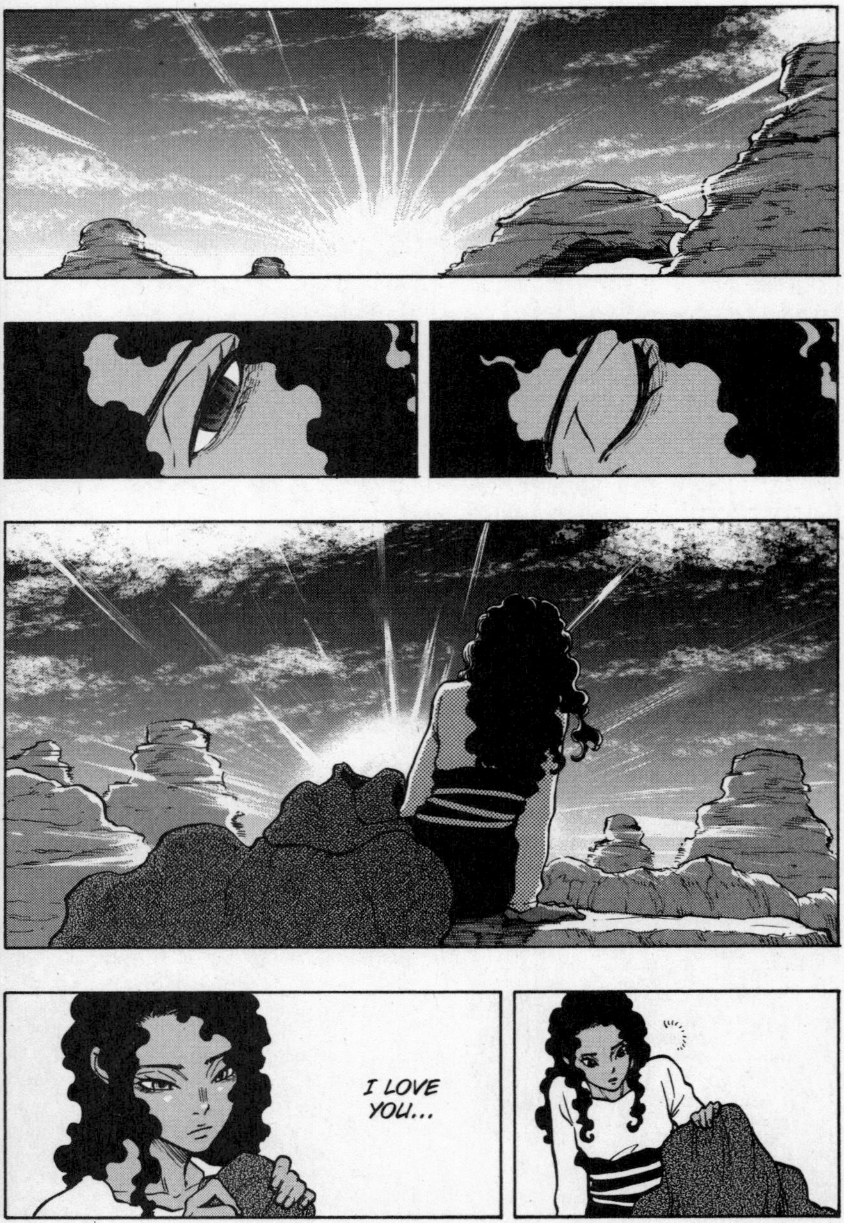
I LOVE YOU...

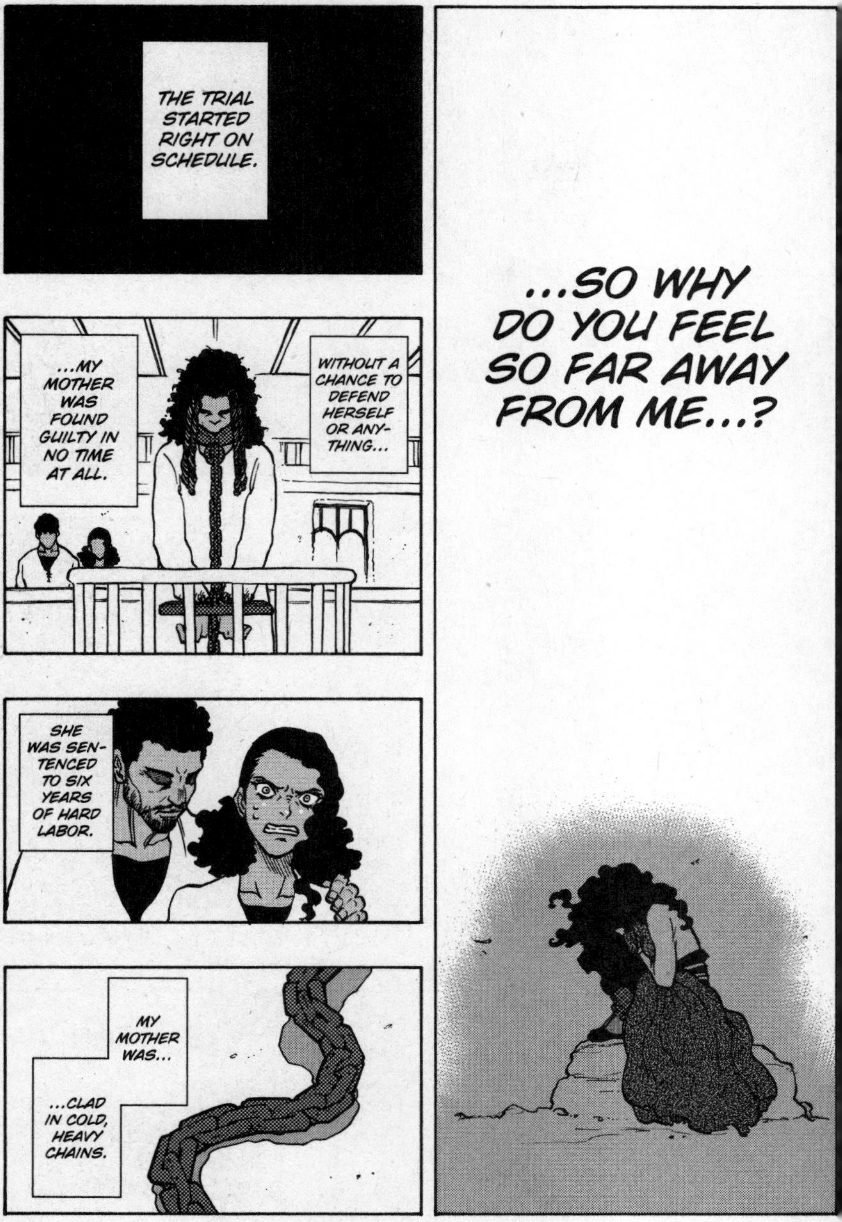
...SO WHY DO YOU FEEL SO FAR AWAY FROM ME...?
THE TRIAL STARTED RIGHT ON SCHEDULE.
WITHOUT A CHANCE TO DEFEND HERSELF OR ANY-THING...
...MY MOTHER WAS FOUND GUILTY IN NO TIME AT ALL.
SHE WAS SEN-TENCED TO SIX YEARS OF HARD LABOR.
MY MOTHER WAS...
...CLAD IN COLD, HEAVY CHAINS.

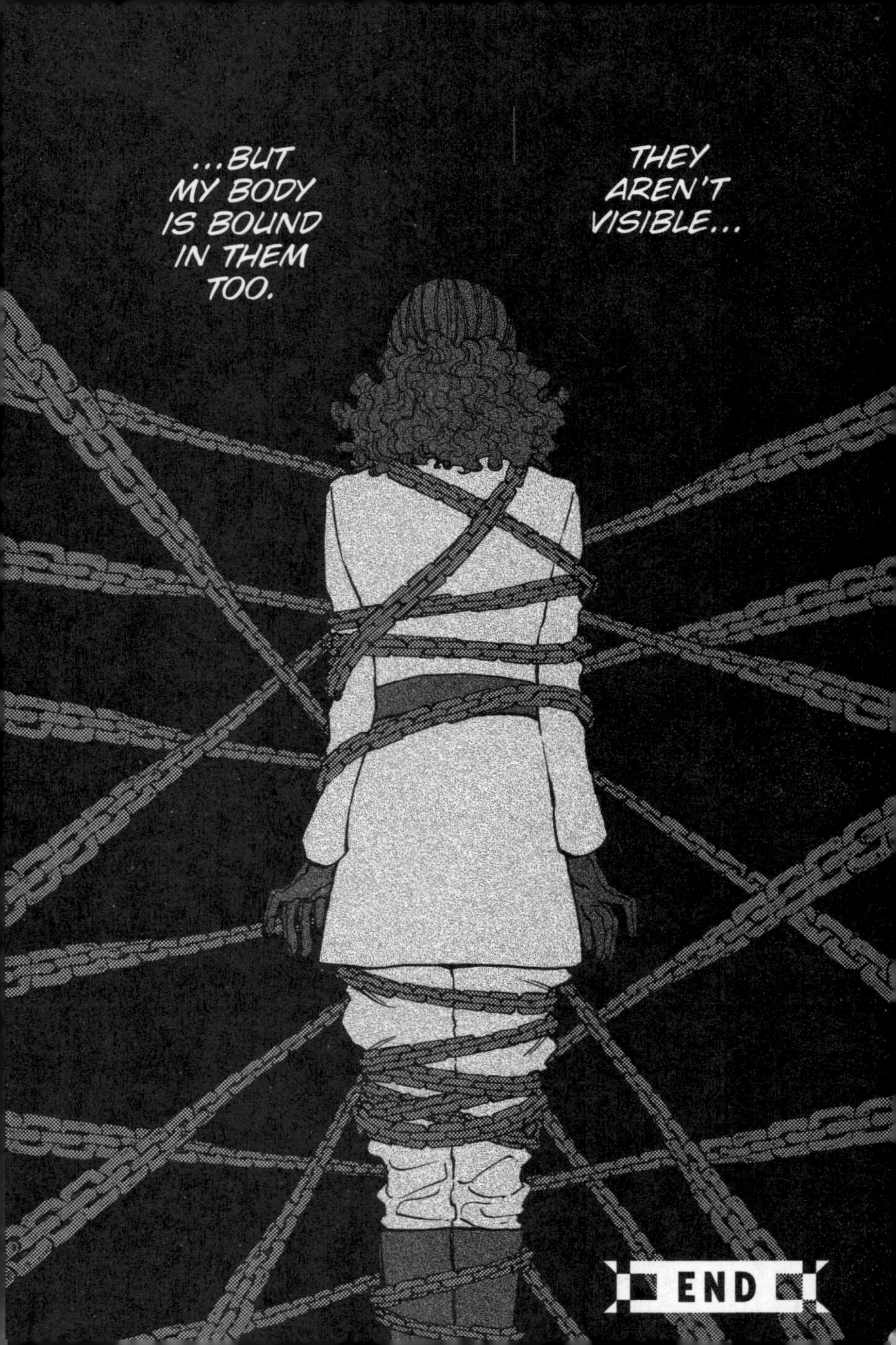
THEY AREN'T VISIBLE...
...BUT MY BODY IS BOUND IN THEM TOO.
END

STAR WARS
LOST STARS

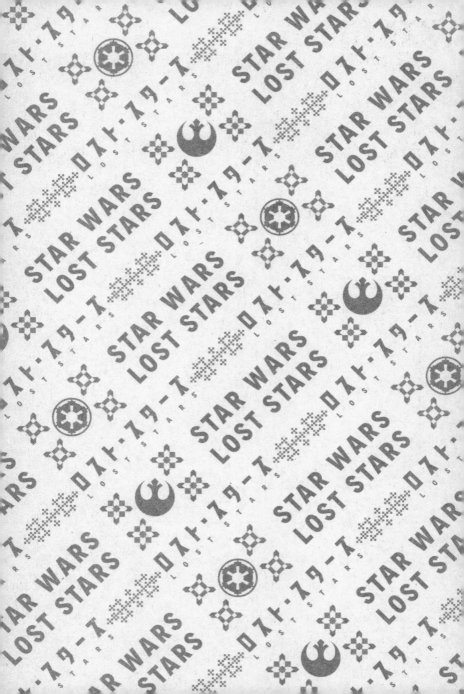

Chapter. 12

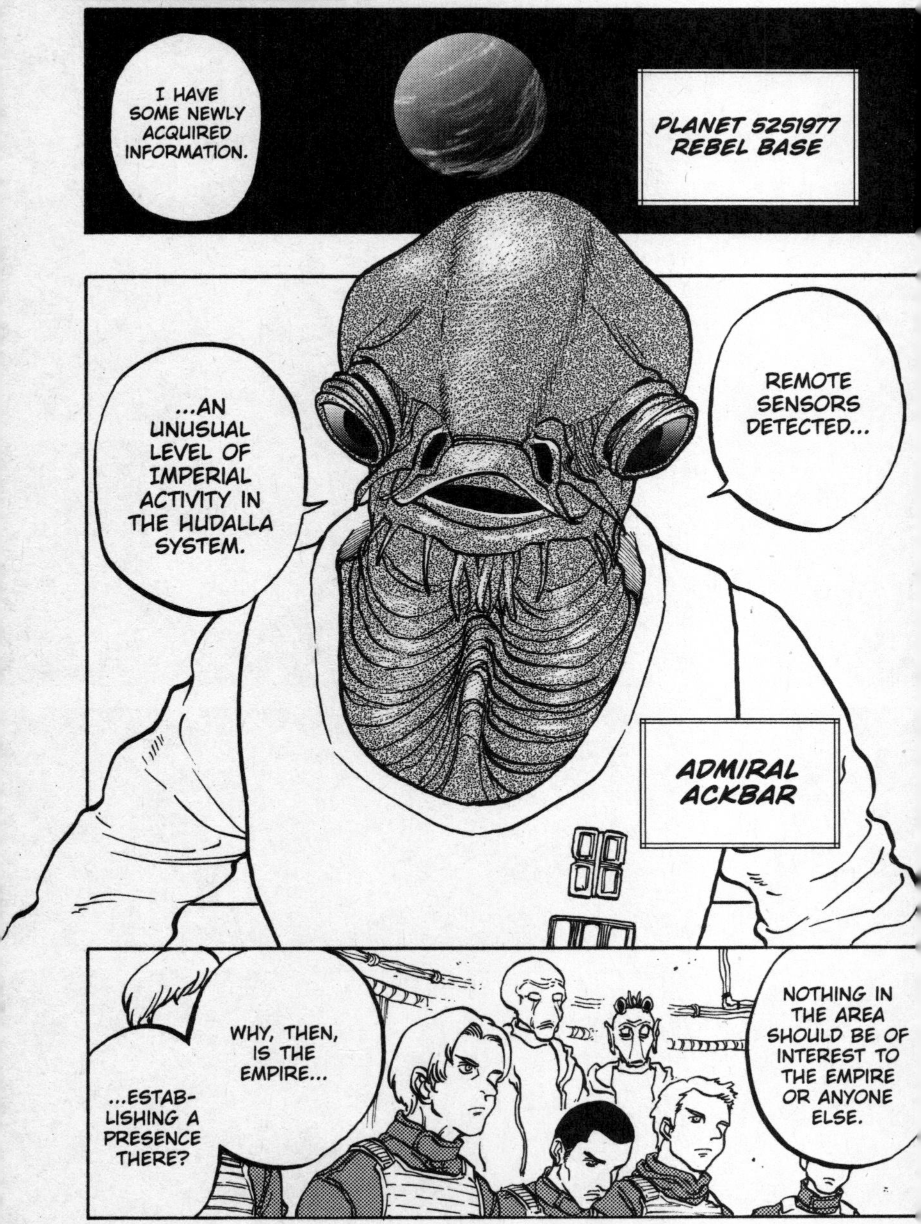

PLANET 5251977 REBEL BASE
I HAVE SOME NEWLY ACQUIRED INFORMATION.
REMOTE SENSORS DETECTED...
...AN UNUSUAL LEVEL OF IMPERIAL ACTIVITY IN THE HUDALLA SYSTEM.
ADMIRAL ACKBAR
NOTHING IN THE AREA SHOULD BE OF INTEREST TO THE EMPIRE OR ANYONE ELSE.
WHY, THEN, IS THE EMPIRE...
...ESTAB-LISHING A PRESENCE THERE?

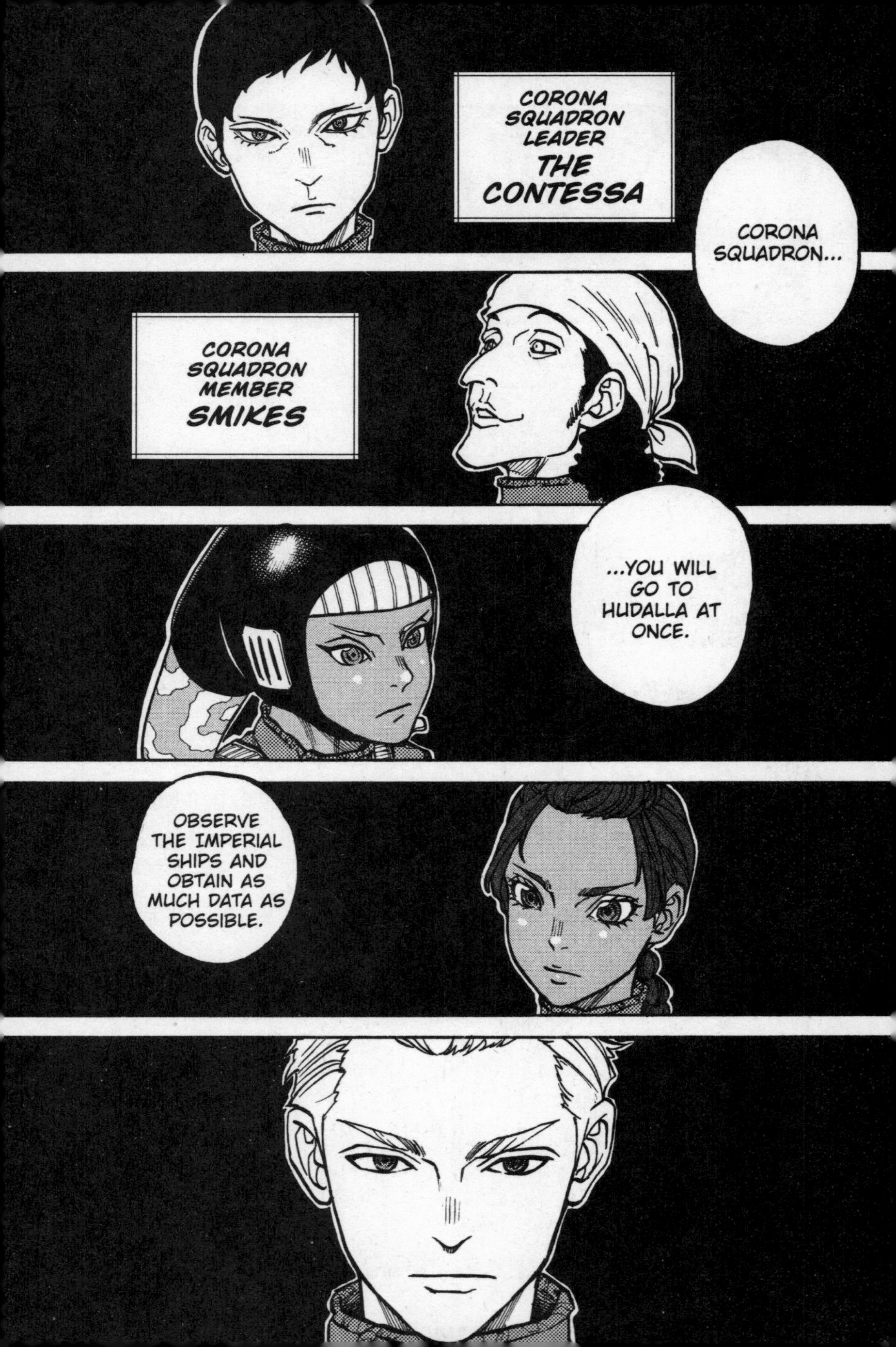

CORONA SQUADRON LEADER THE CONTESSA
CORONA SQUADRON...
CORONA SQUADRON MEMBER SMIKES
...YOU WILL GO TO HUDALLA AT ONCE.
OBSERVE THE IMPERIAL SHIPS AND OBTAIN AS MUCH DATA AS POSSIBLE.

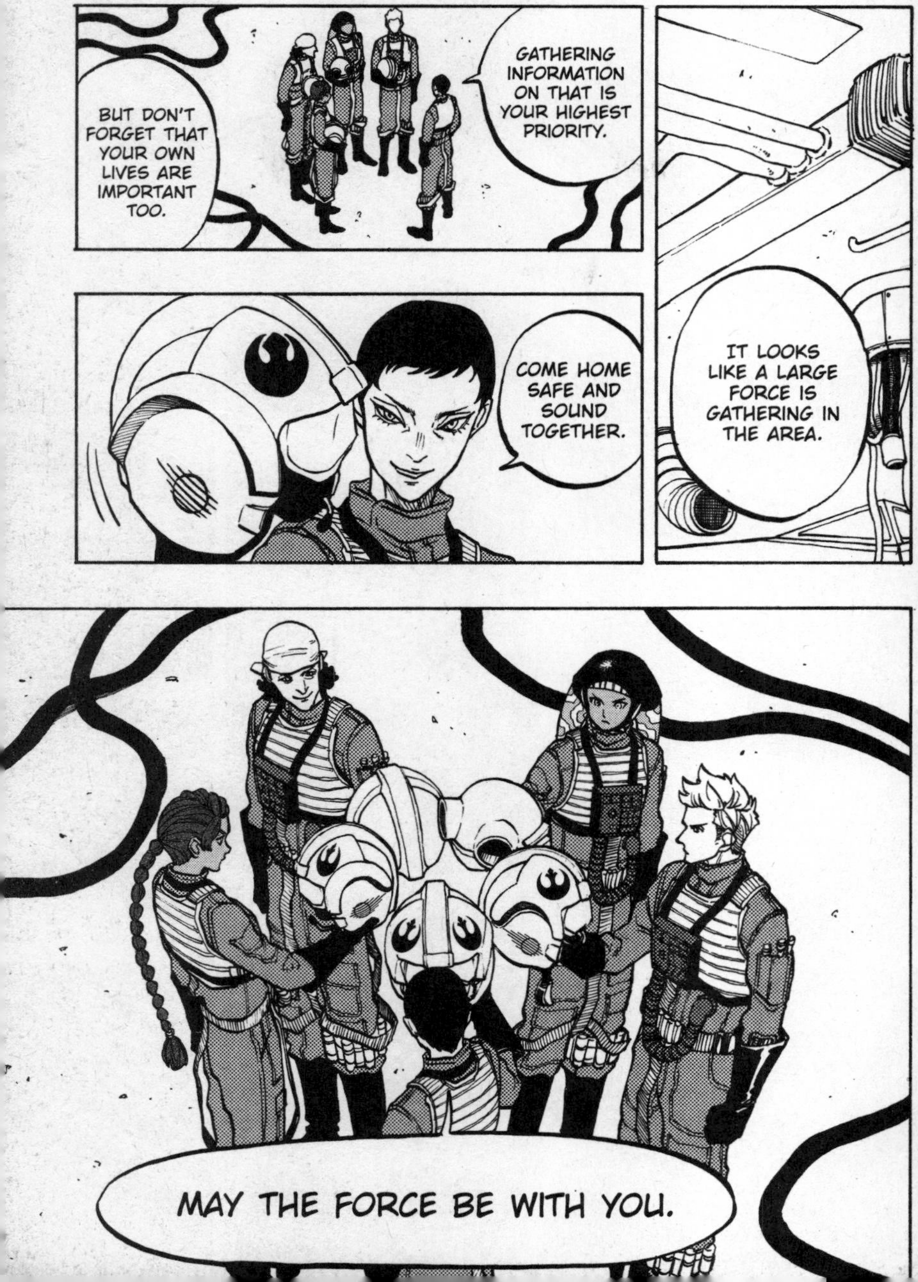
IT LOOKS LIKE A LARGE FORCE IS GATHERING IN THE AREA.
GATHERING INFORMATION ON THAT IS YOUR HIGHEST PRIORITY.
BUT DON'T FORGET THAT YOUR OWN LIVES ARE IMPORTANT TOO.
COME HOME SAFE AND SOUND TOGETHER.
MAY THE FORCE BE WITH YOU.

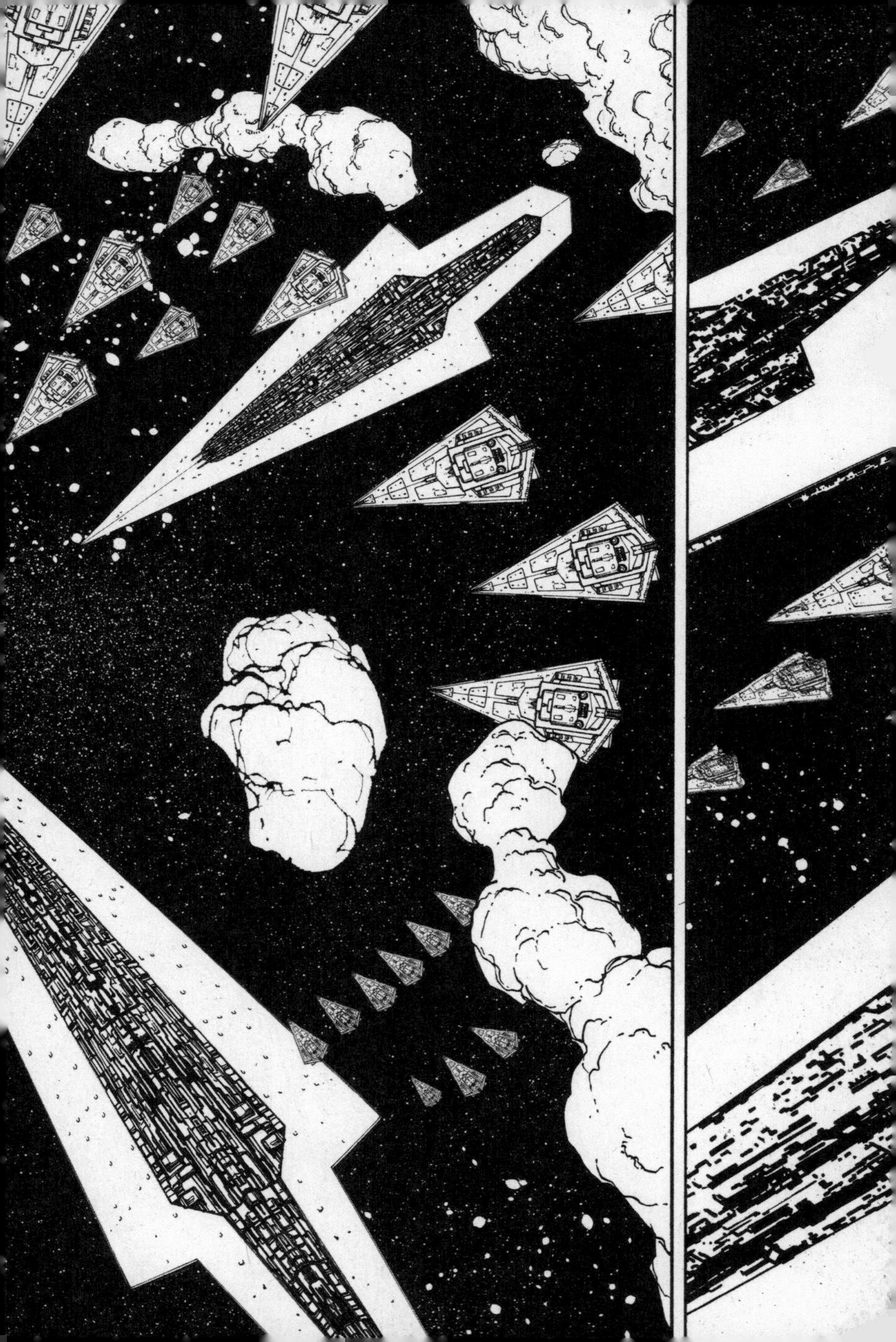

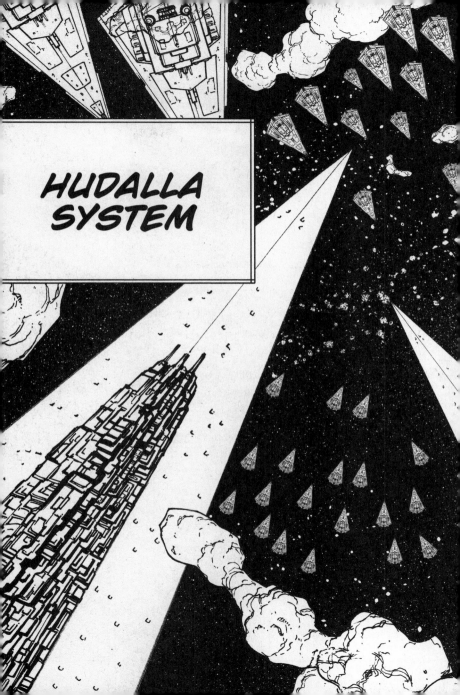

HUDALLA
SYSTEM

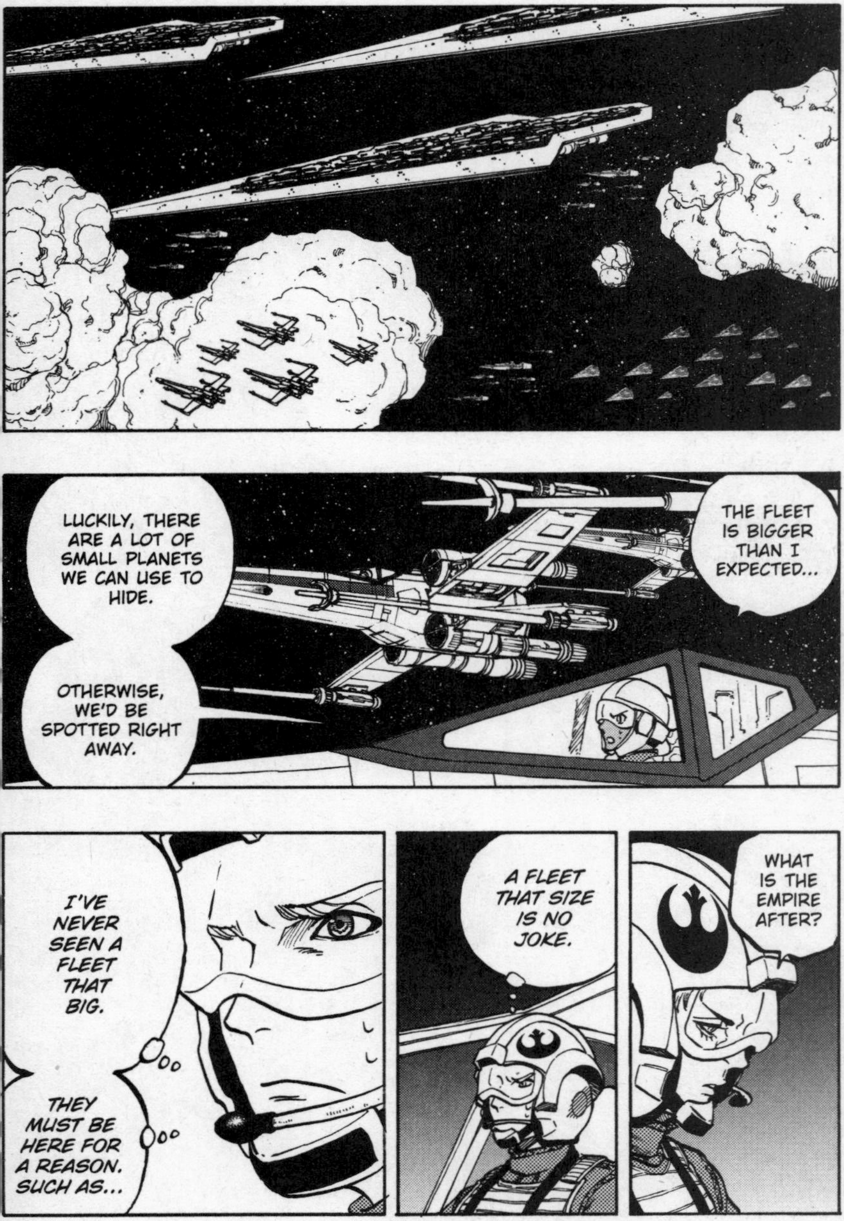
THE FLEET IS BIGGER THAN I EXPECTED...
LUCKILY, THERE ARE A LOT OF SMALL PLANETS WE CAN USE TO HIDE.
OTHERWISE, WE'D BE SPOTTED RIGHT AWAY.
WHAT IS THE EMPIRE AFTER?
A FLEET THAT SIZE IS NO JOKE.
I'VE NEVER SEEN A FLEET THAT BIG.
THEY MUST BE HERE FOR A REASON. SUCH AS...

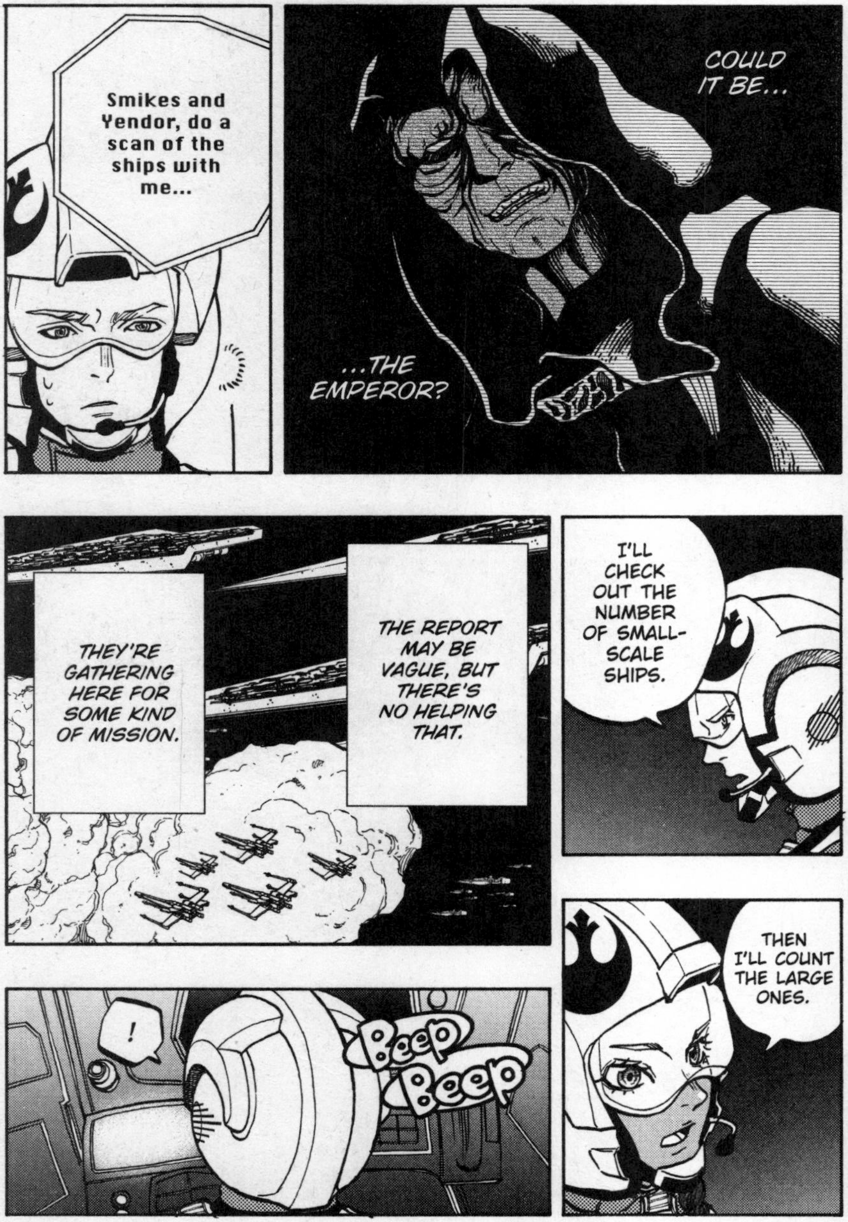
COULD IT BE...
...THE EMPEROR?
Smikes and Yendor, do a scan of the ships with me...
I'LL CHECK OUT THE NUMBER OF SMALL-SCALE SHIPS.
THE REPORT MAY BE VAGUE, BUT THERE'S NO HELPING THAT.
THEY'RE GATHERING HERE FOR SOME KIND OF MISSION.
THEN I'LL COUNT THE LARGE ONES.
Beep Beep
!

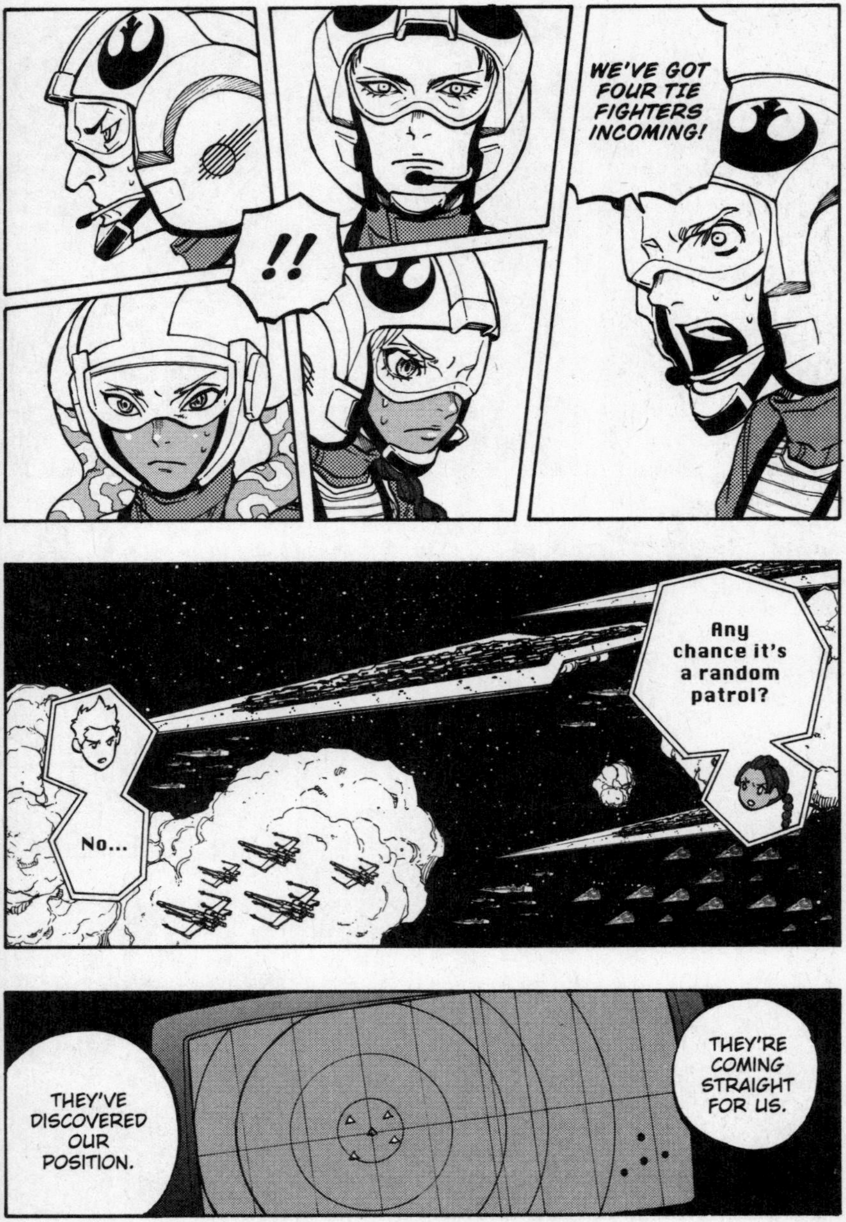
WE'VE GOT FOUR TIE FIGHTERS INCOMING!
!!
Any chance it's a random patrol?
No...
THEY'RE COMING STRAIGHT FOR US.
THEY'VE DISCOVERED OUR POSITION.

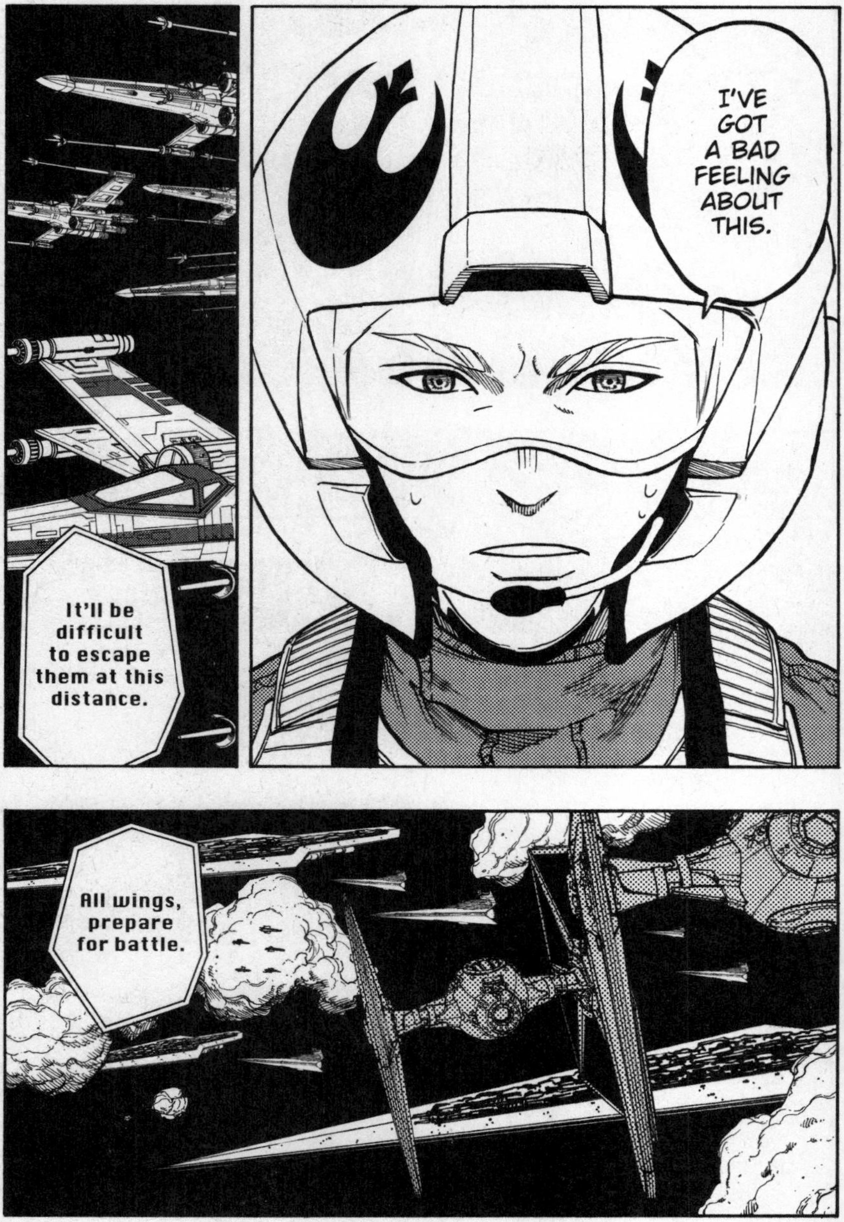
I'VE GOT A BAD FEELING ABOUT THIS.
It'll be difficult to escape them at this distance.
All wings, prepare for battle.

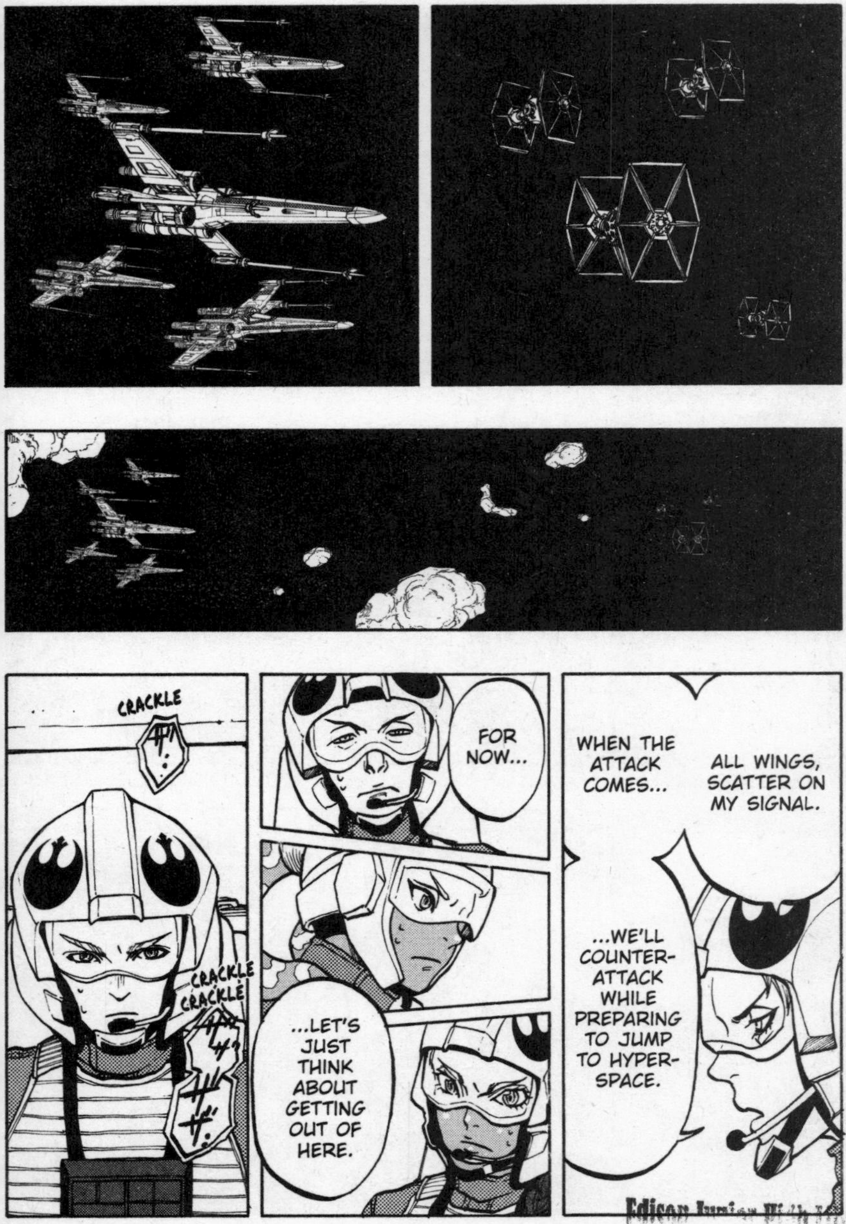
ALL WINGS, SCATTER ON MY SIGNAL.
WHEN THE ATTACK COMES...
...WE'LL COUNTER-ATTACK WHILE PREPARING TO JUMP TO HYPER-SPACE.
FOR NOW...
...LET'S JUST THINK ABOUT GETTING OUT OF HERE.
CRACKLE
CRACKLE CRACKLE

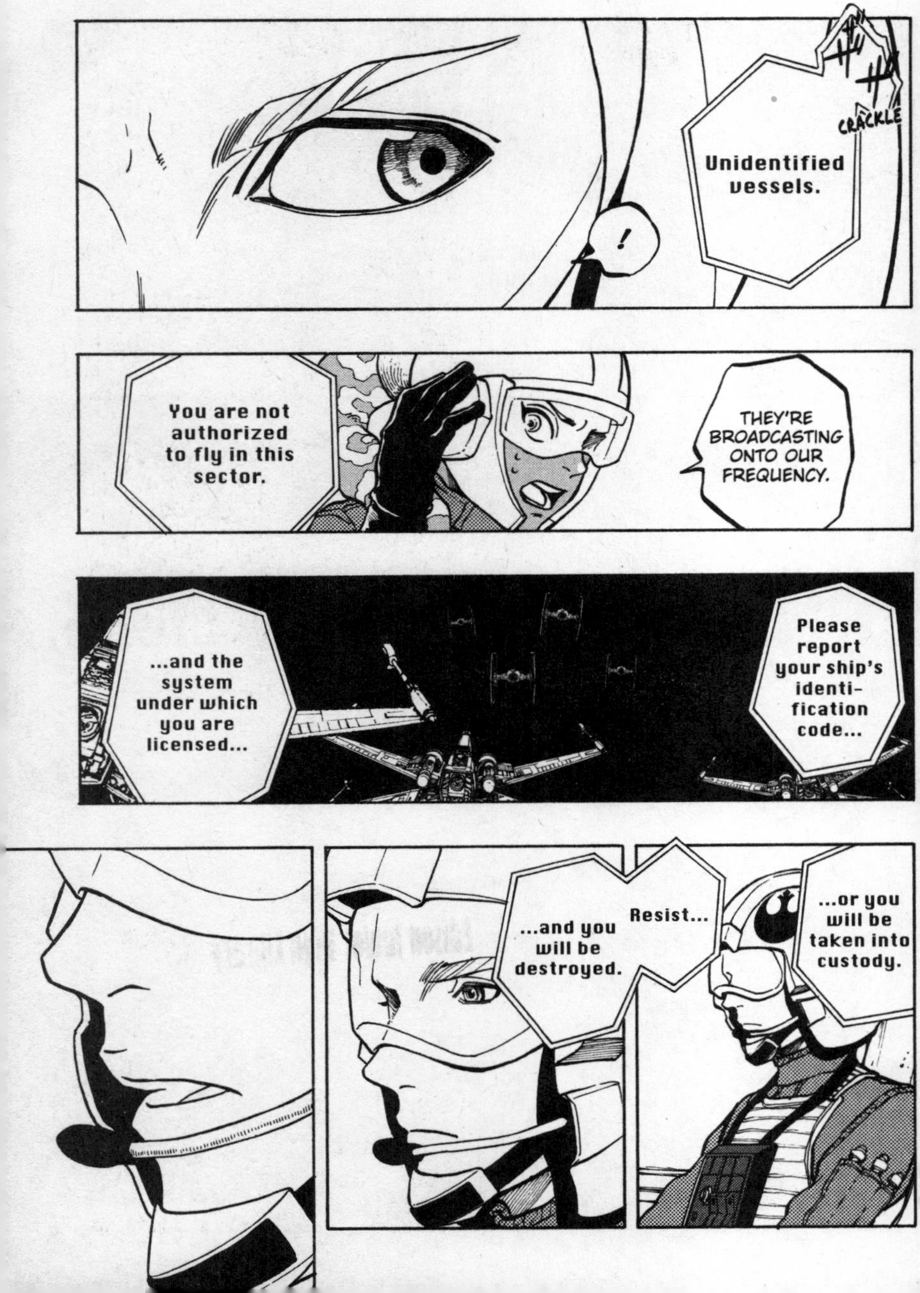
CRACKLE
Unidentified vessels.
!
THEY'RE BROADCASTING ONTO OUR FREQUENCY.
You are not authorized to fly in this sector.
Please report your ship's identi-fication code...
...and the system under which you are licensed...
...or you will be taken into custody.
Resist...
...and you will be destroyed.

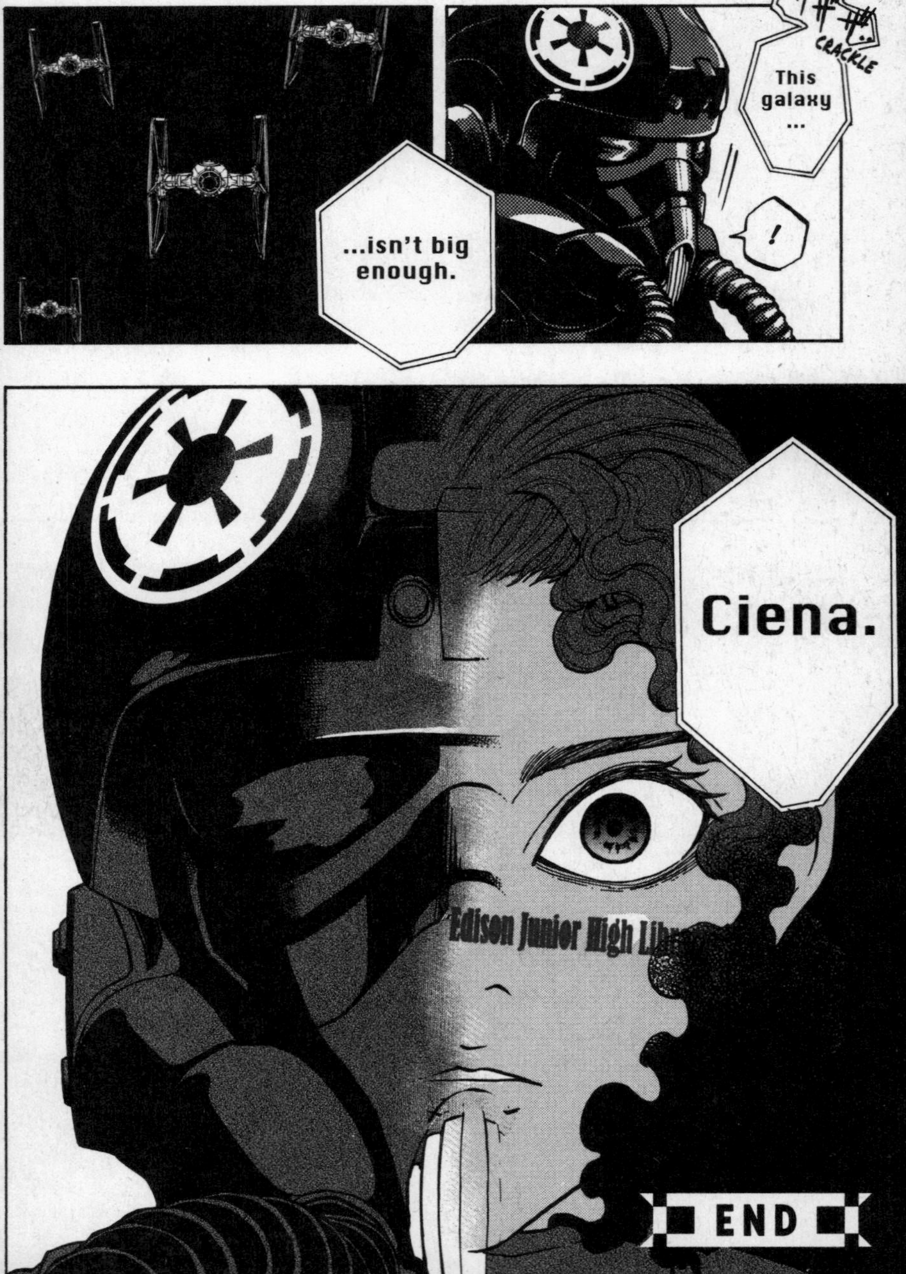

CRACKLE
This galaxy ...
!
...isn't big enough.
Ciena.
END